Phillip Margolin was a practising criminal defence lawyer for twenty-five years, has tried many high-profile cases and has argued before the U.S. Supreme Court. His first book, *Heartstone*, was nominated for an Edgar, and he has also published short stories and contributed articles to law magazines, journals and books. He is married with two children.

Also by Phillip Margolin

WILD JUSTICE

Phillip Margolin

SPHERE

First published in the United States in 2000 by
HarperCollins Publishers Inc.
First published in Great Britain in 2000 by
Little, Brown and Company
Paperback published by Warner Books in 2001
Reprinted 2001
This reissue published in 2010 by Sphere

A CIP catalogue record for this book
is available from the British Library.

ISBN 978-0-7515-4570-8

Typeset in Bembo by M Rules
Printed and bound in Great Britain by
Clays Ltd, St Ives plc

Papers used by Sphere are natural, renewable and
recyclable products sourced from well-managed forests and certified
in accordance with the rules of the Forest Stewardship Council.

Mixed Sources
Product group from well-managed
forests and other controlled sources
www.fsc.org Cert no. SGS-COC-004081
© 1996 Forest Stewardship Council

Sphere
An imprint of
Little, Brown Book Group
100 Victoria Embankment
London EC4Y 0DY

An Hachette UK Company
www.hachette.co.uk

www.littlebrown.co.uk

For Jean Naggar

Thanks for making my dreams come true.

Acknowledgements

Many generous people helped me research and write *Wild Justice*. My thanks to Janet Billups; Ted Falk; Drs. Nathan and Karen Selden; Claudia Gravett; Dr. Jay Mead; Dr. Don Girard; Marlys Pierson; Rabbi Emanuel Rose; Carole Byrum; Debi Wilkinson; Maggie Frost; Brian Hawke; the Honorable Susan Svetkey and the equally honorable Larry Matasar; Joseph, Eleonore, Judy, and Jerry Margolin; Helen and Norman Stamm; Dr. Roy Magnusson; Dr. Edward Grossenbacher; Dr. Michael Palmer; Drs. Rob and Carol Unitan; Dr Stanley Abrams; and Jerry Elshire.

Special thanks go to my tireless and relentless editor, Dan Conaway. Every reader who enjoys reading *Wild Justice* should also thank him. And thanks also to Bob Spizer for his useful insights.

I also want to thank Jean Naggar for finding me a home at HarperCollins and, as always, thank you to everyone else at Jean V. Naggar Literary Agency: You are the best.

And finally to Doreen, Daniel and Ami, thanks for putting up with me.

Revenge is a kind of wild justice.

— Francis Bacon

Part 1

Cardoni's Hand

1

A lightning flash illuminated the Learjet that waited on the runway of the private airstrip moments before a thunderclap startled Dr. Clifford Grant. Grant scanned the darkness for signs of life, but there were no other cars in the lot and no one moving on the tarmac. When he checked his watch his hand trembled. It was 11:35. Breach's man was five minutes late. The surgeon stared at the glove compartment. A sip from his flask would steady his nerves, but he knew where that would lead. He had to be thinking clearly when they brought the money.

Large drops fell with increasing speed. Grant turned on his wipers at the same moment a huge fist rapped on his passenger door. The doctor jerked back and stared. For an instant he thought the rain was distorting his vision, but the man glaring at him through the window was really that big, a monster with a massive, shaved skull and a black knee-length leather coat.

'Open the door,' the giant commanded, his voice harsh and frightening.

Grant obeyed instantly. A chill wind blew a fine spray into the car.

'Where is it?'

'In the trunk,' Grant said, the words catching in his throat as he jerked his thumb backward. The man tossed an attaché case into the car and slammed the door shut. Water beaded the smooth sides of the briefcase and made the brass locks glisten. The money! Grant wondered how much the recipient was going to pay for the heart, if he and his partner were receiving a quarter of a million dollars.

Two rapid thumps brought Grant around. The giant was pounding on the trunk. He had forgotten to pop the release. As Grant reached for the latch another lightning flash lit the view through his rear window – and the cars that had appeared from nowhere. Without thinking, he floored the accelerator and cranked the wheel. The giant dove away with amazing agility as the sedan careened across the asphalt, leaving the smell of burning rubber. Grant was vaguely aware of the screech of metal on metal as he blasted past one of the police cars and took out part of a chain-link fence. Shots were fired, glass shattered and the car tipped briefly on two wheels before righting itself and speeding into the night.

The next thing Clifford Grant remembered clearly was

banging frantically on his partner's back door. A light came on, a curtain moved and his partner glared at him in disbelief before opening the door.

'What are you doing here?'

'The police,' Grant gasped. 'A raid.'

'At the airfield?'

'Let me in, for God's sake. I've got to get in.'

Grant stumbled inside.

'Is that the money?'

Grant nodded and staggered to a seat at the kitchen table.

'Let me have it.'

The doctor pushed the briefcase across the table. It opened with a clatter of latches, revealing stacks of soiled and crumpled hundred-dollar bills bound by rubber bands. The lid slammed shut.

'What happened?'

'Wait. Got to . . . catch my breath.'

'Of course. And relax. You're safe now.'

Grant hunched over, his head between his knees.

'I didn't make the delivery.'

'What!'

'One of Breach's men put the money on the front seat. The heart was in the trunk. He was about to open it when I saw police cars. I panicked. I ran.'

'And the heart is . . . ?'

'Still in the trunk.'

'Are you telling me that you stiffed Martin Breach?'

'We'll call him,' Grant said. 'We'll explain what happened.'

A harsh laugh answered him. 'Clifford, you don't *explain* something like this to Breach. Do you understand what you've done?'

'You have nothing to worry about,' Grant answered bitterly. 'Martin has no idea who you are. I'm the one who has to worry. We'll just have to return the money. We didn't do anything wrong. The police were there.'

'You're certain he doesn't know who I am?'

'I never mentioned your name.'

Grant's head dropped into his hands and he began to tremble. 'He'll come after me. Oh, God.'

'You don't know that for sure,' his partner answered in a soothing tone. 'You're just frightened. Your imagination is running wild.'

The shaking grew worse. 'I don't know what to do.'

Strong fingers kneaded the tense muscles of Grant's neck and shoulders.

'The first thing you've got to do is get hold of yourself.'

The hands felt so comforting. It was what Grant needed, the touch and concern of another human being.

'Breach won't bother you, Clifford. Trust me, I'll take care of everything.'

Grant looked up hopefully.

'I know some people,' the voice assured him calmly.

'People who can talk to Breach?'

'Yes. So relax.'

Grant's head fell forward from relief and fatigue. The adrenaline that had powered him through the past hour was wearing off.

'You're still tense. What you need is a drink. Some ice-cold Chivas. What do you say?'

The true extent of Grant's terror could be measured by the fact that he had not even thought of taking a drink since he saw the police through his rear window. Suddenly every cell in his body screamed for alcohol. The fingers lifted; a cupboard door closed; Grant heard the friendly clink of ice bouncing against glass. Then a drink was in his hand. He gulped a quarter of the contents and felt the burn. Grant closed his eyes and raised the cold glass to his feverish forehead.

'There, there,' his partner said as a hand slapped smartly against the base of Grant's neck. Grant jerked upright, confused by the sharp sting of the ice pick as it passed through his brain stem with textbook precision.

The doctor's head hit the tabletop with a thud. Grant's partner smiled with satisfaction. Grant had to die. Even thinking about returning a quarter of a million dollars was ridiculous. What to do with the heart, though? The surgeon sighed. The procedure to remove it had been performed flawlessly, but it was all for nothing. Now the organ would have to be cut up, pureed and disposed of as soon as Grant took its place in the trunk.

2

The deputy district attorney had asked three questions of Darryl Powers, the arresting officer, before Amanda Jaffe realized that the first question had been improper. She leaped to her feet.

'Objection, hearsay.'

Judge Robard looked perplexed. 'How could Mr. Dart's question possibly be hearsay, Ms. Jaffe?'

'Not that one, Your Honor. I believe it was . . . let's see. Yes. Two questions before.'

Judge Robard looked as though he were in great pain.

'If you thought that question was hearsay, why didn't you object to it when it was asked?'

Amanda felt fires ignite in her cheeks.

'I didn't realize it was hearsay until just now.'

The judge shook his head sadly and cast his eyes skyward, as if asking the Lord why he had to be plagued with such incompetence.

'Overruled. Proceed, Mr. Dart.'

It took Amanda a moment to remember that 'overruled' meant she had lost. She collapsed in her seat. By then, Dart had asked another killer question. Welcome to the real world, a tiny voice whispered in her head. She had earned an A in Evidence at one of the nation's top law schools and had written a note on hearsay for the law review, but she could not think fast enough to make a timely objection in court. Now the judge was certain that she was a moron, and only God knew what the jury thought of her.

Amanda felt a hand patting her forearm. 'Don't feel bad, girlfriend,' LaTricia Sweet said. 'You're doin' fine.'

Great, Amanda thought. I'm screwing up so badly that my client feels she has to console me.

'And were you dressed as you are now, Officer Powers?' Rodney Dart continued.

'No, sir. I was dressed in civilian clothes, because this was an undercover operation.'

'Thank you, Officer. Please tell the jury what happened next.'

'I asked the defendant how much it would cost to have her engage in the sex acts she had suggested. The defendant said that she had her crib in the motel across the street and would feel more comfortable discussing business there. I drove to the motel lot and followed the defendant into room one-oh-seven.'

'What occurred inside the motel room?'

'I asked the defendant to explain the price of the various sex acts, and she mentioned rates ranging from fifty dollars to two hundred dollars for something she described as "a night of ecstasy."'

'What exactly was this "night of ecstasy," Officer Powers?'

'Quite honestly, Mr. Dart, it was too complicated to remember, and I couldn't take out my notebook at that time because I was undercover.'

Darryl Powers had baby blue eyes, wavy blond hair and the type of smile Amanda had seen only in a toothpaste commercial. He had even blushed when he answered the 'night of ecstasy' question. Two of the female jurors looked as if they were about to leap the railing of the jury box and tear off pieces of his clothing.

Amanda grew more despondent as Powers continued to explain the circumstances leading up to LaTricia's arrest for prostitution. Her cross examination was pathetic. When she was through, Rodney Dart said, 'The State rests.' Then he turned toward Amanda, his back to the jury, and smirked. Amanda thought about giving Dart the finger, but she was too depressed to defend herself. What she really wanted to do was finish her first trial, go home, and commit seppuku. Besides, Dart had every right to smirk. He was riding roughshod over her.

Officer Powers smiled at the jury as he left the stand. All five of the women jurors smiled back.

'Any witnesses, Ms. Jaffe?' Judge Robard asked, but

Amanda did not hear him. She was thinking about the previous afternoon when the senior partner in her law firm, her father, Frank Jaffe, had given her LaTricia's case and told her to be ready to try it in the morning.

'*How can I possibly try my first case without interviewing any of the witnesses or doing any investigation?*' Amanda had asked in horror.

'*Believe me,*' Frank Jaffe had replied, '*with LaTricia as your client, the less you know, the better off you are.*'

Amanda had read over the file in State v. Sweet *four times before marching down the hall to her father's office, planting herself in front of his desk and waving it in his face.*

'*What am I supposed to do with this?*' she'd demanded angrily.

'*Put on a vigorous defense,*' Frank had answered.

'*How? There's only one witness, a sworn officer of the law. He's going to testify that our client promised to do things to him for money that I'll bet ninety-five percent of humanity has never heard of.*'

'*LaTricia can take care of herself.*'

'*Dad, get real. She has thirteen priors for crimes like prostitution, prohibited touching and lewd behavior. Who is going to take her word over the cop's?*'

Frank had shrugged. 'It's a funny world, Amanda.'

'*I can't try a case this way,*' Amanda had insisted.

'*Of course you can. Trust me. And trust LaTricia. Everything will work out just fine if you go with the flow.*'

Judge Robard cleared his throat, then repeated himself.

'Ms. Jaffe, any witnesses?'

'Uh, yes, Your Honor.'

The skirt of her black Donna Karan power suit rode up her long legs as Amanda stood. She wanted to tug it down, but she was afraid that everyone in court would see her, so she stood before the court with her thighs partially exposed and color rising in her cheeks.

'The defense calls LaTricia Sweet.'

Before leaving her seat to cross to the witness box, LaTricia leaned over and whispered in Amanda's ear.

'Don't worry about nothin', honey. After I swear to tell the whole truth, you ask me what I do for a living, what I said to that police and why I said it. Then sit back and let me do my thing.'

Before Amanda could reply, LaTricia sashayed across the room. Her bust and butt were so huge that Amanda was afraid that they would rip her tight red sweater and black leather mini skirt. A blond-orange wig, slightly askew, sat atop her head. Amanda compared her client to the radiant Darryl Powers and moaned inwardly.

Since she had no plan, Amanda decided to follow her client's instructions.

'Ms. Sweet,' she asked after LaTricia was sworn, 'what do you do for a living?'

'I walk the streets of Portland and sell my body, Ms. Jaffe.'

Amanda blinked. The confession was a surprise, but she was relieved that her client was not lying under oath.

'Can you tell the jury what happened on the evening of August third of last year?'

'Yes, ma'am.'

LaTricia composed herself and turned toward the jury.

'On August third I was working on Martin Luther King Boulevard when Officer Powers drove by.'

'Did you know that he was a policeman?'

'Yes, I did.'

'You did?'

'Oh, yes. I've seen Officer Powers run a game on several of my friends.'

'Then why did you . . . Uh, what happened next?'

LaTricia straightened her skirt and cleared her throat.

'Officer Powers asked me if I would have sex with him. Now, I knew what he was trying to do. I've seen him arrest my friends, like I said. But I knew he couldn't arrest me if I didn't mention money. So I told him that I had a room in the motel across the street and I would feel more comfortable discussing our mutual interests there. Officer Powers asked me what those interests might be, and I described a few things that seemed to perk him up. At least I thought they did, because his face got all red and I noticed that something more than his temperature was rising.'

Two of the jurors glanced at each other.

'What happened then?' Amanda asked.

LaTricia looked at the jurors, then down at her lap.

'Officer Powers parked in the motel lot and we went to my crib. Once we was inside I . . . This is a little embarrassing for me, Ms. Jaffe, but I know I got to tell the truth.'

'Just take your time, Ms. Sweet,' Amanda advised her. LaTricia nodded, took a deep breath and continued.

'Like I said, I'd seen Officer Powers around and I

thought that he was about the sweetest thing I ever did see, so young and shy. All those friends of mine he'd busted said he was polite and treated them like ladies. Not like the other police. And, well . . .'

'Yes?'

LaTricia cast her eyes down. When she spoke, her voice was barely audible.

'The truth is, I fell in love with Officer Powers and I confessed my love as soon as I shut the door to my room.'

The jurors leaned forward. Someone in the back of the room giggled.

'I know that sounds crazy,' LaTricia said, directing her comment to the spectators, 'and I know Officer Powers didn't say nothin' 'bout my confession when he was on the stand. I don't know if he left that out because he was embarrassed or because he didn't want to embarrass me. He's such a gentleman.'

LaTricia squared her shoulders and turned back to the jury.

'Soon as we was alone I came clean and told him that I knew that he was a policeman. Then I told him that I knew that I was just an old whore, used up by life, but that I had never felt about any man the way I felt about him. Officer Powers, he blushed and looked like he wanted to be anywhere but with me, and I can understand that. He probably has himself a fine white woman, someone foxy. But I told him that all I wanted was one night of love with him and that he could take me to jail when it was over, because one night of his sweet love would be worth an eternity of jail.'

A tear trickled down LaTricia's cheek. She paused, drew a handkerchief from her purse, dabbed at the tear, then said, ' 'Scuse me,' to the jurors.

'Do you want some water, Ms. Sweet?' asked Amanda, who had been swept up in the drama of the moment. Rodney Dart leaped to his feet.

'Objection, Your Honor. This is too much.'

'Oh, I don't 'spect you to believe any of this, Mr. DA. An old bag like me trying to find love with a man half her age. But can't I dream?'

'Your Honor,' Dart begged.

'The defendant is entitled to put on a defense, Mr. Dart,' Judge Robard answered in a tone that let the jurors know that he wasn't buying LaTricia's act, but several of the jurors were casting angry glances at the prosecutor.

'Ain't much more to say,' LaTricia concluded. 'I gambled for love and I lost. I'm ready to take what fate has in store. But I want you to know that I never wanted money from that man. All I wanted was love.'

Frank Jaffe, the senior partner in Jaffe, Katz, Lehane and Brindisi, was a big man with a ruddy complexion and black curly hair that was streaked with gray. His nose had been broken twice in his youth, and he looked more like a teamster or a stevedore than an attorney. Frank was in his office dictating a letter when Amanda walked in waving the *Sweet* file.

'How could you do this to me?'

Frank grinned. 'You won, didn't you?'

'That's beside the point.'

15

'Ernie Katz was in the back of the courtroom. He said you weren't totally awful.'

'You sent Ernie to watch me be humiliated?'

'He also said that you looked scared to death.'

'I was, and giving me this insane case didn't help.'

'You'd have been scared no matter what case you tried first. When I tried my first case I spent the whole trial trying to remember the words you say when you want to introduce a piece of evidence. I never did get it right.'

'Thank you for sharing.'

'Hey, I lost my first trial. I knew you'd have a fighting chance with LaTricia as your client no matter how badly you screwed up. I've been representing her for years, and she usually comes out okay. Ernie said the jury was back in twenty minutes.'

'Twenty-two,' Amanda answered with a grudging smile. 'I have to admit winning was a rush.'

Frank laughed. 'Ernie also said that your closing argument was a doozy. Especially the part where you told the jury that you had scoured the statutes of the state of Oregon and had been unable to find love defined as a crime.'

Amanda grinned. It had been a great line. Then she stopped smiling.

'I still think you're a bastard.'

'You're a warrior now, kiddo. The whole office is waiting at Scarletti's to celebrate.'

'Oh, shit, they're just going to razz me. Besides, I didn't do much. LaTricia won the case with her cocka-mamie story.'

'Hey, trial lawyers should never be humble. Crow about your victories and blame your defeats on biased judges, ignorant juries, and the tricks of fascist prosecutors. As of now, you're the only lawyer in this office who's never lost a case.'

Until she found a place of her own, Amanda was living with Frank in the green, steep-roofed East Lake Victorian where she had grown up. Amanda had not been home, except for summers and holiday visits, since she'd started college, nine years ago. Staying in the second-floor bedroom where she had spent her childhood felt strange after so many years of independence. The room was filled with mementos of her youth: diplomas from high school and college, shelves loaded down with swimming trophies and medals, framed newspaper clippings detailing her athletic feats.

Amanda was exhausted and a little drunk when she climbed into bed at ten, but she was too upset to sleep. Frank had had no business throwing her into court unprepared in the same way he'd thrown her into the pool at the YMCA when she was three to teach her how to swim. Then, at Scarletti's, Frank had embarrassed the hell out of her by giving a speech that compared her victory in court to her surprise win her freshman year at the state high school swimming championships. She wanted her father to stop thinking of her as his little girl and to realize that she was a grown woman who had earned credentials that could open any door in the legal community.

Amanda had forgotten how controlling Frank could be. His assumption that he always knew what was best for her was infuriating. Tonight was not the first time she'd wondered if she had made a mistake by joining Frank's firm instead of going to one of the many San Francisco firms that had courted her or applying for a clerkship at the United States Supreme Court, as Judge Madison had advised.

Amanda stared at the shadows on the bedroom ceiling and asked herself why she had come back to Portland, but she knew the answer. Ever since she had been old enough to understand what her father did, she had been steeped in, and seduced by, the mystery and adventure of criminal law, and no one was better at criminal defense than Frank Jaffe. As a little girl, she had watched her father charm juries and confound hostile witnesses. He had held her in his arms at news conferences and discussed his strategy with her at the kitchen table over hot chocolate. While her law school classmates talked about the money they would make, she thought about the innocents she would save.

Amanda turned on her side. Her eyes had grown used to the dark. She studied the symbols of her successes that Frank had assembled. Frank had lived a lost childhood through her. She knew he loved her and wanted what was best for her. What she wanted was the chance to decide for herself what was best.

3

Mary Sandowski burst through the operating room doors. As the nurse rushed along the crowded hospital corridor, she ducked her head to hide the tears that coursed down her cheeks. Moments later Dr. Vincent Cardoni slammed through the same doors and ran after her. When the powerfully built surgeon caught up with Sandowski, he grabbed the slender woman's elbow and spun her toward him.

'You incompetent cow.'

Visitors, patients and hospital personnel stopped to stare at the outraged physician and the woman he was berating.

'I tried to tell you . . .'

'You switched the cups, you moron.'

'No. You—'

Cardoni shoved her against the wall and leaned forward until his face was inches from the cowering nurse. The pupils in his bloodshot eyes were dilated, and the tendons in his neck swelled.

'Don't you ever contradict me.'

'Vincent, what do you think you're doing?'

Cardoni pivoted. A tall woman with caramel-colored hair and an athletic figure was bearing down on him. She was wearing a loose brown dress and a white doctor's smock. The cold eyes she fixed on the surgeon were the color of jade.

Cardoni turned his rage on the newcomer.

'This is not your business, Justine.'

The woman stopped a few paces from Cardoni and stood her ground.

'Take your hands off her or I'll have you up before the Board of Medical Examiners. I don't think you can stand another complaint, and there will be plenty of witnesses this time.'

'Is there a problem, Dr. Castle?'

Justine glanced at the broad-shouldered man in green OR scrubs who now stood beside her. The white letters on his black plastic name tag identified him as Anthony Fiori.

'There's no problem, because Dr. Cardoni is going to leave,' Justine said, returning her gaze to Cardoni. A pulse throbbed in the surgeon's temple and every muscle in his body tensed, but he suddenly noticed the crowd that had gathered, and he released Sandowski's elbow. Justine stepped closer to Cardoni and studied his eyes.

'My God,' she said in a low tone that was still loud enough to carry beyond them. 'Are you on something? Were you operating on drugs?'

Cardoni's fists knotted. For a moment it appeared that he would strike Justine. Then he spun and stalked away, shouldering through the onlookers. Sandowski sagged against the wall. Fiori caught her.

'Are you okay?' he asked gently.

She nodded as she wept.

'Let's get you someplace less public,' Justine said, taking Sandowski's arm and leading her down a side hall and into a call room where the residents sacked out. Justine eased the shaken nurse onto a narrow metal-frame bed that stood against one wall, and sat beside her. Fiori fetched a cup of water.

'What happened?' Justine asked once Sandowski regained her composure.

'He said I switched the cups, but I didn't. He filled the syringe without looking.'

'Slow down. I'm not following you.'

Sandowski took a deep breath.

'That's better. Just relax.'

'Dr. Cardoni was performing a carpal tunnel release. You anesthetize the hand with lidocaine before you operate.'

Justine nodded.

'Then you irrigate the wound with hydrogen peroxide before suturing it.'

21

Justine nodded again

'The lidocaine and the hydrogen peroxide were in two cups. Dr. Cardoni insisted on filling the syringe himself. He didn't look.'

'He injected the patient with hydrogen peroxide instead of the lidocaine?' Justine asked incredulously.

'I tried to tell him that he had it wrong, but he told me to shut up. Then Mrs. Manion, the patient, started complaining that it was stinging, so he injected her again and she started to scream.'

'I don't believe this,' Justine said, shaking her head in disgust. 'How could he possibly mistake lidocaine for hydrogen peroxide? One of them is clear and the other has bubbles in it. It's like confusing Champagne and water.'

'I really tried to tell him, but he wouldn't let me. I don't know what would have happened if Dr. Metzler hadn't stopped him. It wasn't my fault. I swear I didn't mix up the cups.'

'Do you want to report this? I'll back you up.'

Sandowski looked startled. 'No, no. I don't have to, do I?'

'It's your decision.'

Sandowski's eyes were wide with fear. 'You're not going to report it, are you?'

'Not if you don't want me to,' Justine answered soothingly.

Sandowski's head dropped, and she started to cry again. 'I hate him. You don't know what he's like,' Sandowski sobbed.

'Oh, yes, I do,' she said. 'I'm married to that bastard.'

Fiori looked surprised.

'We're separated,' Justine said forcefully.

She handed Sandowski a tissue. 'Why don't you go home for the rest of the day?' Justine suggested. 'We'll clear everything with the head nurse.'

Sandowski nodded, and Fiori used the phone to make arrangements for the nurse to leave.

'Something's got to be done about him,' Justine said as soon as Sandowski was out of the call room.

'Were you serious when you accused Cardoni of operating on drugs?'

Justine looked at Fiori. She was flushed.

'He can't get through the day without cocaine. He's a malpractice case waiting to happen. I know he's going to kill someone if something isn't done, but I can't say a word. He's an established surgeon. I'm only a resident. I'm also suing him for divorce. No one would take me seriously.'

'I see what you mean,' Fiori answered thoughtfully. 'It puts you in a tough spot. Especially if Nurse Sandowski won't report him.'

'I can't ask her to. She's scared to death.'

Fiori nodded.

'Thank you for stepping in when you did, by the way. I don't know what Vincent would have done if you hadn't been there.'

Fiori smiled. 'You looked like you were handling yourself okay.'

'Thanks anyway.'

'Hey, we lowly residents need to stick together.' Fiori saw the time on a wall clock. 'Oops, got to run or I'll be late for a date with a fatty tumor in Lumps and Bumps.'

The handsome resident took off down the corridor with a purposeful stride. Justine Castle watched him until he disappeared around a corner.

4

Martin Breach's sandy hair was thinning, his drab brown eyes were watery and he had the pale complexion of someone who rarely went outside during the day. He also had dreadful taste in clothes. Breach wore orange or green slacks with garish jackets and loud ties that were unfashionably wide. His outfits made him look silly, but Breach didn't care. By the time his enemies realized that they had underestimated him, they were frequently dead.

Breach had started in the trenches breaking legs for Benny Dee, but he was too intelligent to stay a leg breaker for long. Now Breach ran the most efficient and ruthless criminal organization in the Pacific Northwest. No one knew where to find Benny Dee.

Martin's right-hand man, Art Prochaska, was a giant with thick lips, a broad nose and pencil-thin eyebrows. Rumor had it that in his days as a collector for the mob he had used his huge head to stun debtors as effectively as an electric charge from a Taser. Prochaska had none of Breach's smarts, but he shared his taste for violence. When Martin climbed the ladder of crime, he pulled along the only person in the world he trusted.

Prochaska limped through the door of Breach's office in the rear of the Jungle Club and settled himself across the desk from his boss. He had injured himself when he hit the pavement at the airfield diving to avoid Clifford Grant's car. The office was tiny, and the furniture was rickety and secondhand. Pictures of naked women and a calendar from a motor oil company decorated the paper-thin walls. Raucous music from the strip club made it difficult to hear. Breach wanted the club to look run-down so that the IRS could not get a true picture of the money that flowed through it.

'So?' Breach asked.

'Grant's gone. We checked his place and the hospital. No one's seen him since he split during the raid.'

Breach was very quiet. To someone who did not know, he seemed relaxed, but Prochaska was aware that a rage of monumental proportions was building.

'This is bad, Arty. I'm out a quarter of a million bucks, I'm out my profit and my reputation has taken a hit because of that quack.'

'If he hadn't taken off with the heart, we'd have been arrested.'

Breach stared at Prochaska long enough to make the giant look down.

'Where is he?'

'No one knows. Eugene and me searched his apartment. We didn't find squat. I got the feeling someone had tossed it before we did, but I couldn't say for sure.'

'The cops?'

'No, the place was too neat.'

'The partner?'

'Maybe.'

'Who is he, Arty?'

Prochaska answered hesitantly. He always hated to tell Breach bad news. 'I got one possible lead. My friend at the phone company gave me Grant's records. He made a few calls to a number in the West Hills. The phone belongs to Dr. Vincent Cardoni.'

'Is he a surgeon?'

'Yeah, and he works at St. Francis Medical Center.'

Breach's eyes narrowed. Clifford Grant had privileges at St. Francis.

'The lady across the way from his apartment said that Grant didn't get many visitors, but she saw a woman up there and a man, maybe two. Anyway, the woman was a knockout, so the neighbor kidded Grant about her. She says he got all nervous. He said she was an associate from work named Justine Castle.'

'So what?'

'She's a doctor, Arty, a surgeon, and that ain't all. Castle is married to Vincent Cardoni.'

Breach thought for a moment while Prochaska shifted

nervously in his seat.

'Do you think the cops have Grant?' Breach asked.

'Our people in the Bureau say no.'

'Do a background check on those two, Arty.'

'I'm doin' it already.'

'I want Grant, I want his partner and I want my money back. And once I've got all three, I'm going to get me a replacement for the heart I lost.'

5

Dr. Carleton Swindell, the hospital administrator for St. Francis Medical Center, won his bid on the computer bridge game, then checked his watch. He'd kept his appointment waiting for twenty minutes. Swindell's thin lips drew into a satisfied smile. *Stewing* was probably more accurate, if he knew Dr. Cardoni. Well, that was too bad. It would do Cardoni good to learn a little humility.

Swindell clicked his mouse. The bridge game disappeared and was replaced by a screen saver showing Einstein and Leonardo da Vinci playing tennis – another game at which Swindell excelled. The hospital administrator went into his private washroom and adjusted his bow tie in the mirror. He believed himself to be a handsome man, still as dapper at forty-five in his tweed sports jacket, blue Oxford shirt and sharply creased slacks as he had been at Yale. His blond hair was growing a bit thin in places and he needed his gold wire-rimmed glasses for reading, but he sculled every morning on the Willamette, so his weight was the same as it had been during his university days.

Carleton returned to his office and glanced at his watch again. Twenty-five minutes. Cardoni would be boiling, he thought with satisfaction. Oh, well, no need to overdo it. He leaned forward and buzzed his secretary.

'Please send in Dr. Cardoni, Charlotte.'

Swindell composed himself and waited for the explosion. He was not disappointed. Charlotte opened his office door wide and pressed against it. Cardoni charged in. The scene reminded Swindell of a bullfight he'd seen in Barcelona. Charlotte was the matador, the door her cape, and the bull . . . He had to fight to suppress a smile.

'I've been out there half an hour,' Cardoni said.

'I'm sorry, Vincent. I was on an important long-distance call,' the administrator replied calmly. If Cardoni had seen the unlit lines on Charlotte's phone, he'd know that Swindell was lying, but Swindell bet he wouldn't call him on it. 'Have a seat.'

'What's this about?' Cardoni demanded.

Swindell leaned back and made a steeple of his fingers. 'I've had a disturbing report about you.'

Cardoni glared. The administrator noted the surgeon's flushed pallor, his disheveled hair and unkempt clothes. Cardoni was clearly on the edge. Maybe the rumors of drug use were true.

'Did you accost a nurse in a public corridor yesterday?'

'Accost?' Cardoni mocked. 'What does that mean, Carleton?'

'You know very well, Vincent,' Swindell answered evenly. 'Did you accost Mary Sandowski?'

'Who told you that?'

'That's confidential. Well?'

Cardoni smirked. 'No, Carleton, I did not accost her. What I did was ream her out.'

'I see. And you, um, reamed her out in front of patients and staff at this hospital?'

'I have no idea who was around. The dumb bitch fucked up during an operation. I should have gotten her fired.'

'I'd appreciate a little less profanity, Vincent. Also, you should know that more than one person has informed me that you were responsible for the mistake in the OR. Injecting your patient with hydrogen peroxide instead of lidocaine, I believe.'

'After that moron switched the cups.'

Carleton tapped his fingertips together and studied Cardoni before replying.

'You know, Vincent, this isn't the first complaint of . . . well, to put it bluntly, incompetence that's been made against you.'

Every muscle in the surgeon's body went rigid.

'I want to be frank,' Swindell continued. 'If Mrs. Manion were to file a malpractice case against you, it would make three complaints.' Swindell shook his head sadly. 'I don't want to take action, but I have a duty to this hospital.'

'None of those charges has any foundation. I've consulted my attorney.'

'That may be, but there's a lot of talk. Rumors of drug use, for instance.'

'So you've been chatting with Justine.'

'I can't reveal my sources.' Swindell looked at Cardoni sympathetically. 'You know, there are wonderful programs for doctors in trouble,' he said in a man-to-man tone. 'They're all confidential. Charlotte can give you a list when you leave.'

'She really got to you, didn't she, Carleton? Did you know that Justine's filed for divorce? She'd do anything to blacken my reputation.'

'You seem to have a number of court cases going on. Wasn't there something last year involving an assault?'

'Where is this going?'

'Going? Well, that depends on what I find out after my investigation is complete. I invited you here so you could tell me your side of the story.'

Cardoni stood. 'You've heard it. If there's nothing more, I've got things to do.'

'There's nothing more for now. Thank you for dropping by.'

Cardoni turned his back on the administrator and stalked out without shutting the door. Swindell sat motionless.

'Did you want this closed?' Charlotte asked.

Swindell nodded, then swiveled his chair until he was looking out at the lights of Portland. Cardoni was crude and disrespectful, but the problem he presented could be

dealt with. Swindell's lips twisted into a smile of antici-
pation. It would be a pleasure taking the arrogant surgeon
down a peg or two.

Vincent Cardoni waited for his connection beneath a
freeway off-ramp. Thick concrete pilings straddled the
narrow street. There was a vacant lot across the way, and
a plumbing supply warehouse was the nearest building. At
ten in the evening the area was deserted.

Cardoni was still in a rage as a result of his meeting
with Carleton Swindell. Cardoni never called the administrator 'Doctor.' The wimp may have trained as a
surgeon, but he couldn't cut it. Now he was an administrator who got his rocks off by making life difficult for the
real doctors. What really burned Cardoni was the prick's
refusal to say whether it was Sandowski or Justine who
had informed on him. Cardoni was leaning toward
Justine. The nurse was too afraid of him, and it would be
just like his bitch wife to use Swindell to put on the pressure so that she would have leverage in the divorce
proceedings.

Headlights at the far end of the block flashed on and
off, and Cardoni got out of his car. Moments later Lloyd
Krause pulled under the off-ramp. Lloyd was six-two and
a fat 250 pounds. His long, dirty hair reached the shoulders of his black leather jacket, and there were grease
stains on his worn jeans. Cardoni could smell him as soon
as he climbed out of his car.

'Hey, man, got your page,' Krause said.

'I appreciate the speed.'

33

'You're a valued customer, Doc. So, what can I do you for?'

'I'll take an eight ball, Lloyd.'

'My pleasure,' Krause answered. He walked to his trunk, popped the lid and rummaged around. When he stood up he was holding a Ziploc bag filled with two and a half grams of white powder, which Cardoni pocketed.

'Two fifty, my man, and I'll be on my way.'

'I came straight from the hospital, so I don't have the cash with me. I'll get it to you tomorrow.'

The dealer's easy smile vanished.

'Then you'll get the snow tomorrow,' he said.

Cardoni had expected this. 'Where do you want me to meet you?' he asked, making no move to return the cocaine. Krause held out his hand, palm up.

'The Baggie,' he demanded.

'Look, Lloyd,' Cardoni answered casually, 'we've been friends for almost a year. Why make this hard?'

'You know the rules, Doc. No dough, no snow.'

'I'm going to pay you tomorrow, but I'm using this cocaine tonight. Let's not damage a good relationship.'

Lloyd's hand plunged into his pocket. When it came out, he was holding a switchblade.

'That's a scary knife,' Cardoni said without a trace of fear.

'The coke, and no more fucking around.'

Cardoni sighed. 'I'm certain you're experienced with that knife.'

'That is fucking correct.'

'But you might want to ask yourself one question before you try to use it.'

'This isn't *Jeopardy*. Give me the coke.'

'Think for a moment, Lloyd. You're bigger than me and you're younger than me and you have a knife, but I don't look worried, do I?'

Doubt flickered in the dealer's eyes, and he took a quick look around.

'No, no, Lloyd, that's not it. We're all alone, just the two of us. I wanted it that way because I thought you might act like this.'

'Look, I don't want to hurt you. Just give me the dope.'

'You're not going to hurt me, and I'm not returning the eight ball. I know that for a fact. You better figure out why, quickly, before something bad happens.'

'What the fuck are you talking about?'

'It's a secret, Lloyd. Something I know that you don't. Something I know about what happened the last time someone pulled a knife on me.'

Cardoni noticed that the dealer had not moved closer, and he noted a tremor in Krause's hand.

'There's a lot about me that you don't know, Lloyd.'

He looked directly into his connection's eyes.

'Have you ever killed a man? Have you? With your bare hands?'

Krause took a step back.

'Fear the unknown, Lloyd. What you don't know can kill you.'

'Are you threatening me?' Krause asked with false bravado.

Cardoni shook his head slowly.

'You don't get it, do you? We're all alone here. If something happens, no one can help you.'

Cardoni straightened to his full height, moving sideways to give the dealer a smaller target.

'I honor my debts, and I will pay you tomorrow.'

The dealer hesitated. Cardoni's cold eyes bored into him. Krause licked his lips. The doctor got in his car, and Krause made no move to stop him.

'It's three hundred tomorrow,' Lloyd said, his voice shaky.

'Of course, for the inconvenience.'

'You better fucking bring it.'

'No problem, Lloyd.' Cardoni started the car. 'You have a good evening.'

Cardoni drove off, waving casually, the way he might after finishing a friendly round of golf.

6

Mary Sandowski's eyes opened. Wherever she was, it was pitch black and a blanket of warm, muggy air pressed down on her. Mary wondered if you could feel the touch of air in a dream but was too tired to figure out the answer, so she closed her eyes and dozed off.

Time passed. Her eyes opened again, and Mary willed herself out of the fog. She tried to sit up. Restraints cut into her forehead, ankles and wrists and anchored her in place. She panicked, she struggled, but she soon gave up. Lying in the dark, in the silence, she could hear her heart *tap-tap-tapping.*

'Where am I?' she asked out loud. Her voice echoed in the darkness. Mary took deep breaths until she was calm enough to take stock. She knew that she was naked because she could feel the air on her body. There was a sheet under her, and under the sheet was a firm padded surface. She might be on a gurney or an examining table like the ones at the hospital. A hospital! She must be in a hospital. That had to be it.

'Hello! Is anybody here?' Mary shouted. A nurse would hear her. Someone would come in and tell her why she was in the hospital . . . if she was in a hospital. It dawned on Mary that the air smelled slightly foul. Missing was the antiseptic odor she associated with St. Francis.

A door opened. She heard the click of a switch, and a flash of light blinded her. Mary closed her eyes in self-defense. The door closed.

'I see the patient is awake,' a friendly voice said. It sounded vaguely familiar. Mary opened her eyes slowly, squinting into the light of the bare bulb that dangled directly overhead.

'I hope you're rested. We have a lot to do.'

'Where am I?' Mary asked.

There was no answer. Mary heard the sound of shoes moving across the floor. She strained to see the person who was standing at the foot of the table.

'What's wrong with me? Why am I here?'

A shape moved between Mary and the lightbulb. She saw a section of a green hospital gown that surgeons wore when they operated. Mary's heart lurched. A needle pricked a vein in her forearm.

'What are you doing?' Mary asked anxiously.

'Just giving you a little something that will heighten your sensitivity to pain.'

'What?' Mary asked, not certain she had understood correctly.

Suddenly Mary's throat constricted. She became aware of a warm feeling. Every nerve in her body began to tingle. She heaved for breath and began to sweat. Her pores exuded the smell of fear. Suddenly the sheet beneath her was damp and rough to the touch, and the air that caressed her naked body felt like sandpaper.

Without a word, a hand slid across her left breast. It felt unbearably cold, like dry ice.

'Please,' she begged, 'tell me what's happening.'

A thumb caressed her nipple, and she felt fear so intense that it raised her body a fraction of an inch from the table.

'Good,' the voice remarked. 'Very good.'

The hand slid away. There was complete quiet. Mary bit her lip and tried to stop shaking.

'Talk to me, please,' she pleaded. 'Am I sick?' Mary heard the unmistakable metallic ping of surgical instruments touching accidentally. 'Are you going to operate?'

The doctor did not answer her.

'I'm Mary Sandowski. I'm a nurse. If you tell me what you're going to do, I'll understand, I won't be afraid.'

'Really?'

The doctor chuckled and moved to Mary's side. She saw light dancing off the smooth steel of a scalpel blade. Now she was babbling with fear, but the doctor still refused to answer her question and began to hum a tune.

'Why are you doing this?' Mary sobbed.

For the first time the doctor seemed interested in

Phillip Margolin

something she had said. There was a pause while the surgeon contemplated her question. Then the doctor leaned closer and whispered.

'I'm doing this because I want to, Mary. Because I can.'

7

Amanda Jaffe executed a flip turn and felt her foot slip on the tiles as she somersaulted off the pool wall. The bad turn made her shimmy as she headed into the final lap of her 800-meter freestyle, and she had to fight the water to get her body right. Amanda was on the edge of exhaustion, but she dug in for a final sprint. When she saw the far wall through the churning water, she gritted her teeth for one last, great effort, lunged forward and collapsed against the side of the pool. A clock hung on the wall in front of her. Amanda pulled her goggles onto her forehead. As soon as she saw her time, she groaned. It was nowhere near the time she had registered five years ago in the finals of the PAC-10 championships.

Amanda tugged off her swim cap and shook out her

long black hair. She cut an imposing figure, with shoulders that were broad and muscular from years of competitive swimming. When her breathing leveled, Amanda checked the clock again, noting that her recovery time was also a hell of a lot slower than it had been when she was twenty-one. For a brief moment she thought about working out a little longer, but she knew she'd had it. She hoisted herself out of the pool and headed for the Jacuzzi, where she would soak until the pain in her tired muscles disappeared.

When she was dressed, Amanda went to the reception desk at the Y and stood in line to swap her key for her membership card. She had noticed the woman ahead of her when she was showering. She had the hard, muscled physique of someone who works out with weights and runs long distances, and her looks were as impressive as her body. The woman got her card from the clerk and walked toward an equally striking man in a blue warm-up suit. They made quite a couple. The man looked athletic. He had a dark complexion and blue eyes, and his black hair fell across his forehead in a boyish tangle.

Amanda frowned. There was something familiar about the woman's companion, but she couldn't remember where she'd seen him before. Then he smiled and she knew.

'Tony?'

The man turned.

'I'm Amanda Jaffe.'

Tony Fiori's face lit up.

'My God, Amanda, of course! How many years has it been?'

'Eight, nine,' Amanda answered. 'When did you get back to Portland?'

'About a year ago. I'm a doctor. I'm doing my residency at St. Francis.'

'That's great!'

'What are you up to?'

'I'm a lawyer.'

'Not medical malpractice, I hope?'

Amanda laughed. 'No, I'm with my dad's firm.'

'Hey, I'm forgetting my manners.' Tony turned to the woman. 'Amanda Jaffe, Justine Castle. Justine's a friend from the hospital, another overworked and underpaid resident. Amanda and I went to high school together, and her father and mine used to be law partners.'

Justine had watched quietly while Amanda and Tony spoke. Now she smiled and extended a hand. It was cool to the touch, and her grip was strong. Amanda thought that her smile was forced.

Tony looked at his watch. 'We've got to get back to St. Francis,' he said. 'It was great seeing you. Maybe we can get together for lunch sometime.'

'That would be terrific. Nice meeting you, Justine.'

Justine nodded, and she and Tony walked down to the parking lot. Amanda had parked on the street. She smiled as she headed to her car. Tony had always been a hunk, but she could only fantasize about him in high school when she was a geeky freshman and he was a god-like senior. Then the difference in their ages had been huge. It didn't seem so great now. Maybe she would ask him out for coffee.

Amanda laughed. If he accepted, her social life would improve 100 percent. The only man her age at the firm was married, and she spent most of her working hours out of the office at the law library, which was not heavily populated by swinging singles. She had barhopped a few times with two girlfriends she knew from high school, but she didn't like the forced gaiety. In truth, she found dating painful. Most of the men she'd gone out with hadn't held her interest for long. Her only serious affair had been with a fellow law student. It had ended when a Wall Street firm hired him and she accepted a clerkship on the United States Court of Appeals for the Ninth Circuit, which sat in San Francisco. Todd had made their continuing relationship conditional upon Amanda staying in New York and sacrificing the clerkship. Amanda had decided to sacrifice Todd instead and had never regretted the decision.

Though she didn't miss Todd, she did miss being with someone. Amanda had fond memories of buying the Sunday *New York Times* at one A.M. and reading it at breakfast over toasted bagels and hot coffee. She liked morning sex and studying with someone warm and friendly nearby. Amanda wasn't going to give up her identity for any man, but there were times when it was nice having a man around. She wondered if Tony and Justine were more than friends. She wondered if Tony would say yes to a cup of coffee.

8

The weather in Portland was cold and wet, and Bobby Vasquez was tired and cranky. The wiry vice cop had spent the last two weeks trying to gain the confidence of a low-level junkie whose brother was connected in a big way to some very serious offenders. The junkie was sly and suspicious, and Vasquez was beginning to think that he was wasting his time. He was writing a report about their last meeting when the receptionist buzzed him.

'There's a weird call on line one.'

'Give it to someone else.'

Vasquez still had on the stained jeans, torn flannel shirt and red-and-black Portland Trailblazers T-shirt that he'd been wearing for two straight days. They smelled and he smelled, and he wanted nothing more out of life than a shower, a six-pack and tonight's Blazer telecast.

'You're the only one in,' the receptionist said.

'Then get a number, Sherri, I'm busy.'

'Detective Vasquez, I've got a strange feeling about this. The person is disguising his or her voice with some kind of electronic equipment.'

Sherri had just started, and she treated every new case as if it was the next O.J. Vasquez decided that it would be easier to take the call than argue with her, and it would definitely be more fun than writing the report. He picked up the phone.

'This is Detective Vasquez. Who am I speaking to?'

'Listen to me, I won't repeat myself,' the caller said through a device that produced an eerily inhuman monotone. 'Dr. Vincent Cardoni, a surgeon at St. Francis Medical Center, recently purchased two kilos of cocaine from Martin Breach. Cardoni is hiding the cocaine in a mountain cabin. He is going to sell it to two men from Seattle within the week.'

'Where is this cabin?'

The caller told Vasquez the location.

'This is very interesting,' Vasquez was saying when the line went dead. He gazed at the receiver, then stared into space. The mystery snitch had said the magic word. Vasquez could care less about some junkie doctor. Martin Breach was another matter.

The closest they had come to indicting Breach was two years ago when Mickey Parks, a cop on loan from a southern Oregon police department, infiltrated Breach's organization. Vasquez had been Parks's control, and they had grown close. A week before Breach was going to be arrested, Parks disappeared. Over the next month, the vice and narcotics squad received untraceable packages containing the policeman's body parts. Everyone knew that Breach had killed Parks, knowing that he was a cop, but there was not a shred of evidence connecting Breach to the murder. Breach had cracked jokes during his interrogation while the detectives, including Vasquez, looked on helplessly.

Vasquez swiveled his chair and imagined a doctor in handcuffs slumped forward in an interrogation room, his tie undone, his shirt rumpled, sweat beading his forehead. A doctor in those circumstances would be very vulnerable. Draw a few pictures for him of the downside of spending time in the company of deranged bikers, honkie-hating homeboys and slavering queers and the doctor would drink gasoline to avoid prison. It wouldn't take much effort to convince a terrified physician that ratting out Martin Breach was easier than guzzling premium unleaded.

Vasquez swiveled again and confronted the first problem he foresaw. To arrest the doctor Vasquez needed evidence. The cocaine would do it, but how was he going to find Cardoni's stash? The courts had ruled that the phone tip of an anonymous informant was not a sufficient basis for securing a search warrant. If the informant would not give his name, he could be a liar with a grudge or a prankster. Information provided by an anonymous informant had to be corroborated before a judge would consider it. Vasquez could not get a warrant to search the cabin unless he could present some proof that the cocaine was inside. That was not going to be easy, but nailing Breach was worth the effort.

9

The gravel in the nearly empty parking lot of the Rebel Tavern crunched under the tires of Bobby Vasquez's dull green Camaro. Two Harleys and a dust-coated pickup truck were parked on either side of the entrance. Vasquez checked the rear and found Art Prochaska's cherry red Cadillac parked under the barren limbs of the lot's only tree.

At night, the Rebel Tavern looked like a scene from a postapocalyptic sci-fi flick. Bearded, unwashed bodies clad in leather and decorated with terrifying tattoos stood four deep at the bar, eardrum-busting music made speech impossible and blood flowed at the slightest excuse. But at three on a Friday afternoon the cruel sun spotlighted the tavern's fading paint job and the jukebox was turned low enough for the hung-over to bear.

Vasquez entered the tavern and waited while his eyes adjusted to the dark. His investigation was not going well. Vincent Cardoni was under investigation by the Board of Medical Examiners, and his behavior at St. Francis Medical Center was becoming increasingly erratic and violent; there were even rumors about cocaine use. But none of this information provided probable cause to search Cardoni's mountain cabin for two kilos of cocaine. Vasquez was desperate, so he had set up this meeting with Art Prochaska, who had been busted by the DEA recently. Vasquez would have to help Prochaska with his federal beef if he wanted information, a prospect he found as appealing as a prostate examination, but it was starting to look as though Breach's enforcer might be his only hope.

Prochaska was nursing a scotch at the bar. While Vasquez bought a bottle of beer, Prochaska went to the men's room. Vasquez followed a moment later. As soon as the door closed, Prochaska locked it and slammed Vasquez face forward into the wall. Vasquez could not stand the feel of Prochaska's hands on him, but he expected the frisk and stifled his impulse to smash his beer bottle into the gangster's face. When the pat-down was finished, Prochaska stepped back and told Vasquez to turn around. The vice cop was standing close enough to smell the garlic on Prochaska's breath.

'Long time, Art.'

'If I never saw you, it wouldn't be too long, Vasquez,'

Prochaska answered in a voice that sounded like a car driving over crushed gravel.

Vasquez took a sip of his beer and leaned back against the bathroom wall. 'I hear you're under indictment for possession with intent to distribute. I want to help you with the feds.'

Prochaska laughed. 'You born again?'

'Don't be so cynical. I've been known to help bigger turds than you when it worked to my advantage.'

'Why don't you quit wasting my time and tell me what you want?'

'I need some information about Dr. Vincent Cardoni, a surgeon at St. Francis.'

'Don't know him.'

'Look, Art, you know I'm not wired. This is between us. I'm just trying to corroborate some information I received.'

'How can I help you if I don't know this guy?'

'By telling me if Martin Breach sold him two kilos of cocaine.'

Prochaska moved very quickly for a man his size. Before Vasquez could react, Prochaska pinned him to the wall and pressed his forearm against Vasquez's windpipe. The beer bottle crashed to the floor. Prochaska tilted Vasquez's chin up, so he was forced to stare into the hit man's eyes.

'I should crush your throat and kick you to death for even suggesting that I rat out my best friend.'

Vasquez tried to struggle, but Prochaska had a hundred pounds on him. Panic made him twitch as he consumed the last of his air, but Prochaska confined him like a strait-jacket. Just as Vasquez became light-headed, Prochaska eased off and stepped back. Vasquez sagged against the wall and gulped in the urine-scented air. Prochaska smiled wickedly.

'That's how easy it is,' he said. Then he was gone.

10

An hour later Bobby Vasquez turned onto the two-lane highway that led into the mountains near Cedar City. The highway gained altitude quickly. Low-hanging clouds shrouded the tops of high green foothills, and the air was heavy with the threat of snow. On the north side of the highway, through a break in the towering evergreens, the cold, clear water of a runoff rushed downhill over large gray stones polished smooth by the constant torrent. On the south side, the highway ran beside a river that boiled with white water in some spots and crept along with lazy indifference in others.

While Mickey Parks had been undercover, Vasquez was the only person Parks could talk to without fear of giving himself away. He'd confided his fears and hopes to

Vasquez as if Bobby were a priest in a confessional, and Vasquez had grown to like and admire the naïve, dedicated cop. Parks's death hit Vasquez hard. Prochaska's refusal to corroborate his tip did not dissuade Vasquez from going after his killers. It only made him more determined to bring down Breach.

A narrow dirt driveway led from the highway to the cabin. The weak light from the setting sun was cut off by thick rows of towering evergreens and the driveway was covered with dark shadows. At the end of a quarter mile the headlights settled on a modern home of rough cedar with high picture windows and a wide deck along the north and west sides. A stone chimney was part of the east side of the house and rose above the peaked shake roof. Vasquez wondered how much Cardoni's 'cabin' cost. Even before his divorce, the best Vasquez had been able to afford had been a house half its size.

Vasquez parked the car so that it was pointing back toward the road. He pulled on latex gloves and walked toward the cabin. Crime was almost nonexistent in this mountain community and the house did not have an alarm. Once he stepped inside he would be committing a felony, but Vasquez had to know if Cardoni really had two kilos hidden in this house. If he found the stash, he would leave and figure out a way to get a warrant. He could even tail Cardoni and try to catch him selling. The main thing was to find out if he was on a wild-goose chase.

Vasquez turned his collar up against the chill and worked his way around the house, trying the exterior doors before resorting to forced entry. He got lucky when he turned the knob of a small door in the rear of the garage and it opened. Vasquez turned on the garage lights and searched. The garage had an unused feel to it. No tools hung from the walls; Vasquez saw no gardening equipment or junk lying about. He also found no cocaine, but he did find a key for the house hanging on a hook. A moment later Vasquez was standing in a downstairs hall at the foot of a flight of stairs.

At the top of the stairs was a living room with a wall of glass that provided a panoramic view of the forest. Something moved on the periphery of his vision, and Vasquez went for his gun, stopping when he realized that he'd seen a deer bounding into the woods. Vasquez exhaled and turned on the lights. He had no fear of being discovered. Cardoni's nearest neighbors were half a mile away.

The living room was sparsely furnished; the furniture was cheap and looked out of place in such an expensive home. It occurred to Vasquez that there was no dust or dirt anywhere, as if the living room had been cleaned recently. There were plastic plates and cups in the cupboards, a few mismatched utensils in the drawers. A pottery mug half filled with cold coffee sat on the drain board next to the sink. Vasquez also noted a coffeepot still holding a small amount of coffee. He touched the pot. It was cold.

The master bedroom had the same unlived-in feel. Vasquez saw an empty bookcase, a wooden straight-back chair and a cheap mattress that rested on the floor. There were no sheets on the mattress, but there were several dried brown spots that looked like blood. Vasquez searched the closets and the connecting bathroom. Then he moved on to the other rooms on the main floor. The more Vasquez searched, the more uneasy he felt. He had never seen such a tidily desolate home. Aside from the coffee cup and the coffeepot, there were no signs of life anywhere.

When Vasquez finished with the main floor he headed downstairs to the basement. There were four rooms, one of which was padlocked. Vasquez searched the other rooms. All were empty and devoid of dust or dirt.

Vasquez returned to the padlocked door. He had a set of lock picks with him and was soon inside a long and narrow room with walls and floor of unpainted gray concrete. A faint unpleasant odor permeated the air. Vasquez looked around. A sink was in one corner and a refrigerator in another. Between them, in the center of the room, was an operating table. Hanging from the padded tabletop were leather straps that could be used to secure a person's arms, legs and head. A metal tray that would hold surgical implements during an operation was completely empty.

The detective studied the floor around the operating table more closely and spotted several bloodstains. Vasquez knelt to get a better look at the blood and caught sight of something under the table. It was a scalpel. Vasquez picked it up gingerly and examined it closely. Flecks of dried blood covered the blade and the handle. He laid it carefully on the tray, then turned his attention to the refrigerator.

Vasquez grasped the handle. The door caught briefly, then popped free. The detective blinked hard, then released the handle as if his fingers had been burned. The refrigerator door slammed shut, and Vasquez fought the urge to bolt from the room. He took a deep breath and opened the door again. On the top shelf were two glass jars with screw-on tops labeled VIASPAN. The jars were full of a clear liquid with a faint yellow tinge. Vasquez spotted a plastic bag filled with a white powder on the bottom shelf. Not two kilos' worth. Nowhere near that amount. Days later the state crime lab would report that the powder was indeed cocaine. By that time, Vasquez would have trouble remembering that cocaine was even involved in the case against Dr. Vincent Cardoni. What Bobby Vasquez would remember for the rest of his life were the dead eyes that stared at him from the two severed heads that sat on the middle shelf.

11

Milton County sheriff Clark Mills, a sleepy-eyed man with shaggy brown hair and a thick mustache, struggled valiantly to maintain his composure when Vasquez showed him the severed heads. Both belonged to white women. One head was oval in shape and covered with blond hair that was stiff and stringy from the extreme cold. It leaned against the interior wall of the refrigerator like a prop in a horror film. The second head was covered with brunette hair and leaned against the first. The eyes in both skulls had rolled back so far that the pupils had almost disappeared. The skin looked like a pale rubber compound created by a special-effects wizard and was ragged and uneven where the neck had been severed from the body.

Jake Mullins, Mills's deputy, had blinked furiously for a few seconds before backing out of the room. The person who seemed the least affected by the horror in the refrigerator was Fred Scofield, the Milton County district attorney. Scofield, a heavy man tottering on the brink of obesity, had been in Vietnam and was a big-city DA before burning out and moving to the peace and seclusion of the mountain community of Cedar City.

'What should we do, Fred?' the sheriff asked.

Scofield was chewing on an unlit cigar and staring dispassionately at the heads. He turned his back to the refrigerator and addressed the shaken lawman.

'I think we should clear out of here so we don't mess up the crime scene. Then you should get on the horn and have the state police send a forensic team up here ASAP.'

They collected the deputy, whose complexion was as pale as the heads in the refrigerator. While Sheriff Mills phoned the state police and the deputy collapsed on the living room couch, Scofield led Bobby Vasquez outside onto the deck and lit up his cigar. The temperature was in the low thirties, but the cold country air was a welcome relief after the close, fetid smell in the makeshift operating room.

'What brought you to this house of horrors, Detective?'

Vasquez had worked on his story while waiting for the police, and he had it down pat. He figured he could get it past anyone if he could get it by the flinty district attorney.

'I've been investigating an anonymous tip that a doctor

named Vincent Cardoni was planning to sell two kilos of cocaine he had purchased from Martin Breach, a major narcotics dealer.'

'I know who Breach is,' Scofield said.

'The cocaine was supposed to be hidden in this house.'

'I assume you corroborated this tip before barging into Dr. Cardoni's domicile?'

There was not much of a moon, but Scofield could see Vasquez's eyes in the light from the living room. He watched them carefully while Vasquez answered his question. The vice cop's gaze never wavered.

'Art Prochaska, Breach's lieutenant, was arrested recently by the DEA. I leaned on him, and he agreed to talk about Cardoni if I helped him with his federal case and kept him out of this one.'

'But you're not keeping him out of it.'

'No, sir. Not now. We're talking serial murders. That changes a lot of things.'

Scofield nodded, but Vasquez thought he saw a glimmer of skepticism in the older man's features.

'Prochaska confirmed that Cardoni had been buying small, personal-use quantities from one of Breach's dealers until a few weeks ago, when he suddenly asked for two kilos. Cardoni checked out, so Breach sold him the dope. Prochaska told me that the doctor had a buyer and the sale was going down today.'

Scofield's jaw dropped and he almost lost his cigar.

'You mean Cardoni and his buyer could be on their way here right now?'

'I don't think so. I think we missed the sale. I searched

everywhere. The only cocaine I found was the small amount in the refrigerator.'

Scofield puffed on his cigar thoughtfully. 'We just met, Detective. The only thing I know about you is that you're a sworn officer of the law. But I do know a thing or two about Martin Breach and Art Prochaska. Frankly, I am having a hard time believing that Prochaska would give any police officer the time of day, much less discuss Martin Breach's business.'

'That's what happened, Mr. Scofield.'

'Prochaska is going to deny everything.'

'Probably, but it will be my word against his.'

'The word of an experienced police officer against that of a scumbag dope dealer,' Scofield reflected, nodding thoughtfully.

'Exactly.'

Scofield did not look like he was buying anything Vasquez was selling.

'Why didn't you put all of this information in an affidavit and present it to a judge, who could give you a warrant to search Dr. Cardoni's home?'

'There wasn't time. Besides, I didn't need a warrant. I had exigent circumstances here,' Vasquez said, naming one of the exceptions to the rule that searches must be conducted with a warrant. 'Prochaska said that the sale was going down today, but he didn't know when it was going down. I figured that I might miss the sale if I took the time to get a warrant. As it turned out, I missed it anyway.'

'Why didn't you bring backup or call ahead to Sheriff Mills or the state police?'

'I should have done all those things,' Vasquez said, looking properly chagrined. 'It was bad judgment on my part to handle this alone.'

Scofield looked off into the forest. The only sound was the occasional rustle of leaves in the wind. He puffed on his cigar. Then he broke the silence.

'I guess you know that I'll be prosecuting this mess right here in Cedar City and you're gonna be my star witness.'

Vasquez nodded.

'Do you want to add to anything you've told me or correct anything you've said?'

'No, sir.'

'All right, then, that's it. And I hope it is what happened, because this whole case will go down the toilet if I can't convince Judge Brody that he can rely on your word.'

12

Sean McCarthy came to the crime scene because of an inquiry by Bobby Vasquez, who remembered that Cardoni had recently assaulted a nurse who had disappeared. McCarthy was forty-seven, meticulously dressed and as pale and cadaverous as the corpses that were the subject of his homicide investigations. The detective's red hair was spotted with gray, the freckles that dotted his alabaster skin were dull pink and his eyes were rimmed with dark circles.

Detective McCarthy stood inches from the open refrigerator and gazed at the severed heads thoughtfully while Vasquez and Scofield looked on. Then he took out a stack of snapshots and raised a Polaroid to eye level. He studied it, then he studied the heads. McCarthy had shown none of the revulsion or shock expressed by the other officers who viewed the remains. Instead, his lips creased, forming a smile that was as enigmatic as it was out of place. When he was satisfied he closed the refrigerator door.

'Those fucking heads don't bother you?' Vasquez asked.

McCarthy did not answer the question. He glanced at the forensic experts who were photographing and measuring the basement room.

'Let's get out of here so these gentlemen can work undisturbed.'

McCarthy led Vasquez and Scofield upstairs and onto the deck. Vasquez was exhausted and wanted only to sleep. Scofield seemed edgy. McCarthy gazed at the morning sky for a moment, then held up one of the Polaroids so that Vasquez and Scofield could see it.

'One of the victims is Mary Sandowski. I don't know the identity of the other one.'

McCarthy was about to continue when a deputy emerged from one of the hiking trails that led into the forest.

'Sheriff,' he called to Mills, who was conferring with two men at the side of the house. 'We found something.'

'Ah,' McCarthy said, 'I've been expecting this.'

'Expecting what?' Vasquez asked, but the homicide detective set off after Mills and the deputies without answering. Vasquez looked at Scofield, who shrugged and followed the lanky detective into the woods. The men marched silently along a narrow trail. The sound of their footsteps was dulled by the thick dark soil. A loamy scent mixed with the smell of pine. A sign announced that the men were entering national forest; a quarter of a mile later, the trail bent right and they were suddenly in a clearing. A shovel was sticking out of a pile of dirt in the middle of the field.

'It looked like the earth had been turned recently,' the deputy explained, 'so I got a shovel and came back out here.'

He stepped aside so that the other men could see his discovery. Vasquez walked over to the narrow hole that the deputy had dug. At the bottom was a human arm.

Dr. Sally Grace, an assistant medical examiner, arrived shortly before the last of nine bodies was exhumed from the damp ground. All of the corpses were naked. Two were headless females. Of the remaining corpses, four were female, three were male and all but one appeared to be young. After a cursory examination, Grace informed the law enforcement officials gathered around her that, with the exception of the middle-aged male, all of the victims showed evidence of torture. Furthermore, Grace told them, one of the headless females had been ripped open from the breastbone to the abdomen and was missing her heart, and one of the males and another female had midline cuts from the area beneath the sternum to the pubic bone and were missing kidneys.

While Dr. Grace talked, Vasquez studied the corpses. All of the victims seemed pathetically frail and defenseless. Their rib cages showed. Their shoulder blades looked sharp and visible under their translucent skin, more like wire hangers than bones. Vasquez wanted to do something to comfort the dead, like brushing off the clumps of dirt that clung to their pale skin or laying a blanket over them to keep them warm, but none of that would help now.

When Dr. Grace finished her briefing, McCarthy wandered up and down the row of corpses. Vasquez watched him work. McCarthy gave eight of the bodies a cursory examination, but he squatted next to the seemingly untouched middle-aged male and withdrew another Polaroid from his jacket pocket. McCarthy glanced back and forth between the photograph and the corpse, then spent a few moments in deep thought. When he stood up he summoned the medical examiner. Vasquez could not hear what the detective said, but he watched Dr. Grace squat next to the corpse and examine the back of its neck. She beckoned McCarthy and he squatted next to her, nodding as she pointed to an area of the neck and gestured with her hands.

'Thank you, Dr. Grace,' McCarthy said to the medical examiner. He stood up.

'Want to fill us in, Detective?' Scofield asked, making it clear that he did not appreciate mysterious behavior in a fellow investigator.

McCarthy started back toward the cabin. 'About a month ago, a detective from Montreal contacted me with information about an ailing Canadian millionaire who was negotiating with Martin Breach to secure a heart on the black market. Do you know who Breach is?'

Scofield and Vasquez nodded.

'We've long suspected that Breach has a small but lucrative sideline: the sale of human organs on the black market to wealthy individuals who are unwilling to wait for a donor. We also suspected that the organs are frequently obtained from unwilling donors. The investigation in Canada included wiretaps. Dr. Clifford Grant was mentioned several times. He was a surgeon at St. Francis Medical Center.' McCarthy showed them the photograph he had examined earlier, then nodded back toward the bodies. 'He's the middle-aged victim who bore no marks of torture.'

Scofield and Vasquez examined the picture, and they walked in silence for a while. When Scofield returned the photo the homicide detective continued.

'We put Grant under twenty-four-hour surveillance as soon as we learned he was going to be involved in harvesting the heart. A few evenings after we received the tip, Grant was observed picking up a cooler from a locker at the bus station and placing it in the trunk of his car. If the cooler contained the heart, Grant could not have been the person who harvested it. You've only got a leeway of four to six hours between removing a heart and transplanting it into the body of the new recipient, and Grant was under constant surveillance. That meant that Grant had a partner.'

'Cardoni,' Vasquez said.

'Possibly.'

Scofield lit a cigar and took a few puffs. The smoke curled up and spread out until it disappeared.

'I was one of several officers who followed Grant to a private airfield. We observed Art Prochaska, Martin Breach's lieutenant, place an attaché case in Grant's car. Grant spotted us and took off before giving Prochaska the cooler. A few days later his car was discovered at the long-term parking lot at the airport.'

'And now we've found Grant and the operating room where the organs were harvested,' Vasquez said.

'And since we found Grant here,' Scofield added, 'it's not much of a stretch to say that Grant's partner probably killed him.'

They walked in silence for a few moments. As they came in sight of the cabin, Vasquez put out his hand to stop McCarthy.

'I want to ask you a favor,' he said. 'I want Breach, and I want Cardoni. I want to be part of this investigation. It was my case to begin with. I don't want to be cut out. What about it?'

McCarthy nodded thoughtfully.

'Let me talk to some people. I'll see what I can do.'

13

Frank Jaffe was an excellent storyteller. Amanda's favorite tale was the account of her miraculous birth, which Frank told her for the first time on her fifth birthday during a visit to Beth Israel cemetery. It was terribly cold that afternoon, but Amanda didn't notice the raw wind or the stark gray and threatening sky, so intense was her concentration on the grave of Samantha Jaffe, born September 3, 1953, died March 10, 1974. The headstone was small because Frank had not been able to afford elegance when he purchased it. The grave lay beneath the swaying leafless branches of an ancient maple tree, third in from a narrow road that roamed through the graveyard. Frank had gazed with sad eyes at the headstone. Then he had looked down on his little girl. Amanda was all that was good in the world and the reason that Frank persevered. In his mid-twenties Frank had been tall and strong, but a single father who worked all day and struggled in law school each night needed more than strength and youth to keep from folding.

'You were born on March the tenth,' Frank had begun, 'coincidentally the very same day as today, at three-oh-eight in the afternoon, which is almost the time it is now, in the year nineteen hundred and seventy-four.'

'At three-oh-eight in the afternoon?'

'Three-oh-eight on the dot,' Frank assured her. 'Your mother was lying in a wide bed on soft white sheets . . .'

'How did she look?'

'She was smiling a wonderful smile because she knew you were about to be born, and that smile made her look like an angel – the most beautiful of angels. Except, of course, she didn't have wings yet.

'Did she get wings?'

'Certainly. It was part of the bargain, but the angel and your mother did not make their bargain right away, so your mother had to wait for her wings.'

'When did the angel come?'

'She appeared in the hospital in your mother's room just as you were about to be born. Now, angels are usually invisible, but your mother could see this angel.'

'Only my mother?'

'Only your mother. And that was because she was so like an angel herself.'

'What did the angel say?'

'"Samantha," she said, in a voice that sounded like a

light rain falling, "God is very lonely in heaven and he wants you to visit." "Thank God for me," your mother said, "but I am about to bring a wonderful baby girl into the world, so I must stay with her." "God will be very sad to hear that," the angel replied. "It can't be helped," your mother told the angel. "My little girl is the most precious little girl in the world, and I love her to bits. I would be very sad myself if I couldn't be with her always.'"

'What happened then?'

'The angel flew back to heaven and told God what your mother had said. As you can imagine, God was very sad. He even cried a few tears. But God is very smart and an idea occurred to him, so he sent the angel back to earth.'

'Did the angel tell Mother God's idea?'

'She certainly did. "Would you come and visit God in heaven if you could be with your little girl always?" she asked. "Of course," your mother answered. She was a wonderful person and never liked to see anyone sad. "God has an idea," the angel told your mother. "If you will come with me right now, God will put your soul in your little girl, right next to her heart. Then you will be with her always. It will even be better than the way other mothers are with their children. You'll be with her everywhere she goes, even if she is at school or on the playground or on a trip." "How wonderful," Samantha said, and she shook hands with the angel to seal the bargain.'

'Then what happened?'

'A miraculous thing. As you know, you can't get to heaven unless you die, so your mother died, but she didn't die until the second that you opened your mouth and took your first breath. When your mouth was its widest, the soul of Samantha Jaffe jumped right inside of you and went straight to a spot next to your heart.'

'Which is where she is today?'

'Which is where she is every minute of every day,' Frank had answered, giving Amanda's hand a gentle squeeze.

Amanda remembered the story of her miraculous birth every time she and Frank made their birthday pilgrimage to the cemetery. For years Amanda really believed that Samantha lived next to her heart. As a small girl, at night, snug in her bed, she talked to Samantha about the things daughters confide to their mothers. As a teenager, it became a ritual before she mounted the blocks in each swim meet for Amanda to press her fist against her heart and silently ask her mother for strength.

Frank had never remarried, and an older Amanda wondered if her father really believed that Samantha dwelt with them. She had asked him once why he never married again. Frank told her that he had come close twice but had backed out in the end because neither woman could make him forget the love of his life. This saddened Amanda, because she wanted her father to be happy, but Frank always seemed at peace with himself, and she guessed that someone as strong as Frank would have married again if he had fallen in love.

Frank's sacrifice, if it was one, also impressed upon Amanda the power of true love. The emotion was not something to be trifled with, and she did not give herself easily. Love was very serious business. It was, as she learned from her father's example, something that could truly last forever.

Frank and Amanda had been lucky. A hard rain had fallen on the morning of March tenth, but it quit a little after noon and never resumed. The sun had even come out for a while when they were visiting Samantha's grave. As usual, Frank and Amanda were silent after leaving the cemetery. March tenth was always a hard day for both of them, and they used the drive home as a time to think.

A Porsche was idling in their driveway. As soon as Frank pulled next to it, the door to the Porsche opened and Vincent Cardoni started toward them wearing loose-fitting sweatpants and a faded UCLA sweatshirt. He was six-two and well muscled, with long black hair combed back from a high forehead. Cardoni's jaw was square and his nose classically Roman, but his complexion was washed out and his cheeks were sunken, as if he was not eating properly. A hard edge showed in the doctor's eyes, and anger forced his lips into a tight line.

'There are cops at my house,' Cardoni said as soon as Frank's door was open.

'It's a bit cold out here, Vince,' Frank said with a friendly smile. 'Why don't we talk inside?'

'Did you hear me, Frank? I said cops. More than one. I counted three cars. They were looking in the bushes around my house. The door was open. They were inside.'

'If they're in your house, the damage is done. We'll need to discuss this calmly if I'm going to repair it.'

'I want those motherfuckers out of my house, now!'

Frank's face darkened when Cardoni swore. 'I don't believe I've ever introduced you to my daughter. Amanda is a fine attorney. She's just finished a clerkship at the Ninth Circuit Court of Appeals. That's a very prestigious job. Now she's lowered herself and is working in my firm. Amanda, this is Dr. Vincent Cardoni. He's a surgeon at St. Francis.'

Cardoni stared at Amanda as if seeing her for the first time.

'Pleased to meet you, Dr. Cardoni,' Amanda said, extending her hand.

Cardoni gripped her hand hard, and his eyes stayed on hers for a brief moment before sliding down her body. Amanda felt the heat rise in her cheeks. She released Cardoni's hand. His eyes held hers for a moment, then shifted back to her father.

'Let's go inside,' Cardoni said in a tone that made the words sound more like an order than the acceptance of an invitation. Frank led the way, and the doctor followed. Amanda hung back to allow a bit of distance between her and Frank's client. Inside, Frank turned on the lights and escorted Cardoni into the living room, where he indicated a couch.

'Tell me what's going on,' Frank said when they were all seated.

'I have no idea. I was out for a run in Forest Park. When I drove back, I saw cops swarming over my yard and my house. I didn't stop to ask them why.' He paused for a moment. 'This can't have anything to do with the scrape you got me out of last year, can it?'

'Doubtful. The case was dismissed with prejudice.'

'Then what's going on?'

'No use speculating. What's your phone number at home?'

Cardoni looked puzzled.

'I'm going straight to the horse's mouth. The police are probably still at your house. I'll ask the man in charge what's going on.'

Cardoni rattled off his number, and Frank left the room. Amanda did not like being left alone with Cardoni, but he showed no interest in her. He fidgeted, then stood and began to pace around the living room, glancing briefly at the artwork and fingering curios. Cardoni walked behind Amanda and stopped moving. She waited for Cardoni to move again, but he did not. When she could not stand the stillness any longer, Amanda turned sideways on the sofa so she could see the surgeon. He was standing behind her, his eyes on the painting across the room from him. If he had been watching her, there was no way Amanda could prove it.

'We're going to drive over to your house, Vince,' Frank said as he reentered the living room.

'Did they tell you what's going on?'

'No. I spoke with Sean McCarthy, the detective in charge. He wouldn't answer any of my questions. Vince, Sean is a homicide detective.'

'Homicide?'

'Frank nodded, watching Cardoni for his reaction. 'Sean is a sharp cookie, very sharp. He said he wants to talk to you. When I hemmed and hawed, he threatened to get an arrest warrant.'

'You're kidding.'

'He sounded very serious. Is there something we need to worry about? I don't like walking a client into a meeting with a homicide detective when I'm not fully prepared.'

Cardoni shook his head.

'Okay, then. Listen up. I have lost damn few cases, but when a client of mine has been convicted it is usually his mouth that's done him in. Do not speak unless I give you the okay, and when you do respond to questions, listen to what you're asked. Do not volunteer anything. Do you have that straight?'

Cardoni nodded.

'Then let's go.'

Frank turned to Amanda. 'I'll ride with Vincent. You follow in our car.

On the ride to Cardoni's house, Amanda decided that she did not like Frank's client. She didn't appreciate the way he had moved his eyes over her when Frank had introduced her. It was unnerving to be examined so clinically, without lust or friendliness. The speed with which the doctor had switched off his anger while he studied her was also unsettling. However, Amanda's concerns about the doctor were quickly forgotten in the excitement of being included by Frank in what might be a murder investigation.

Since joining Jaffe, Katz, Lehane and Brindisi,

Amanda, like most first-year associates, had been given the jobs no one else wanted to do. She liked legal research, so she had not resented her time in the law library. But she really wanted to try cases, and the bigger the stakes, the better. She wasn't certain if Frank had asked her along because he wanted her involved in Cardoni's case or because he might need a ride home. She didn't care. Either way, she would be in at the start of a murder case.

Cardoni lived in a sprawling yellow-and-white Dutch Colonial on half an acre of land shaded by beech, oak and cottonwood. When Amanda drove up she saw black-jacketed PPB officers scouring the grounds. Police cars were blocking the garage, so Cardoni parked his Porsche in the street and Amanda parked behind him. Sean McCarthy was waiting for them at the front door.

'Frank,' McCarthy said with a smile.

'Good to see you again, Sean. This is Dr. Cardoni, and this is my daughter, Amanda. She's an attorney with my firm.'

McCarthy nodded to Amanda and extended a hand toward Cardoni, which the surgeon ignored. McCarthy seemed unconcerned about the rebuke.

'I apologize for the intrusion, Doctor. I've given strict orders to my men to respect your property. If there's any damage, please notify me and I'll see that you're compensated.'

'Cut the bullshit and get your men out of my house,' Cardoni responded angrily.

'I can understand why you're upset,' the detective

answered politely. 'I'd be too if I found strangers prowling through my home.' McCarthy withdrew a document from his jacket and handed it to Frank. 'However, we do have court authorization to search. All I can promise is that we'll be out of your hair as soon as possible.'

'Is that legal?' Cardoni asked.

'I'm afraid so,' Frank answered after reading the search warrant.

'You have a very pleasant den. Why don't we go in there and talk? It will be warmer, and we won't be in the way of my men. That will speed up the search.'

Cardoni glared at the detective. Frank placed a hand on his arm and said, 'Let's get this over with, Vince.'

McCarthy led them down a hall and into a comfortable wood-paneled den where several other men waited. McCarthy introduced them.

'Frank, this is Bobby Vasquez. This is the Milton County sheriff, Clark Mills. And this is Fred Scofield, the Milton County district attorney. Gentlemen, this is Dr. Vincent Cardoni and his attorneys, Frank and Amanda Jaffe. Dr. Cardoni, why don't you have a chair?'

'Thanks for inviting me to sit down in my own home,' Cardoni replied. Amanda heard the edge in his voice but wasn't certain if it came from anger, fear or both.

'What's going on here, Sean?' Frank asked.

'I'll answer you in a minute. First I'd like to ask your client a few questions.'

'Go ahead,' Frank said to McCarthy. Then he turned to Cardoni and told him to wait to answer each question until after they consulted.

'Dr. Cardoni, do you know Dr. Clifford Grant? I believe he also practices at St. Francis.'

Cardoni and Frank leaned toward each other and had a whispered conversation.

'I know who Dr. Grant is,' Cardoni said when they were through. 'I've even spoken to him a few times. But I don't know him well.'

'Do you know a woman named Mary Sandowski?'

Cardoni looked disgusted. He didn't bother consulting with Frank before answering.

'Is this about Sandowski? What happened? Did she swear out a complaint?'

'No, sir. She didn't.'

Cardoni waited for more explanation. When it did not come, he answered McCarthy.

'I know her.'

'In what capacity?'

'She's a nurse at St. Francis.'

'That's it?' Vasquez pressed.

The interruption seemed to annoy McCarthy. Cardoni's eyes swung slowly between the vice cop and McCarthy. Cardoni was so focused and tight that it made Amanda uneasy.

'What's going on here?' the surgeon demanded.

'When was the last time you were at your cabin in Milton County, Dr. Cardoni?' McCarthy asked.

'What the fuck are you talking about? I don't own a cabin in Milton County, and I'm not going to play this game anymore. Either tell me why you're ransacking my home or get the fuck out.'

Frank raised his hand to quiet Cardoni.

'I'm going to instruct my client not to answer any more questions until you explain the reason for them,' he said.

'Fair enough,' McCarthy replied. He walked over to a television and VCR that sat in a gap between books in a floor-to-ceiling bookshelf and turned on the TV. There was a videocassette on top of the VCR. McCarthy took the cassette out of its case and put it in the machine.

'We found this cassette in your bedroom, Dr. Cardoni. I'd be interested in your comments on the contents, if your attorney gives you permission to give them. It appears to have been shot in a basement room in a house in the mountains in Milton County. We found several items at the house that bore your fingerprints. One of the items is a scalpel that looks a lot like the scalpel you'll see on the tape. By the way, the cassette has already been dusted for prints, and yours are on it.'

'So what? I have dozens of videocassettes in the house.'

'Vincent, from this point on, I don't want you talking to anyone but me unless I say it's okay,' Frank said. 'Understood?'

Cardoni nodded, but Amanda could see that he was upset by the restriction. McCarthy turned on the set and the VCR. Amanda noticed that none of the law enforcement officers was looking at the TV; they were all focused on Cardoni.

A woman's terrified face filled the screen. She was saying something, but there was no sound on the tape. The camera panned down her naked body. She was gaunt, as if she had not eaten in days. The camera focused on her breasts and zoomed in on the woman's left nipple. It was flaccid. A gloved finger moved into view and stimulated the nipple until it became erect. The finger withdrew, and the woman's face filled the screen again. Suddenly her eyes grew impossibly wide and she screamed. Amanda froze. The woman screamed again and again. Then her eyes rolled back in her head and she passed out.

The gloved hand slapped the woman's cheeks until she came around. She began to sob. The camera was still tight on her face, and Amanda could read her lips. They formed the word *please*, and she said it repeatedly as tears streamed down her cheeks.

The camera moved, and the woman's face disappeared from the screen as it panned the surroundings. Amanda saw concrete walls, a sink, and a refrigerator. Then the camera returned to the woman. It pulled back and showed her from a side view. Blood was trickling down her heaving ribs. The camera shifted upward for a shot above the woman. There was a red puddle on her chest. The camera moved in. The nipple was missing.

Amanda's breath caught. She squeezed her eyes shut, and only a great effort of will kept her together. When she was under control, Amanda opened her eyes, making sure that she was not looking at the screen.

All the blood had drained from her father's face, but Cardoni's complexion had not changed. The detective switched off the set. Cardoni turned slowly until he was looking directly at McCarthy.

'Will you please tell me what the fuck that was all about?' he asked in a hard, emotionless voice.

'Recognize the woman?' the detective asked.

Frank regained his composure. He reached out and grabbed Cardoni's forearm. 'Not a word.' Then he stared at McCarthy. 'I thought better of you, Sean. This is a cheap trick, and this interview is at an end.'

McCarthy did not look surprised.

'I thought you'd be interested in the type of person you're representing.'

Frank stood. He still looked shaky, but his voice was steady.

'I didn't see Dr. Cardoni in that horror movie. I assume you didn't either or you would have shown us a different segment.'

'You'll receive full discovery, including a copy of this tape, at the appropriate time.'

McCarthy switched his attention to the doctor. 'Vincent Cardoni, I must inform you that you have the right to remain silent. Anything you say can and will be used against you in a court of law. You have a right to an attorney. If you cannot afford to retain an attorney, one will be appointed to represent you. Do you understand these rights?'

Cardoni stood up and glared at McCarthy.

'You can kiss my ass,' he said slowly and distinctly.

Frank stepped between his client and McCarthy.

'Are you arresting Dr. Cardoni?'

'Sheriff Mills is placing Dr. Cardoni under arrest. Multnomah County may have its own charges in the near future.'

'Is Dr. Cardoni charged with the murder of the woman on the tape?' Frank pressed.

Fred Scofield stood up and answered Frank.

'Sheriff Mills will be arresting Dr. Cardoni on the charge of murdering Mary Sandowski and for possession of cocaine, which was found in the doctor's bedroom, but I'll be going to a grand jury very soon to ask for indictments on eight other charges of aggravated murder. I anticipate that Dr. Cardoni will be spending a lot of time in Milton County in the near future.'

'I'd like you to step aside, Mr. Jaffe,' Sheriff Mills said. 'We're going to cuff your client.'

Cardoni switched into a fighting stance. Vasquez reached for his weapon. Frank laid his hand on Cardoni's arm.

'Don't resist, Vince. I'll deal with this.'

'Then deal with it. I'm not going to jail.'

'You have to. If you resist, it will make things worse. It could affect release, and it can be used against you at a trial.'

Amanda could see Cardoni processing this information. He relaxed instantly, again amazing Amanda at the speed with which he could change his emotions.

'Can I speak with my client in private for a few moments?' Frank asked.

McCarthy thought about the request, then nodded. 'You can do it in here, but I want Dr. Cardoni in handcuffs.'

Cardoni's hands were cuffed behind his back, and Sheriff Mills conducted a pat-down search of the prisoner.

'Do you need me?' Amanda asked, trying to sound casual.

'It would be better if Dr. Cardoni and I talked alone. We'll only be a minute.'

'No problem,' Amanda answered, smiling to mask her disappointment.

'I'm not going to pull any punches,' Frank said as soon as the door closed. 'You're in a lot of trouble. Aggravated murder is the most serious crime you can face in Oregon. It carries a potential death sentence.'

For the first time Cardoni looked worried.

'Where are they going to take me?'

'Probably to the Cedar City jail.'

'How quickly can you get me out?'

'I'm not sure. There is no automatic bail in a murder case, and I don't want to move for a bail hearing until we're in the best position to get you out.'

'I'm not some car mechanic who can afford to sit around and collect unemployment. I'm a physician. I have patients scheduled for surgery.'

'I know, and I'll try to get the administration at St. Francis involved on your behalf.'

'Those bastards won't help me. They've been trying to get rid of me. This will give them their opening. Do you have any idea how long it takes to become a doctor? Do you know how hard I've worked? You've got to keep me out of jail.'

'I'm going to do everything I can, but I don't want to lie to you and build up your hopes. Scofield said that they were thinking of adding eight more counts of aggravated murder to the indictment. That could mean that they have eight other bodies. This is not going to be simple, like your assault case.

'Now listen to me. Following my instructions could save your life. I mean that literally. You will be in a police car and then the jail, where they will process you in. Do everything they tell you. Do not resist. But do not, under any circumstances, discuss this case with anyone. I'm talking about cops, DAs and other prisoners, especially other prisoners. You're going to feel isolated and in need of a friend. There are going to be prisoners who will be your friend. They'll get you to feel comfortable. You'll unburden yourself to them. The next time you see your friend he will be testifying against you in exchange for having his case dropped. Do you understand what I just said?'

Cardoni nodded.

'Good. I'll be out to see you tomorrow. Try to think of people who can vouch for you at a bail hearing, and see if you can figure out why McCarthy wanted to know if you knew Dr. Clifford Grant.'

Frank laid a gentle hand on Cardoni's arm. 'One last thing, Vince. Don't give up hope.'

Cardoni looked directly into Frank Jaffe's eyes. His voice was steady and hard.

'I never give up, Frank, and I never forget, either. Someone has set me up. That means that someone is going to pay.'

'So,' Frank asked Amanda when they were alone in the car and headed home, 'what do you make of all that?'

Amanda had been very quiet since the videotape started to roll, and she was subdued when she answered Frank's question.

'The police seem pretty certain that Cardoni is guilty.'

'What do you think?'

Amanda shivered. 'I don't like him, Dad.'

'Any specific reason, or just your gut?'

'His reactions aren't normal. Have you noticed that he switches emotions the way you and I switch TV channels? One second he's in a rage, the next he's cold as ice.'

'Vince isn't Marcus Welby, MD. That's for sure.'

'What was the other case you handled for him?'

'An assault. Vince was trying to score some cocaine.' Amanda's eyebrows raised. 'He was in a bar that doesn't usually cater to members of the medical profession. He also tried to score with someone's girlfriend. When the boyfriend objected, Vince beat him so badly that he had to be taken to the hospital. Fortunately for Vince the man was an ex-con, and no one in that type of bar has decent eyesight or much of a memory when it's the police asking the questions.'

The mention of violence made Amanda flash on Mary Sandowski's tearstained face. She felt a little dizzy and squeezed her eyes shut. Frank noticed that Amanda's face was drained of color.

'Are you okay?' he asked.

'I was just thinking about that poor woman.'

'I'm sorry you had to see that.'

Amanda grew thoughtful. 'When I was a little girl,

you never took me to court when you tried the really bad cases, did you?'

'You were too young.'

'You didn't even do it when I was in high school. I remember asking you about the Fong case and the one where the two girls were tortured, but you never seemed to have the time.'

'You didn't need to hear about stuff like that at that age.'

'You always did shelter me when I was growing up.'

'You think it was easy for me raising a little girl by myself?' Frank answered defensively. 'I always tried to figure out what your mother would have done, and I could never see Samantha letting me take an eleven-year-old to a rape trial.'

'No, I don't suppose she would have,' Amanda answered with a brief smile. Then she thought about the videotape again and grew somber.

'I guess it doesn't get much worse than what I just saw,' she said.

'No, it doesn't.'

'I never really understood what you did, until now. I mean I knew intellectually, but . . .'

'There's nothing intellectual about criminal law, Amanda. There are no ivory towers, just tragedy and human beings at their worst.'

'Why do you do it?'

'Good question. Maybe because it is real. I'd be bored silly closing real-estate deals or drawing up contracts. And every once in a while you do make a difference in some poor bastard's life. I've represented a lot of very bad people, but I've also freed two people from prison who were sentenced to death for crimes they didn't commit, and I've kept people out of jail who didn't deserve to be there. I guess you can say that I spend a lot of my time in the shit, but every so often I come up with a pearl, and that makes the bad stuff worthwhile.'

'You don't have to take every case, though. You can turn some away.'

Frank glanced at his daughter. 'Like this one, you mean?'

'What if he's guilty?'

'We don't know that.'

'What if you knew beyond any doubt that Cardoni tortured that woman? How could you help a person who could do what we saw on that tape?'

Frank sighed. 'That's the question every criminal lawyer asks at some point in his or her career. I expect you'll be mulling it over while we work on this case. Those who decide they can't do it switch to some more refined type of law.'

'Are there enough pearls to justify working for someone like Cardoni?'

'Do you remember the McNab boy?'

'Vaguely. I was in junior high school, wasn't I?'

Frank nodded. 'I fought that case and fought that case. He was convicted in the first trial. I cried after the verdict because I knew he was innocent. I wasn't experienced in handling death cases. I truly believed that the verdict was my fault. Guilt drove me, and I didn't stop until I'd won the appeal and a new trial.

'The jury hung at the retrial. I couldn't sleep, I lost weight and I charged every moment that poor boy spent in jail to my soul. Then my investigator talked to Mario Rossi's mother.'

'The snitch?'

Frank nodded. 'Rossi's testimony kept Terry McNab on death row for four years, but he confessed to his mother that he lied to get a deal for himself. When Rossi recanted, the prosecutor had to dismiss.'

Frank was silent for a moment. Amanda saw the color rise in his cheeks and his eyes water. When he spoke again, Amanda heard his voice catch.

'I can still remember that afternoon. We ended the hearing around four, and Terry's father and mother and I had to wait another hour for Terry to be processed out of jail. Terry looked stunned when he stepped outside. It was February and the sun had gone down, but the air was clear and crisp. When he stood on the steps of the jail Terry looked up at the stars. He just stood there, looking up. Then he took a deep breath.

'My plane didn't leave until the morning, so I was staying at a motel on the edge of town. Terry's folks invited me to dinner, but I begged off. I knew they were just being polite and that the family would much rather be alone. Besides, I was wrecked. I'd left everything in the courtroom.'

Frank paused again.

'Do you know the thing I remember most about that day? It was the way I felt when I entered my motel room. I hadn't been alone until then, and the enormousness of what I had done had not sunk in. Four and a half years of fighting to do the right thing, the lost sleep, the tears and the frustration . . . I closed the door behind me and I stood in the middle of my motel room. I suddenly understood that it was over: I had won, and Terry would never have to spend another moment caged up.

'Amanda, I swear my soul rose out of my body at that moment. I closed my eyes and tilted my head back and felt my soul rise right up to the ceiling. It was only a moment, and then I was back on earth, but that feeling made every moment of those horrible four years worthwhile. You don't get that feeling doing anything else.'

Amanda remembered how she had felt when she heard 'Not guilty' in LaTricia Sweet's case. It had been so heady to win, especially when she hadn't thought she would. Then Amanda remembered what she had seen on the tape, and she realized that there was no comparison between LaTricia Sweet's case and the murder of Mary Sandowski. LaTricia wasn't hurting anyone but herself. No one had to fear her after she was set free. It would be totally different to help free the person who tortured Mary Sandowski.

Amanda had no doubt that her father meant what he had said. What she didn't know was whether she believed that the chance to save a few deserving people would ever be enough compensation for representing a monster who could coldly and cruelly cut the nipple off a screaming human being.

14

Bobby Vasquez parked in his assigned spot in the lot of his low-rent garden apartment. On one side of the complex was the interstate and on the other a strip mall. Truth was, between the IRS and his child support payments, this was the best he could afford. There were two rows of mailboxes near the parking spot. Vasquez collected his mail and thumbed through it while he climbed the stairs to his second-floor apartment. Ads and bills. What did he expect? Who would write him?

Vasquez opened his door and flipped on the light. The furniture in the living room was secondhand and covered by a thin layer of dust. Sections of a three-day-old *Oregonian* littered the floor, the threadbare couch and one end of a low plywood coffee table. Each weekend

Vasquez vowed to clean up, but he made an effort only when the dirt and debris overwhelmed him. He was rarely home, anyway. Undercover work kept him out at odd hours. When he wasn't working he kept company with Yvette Stewart, a cocktail waitress at the cop bar where he did his serious drinking. His wife had left him because he was never around, and he had continued the tradition after moving to this shithole.

Vasquez tossed his mail onto the coffee table and walked into the kitchen. There was nothing in the refrigerator but a six-pack, a carton of spoiled milk and a half-eaten loaf of stale bread. Vasquez didn't care. He was too exhausted to be hungry, anyway. Too exhausted to sleep, too.

Vasquez flopped onto the couch, popped the top on a beer can and flipped channels until he found ESPN. He closed his eyes and ran the cold can across his forehead. Everything was going just fine so far. Cardoni was in jail, and everyone seemed to have bought his story about the search. It felt good on those rare occasions when things went right for a change. Another thing that cheered Vasquez was Cardoni's claim that he did not own the Milton County house. Something like that was easy to check.

Vasquez turned off the set and pushed himself off the couch. He crumpled the sections of the newspaper and the beer can and threw them in the trash. Then he dragged himself into the bathroom. While he brushed his teeth he savored the fact that Dr. Vincent Cardoni was spending the first of what would be an endless number of days behind bars.

15

Frank Jaffe sat in a back booth in Stokely's Café on Jefferson Street in Cedar City and finished his apple pie while reading the final page of the police reports Fred Scofield had given him earlier that morning. The café had always been an oasis for Frank, his father and other weary hunters exhausted from hours of trudging through thick underbrush with nothing to show for their efforts but scratches, running noses and tales about the giant bucks that got away. It was the first place Frank had ordered a cup of coffee and sipped a beer. When Amanda was old enough, Frank had taught her how to shoot and introduced her to the wonders of Stokely's chicken-fried steak and hot apple pie.

Frank finished his coffee and paid the check. The

Milton County jail was three blocks away on Jefferson in a modern annex behind the county courthouse, and Frank set off in that direction. In the days of Frank's youth, the population of Cedar City hovered around thirteen hundred and Jefferson had been the only paved street, but developers had ruined the town. Family-owned hardware and grocery stores were dying a slow death as national chains moved in; there was a mall with a multiplex cinema at the east end of town; Stokely's was forced to include caffè latte on its menu in order to survive; and the three-story red-brick courthouse on Jefferson was one of the few buildings that was more than thirty years old.

After checking in with the deputy at the reception desk, Frank was led to the attorney visiting room. A few moments later the thick metal door opened and Vincent Cardoni was brought in. The surgeon was dressed in an orange jail-issue jumpsuit, and there were dark circles under his eyes. As soon as the guard locked them in, Cardoni glared at Frank.

'Where the hell have you been? I thought you were coming first thing this morning.'

'I met with Fred Scofield first,' Frank answered calmly. 'He gave me some discovery that I needed to read through before we met.'

Frank placed a stack of police reports on the cheap wooden table that separated them.

'This set is for you. I thought we could go over some of it before the bail hearing.'

Frank handed Cardoni a copy of the criminal complaint.

'There are two counts against you now. The first involves the cocaine that the cops found in your bed-room.' Frank paused. 'The other is a charge of aggravated murder for killing Mary Sandowski, the woman on the tape.'

'I didn't— '

Frank cut him off. 'Sandowski was found on property about twenty-five miles from here. More corpses were buried a short distance from the cabin where they dis-covered two severed heads. Most of the victims were tortured.'

'I don't care what happened at that cabin. I didn't do it.'

'Your word alone isn't going to be enough to win this case. Scofield has several witnesses who will testify that you attacked Mary Sandowski in the hallway of St. Francis.'

Cardoni looked exasperated. He addressed Frank the way he might talk to a not-too-bright child.

'Haven't I made myself clear, Frank? I do not own a house in Milton County, and I do not know a thing about these murders.'

'What about the videocassette? McCarthy says your prints are on it.'

'That's easy. The person who planted it obviously stole it from my house, taped over what was on it and returned it.'

'And the cocaine they found in your bedroom?'

The question surprised Cardoni. He colored and broke eye contact with Jaffe.

'Well?' Frank asked.

'It's mine.'

'I thought you were going to get help after I got you out of that last scrape.'

'Don't preach at me, Frank.'

'Do you hear me preaching?'

'What? Now you're disappointed in me? Fuck that. You're my lawyer, not a priest or a shrink, so let's get back to these bullshit charges. What else do the cops have?'

'Your prints are on a scalpel with Sandowski's blood on it. They were also on a half-filled coffee mug that was found next to the kitchen sink.'

Suddenly Cardoni looked interested.

'What kind of coffee mug?'

'It's in here someplace.'

Frank shuffled through the stack of police reports until he found what he was after. He gave two photocopied sheets to Cardoni. One showed the mug sitting on the kitchen counter, and the other was a close-up. Cardoni looked up triumphantly.

'Justine bought this mug for me in one of those boutiques on Twenty-third Street when we were dating. It was in my office at St. Francis until it disappeared a few weeks ago. I thought one of the cleaning people stole it.'

'What about the scalpel?'

'I'm a surgeon, Frank! I handle scalpels every day. It's obvious. Someone is framing me.'

Frank thought about that possibility. He thumbed through the police reports.

'This whole thing started with Bobby Vasquez, the

cop with the mustache who watched the tape with us. He got a tip that you purchased two kilos of cocaine from Martin Breach and were storing them in a cabin you owned in the mountains near Cedar City. Vasquez claims that an informant corroborated the tip. He went to the cabin to search and found the severed heads in a refrigerator in the makeshift operating room we saw on the tape.'

'Who gave Vasquez the tip?' Cardoni asked.

'It was anonymous.'

'Really? How convenient.'

A thought occurred to Frank.

'Does Martin Breach supply your cocaine?'

'I said I didn't want to talk about the blow.'

'I have a reason for asking. Do you buy from Breach?'

'No, but the guy I buy from might. I don't know his source.'

Frank made some notes on a yellow pad.

'Let's talk about Clifford Grant.'

Cardoni looked confused. 'What's this about Grant? That cop asked me about him at the house.'

Frank told Cardoni about the investigation into Breach's blackmarket organ sales, the tip from the police in Montreal and the failed raid at the private airport.

'It looks like the organs were being removed at the Milton County house, but the police are certain that Grant didn't harvest the heart. They think he had a partner.'

'And they think the partner is me?' Cardoni asked calmly.

Frank nodded.

'Well, they're wrong.'

'If they are, someone went to a hell of a lot of trouble to frame you. Who hates you enough to do that, Vince?'

Before Cardoni could answer, the door opened and the guard entered carrying a plastic clothing bag. Frank looked at his watch. It was nine-forty.

'We've only got twenty minutes until the bail hearing. I brought a suit, shirt and tie for you from your house. Put them on and I'll meet you in court. Read through the discovery carefully. You're a very bright guy, Vince. Help me figure this out.'

The bail hearing in *State v. Cardoni* was held on the second floor of the county courthouse in the pre-World War I courtroom of the Honorable Patrick Brody. Frank and his client sat at one counsel table and Scofield at another. Beyond the bar of the court were rows of hard wooden benches for spectators. Most days a few retirees and a sprinkling of interested parties were the only visitors, but the benches were packed for the hearing. Vans with network logos on their sides and satellite dishes on their roofs jammed the street in front of the courthouse; parking, which was usually a breeze, was impossible to find, as were accommodations at any motel within twenty miles. The combination of mass murder, black-market organ sales, torture and a handsome physician who had already been dubbed Dr. Death by the tabloids had lured reporters from all over the United States and several foreign countries to Cedar City.

While he waited for Fred Scofield to call his first witness, Frank glanced around the courtroom and spotted Art Prochaska watching the proceedings from a seat near the window at the back. Frank had represented several of Martin Breach's 'employees,' but never Prochaska. Nonetheless, Frank recognized him instantly and wondered what he was doing at the hearing.

Judge Brody rapped his gavel, and Scofield called Sean McCarthy to lay out the case against Cardoni. Then the prosecutor put on several forensic experts before calling his final witness.

A woman crossed the courtroom and took the witness stand. She was beautifully dressed in a pale gray pantsuit, a green cashmere turtleneck and pearl earrings. The woman's caramel hair fell gently across her shoulders. Her jade-colored eyes flicked toward Cardoni for a second, then she ignored him. Frank had never seen her before, but his client obviously had, because he stiffened and stared angrily.

'Could you please state your name for the record?' the bailiff asked.

'Dr. Justine Castle,' she replied in a firm voice that carried easily to all corners of the courtroom.

'How are you employed, Dr. Castle?'

'I'm a physician, and I'm currently in a residency program in general surgery at St. Francis Medical Center in Portland.'

'Where did you attend college and medical school?'

'I received a BS in chemistry at Dartmouth and a master's in biochemistry from Cornell, and I attended medical school at Jefferson in Philadelphia.'

'Did you work between college and medical school?'

'Yes. I spent two years working as a research chemist for a pharmaceutical firm in Denver, Colorado.'

'What is your relationship to the defendant, Vincent Cardoni?'

'He is my husband,' Justine answered tersely.

'Were you living together at the time of his arrest on the present charges?'

Justine turned toward Cardoni and stared directly at him.

'No. I moved out after he beat me.'

There was a stir in the crowd, and Judge Brody called for order as Frank stood.

'Objection, Your Honor. This is not relevant to the issue before the court, which is whether there is strong proof of my client's guilt of the murders in Milton County.'

'Overruled.'

'Can you tell Judge Brody the circumstances of this beating?' Scofield continued.

Justine's voice did not waver and she did not flinch when she answered.

'It occurred during a rape. Vincent wanted me to have sex with him. He was using cocaine and I refused. He pounded me with his fists until I submitted. Afterward he beat me some more for sport. I moved out that night.'

'And when was this?'

'Two months ago.'

Judge Brody was old-fashioned. He had been married to the same woman for forty years, and his weekly attendance at church was not for show. His expression reflected the way he felt about men who abused women. Frank saw his chances of obtaining bail fading with each word Justine Castle spoke.

'You mentioned drug use. Is the defendant addicted to drugs?'

'My husband is a cocaine addict.'

'Does this affect his judgment?'

'His behavior has become increasingly erratic during our marriage.'

'Did you recently witness erratic behavior on the part of your husband during an incident involving a nurse at St. Francis Medical Center named Mary Sandowski?'

'Yes, I did.'

'Please tell Judge Brody what you saw.'

When Justine finished recounting Cardoni's assault on Sandowski, Scofield changed the subject.

'Dr. Castle, do you have any reason to believe that the defendant would be a flight risk if he is released on bail?'

'Yes, I do.'

'Please explain to the judge why you believe the defendant might flee.'

'I have filed for divorce. My divorce attorney has been trying to locate my husband's assets. Almost immediately after I filed, my husband tried to withdraw large sums of money from our joint accounts and our investment accounts. We were able to anticipate some of these moves, but he still sent a lot of this money to offshore accounts. We also believe that he has accounts in Switzerland. These accounts would provide him with enough money to live in luxury if he was to flee the country.'

The cords in Cardoni's neck were tight with anger. He leaned his head toward Frank without taking his eyes off Justine.

'You asked me who would want to set me up,' Cardoni whispered. 'You're looking at her. The bitch has access to my office at the hospital, and she has keys to my house. It would have been easy for Justine to steal the coffee mug, the scalpel and the videocassette. And Justine knew Grant.'

'You're suggesting that Justine was Grant's partner?'

'She's a surgeon, Frank. Harvesting those organs would be a piece of cake.'

'What about murder? Do you think she's capable of that?'

'As capable as she is of lying under oath. I never raped Justine and I don't have any offshore accounts. Her whole testimony is a lie.'

'What happened?' Amanda asked as soon as Frank walked through the door to her office.

'Bail denied,' her father answered. He looked exhausted. 'I wasn't surprised. Cardoni couldn't come up with a single character witness, and Scofield's case is very strong.'

'How did Cardoni take the judge's decision?'

'Not well,' Frank answered without elaborating. He had no desire to relive Cardoni's tirade, which was peppered with threats against Justine Castle and every member of every branch of government that was involved in his prosecution.

'Where do you go from here?'

'I'm already working on a motion to suppress, but I don't have much hope that I'll win.'

'Let me take a crack at it,' Amanda asked eagerly.

Frank hesitated. Amanda took a breath and plunged in.

'Why did you ask me to come to work for you, Dad? Were you being charitable?'

Frank was taken aback by the question. 'You know that's not it.'

'I know I don't need charity. I was law review at one of the top schools in the country, and I just finished clerking for a federal appeals court. I can get any job I want, and I'm going to start looking if you don't give me some responsibility.'

Frank looked angry and started to say something, but Amanda pressed her case.

'Look, Dad, I might be a neophyte in a trial court, but I'm a sixth-degree black belt when it comes to legal research. You tell me where you could get someone better to work on this motion.'

Frank hesitated. Then he threw his head back and laughed.

'You're damn lucky you're my daughter. If any other associate talked to me like that, I'd kick their ass into the center of Broadway.'

Amanda grinned but held her tongue. One thing she knew from watching tons of appellate arguments was that you shut up when you'd won.

'Come down to my office for the file,' Frank said. An idea occurred to him. 'Since you're so anxious to get your hands dirty, why don't you keep Herb Cross company when he interviews Justine Castle, Cardoni's wife? She killed us at the bail hearing. Her testimony at a sentencing hearing could send Cardoni to death row.'

'Is Castle a doctor?'

'Yes. Why?'

'And she's very attractive?'

'A knockout.'

'I've met her.'

16

Every weekday morning Carleton Swindell rowed the Willamette, then showered at his athletic club. His hair was still a tad damp when he entered the anteroom of his office at seven-thirty sharp a few days after Vincent Cardoni's bail hearing. As soon as the hospital administrator walked in the door, Sean McCarthy stood up and displayed his badge.

'I hope you don't mind my waiting in here, Dr. Swindell,' McCarthy said while Swindell inspected his identification. 'There wasn't anyone around.'

'No problem, Detective. My secretary doesn't get in until eight.'

McCarthy followed Swindell into the administrator's office. Diplomas from several prestigious universities, including a medical degree and a master's in public health from Emory University, were prominently displayed next to photographs of Swindell posing with President Clinton, Oregon's two senators and several other dignitaries. A tennis trophy and two plaques for rowing victories graced a credenza under a large picture window with a view of downtown Portland, the Willamette River and three snow-capped mountains. McCarthy did not see any family photographs.

'I don't have any overdue parking tickets, do I?'

'I wish it were that simple. I assume you know that one of the doctors at your hospital has been charged with murder.'

Swindell's smile disappeared. 'Vincent Cardoni.' He shook his head. 'It's unbelievable. The whole hospital's been talking about nothing else.'

'So you were surprised by the arrest.'

Swindell looked thoughtful. 'Why don't you sit down?' he said as he walked around his desk. When he was seated, Swindell swiveled toward his view, leaned back and steepled his fingers.

'You asked if I'm surprised. The type of crime – a mass serial killing – of course that shocks me. How could it not? But Dr. Cardoni has been a problem for this hospital since we hired him.'

'Oh?'

Swindell looked pensive.

'Your visit presents me with a problem. I'm not certain I can discuss Dr. Cardoni with you. Confidentiality and all that.'

McCarthy took a document out of his inside jacket pocket and held it out across the desk.

'I had a judge issue a subpoena before I came. It's for Dr. Cardoni's records.'

'Yes, well, I'm sure it's in order. I'll have to have our attorneys review it. I'll expedite the matter, of course.'

'Thank you.'

'Shocking. The whole business.' Swindell hesitated. 'May I speak off the record?'

'Of course.'

'Now, I don't have proof of anything I'm going to tell you. It's what I believe you call deep background.'

McCarthy nodded, amused by the TV cop lingo.

'A week or so ago, Dr. Cardoni attacked Mary Sandowski, one of our nurses.' Swindell shook his head. 'I read that she was one of the poor souls you found in that mountain graveyard.'

McCarthy nodded again.

'He's a violent man, Detective. Last year he was arrested for assault, and I've had complaints of abusive behavior from our staff. And there are rumors of drug use.' Swindell looked grim. 'We've never substantiated the rumors, but I've got a gut feeling that there is something to them.'

'Another doctor who worked here was found in the graveyard.'

'Ah, Clifford.' Swindell sighed. 'You know, of course, that he was in danger of losing his privileges here?'

'No, I didn't.'

'Drinking,' Swindell confided. 'The man was a hopeless alcoholic.'

'Did Cardoni know Clifford Grant?'

'I assume so. Dr. Grant was supervising Justine Castle's residency until we convinced him to take a leave of absence. Dr. Castle is married to Vincent.'

'Interesting. Is there anything else that would tie Grant to Cardoni?'

'Not that I can think of right now.'

McCarthy stood. 'Thank you, Dr. Swindell. Your information has been very helpful. And thank you for expediting the subpoenas.'

Swindell smiled at the detective and said, 'My pleasure.'

As soon as McCarthy was out of the office, Swindell phoned Records. He wanted to make sure that the police received anything on Cardoni as soon as possible. It was the least he could do to thank them for taking care of a very annoying problem.

Walter Stoops made a living scrambling after personal injury clients and pleading out drunk drivers. Three years earlier Stoops had been suspended from the practice of law for six months for misusing client funds. Late last year the thinnest of technicalities had enabled him to avoid a count of money laundering when a Mexican drug ring was busted.

Stoops practiced out of an office on the top floor of a run-down, three-story building near the freeway. The cramped reception area was barely big enough to accommodate the desk of the secretary/receptionist, a young woman with stringy brown hair and too much makeup. She looked up uncertainly when Bobby Vasquez stepped through the door. He guessed that Stoops did not have many clients.

'Could you please tell Mr. Stoops that Detective Robert Vasquez would like to talk to him?'

He flashed his badge and dropped into a chair beside a small table covered with year-old issues of *People* and *Sports Illustrated*. The young woman hurried through a door to her left, returned a moment later and showed Vasquez into an office not much larger than the reception room. Seated behind a scarred wooden desk was a fat man in a threadbare brown suit wearing tortoiseshell glasses with thick lenses. His sparse hair was combed sideways across the top of his head, and the collar of his white shirt was frayed.

Stoops flashed Vasquez a nervous smile. 'Maggie says you're with the police.'

'Yes, I am, Mr. Stoops. I'd like to ask you a few questions in connection with an investigation that I'm conducting. Mind if I sit?'

'No, please,' Stoops said, pointing to an empty chair. 'But if this is about one of my clients, I may not be able to help you, you understand,' he said, trying hard to sound nonchalant.

'Sure. Just stop me if there's a problem,' Vasquez answered with a smile as he pulled a stack of papers out of a briefcase he was carrying. 'Are you familiar with Northwest Realty, an Oregon corporation?'

Stoops's brow furrowed for a moment. Then a light went on.

'Northwest Realty. Sure. What about it?'

'You're listed as the corporate agent. Would you mind telling me a little about the company?'

Stoops suddenly looked concerned. 'I'm not certain I can do that. Attorney-client confidence, you know.'

'I don't see the problem, Mr. Stoops.' Vasquez thumbed through the printouts. 'For instance, it's public record that you purchased a three-acre lot in Milton County in 1990 for the company. Your name is on the deed.'

'Well, yeah.'

'Have you purchased any other property for the corporation?'

'Uh, no, just that one. Can you tell me what this is about?'

'What other things have you done for Northwest Realty besides buying the land in Milton County?'

Stoops twisted nervously in his chair. 'I'm very uncomfortable discussing a client's business. I don't think I can continue unless you explain why you're asking these questions.'

'That's fair,' Vasquez answered cordially. He pulled two photographs out of his briefcase and tossed them on the blotter. The photos were upside-down for Stoops. He leaned forward, not yet processing what he was seeing. He reached out gingerly and rotated the snapshots. Then his face lost all color. Vasquez pointed to the photograph on the right.

'These heads were found in a refrigerator in the basement of the house you bought for Northwest Realty.'

Stoops's mouth worked, but no sound came out. Vasquez pointed at the other photo.

'This is a picture of a graveyard we found. It's a short distance from the house. There are nine corpses. Two of them were decapitated. All of these people were probably tortured in the basement room where we found the heads.'

'Jesus,' was all Stoops managed. He was sweating profusely. 'Why the fuck didn't you warn me?'

'I didn't know if that was necessary. I thought you might have seen these bodies before.'

Stoops's eyes widened, and he bolted upright. 'Wait a second here. Wait one second. I read about this in the paper this morning. Oh, no. Now wait a minute. You can't come into my office and show me pictures like these.'

'Let me ask you again: What can you tell me about Northwest Realty?'

The lawyer sank back in his chair. He pulled a handkerchief out of his pocket and mopped his brow.

'I've got a heart condition. Did you know that?' Stoops glanced at the photographs again, then pulled his eyes away. 'What did you think you were doing?'

Vasquez leaned forward. 'Let's not play games, Walter. I usually work narcotics. I know all about your arrangement with Javier Moreno. You're a fucking crook who got lucky. You owe one to the criminal justice system, and I'm here to collect. Talk to me, now, or I'll bring you in as an accessory to murder.'

Stoops looked shocked. 'You can't think . . . Hey, this is bullshit.'

Vasquez stood up and took out his handcuffs. 'Walter

111

Stoops, the law requires me to advise you that you have a right to remain silent. Anything you say—'

Stoops held out his hands, palms out. 'Wait, wait. I wasn't involved in that,' he said, pointing toward the photographs. 'I don't know a thing about these murders. I overreacted, that's all. It was a shock seeing those heads. I'm gonna see the goddamn things in my sleep.' Stoops wiped his brow again. 'Go ahead and ask your questions.'

Vasquez sat down, but he set the handcuffs on the desk where Stoops could see them.

'Who owns the Milton County property?'

'I can't tell you.'

Vasquez reached for the cuffs.

'You don't understand,' Stoops said desperately. 'I don't know who owns it. The guy contacted me by mail. I can't even say it's a guy. It could be a woman. The deal was that I was supposed to find rural property with a house on it. It had to be isolated. There was a whole list of conditions. I would have said no, but . . . Well, to be honest, I was in trouble with the IRS, and I was suspended for a while from practice, so there was hardly any money coming in. And, well, the price was right and there didn't seem to be anything wrong with what the buyer was asking. It was just a real-estate transaction.'

'Where did the corporation come in?'

'That was the buyer's idea. I was supposed to set one up and use it to buy the property. The deal was I would get cashier's checks, money orders and stuff like that to set up the corporation. Then I would send pictures and descriptions of properties I thought would work to a box number. When the client found a place he wanted, the corporation would buy it. It sounded peculiar, but it didn't sound illegal. That was the only transaction I was ever involved with for Northwest Realty. After I bought the land I never heard from the guy again.'

'Does the name Dr. Vincent Cardoni mean anything to you?'

'Just from the morning paper.'

'Would you have any objection to my seeing your file on Northwest Realty?'

'No, not now.'

Stoops stood up and opened a gray metal filing cabinet that stood in one corner of his office. He handed a file to Vasquez and sat down. Vasquez thumbed through the documents. The only thing that interested him were photocopies of cashier's checks and money orders, all in amounts less than ten thousand dollars, that added up to almost three hundred thousand dollars. The significance of the amount of each money order was obvious to anyone who dealt with drug dealers. Selling dope was easy; using the cash you got for it was the hard part. The Bank Secrecy Act required banks to report cash transactions of $10,000 or more and to keep records of individuals who engaged in such transactions. In order to avoid this problem drug dealers structured their cash transactions in amounts less than $10,000.

'Can I get a copy of the file?' he asked.

'I can't give you copies of the correspondence, but I can give you everything else.'

Vasquez could have pressured him for copies of the

few letters in the file, but there was nothing in them of use. All of the letters of instruction were unsigned and written on a computer. He settled for the rest of the file.

Vasquez sat in the waiting room while Stoops's secretary brought the material down the hall to a copier. He was disappointed. He had counted on Stoops to link Cardoni to the land, but it looked as though Cardoni had covered his tracks. It probably didn't matter. There was overwhelming evidence against the surgeon. There were the items with his prints that had been found in the cabin and the videocassette that had been found in his house in Portland. Once the jury saw that videotape, Cardoni was dead. Still, Vasquez thought, it would have been nice to have another piece of evidence tying him to the killing ground.

17

Seven years ago a white grocery clerk had mistakenly accused Herb Cross, an African-American, of robbing a convenience store. Cross hired Frank Jaffe to represent him. When Frank's investigator failed to find witnesses to support Cross's alibi, Frank's client took matters into his own hands and used his contacts to track down the real robber. Frank was so impressed that he offered his client a job.

'I'll ask the questions,' Cross instructed Amanda as they walked down the fifth-floor corridor of St. Francis Medical Center toward the conference room in the Department of Surgery where Justine Castle was waiting. 'You listen and take notes. If there's something you think I haven't covered, chime in when I'm through. Our object today is to get as much information as possible from Dr. Castle, so let her talk. And don't defend Cardoni, no matter what she says. We want to see how she feels and what she knows. We're not here to convert her to our cause.'

Cross got no argument out of Amanda. She had never interviewed a witness before and was relieved that Herb would be doing the questioning.

The windowless conference room was narrow and stuffy, and the air was permeated by the faint smell of sweat. A flickering fluorescent light fixture hung above shelves of medical books and journals. Justine Castle was sitting on one side of a conference table sipping a cup of black coffee. She had been in surgery for a good part of the afternoon, and Amanda thought that she looked worn out. Her hair was swept back in a ponytail, and she was not wearing makeup.

'I'm Herb Cross, Frank Jaffe's investigator. We spoke on the phone. This is Amanda Jaffe. She's an attorney with the firm.'

'We met at the Y,' Amanda reminded Castle, who showed no sign of recognition. 'You were with Tony Fiori.'

'Oh, yes,' Castle answered dismissively. 'Tony's high school friend.'

The cold response surprised Amanda, but she did not show it.

'I want to thank you for seeing us, Dr. Castle,' Herb said.

'I only agreed to see you to be polite, Mr. Cross.

Nothing I say will help your client. Our divorce is not amicable, and I find Vincent repulsive.'

'Yet you married him,' Cross said. 'You must have seen something good in him.'

Justine smiled ruefully. 'Vincent can be charming when he's not coked up.'

Amanda and Cross sat opposite Dr. Castle. Amanda took out a pad and prepared to take notes.

'You've read the newspaper account of the murders in Milton County,' Herb began. 'Had Dr. Cardoni ever said or done anything that made you suspect that he was killing these people?'

'Mr. Cross, if I had any idea that my husband had done something like that, I would have called the police immediately.'

'Do you think he's capable of this type of violence?'

'Vincent is a violent man,' she answered without hesitation. 'I assume you know about my testimony in court.'

'You testified that he beat you and raped you.'

'It's not a far stretch from rape and assault to murder.'

'The murders in Milton County were not acts of passion,' Cross said. 'They were well-thought-out acts of sadism.'

'Vincent is a sadist, Mr. Cross. The rape was very methodical. The beating was not administered in some sort of insane rage. Vincent looked very satisfied with himself when he was through.'

'Dr. Cardoni denies raping or beating you.'

'Of course he does. You don't expect him to admit it, do you?'

'Did you report the rape to the police or seek medical assistance?'

Justine looked disgusted. 'You mean, can I prove Vincent raped me?'

'It's my job to check the facts in a case.'

'Let's not kid each other, Mr. Cross. It's your job to trick me into saying something that will help Vincent escape the punishment he deserves. But to answer your question, no, I did not report the rape or seek medical assistance. So it's Vincent's word against mine. That possibility does not intimidate me in the least.'

'Dr. Castle, did you know that your husband owned a home in Milton County?'

'The police asked me about that. If he does own that place, he never told me.'

'Your divorce lawyer never ran across a reference to it or property owned by Northwest Realty when you were trying to discover Dr. Cardoni's assets?'

'No.'

'Did you know Dr. Clifford Grant?'

Justine's anger faded away and was replaced by a weary sadness.

'Poor Clifford,' she said. 'He was my attending until the administration started taking his responsibilities away from him. Not that I can blame them. He couldn't stop drinking. That's why his wife left, and that made him drink even more. Then there was that incident in surgery. He almost killed a four-year-old boy.'

'And yet I get the impression that you liked Dr. Grant.'

Justine shrugged. 'He was going through his divorce

while he was supervising me. We went out for dinner every now and then. He trusted me and unburdened himself on occasion.'

She stopped talking, and her eyes grew distant. 'I can't help wondering if I'm responsible for his death.'

'Why would you say that?'

'Vincent and Clifford didn't become friendly until we were engaged. The papers say that they were harvesting organs for the black market. I wonder if Clifford would have trusted Vincent if I hadn't brought them together.'

'What can you tell us about the incident with Mary Sandowski?' Cross asked.

'I was there when he attacked her. The poor woman was speechless with fright. He had her by the arm and he was screaming at her.'

'Do you know why he was so angry?'

'Mary told me that Vincent screwed up during an operation and became furious with her when she tried to warn him. I'm certain she was right.'

'Why is that?'

'I saw Vincent's eyes. He was coked to the gills.'

'What's your husband's reputation among the other doctors at St. Francis?'

'I can't speak for them. If you want gossip, you might want to talk to Carleton Swindell, the hospital administrator. I do know that the Board of Medical Examiners is looking into several complaints of malpractice that are probably legitimate. If it was up to me I would never let him in an operating room. I think he's a drug addict and an incompetent.'

'He's also rich, isn't he?'

Justine raised an eyebrow suspiciously. 'What if he is?'

'I don't want to offend you, Dr. Castle, but isn't it true that you'd come away from the divorce with a lot of property and money if your husband is convicted of murder?'

Justine pushed away from the table and stood up.

'Anything I take out of this marriage I've earned, believe me. And now I'm afraid that I have to end this interview. I've been working since early this morning and I need to get some rest.'

'What do you think?' Amanda asked as they headed toward the elevator.

'I think that Dr. Justine Castle is one pissed-off lady.'

'Wouldn't you be if you were the victim of rape and assault?'

'Then you believe her?'

Amanda was going to answer when she noticed Tony Fiori walking toward them. He was wearing green surgical scrubs under a white coat that looked as though it had never been washed. Scraps of paper poked out of the jacket's bulging pockets.

'Tony!'

Fiori looked puzzled for a moment. Then he smiled.

'Hey, Amanda. What are you doing up here?'

'We just finished interviewing a witness in a case. This is Herb Cross, our investigator. Herb, this is Dr. Tony Fiori, an old friend from high school.'

Herb shook Tony's hand.

'Do you have time for a cup of coffee?' Tony asked

Amanda. 'I got bumped out of the OR by an emergency and I've still got half an hour before I have to be back.'

'I don't know,' Amanda said hesitantly, looking at Cross.

'That's fine,' the investigator replied.

'You're sure you don't need me?'

'I'm just going back to the office to write my report. We'll catch up later.'

'Okay, then. I'll see you at the office.'

She turned to Tony. 'I can use a caffeine fix. Let's go.'

It was raining when Amanda and Tony walked outside. They sprinted across the street to Starbucks, and Amanda found a table while Tony ordered for them.

'One grande skinny caramel latte,' he said, placing the drink in front of Amanda.

'That looks like regular coffee,' Amanda said, pointing to Tony's cup.

'Hey, I'm a barbarian. What can I say?'

Amanda laughed. 'It's strange – we don't see each other for years, and now we bump into each other twice in less than a month.'

'It's fate,' Tony answered with an easy smile.

'You look like you're working hard.'

'Like the proverbial dog. Fortunately, my senior resident is a good guy, so it's not as bad as it could be.'

'What are you doing?'

'I've been on the surgical intensive care rotation for two months, but I've been doing elective surgeries for the past two days – hernias, appendectomies. It's two-for-one day today. Let me take out your appendix and I'll remove your spleen for free.'

'No, thanks,' Amanda answered with a laugh. 'I gave at the office.'

Tony took a long drink of coffee. 'Man, I needed that. I've been at it since six this morning without a break.'

'I'm glad I came along.'

Tony leaned back and studied Amanda.

'You know what I remember about you?' he asked with a smile. 'The swimming. You were so great at the state meet my senior year, and you were only a freshman. Did you keep it up in college?'

'All four years.'

'How'd you do?'

'Pretty well. I won the two hundred free in the PAC-Ten my junior and senior years and placed at nationals.'

'Impressive. Did you try for the Olympics?'

'Yeah, but I never really had a chance to make the team. There were three or four girls who could kick my butt on my best day. To tell you the truth, I was burnt out by my senior year. I didn't swim at all when I was at law school. I'm just getting back to it now.'

'Where did you go to law school?'

'NYU. The last two years I had a clerkship at the Ninth Circuit Court of Appeals in San Francisco. You went to Colgate, right?'

'Only for a year. My dad died and it hit me hard.' Tony's eyes grew moist, and he looked down at the table.

Now Amanda remembered. Dominic Fiori had been Frank's law partner. He was raising Tony after a bitter divorce. During winter break of Amanda's sophomore year in high school, Dominic had died in a fire. The sudden death of a parent was bound to be traumatic.

'Anyway, I dropped out for a while and bummed around Europe and South America for a year after that,' he continued in a subdued tone. 'Then I was a ski instructor in Colorado for a while before I got my act together and went back to school at Boulder. My grades weren't good enough for an American medical school, so I ended up in Peru. I took some tests when I graduated and was accepted at St. Francis for my residency.'

'That's a tough road.'

Tony shrugged. 'I guess,' he answered, looking a little embarrassed. 'So you were interviewing Justine for your case?' he asked, changing the subject.

'How did you know?'

'I have amazing psychic powers. Also, I read the papers. Your father and Cardoni have been all over the news since they found those heads.' Tony was suddenly serious. 'You know, I was there when Cardoni had his run-in with Sandowski.'

'No, I didn't.'

'Did he really decapitate her?'

Amanda's legal training reared its head. 'I can't really talk about that.'

'Sorry, I didn't mean to be nosy. It's just . . . I knew 'em both.' He shook himself, as if trying to clear away an unpleasant image.

Amanda hesitated, then made a decision. 'I guess I can tell you. It'll come out at the trial anyway. There's a videotape of Mary Sandowski being killed. Whoever did it operated on her while she was conscious.' She shivered. 'You're probably used to seeing people in pain, but I've never seen anything like that.'

'I haven't seen anything like that either, Amanda. A doctor tries to ease suffering. I'd have been just as upset as you.'

Tony glanced up at the clock on the wall. 'I'm going to have to get back.' He hesitated. 'Uh, look,' he asked nervously, 'do you want to get together sometime? You know, dinner, a movie?'

Amanda flashed a reassuring smile. 'Sure. I'd like that.'

Tony grinned. 'Great. Give me your number.'

Amanda took out a business card and wrote her home number on the back. Tony stood up.

'Don't rush off,' he told her. 'Finish your latte. I'll call soon.'

Amanda watched Tony duck into the rain and jog back toward the hospital. She wondered if he'd really call. It would be tough giving up an evening in the library to go to dinner with a drop-dead gorgeous doctor, but Amanda believed she was woman enough to make the sacrifice.

'And she sent us on our way,' Herb Cross told Frank Jaffe as he concluded his account of the Justine Castle interview.

'What was your opinion of her?' Frank asked. Cross slouched in the client chair in Frank's office and stared at the West Hills through the window at Frank's back while he gathered his thoughts.

'She's very bright and very dangerous. She hates our client and will do everything she can to put him on death row if she's called as a witness.'

'Cardoni thinks she set him up.'

Cross looked surprised. 'He thinks Castle is a serial killer?'

'That's what he says. She's a surgeon, she knew Grant.'

Cross looked skeptical.

'I don't buy it either,' Frank said, 'but we have to worry about Castle. I need to know if there's some way to get to her if she testifies. Go to the jail. Talk to our client. Get as much background on her as you can, then go after her.'

18

Bobby Vasquez found Sean McCarthy neck deep in paperwork when he walked into the squad room and pulled up a chair to the detective's desk.

'Hey, Bobby,' McCarthy said. 'What have you got?'

'A lot,' he answered, opening a file he was carrying. 'Cardoni grew up outside of Seattle. His parents were divorced and Cardoni started getting in trouble soon after the split. He was a star wrestler in high school, excellent grades, but he was also arrested for assault. The case never came to trial. I don't know why it was dismissed.

'After high school Cardoni went to Penn State on a wrestling scholarship, but he lost it in his sophomore year when he was arrested for assault.'

'Any specifics?'

'I got the police report on that one. It was a bar fight. He really fucked up the other guy. Cardoni went into the army as part of a plea bargain. Charges were dismissed.'

'How'd he do in the army?'

'No trouble I could find. He qualified for the wrestling team and trained during his hitch. He also excelled at unarmed combat. After the army, Cardoni went to Hearst College, in Idaho. Good grades, NCAA Division Two nationals as a junior and a senior, then medical school in Wisconsin and a residency at New Hope Hospital in Denver.'

'Any trouble in Idaho, Wisconsin or Colorado?'

'Cardoni was the defendant in a malpractice suit in Colorado. The insurance company settled it. I've got rumors of cocaine use, and there were a couple of sexual harassment complaints that went nowhere. After Cardoni finished his residency, he moved to Portland.'

'Where does Cardoni's money come from?' McCarthy asked.

'Some of it comes from an inheritance. His folks are dead. I also hear that he's invested wisely.'

McCarthy leaned back in his chair and tapped his fingers together thoughtfully.

'If Cardoni is a serial killer, he may have cut his teeth before moving to Portland. Find out if a killing field like the one near the cabin was ever found in Washington, Pennsylvania, Idaho, Wisconsin, Colorado or any other place Cardoni lived.'

'Okay.'

'And while we're on the subject, did you have any

luck tracing the ownership of the Milton County property?'

'None. I went to the banks that cut the cashier's checks, but there was no record of the purchases because they were under ten thousand dollars. Is there anything new on your end?'

'A little. I'm certain that the Milton County cabin is the place where the illegal organs were harvested. Remember those jars in the refrigerator?'

'The ones with Viaspan written on them?'

'Right. Viaspan is a cardiac preservation fluid. Before you cut the heart out of a donor's body, you inject Viaspan into it. It replaces the blood, fills up the vessels and preserves the heart so the metabolic processes don't continue when the heart stops beating. After you remove the heart, you place it in a plastic bag filled with Viaspan. Viaspan would also be used when transplanting other organs.'

'Like a kidney?'

'Exactly. We've also identified several of the victims. The decapitated woman without the heart is Jane Scott, a runaway. One of the victims is Kim Bowers, a prostitute who disappeared a year and a half ago, and another is Louise Pierre.'

'The Lewis and Clark student who went missing in June?'

McCarthy nodded. 'One of the males is Rick Elam, a shipping clerk who was reported missing in September. Elam and Pierre were missing kidneys. Now, here is the interesting part. Scott, Elam and Pierre were patients at St. Francis within months of their disappearances.'

'No shit! Were any of them a patient of Cardoni?'

'No, but they didn't have to be. All you need to do to find a donor for a heart is to find a person whose blood type is compatible with the recipient's and who is within twenty percent of the recipient's body weight. The heart of a person with type O blood can be given to anyone. All Cardoni or Grant had to do was look at their files.'

'Were any of the other victims missing organs?'

McCarthy shook his head sadly. 'It looks like Cardoni was just having fun with some of those poor bastards and mixing business with pleasure with the others.'

19

Amanda was half an hour late for her date with Tony Fiori when she finally arrived at the YMCA. On the ride over she had worried that he would think she'd stood him up, but he smiled when he saw her.

'I'm sorry,' Amanda apologized. 'I had a jury out and they came back just before five.'

'Did you win?'

Amanda let her grin answer the question.

'It was so great, Tony. Dad put me on the court appointment list so I could get more trial experience, and they appointed me to help this poor woman, Maria Lopez. She's a single mother and she's got these three maniac kids. So she's at Kmart and José, her two-year-old, streaks down the aisle toward these toys, so she stuffs a roll of Scotch tape and a bottle of aspirin in her coat pocket and goes after him. José knows how to run, but he hasn't figured out stopping yet. *Bam*, he goes headfirst into this display counter. Maria is holding José, who is screaming his head off, and trying to comfort Teresa, who's three and is screaming to keep José company, and trying to keep an eye on Miguel, who's four. Naturally she forgets about the tape and the aspirin, and some idiot security officer arrests her for shoplifting.'

'How did you get her off?'

'I slam-dunked the security officer. He testified that Maria was looking around "stealthily" when she "slipped" the stuff in her pocket. And he said that José didn't take off for a second or so after she "secreted the goods on her person." He made Maria sound like some master thief. Then I showed him the videotape from the store's security camera. You should have heard him stammer and stutter after that. Maria was so grateful. She just manages to get by, and she was scared to death of what would happen to her kids if she went to jail.'

'Sounds like you did a super job.'

'Bet your ass I did,' Amanda said, puffing up like a peacock.

'Then you deserve an amazing dinner as a reward.'

'Oh? Where are we going?'

'It's a surprise. I'll tell you when we're finished working out.'

They swam hard for an hour, and Amanda found that the time went quickly with Tony as her workout partner.

She showered, toweled her hair dry and emerged from the locker room moments before Tony came out.

'Tell me where we're going to dinner,' she demanded. 'I'm famished.'

'Great, because it's a very exclusive Italian place I know. Did you drive?'

Amanda nodded.

'Then follow me.'

Tony took the freeway, then exited onto the winding streets of a residential neighborhood with which she was unfamiliar. Finally Tony pulled into the driveway of a blue two-story Victorian with white gingerbread trim. A high hedge enclosed a small backyard, and a shaded porch fronted the street.

'Welcome to Papa Fiori's, home of the finest Italian food in Portland,' Tony said when Amanda got out of her car.

'You're cooking?'

'*Si, signorina.*'

Tony opened the front door and flipped on the lights.

'This is lovely,' Amanda said as she admired the stained-glass windows above the front door.

'It was the windows that sold me. The place was built in 1912, and those are original.'

There was a television, a VCR and a stereo in the living room, but most of the furnishings in the house were in keeping with its age. Tony led Amanda through the dining room. The dining table was polished mahogany, ornate molding created a border for the high ceiling and the cherrywood mantel over the fireplace was decorated with intricately carved cherubs, dragons and devils.

'Is all this original, too?'

'Mostly, yeah. It's all from the general period.'

Tony flipped on the kitchen light and pointed to a table near the stove. 'Why don't you sit over there while I prepare spaghetti and meatballs alla Fiori. Do you like garlic bread?'

'I love it.'

'Then you're in for a treat.'

'This was as good as advertised,' Amanda said after finishing a second piece of garlic bread. She felt fat and drowsy after consuming too much pasta and two glasses of Chianti.

'Some more wine?'

'Just a little. I've got to drive home.'

Tony topped off her glass and watched as Amanda took a sip. She caught him looking and smiled to let him know that she didn't mind. Amanda could not remember spending a more relaxing evening with a man.

They carried their wineglasses into the living room.

'How's work coming?' Tony asked as he lit the logs in the fireplace.

'I'm pretty busy.'

'You seem to like what you're doing.'

'Yeah, for the most part,' she answered wistfully. 'I'd like more responsibility.'

'You're working on the Cardoni case, aren't you?'

'A little. The motion to suppress is set for Monday, and

Dad's got me researching it. And I've gone out with Herb Cross, our investigator, the guy you met at the hospital.'

'How's it going?' Tony asked when they were settled on the couch.

'I think we're going to get clobbered at the motion.'

'How come?'

'Do you understand what happens at a motion to suppress?'

'I watch *The Practice* when I get a chance.'

Amanda took another sip of wine. Her stocking feet were up on Tony's coffee table and she could feel the heat from the fire on her soles. She decided that she wouldn't mind staying like this for a long time.

'Police usually need a warrant when they search a house, but there are exceptions. One of them comes into play when an officer doesn't have time to get a warrant because the evidence he's looking for might be destroyed or moved while he goes to a judge. That's what the cop who searched the cabin is claiming, and we can't find a way of getting around that.'

Tony was curled up on the couch beside Amanda. His hair was mussed, and the wine had put a glow in his cheeks. Amanda had a hard time keeping her eyes off him.

'What happens if you lose?' Tony asked.

'The state gets to introduce all of the evidence it took from the mountain cabin and Cardoni's house in Portland, and our case is in big trouble.'

'If Cardoni killed all of those people, maybe that isn't such a bad thing.'

'That's one way to look at it.'

'But really, if he's that cold, that cruel, wouldn't you want him locked away someplace where he couldn't hurt people?'

'That's a question of punishment. It's for a judge to decide. You don't ask for the personal history of everyone you operate on, do you? If you found out a patient was a serial killer, would you refuse to treat him?'

'I guess not.' Tony looked at the fire for a moment. 'I wonder how a guy like that thinks. I mean, if he did it. Everyone has a dark side, but what he did . . .'

'Some people just aren't made like the rest of us, Tony. I sat in when Dad talked to Albert Small. He's a psychiatrist Dad consults with on tough cases.'

'What did he say?'

'The serial killer who murdered the people at the cabin is called an organized nonsocial. They are very adept at fitting into society and have above-average intelligence, respectable looks and an uncanny ability to tune in to the needs of others, a skill they use to manipulate people and disarm potential victims. They also have active fantasy lives and visualize their crimes in advance. That helps them anticipate errors that could lead to their capture.'

'I guess Cardoni fits that profile, right? He's a medical doctor and a good-looking man with above-average intelligence, and he was able to convince a bright woman like Justine Castle to marry him.'

'That's true, but there are several differences between the profile and Cardoni. His outrageous behavior attracts attention. He botched operations, used drugs blatantly and made himself generally hated.'

'I see what you mean,' Tony said thoughtfully. 'He sure didn't anticipate errors that could lead to his capture. Leaving that mug and scalpel with his fingerprints at the scene of the murder was really dumb.'

'If he left them.'

'What do you mean?'

'Cardoni claims that he's being framed. Planting those objects at the scene would be a smart move if Cardoni isn't the killer and the real killer wanted to set him up.'

'Do you believe him? Do you think that's what's happening?'

Amanda sighed. 'I don't know. We pointed this out to Dr. Small, and he had an alternative explanation. Organized nonsocials are people who have never grown out of the 'me' stage that most children are in until they're socialized. They think only of their own needs and see themselves as the center of the universe. They can't conceive of themselves as ever being wrong, which leads them to have very poor judgment on occasion. Their very belief in their own infallibility leads them to make mistakes. Add cocaine use to an already impaired ability to make sound judgments and you end up with someone who leaves incriminating evidence at a crime scene because he can't conceive of being caught.'

Amanda stifled a yawn, then blushed and laughed.

'Oh, my gosh. I'm boring you,' Tony said with a grin. 'Should I tell you some dirty jokes or juggle?'

Amanda gave him a sleepy smile. 'It's not you. I'm just wiped from the workout and my trial.'

She yawned again.

Tony laughed. 'Time for you to go home. Do you feel awake enough to drive?'

Amanda wondered if Tony would offer his guest bedroom if she answered in the negative and where that might lead. Before she could get too deep into those woods, Tony stood up.

'Let me fix you a cup of espresso,' he said. 'I make it strong enough to get you to the moon and back without blinking.'

Frank was working in the den when Amanda came home a little after eleven. She stuck her head in the door and said, 'Hi.'

Frank looked up and smiled. 'Where've you been?'

'Remember Tony Fiori?'

'Dominic's son?'

'I had dinner with him.'

'Really? I haven't seen Tony since . . . It must be at least ten years. How did you two get together?'

'I talked to him at the Y a few weeks ago. Then we bumped into each other at St. Francis after Herb and I interviewed Justine Castle. We had coffee and he asked me out a few days later.'

'What was he doing at St. Francis?'

'He's a doctor.'

'No kidding.'

'Why are you so surprised?'

'He had a tough time after Dom died. I heard he dropped out of school. I'm glad to hear that things have worked out for him. Did you have a good time?'

'Very.'

'How'd your trial go?'

Amanda gave Frank a thumbs-up, then told him about the case.

'All right,' Frank answered enthusiastically just as the phone rang.

Frank held up his hand and answered it.

'Is this Frank Jaffe?' a man asked.

Amanda looked at him expectantly, hoping that Tony was calling to say good night. Frank said, 'This is he,' as he shook his head.

'I'm beat, Dad. I'm going to hit the hay,' Amanda told him, and headed to her room. Frank waved at her, then returned to the phone.

'What can I do for you?' Frank asked the caller.

'It's what I can do for you.'

'Oh?'

'I know something about the Cardoni case. We should talk.'

20

On hot summer nights the Carrington, Vermont, marching band performed concerts in a gazebo on the town square, and you could lie back in the grass, look up at the stars and believe that you were living in a slower, more peaceful time when kids ate ice cream and played tag and adults whiled away the time strolling arm in arm down by Hobart Creek. On those nights the darkness hid the fact that many of the quaint nineteenth-century shops that surrounded the square were out of business or barely hanging on. In daylight there was no way to hide the poverty of the town where Justine Castle had grown up.

As Herb Cross drove to James Knoll's farmhouse, he wondered what Justine's life had been like in this town of trailer parks, taverns and failing mills, and he hoped that the former chief of police could give him the answer. Knoll had seemed excited about the opportunity to talk about police work when Cross phoned him from the police station. He had even offered lunch.

A tall, lanky man with a full head of snow-white hair, leathery skin and bifocals walked down from the porch as soon as Herb parked. Cross shook hands with Knoll.

'Come on inside. My wife fixed us some sandwiches and coffee.'

When they were seated at the kitchen table, Knoll studied the investigator.

'Portland to Carrington is a long way to travel.'

'Our client is facing the death penalty.'

Knoll nodded to indicate that no other explanation was necessary.

'It's been some time since I've thought about Justine Castle.' Knoll shook his head. 'That was a bad business.'

'What happened, exactly? I read a newspaper account, but the details were sketchy.'

'We kept it that way. Didn't want a scandal. Gil was dead and there was a young woman's reputation at stake.'

Knoll took a bite of his sandwich and a sip of coffee before going on.

'Gil Manning was our star quarterback and star basketball player . . . and a star asshole. 'Course, everyone overlooked the asshole part because he was . . .'

'A star?' Herb smiled.

'Exactly. Justine was the prettiest girl in school, and they were an item starting in their junior year. Justine was our valedictorian. They were a glamorous couple.

Homecoming weekend their senior year, Gil won the game with a ninety-yard run in the final minutes. It was all anyone talked about until they announced their engagement.

'Gil was a good high school athlete, but he wasn't good enough for a college athletic scholarship. He didn't have the grades, anyway. Justine could have gone to any college. She was accepted at quite a few, if I recall. Then she got pregnant and that was that. She and Gil were married the day after graduation and they moved in with his parents. That's when the trouble started.

'Gil couldn't handle life after high school. He wasn't important anymore. He always drank a lot, but that was boys-will-be-boys stuff while he was the big man on campus. After high school he was just another town problem when he got tanked up.

'The real trouble began when he started taking out his frustrations on Justine. One night Gil beat her up so bad she lost the baby. I tried to get her to tell the truth about what happened. It was pretty obvious that she hadn't fallen down any stairs. But Gil was at the hospital, hovering over her, real solicitous, and she wouldn't speak against him.'

Knoll shook his head sadly. 'Justine had always been so pretty and so bright, but the woman I saw at the hospital looked dragged out and used up, and she was only eighteen. It would have given me great pleasure to haul Gil's sorry ass to jail, but we had no case without Justine.'

Knoll paused to take a bite from his sandwich.

'Two months later we got a nine-one-one from the

Manning place. It was Justine, scared to death. She was gulping air and could hardly speak. I got there about one in the morning. Gil was stretched out by the front door, facedown. She'd killed him with his hunting rifle, one shot, right through the heart. When I got to the farm Justine was sitting at the kitchen table. She was still holding the phone. Dispatch had told her to stay on the line until we got there. I had to pry the receiver out of her hand. She was shaking like a leaf.'

'Did she tell you what happened?'

'Oh, yeah. We talked about it once I got her settled down. Gil had insisted she go drinking with him. She didn't want to, but he made a scene. Gil got drunk and nasty at Dave Buck's tavern, and Dave tossed him after he tried to start a fight with some kid from a rival high school. On the way home Gil started blaming her for his life being shit. He said she was a fat pig, claimed she was holding him back.' Knoll shook his head. 'From what, I could never guess. Then he cracked her on the jaw. There was a bad bruise. We took pictures. He hit her in the eye, too. Then he pushed her out of the car and tried to run her down.

'Justine ran away, and Gil was too tanked to catch her. When he stopped looking she headed home in the dark. By the time she reached the farm she was hysterical and scared to death. She said that she was certain that Gil would kill her when he came home. Gil's folks were visiting their other son in Connecticut, so she was all alone. She grabbed Gil's rifle and sat on the couch in the front room.

'Meanwhile Gil had crashed the car. He wasn't hurt, but the car was totaled. Gil got a ride home from Andy Laidlaw, one of his drinking buddies. Andy told me that Gil admitted trying to run down Justine, but he also said that Gil was real remorseful about what he'd done. When they got to the farm, Andy offered to go inside with Gil, but Gil sent him off. Andy said that Gil was standing in the front yard when he drove away.'

'How did Gil end up dead?'

'Justine said she heard the car drive in and thought it was Gil's. She didn't know he had wrecked it. When he came through the door, she told him to leave or she would shoot him. He took a step forward, she fired and that was that.'

'How close to town was Justine's parents' house?'

'Closer than the farm, but she said that she was so scared after Gil tried to kill her that she just ran back to the farm without thinking. She didn't want her parents to know, anyway. She was ashamed that the marriage wasn't working.'

'Didn't she cool down while she was sitting there with the gun?'

'Didn't have time.'

'When did they leave the bar?'

'About eleven o'clock.'

'When did she phone in the nine-one-one?'

'About one.'

'That means there was probably an hour and a half between the time she ran away from her husband and the time she shot him.'

'We knew that, but you have to remember that she ran the four and a half miles from town. It took her close to an hour. During that time, Gil was wrecking the car, going to Andy's house and getting a lift. Justine said that Gil walked in about five to ten minutes after she got home.'

'So you figured the shooting was justifiable?'

'I talked it over with the county prosecutor, and he didn't want to go with it,' Knoll said, not answering Herb's question. 'Justine was a good girl who was stuck with a bad man. Everyone knew it. Everyone knew about the baby, too. There wasn't much sympathy for Gil. The only ones who wanted Justine prosecuted were Gil's parents, but that's to be expected. They claimed that Justine murdered Gil to get the insurance.'

Cross raised an eyebrow. 'How much was that?'

'About a hundred thousand dollars, if I recollect correctly.'

'That's a lot of money for a farm girl.'

'That's a lot of money for anyone.'

Cross watched Knoll carefully when he asked his next question.

'Did you believe Dr. Castle's story?'

Knoll never broke eye contact. 'I never had any reason not to, but then I never pushed much to prove she was lying. It was one of those times when no one wanted me to be much of a detective.'

21

The Cardoni case had created big-city parking problems in Cedar City, and Amanda drove around town for fifteen minutes looking for a space. At the courthouse, Amanda went to the head of the line of people waiting for the first available seat in Judge Brody's courtroom and showed her bar card to the guard. Frank was conferring with Cardoni at the defense counsel's table while they waited for the judge to make his entrance. Their client was wearing a charcoal gray business suit, a white silk shirt and a blue tie with narrow yellow stripes. Amanda could understand why someone as sophisticated as Justine Castle would fall for the surgeon. He had rugged good looks and broad shoulders. He also looked dangerous, leaning slightly forward, tense, like a hunted animal.

'You made it,' Frank said with a smile.

'I almost didn't. There isn't a place to park in the whole town. I got lucky over by Stokely's.'

'Vince, you remember my daughter, Amanda? She helped me research the motion, and I wanted her as second chair in case we're faced with a tricky legal issue.'

Cardoni barely acknowledged Amanda. She forced herself to smile at him and took her seat. She was glad that her father was sitting between her and their client.

Amanda had barely gotten her papers out of her attaché case when a door opened behind the dais and the judge entered the courtroom. The bailiff rapped his gavel, and everyone stood until Judge Brody indicated that they could be seated.

'Are you gentlemen ready to proceed?' Brody asked. Scofield nodded from his counsel table.

'Ready for Dr. Cardoni, Your Honor,' Frank Jaffe said.

'Opening statement, Mr. Jaffe?'

'A brief one, Your Honor. We are seeking to suppress every piece of evidence gathered at a cabin in Milton County and Dr. Cardoni's home in Multnomah County. The state searched the Milton County house without a warrant, so it bears the burden of convincing the court of the existence of an exception to the state and federal rules requiring government agents to procure a warrant before searching a citizen's home.

'The search of Dr. Cardoni's Portland residence was conducted pursuant to a warrant, but the warrant was issued because of information in an affidavit. We contend that the evidence discussed in the affidavit was obtained during an illegal warrantless search of the Milton County home. If the court agrees, we ask you to suppress the evidence gathered in Portland under the "fruit of the poisonous tree" doctrine, which I have discussed in the memorandum of law submitted by me in support of this motion.'

'Very well. Mr. Scofield, what is your position?'

Scofield rose slowly. He rocked in place as he spoke.

'Well, Judge, Detective Robert Vasquez, a Portland police detective, received an anonymous tip informing him that the defendant was holding two kilos of cocaine in his home up here in Milton County. He'll tell you that he corroborated the tip, then had to act fast because he learned that the sale of the coke was imminent. He rushed up here and searched the house without a warrant because he had established exigent circumstances. As it was, he missed the sale.

'As the court knows, a police officer does not have to stop and get a search warrant if he has reason to believe that stopping to get the warrant will lead to the loss or destruction of the very evidence that he wants to seize. Of course, if the search here in Milton County was okay, there was nothing wrong with using the evidence found in the mountain home as the basis for probable cause in the warrant affidavit for the defendant's Portland house.'

'Who's your first witness, Mr. Scofield?' Judge Brody asked.

'The State calls Sherri Watson.'

Watson was the receptionist at vice and narcotics who had transferred the anonymous call to Vasquez. After she testified that the call had in fact been phoned in to police headquarters, Scofield called Bobby Vasquez to the stand.

Vasquez was wearing a navy blue sports jacket and tan slacks. Amanda thought he looked nervous when he took the oath. He took a sip of water as he waited for the district attorney's first question.

'Please tell the court the circumstances that led you to search the Milton County cabin without a warrant,' Scofield asked after the detective recounted his background in police work.

'I was at my desk in vice and narcotics writing a police report when the receptionist put through a caller who wanted to report a crime. I was the only one available, so it was chance that I caught the call.'

'What did the caller tell you?' Scofield asked.

'The informant said that Dr. Vincent Cardoni was going to sell two kilos of cocaine.'

'Did the caller tell you where the defendant was keeping the cocaine?'

'Yes, sir. In a mountain cabin here in Milton County.'

'Did you obtain a warrant to search the cabin?'

'No, sir. The caller never identified him- or herself. The tip was anonymous. I knew I needed corroboration before I could go to a judge.'

'Did you try to corroborate the call?' Scofield asked.

'Yes, sir. I confronted a known drug dealer who knew the person who had sold Dr. Cardoni the cocaine, and he confirmed that Cardoni was going to sell the two kilos.'

'Did your informant know who was buying the two kilos of cocaine from the defendant?'

'No. Just that Dr. Cardoni was selling and that the two kilos were supposedly in the doctor's cabin.'

'So he corroborated the anonymous caller's statement that the drugs were in Milton County?'

'Yes, sir.'

'Now that you had corroboration, why didn't you get a warrant?'

'There wasn't time. I talked to this informant in the afternoon. He said the sale was going down that day. It takes about an hour and a half to drive to the defendant's house from Portland. I was afraid that I would miss the sale if I waited for a judge to issue a warrant.'

'Tell the judge what happened when you arrived at the cabin.'

'I gained entry to the house. Once I was inside I noticed a padlock on one of the doors on the bottom floor. This made me suspicious, and I concluded that it was probable that the defendant had locked the room to protect his contraband.'

'How did you open the lock?'

'With a lock pick I had with me.'

'Did you find cocaine in the ground-floor room?'

'Yes, sir,' Vasquez answered grimly.

'What else did you find?'

'The severed heads of two Caucasian females.'

There was a stir in the courtroom, and Judge Brody rapped his gavel. While order was being restored, Vasquez took a drink of water.

'Can you identify these items, Detective Vasquez?' Scofield asked.

Vasquez took three photographs from the district attorney and identified them as different views of the refrigerator and its contents. Scofield handed the photos to the judge and moved to enter them into evidence for purposes of the hearing. Brody's face drained of color when he saw the pictures. The judge looked at the evidence quickly, then turned the photographs facedown.

'After finding the severed heads, did you call the Milton County Sheriff's Department?'

'Yes, sir.'

'What happened then?'

'Representatives of that department, the Oregon State Police, and the Portland Police Bureau arrived at the scene and conducted a thorough examination of the premises.'

'Were a number of physical items, including numerous pieces of scientific evidence, seized from the cabin?'

'Yes, sir.'

'Your Honor, I am handing you State's exhibit one. It is a list of all the items seized from the cabin. Rather than having Detective Vasquez take up court time, Mr. Jaffe and I have stipulated that this is the evidence that the defendant wishes to suppress.'

'Do you so stipulate, Mr. Jaffe?' the judge asked.

'Yes, Your Honor.'

'Very well, the stipulation will be accepted and the list will be admitted into evidence. Proceed, Mr. Scofield.'

Scofield walked Vasquez through the search of the Portland home, then concluded his questioning.

'Your witness, Mr. Jaffe.'

Frank leaned back in his chair and studied the policeman. Vasquez sat quietly, looking very professional.

'Detective Vasquez, how many other officers accompanied you to the cabin when you made the search?'

'None.'

Frank looked bewildered. 'You expected to meet two or more men who were trafficking in cocaine, did you not?'

'Yes, sir.'

'You presumed that they would be dangerous, didn't you?'

'I didn't know.'

'Isn't it true that drug dealers often carry guns?'

'Yes.'

'Are they frequently violent men?'

'They can be.'

'And you went to meet these drug dealers, who were most probably armed, without backup?'

'It was stupid. In retrospect, I guess I should have brought help or called on Sheriff Mills to assist me.'

'So you lay your failure to bring backup to stupidity?'

Vasquez nodded. 'I should have known better.'

'Could there have been another reason why you drove to the cabin alone?'

Vasquez thought for a moment.

'I'm afraid I don't understand the question.'

'Well, Detective, if there had been other officers there, they would have witnessed your illegal entry into the cabin and could have testified against you, couldn't they?'

'Objection,' Scofield said. 'The court will decide if the entry was illegal.'

'Sustained,' Judge Brody agreed.

'Detective Vasquez, have you read the fingerprint report from the Oregon State Police?'

'Yes, sir.'

'Were your prints lifted from the crime scene?'

'No.'

'And why is that?'

'I wore latex gloves.'

'Why would you do that?'

Vasquez hesitated. He had not anticipated this question.

'I, uh . . . It was a crime scene, Counselor. I didn't want to confuse the forensic experts.'

'What confusion could there be? Your prints are on file. It would be very easy to eliminate them.'

'I didn't want to cause the lab extra work.'

'Or leave incriminating evidence of an illegal break-in?' Frank asked.

'Objection,' Scofield said.

'Sustained,' Brody said. 'Stop throwing mud on this officer's reputation and move on, Mr. Jaffe.'

'Yes, Your Honor. Detective Vasquez, you testified that you met the informant who corroborated the anonymous caller on the afternoon of the day you searched the cabin?'

'That's correct.'

'As soon as you had your corroboration, you drove to Milton County?'

'Yes. I felt I had to go immediately or risk missing the sale of the cocaine.'

'I gather that the informant who corroborated your

information was the only witness you talked to that day before heading for Milton County?'

'Right.'

'What is the name of the person who corroborated your information on the day of the search?'

'I'm afraid I can't reveal that, Mr. Jaffe. He spoke to me on a guarantee of confidentiality.'

'Your Honor, I ask the court to instruct the witness to answer. Otherwise you will be in the position of having one anonymous informant corroborating another.'

Brody turned to Vasquez. 'Why won't you reveal this man's name?'

'He would be in great danger, Your Honor. He could even be killed.'

'I see. Well, I'm not going to risk that, Mr. Jaffe. If you are implying that no such witness exists, I'll just have to judge Detective Vasquez's credibility.'

'And I assume that you will suppress all of the evidence if you conclude that the officer is lying?'

'Of course,' Brody answered with a scowl, 'but you're a far way from establishing that, Mr. Jaffe.'

The ghost of a smile played on Frank's lips as he told the court that he had no more questions of the witness.

After a brief redirect examination of Vasquez, Fred Scofield summoned several more police witnesses. Judge Brody called a halt to the proceedings a little before noon, and the spectators rushed for the door. Frank and Fred Scofield walked over to the judge and had a quiet conversation at the bench while Amanda started collecting her papers.

'How do you think your father did?' Cardoni asked.

'I think he scored some points,' Amanda answered without looking at the doctor.

Cardoni grew quiet. Amanda finished packing her attaché case.

'You don't like me, do you?'

The question startled Amanda. She forced herself to look at Cardoni. He was slouched in his chair, studying her.

'I don't know you well enough to like you or dislike you, Dr. Cardoni, but I am working very hard to help you.'

'That's nice of you, considering the fee I'm paying your firm.'

'This has nothing to do with the fee, Doctor. I work hard for all of our clients.'

'How hard can you work when you think I killed those people?'

Amanda colored. 'My belief in your guilt or innocence has no effect on my professional performance,' she answered stiffly.

'Well, it matters to me,' Cardoni said just as the guards who were going to escort him to the jail appeared. Cardoni turned away from Amanda and put his hands behind his back. Amanda was relieved that their conversation was over. Frank returned to the table while the guards were securing Cardoni's handcuffs.

'The judge has some matters in other cases at one-thirty,' he said to his client. 'We should start at two. Fred is resting, so it's our turn to put on witnesses after lunch. I'll see you in court.'

The guards led Cardoni away.

'You going to Stokely's?' Frank asked Amanda.

'Where else? Want to join me?'

'Sorry, I can't. I have a lot to do during the lunch hour. Eat a big slice of pie for me.'

'You bet,' Amanda said. Just as she reached the courtroom door she turned slightly and saw Cardoni watching her. His scrutiny unsettled her, but she forced herself to meet his eyes. For a moment she refused to back down. Then a thought occurred to her. It did not take much courage to confront a prisoner in manacles who was surrounded by guards. Would she have the courage to stare him down if he was loose? The odds were that Cardoni would be convicted, but Frank was very good. What if he won freedom for the surgeon? Would he remember her brazen stare?

Amanda's mouth went dry. She decided that she did not want to antagonize Cardoni; she did not want him thinking about her at all. Amanda broke eye contact and hurried out of the courtroom.

22

'Any witnesses for the defendant, Mr. Jaffe?'

'I do have a witness, Your Honor. He's waiting in the hall. May I get him?'

Amanda watched her father walk up the aisle and into the courthouse corridor and return with a hulking, bald-headed man. Fred Scofield frowned, and Bobby Vasquez turned ash gray.

'Please state your name for the record,' the bailiff instructed the witness after swearing him in.

'Arthur Wayne Prochaska.'

'Mr. Prochaska, how are you employed?' Frank asked.

'I manage a couple of bars in Portland.'

'Would one of those bars be the Rebel Tavern?'

'Yeah.'

'Mr. Prochaska,' Frank asked, 'do you know a police officer named Robert Vasquez?'

'Sure, I know Bobby.'

'Can you point him out for the record?'

Prochaska grinned and pointed directly at Vasquez.

'He's the good-lookin' fella sitting behind the DA.'

'When is the last time you spoke with Officer Vasquez?'

Prochaska looked thoughtful for a moment. 'We met at the Rebel the day he found those heads. It was afternoon. I read about them heads in the paper the next day.'

'Why did you meet with Officer Vasquez on that day?'

'He asked me to,' Prochaska answered with a shrug. 'I wasn't doing anything, so I said okay.'

'Did Officer Vasquez explain why he wanted to talk to you?'

'Yeah. He said a friend of mine sold some doctor cocaine. I told Bobby I didn't know anything about it. To tell the truth, I was pissed off that he would ask me to rat out a friend.'

'Was the doctor he asked you about Vincent Cardoni?'

'Right. That was the guy. Cardoni.'

'Did you know Dr. Cardoni?'

'Never heard of him until Bobby showed up.'

'Did you tell that to Officer Vasquez?'

'Yeah.'

'Did Officer Vasquez try to bribe you?'

'I don't know if you'd call it a bribe. The cops do it all the time. You know, they bust you, then they tell you they'll go easy on you if you'll tell them about someone else.'

'And Officer Vasquez tried to bargain with you in that manner?'

'Yeah. I was waiting on charges of possession with intent. He said he'd talk to the feds if I told him about this doctor. Only I couldn't, because I didn't know him.'

'Mr. Prochaska, Officer Vasquez has testified under oath about a conversation he alleges occurred on the afternoon of the day that he discovered the heads of the dead women. Was anyone else with you when you spoke with Officer Vasquez?'

'No.'

'Officer Vasquez testified that the person he talked to said that Dr. Cardoni purchased two kilos of cocaine from someone the informant knew. Dr. Cardoni allegedly was holding the cocaine in a cabin in Milton County and was going to sell it that afternoon. Do you remember saying anything like that to Officer Vasquez?'

Prochaska laughed. 'I think Bobby got caught with his pants down when he broke into the cabin, so he made this stuff up.'

'Objection, Your Honor,' Scofield said. 'Speculation, nonresponsive. I move to strike the answer.'

'Objection sustained,' Brody said. He looked angry, and his tone was harsh when he ordered Prochaska to confine his answer to the question he had been asked.

'Mr. Prochaska, do you deny that you gave Officer Vasquez information about Dr. Cardoni?'

'Yeah, absolutely. That's why I'm testifying. I don't want no one spreading lies about me.'

'Your witness, Mr. Scofield.'

Fred Scofield's lips formed a grim smile as he studied Art Prochaska. The dealer's reputation was well known, and he could not wait to get at him.

'Have you ever been convicted of a crime, Mr. Prochaska?' he asked calmly.

'Yeah, several. But none lately.'

'Why don't you tell Judge Brody your criminal history?'

'Okay. Let's see. I got a couple of assaults. I was down at the state pen for two years. There's some drug stuff. I was busted a few times, but they didn't prove it except once. I did do a few years on that.'

'Mr. Prochaska, you are the right-hand man of Martin Breach, a notorious drug dealer, are you not? His enforcer?'

'Martin is my business partner. I don't know about that other stuff.'

'Mr. Breach has a reputation for killing people who inform on him, doesn't he?'

'I never seen it.'

'If you admitted that you informed on Mr. Breach, it would put you at some risk, wouldn't it?'

'I would never do something like that. I don't believe in it.'

'Not even to save yourself from serving a fifteen-year sentence in a federal penitentiary?'

'No, sir. Besides, those charges are gonna be dropped.'

'But you didn't know that when Officer Vasquez talked to you.'

'I suspected they might be,' Prochaska answered with a smirk.

'Isn't it true that you did corroborate Officer Vasquez's information but are afraid to admit it for fear that Martin Breach will kill you?'

'Vasquez was lying if he says I told him that stuff.'

Scofield smiled. 'We have only your word for that against the word of an officer of the law, don't we?'

'Hey, I got proof he lied.'

Scofield paled. 'What proof?'

'Do you think I'm dumb enough to meet a cop and not protect myself? Bobby and me had our chat in the men's john, where I got surveillance equipment. I taped the whole conversation.'

Scofield turned toward Vasquez. The policeman looked sick. Frank leaped to his feet, a cassette in his hand. He had been waiting for this moment.

'I have the tape of the conversation, Your Honor. I think we should play it and resolve this dispute between the witnesses.'

'Objection, Your Honor,' Scofield said. His voice was shaking.

'On what grounds?' Brody asked angrily.

'Uh, if . . . if there is such a tape, it was recorded surreptitiously. That violates Oregon law.'

Brody glared at the district attorney. 'Mr. Scofield, your question opened the door for this evidence. And I'll tell you something else: If someone is lying in my courtroom, I want to know about it. I don't care if that tape was made by Iraqi terrorists. We are going to hear it right now. Play the tape, Mr. Jaffe.'

Frank placed the cassette in a boom box that he had brought with him from Portland. When he hit the play button, everyone in the court heard a door slam shut and the sound of a brief struggle. Then Bobby Vasquez said, 'Long time, Art.'

The tape spun along. When Prochaska turned down Vasquez's offer to help him with his federal charges, Judge Brody's eyes narrowed, and he cast a withering glance at Vasquez. Then Prochaska told Vasquez that he did not know Vincent Cardoni and refused to talk about Martin Breach. By the time the tape wound to a halt Judge Brody was furious, Scofield was shell-shocked and Vasquez was staring at his feet. Vincent Cardoni smiled triumphantly.

'I want Officer Vasquez back on the witness stand immediately,' Brody ordered Scofield.

'I believe Officer Vasquez should seek counsel before answering any questions about the tape we've just heard,' Scofield said, casting a quick, angry look at the detective.

'Quite right, quite right, Mr. Scofield. Thank you for correcting me. Officer Vasquez better get one hell of a lawyer, because his criminal conduct has forced me to suppress every piece of evidence seized at the house in Milton County and every piece of evidence seized from Dr. Cardoni's home in Portland. I grant this motion regretfully, but I have no choice, Mr. Scofield, because your star witness is a damned liar.'

Judge Brody glared at Vasquez.

'Nine people have been slaughtered, Detective. Horribly butchered. I make no pronouncement as to the guilt or innocence of Dr. Cardoni. I haven't heard the evidence in this case. I do know that the person who killed those people is probably going to escape his justly deserved punishment because of you. I hope you can live with that.'

Frank stood up to speak. 'Your Honor, will you reconsider your decision on bail for Dr. Cardoni? In order for bail to be denied in an aggravated murder case it must appear to the court that the state will be able to prove its case at trial by clear and convincing evidence. Now that the court has suppressed all of the state's evidence, it is unlikely that the case will go to trial. I don't even see how Mr. Scofield can appeal your ruling in good faith. I ask that the court release Dr. Cardoni on his own recognizance.

'I am also putting Mr. Scofield on notice that I am moving against his indictment on the grounds that it was obtained through the submission to the grand jury of illegally obtained evidence and police perjury.'

Frank handed the original of his motion, which he had prepared in advance of the hearing, to Judge Brody and gave a copy to the district attorney. As soon as Brody finished skimming the new motion his head dropped. When he raised it, his eyes blazed with anger.

'You have tied my hands with your unprofessional conduct, Mr. Scofield. I have no idea how Vasquez took you in. Your preparation for this motion to suppress borders on the criminal. You won your motion to deny bail by promising that you would produce all sorts of evidence against Dr. Cardoni. Now you can't present any of it.

'Your motion to release Dr. Cardoni on his own recognizance is granted, Mr. Jaffe. I will take the motion to dismiss under advisement. Mr. Scofield, you have thirty days to file a notice of appeal from any of my rulings or they will become final. Court is in recess.'

Judge Brody fled to his chambers.

'Thank you, Frank,' Cardoni told Amanda's father. Then he looked at her. 'And thank you, Amanda. I know you think I'm guilty, but Frank's told me how hard you've worked for me, and I appreciate it.'

Amanda was surprised at how sincere Cardoni sounded, but it didn't change her opinion. What had just happened frightened her. Frank was a magician in the courtroom, but his latest trick could have horrifying consequences.

Reporters mobbed Frank in the corridor outside the courtroom. Amanda forgot her misgivings as she was caught up in the action. Some of the reporters directed their questions to her, and it dawned on Amanda that she was a celebrity, if only for the length of a sound bite. After the furor died down, father and daughter walked to Stokely's to eat dinner. Frank was uncharacteristically quiet after a victory of this magnitude.

'What happens to Cardoni now?' Amanda asked.

'He'll be processed out of jail, Herb will drive him home and he'll try to put his life back together.'

'So it's over?'

'It should be. Art Prochaska's testimony was the legal equivalent of a nuclear weapon. There isn't any evidence left for the State to use.'

'How long have you known about Prochaska?'

'He called Friday evening.'

'So you knew we'd win all along.'

'There's no such thing as a sure thing, but this is as close as I've ever gotten.' Frank noticed the look on Amanda's face and added, 'I hope you're not upset that I didn't tell you about Art.'

'No, that's okay,' Amanda answered, but she was upset. They walked in silence for half a block. Then Amanda's thoughts shifted to Cardoni.

'I know I should be excited because we won, but I just . . . I think he killed those people, Dad.'

'I don't feel so good about this one myself,' Frank admitted.

'If he's guilty, they can't try him, can they?'

'Nope. I did too good a job. Vincent's free and clear.'

'What if he does it again?'

Frank put his arm around Amanda's shoulders. His closeness was comforting, but it could not make her forget the videotape or the still pictures of the nine corpses.

'About three years after I started out I second-chaired a terrible case with Phil Lomax. Two young children and their baby-sitter were murdered during a home burglary. The crime was brutal. The defendant was a very bad actor. Totally unrepentant, cruel, with a long history of prior vicious assaults. The DA was certain she had the right man, but the evidence was paper thin. We fought our guts out, and the chances of conviction were about fifty-fifty by the end of the trial.

'After the jury went out, Phil and I went to one bar to wait and the DA and her staff went to another. The jury came back four hours later with a guilty verdict. About a month later I bumped into one of the DA's investigators. He told me that Phil and I had been the subject of discussion while the prosecutor and her assistants were waiting for the verdict. They thought that we were very ethical lawyers who had fought hard but had also fought clean. They respected us as people and they had come to the conclusion that we'd sleep better with a conviction than an acquittal. They were right. I was actually relieved that we had lost, even though I gave one hundred and ten percent for our client.'

'Do you feel bad now?'

'Do you hear me bragging about our victory, Amanda? As a professional, I'm proud that I did my job. As an officer of the court, I feel good about exposing perjury by someone who is sworn to protect us and uphold the Constitution. What Vasquez did was inexcusable. But I'm also a human being and I'm worried. So I pray that Vincent Cardoni is an innocent man who has been wrongly accused. If he's guilty, I pray that this experience has frightened him so much that he won't hurt anyone else.'

Frank gave Amanda's hand a squeeze.

'This is not an easy business, Amanda. It's not easy at all.'

23

Martin Breach was hunkered down over a slab of ribs when Art Prochaska walked into the restaurant. He motioned Prochaska into a chair with a hand stained with barbecue sauce.

'You want a plate?' Breach asked. His mouth was stuffed with meat, and the question was barely intelligible.

'Yeah.'

Breach waved. A waiter appeared immediately.

'The deluxe combo and another pitcher of beer,' Breach said. The waiter scurried away.

'So?' Breach asked.

'Cardoni is out.'

'Good work. I was worried that puke would cut a deal with the DA if he went down.' Breach ripped a chunk of meat off a long bone. A sloppy scarlet ring of sauce circled Breach's mouth. 'Now I want my money. Put Eugene and Ed Gordon on Cardoni. The first chance they get, I want him snatched.'

Prochaska nodded. Breach handed Prochaska a fat rib. The enforcer started to protest, but Breach insisted.

'Take it, Arty. I'll get one of yours when your order comes.'

Breach wiped his face with a napkin, then reached for another rib.

'I want Cardoni in good enough condition to chat,' he told Prochaska between bites. 'No brain damage. Tell the two of 'em. If Cardoni is too fucked up to tell me where my money is, I'll take it out on them.'

24

There was a message from Herb Cross on the answering machine when Frank and Amanda arrived home from Cedar City. Frank shucked his jacket and tie, fixed himself a glass of scotch and dialed a number in Vermont.

'What's up?' Frank asked when he was connected to Cross's hotel room.

'I may be on to something.'

'Oh?'

Frank listened quietly while Herb told him what he had learned during his meeting with James Knoll.

'It doesn't sound like there's anything we can use,' Frank said when Herb was through. 'Evidence that Dr. Castle shot an abusive husband in self-defense when she was in her teens isn't going to be admissible to prove that she kidnapped and tortured people.'

'I'd agree if that was all I found. Gil Manning was insured for one hundred thousand dollars. When the police cleared Castle, the insurance company paid off. She used the money to pay her tuition at Dartmouth. In her senior year she married a wealthy classmate, and they moved to Denver after graduation. Eight months later Castle's husband was dead.'

'You're shitting me.'

'It was a one-car accident. He was heavily intoxicated. He was also heavily insured and he had a fat trust fund. Castle inherited the money from the trust fund and she received the insurance money.'

'Now that is interesting.'

'I phoned the dead husband's parents in Chicago. They swear that their son was never more than a social drinker. They pressed for an investigation, but the cops told them that they were satisfied that their son's death was an accident. Castle's in-laws think that Justine was a gold digger. They were opposed to the marriage.'

'Was there any evidence of foul play?'

'I haven't looked into the accident yet. Do you want me to go to Denver?'

'No, come home.'

'I think I'm on to something with this, Frank. I think we should pursue it.'

'That's not necessary. I won the motion to suppress. Cardoni is free and it's unlikely he'll be prosecuted.'

'What! How did that happen?'

'If you've got a few minutes, I'll tell you.'

25

Granite cherubs and gargoyles peered down on passersby from the ornate stone scrollwork that graced the façade of the Stockman Building, a fourteen-story edifice that had been erected in the center of downtown Portland shortly after World War I. The law firm of Jaffe, Katz, Lehane and Brindisi leased the eighth floor. Frank Jaffe's spacious corner office was decorated with antiques. He sat behind a partner's desk that he had picked up for a song at an auction. Currier and Ives prints graced one wall, and a nineteenth-century oil of the Columbia Gorge, which Frank had discovered at another auction, hung across from him over a comfortable sofa. The only jarring note was the computer monitor that sat on the edge of Frank's desk.

Vincent Cardoni showed no interest in the décor of Frank's office. The physician's attention was riveted on his attorney, and he shifted anxiously as Frank explained Fred Scofield's latest legal maneuver.

'So you're saying we have to go back to court?'

'Yes. Judge Brody has set the hearing for next Wednesday.'

'What kind of bullshit is this? We won, didn't we?'

'Scofield moved to reopen the motion to suppress. He has a new theory, inevitable discovery.'

'What's that mean?'

'It comes out of *Nix v. Williams*, a United States Supreme Court opinion. Around Christmas of 1968 a ten-year-old girl disappeared from a YMCA building in Des Moines, Iowa. Shortly after she disappeared, Robert Anthony Williams was seen leaving the YMCA carrying a large bundle wrapped in a blanket. A young boy who helped Williams open his car door saw two skinny white legs under the blanket.

'The next day Williams's car was found a hundred and sixty miles east of Des Moines in Davenport, Iowa. Later clothing belonging to the child and a blanket similar to the one Williams carried from the Y were found in a rest stop between Des Moines and Davenport. The police concluded that Williams had left the girl's body between Des Moines and the rest stop.

'The police used two hundred volunteers to conduct a large-scale search in an attempt to find the body of the victim. Meanwhile, Williams surrendered to the police in Davenport and contacted an attorney in Des Moines.

Two Des Moines detectives drove to Davenport, picked up Williams and drove him back to Des Moines. During the trip, one of the detectives told Williams that snow might cover the little girl, making it impossible to find her body. Then he said that the girl's parents were entitled to a Christian burial for the little girl who had been snatched away from them on Christmas Eve. Later in the ride, Williams told the detectives how to find the body.

'Before trial, Williams's attorney moved to suppress evidence of the condition of the body on the ground that its discovery was the fruit of Williams's statements and those statements were the product of an interrogation that was illegal because it had been conducted out of the presence of his attorney.

'I'm not going to bore you with all the in and outs of the appeals that eventually brought the case to the United States Supreme Court twice. What you need to know is that the justices adopted the inevitable-discovery rule. They concluded that the evidence supported a finding that the search party would inevitably have discovered the body of the little girl even if Williams had not led the police to it. Then the Court ruled that evidence that would normally be excluded because of police miscon-duct is still admissible if it would have been discovered inevitably.'

'How does that help Scofield?'

'The cabin is on private land, but the graveyard is on a trail that goes through national forest land. Scofield is arguing that the graveyard was so obvious that Vasquez, a hiker, a forest ranger, somebody would inevitably have discovered it, giving a judge grounds to issue a search warrant for the cabin.'

Cardoni laughed. 'That's bullshit. Vasquez never went back there and there wasn't anyone near the cabin until Vasquez called the cops.'

'You're right, Vince. The argument is total horseshit, but Brody might jump on this with both feet. There's an election coming up. Word is that Brody is going to run for one more term, then retire. If he lost the election, he would be humiliated. Granting Scofield's motion would get him off the hook for the most unpopular decision that he's ever made. Most Milton County voters don't understand the subtleties of search-and-seizure law. All they know is that Brody let you out and that the cops think you're Jack the Ripper's meaner cousin.'

'Even if that tub of lard does rule for Scofield, you'd win on appeal, wouldn't you?'

'I'm pretty sure I would. The problem is that Brody will put you back in jail pending trial.'

Cardoni's toe tapped rapidly.

'I pay you to anticipate things like this.'

'Well, I didn't. Hell, Vince, there's no way I could.'

Cardoni glared at Frank. He was rigid with anger.

'I am not going back to jail because some fat-ass judge wants to win an election. Either you handle this or I will.'

26

Eugene Pritchard and Ed Gordon were intelligent muscle whom Martin Breach used when more than simple violence was needed. Pritchard had been a professional fighter with a decent record until he was busted smuggling cocaine into the country after a fight in Mexico. Gordon was an ex-marine. He had been dishonorably discharged for assaulting an officer.

At eight o'clock on the day that Frank Jaffe told Cardoni about Scofield's motion to reopen, Pritchard and Gordon were debating the pros and cons of a home invasion when Cardoni's car drove out of his garage. They followed without lights until Cardoni turned onto a major thoroughfare. Then they stayed a few cars behind the doctor and tried to guess where he was headed. After a while it got confusing. Cardoni seemed to be wandering aimlessly. He cruised the streets of downtown Portland for a while, then headed out of town along Burnside. Several miles later Cardoni turned onto Skyline Boulevard and followed it past the cemetery until he reached a bumpy dirt track that ended abruptly at Forest Park, a vast wooded area.

Gordon turned off the headlights and followed at a safe distance. Cardoni got out of his car and started off along a narrow trail.

'What's he doing out here?' Pritchard asked.

'Maybe he's got a few more bodies stashed in the woods.'

Pritchard shook his head. 'He is one sick fuck.'

'Don't make disparaging remarks about someone who's making our job so easy. We'll take him here. It's isolated and there are no witnesses.'

Pritchard grabbed a flashlight and they set off after Cardoni.

The Wildwood Trail runs for more than twenty miles through Portland's park system. The part of this trail Cardoni was walking led into the deep central section of Forest Park, far from roads or houses. Even though Pritchard was in the middle of a big city, he felt that he was standing in the dark heart of an unexplored jungle. Gordon had hiked and camped in the army, but Pritchard was a city boy who preferred watching TV and drinking in bars to trekking through the forest primeval. He definitely did not like wandering through the woods in the dark.

Following the faint glow of the doctor's flashlight was easy, and Pritchard kept his off. The rotting corpse of a tree felled by the violent storms of winter blocked part of the trail, and Gordon tripped over a root. He swore under his breath and squinted, trying to make out the floor of the forest in the dark. Pritchard turned his head and told his partner to shut up and watch where he was going. When he looked forward he could not find Cardoni's light. The men froze. The only sounds they heard were the swish of tree branches and the scratch of tiny claws in the underbrush.

Then Pritchard heard a crack, a grunt and a second sharp blow. He spun toward the sound and turned on his flashlight. Gordon was down and blood was pooling under him. Pritchard felt for a pulse. Gordon was breathing, but he was not moving.

'It's spooky in the woods at night.'

Cardoni was behind him. Pritchard pulled his gun and spun around.

'Do you feel like Hansel and Gretel all alone in the forest of the wicked witch?'

'You can stop with the games, ' Pritchard said, fighting hard to keep the fear out of his voice.

'You're the one who's been playing hide-and-seek all week, or didn't you think I'd notice?' Cardoni answered from a new location. Pritchard had not heard him move. He aimed his flashlight at Cardoni's voice. The beam cut between a western hemlock and a red cedar, but it did not find the surgeon.

'Let's cut the shit,' Pritchard shouted into the darkness.

He waited for an answer, but none came. Pritchard turned slowly in a circle, pointing his gun and the flashlight at the trees. A twig snapped and he almost fired. Two tree limbs rubbed together and he jumped sideways off the trail.

'That's enough, goddamn it. Get out here,' Pritchard yelled, but he heard only the sound of his own labored breathing. He began backing down the trail toward the car, shifting the gun back and forth across the path every time he heard a sound. The muscles in his shoulders and arms ached from tension. His heel caught on a tree root. Pritchard flailed his arms to arrest his fall, and the gun flew from his hand. He landed hard on the packed earth and rolled toward the gun. He expected to feel a knife blade slice into his body or a club smash across his back as he groped for his weapon, but the only sounds he heard were those he made.

Pritchard could not find the gun, and he was too vulnerable on his hands and knees. He got to his feet and spun in place, keeping the flashlight in front of him to use as a weapon. Something hard smashed into Pritchard's right kneecap. His leg gave out and toppled sideways. As he fell, Cardoni broke his right shoulder. Pritchard's eyes squeezed shut involuntarily from the intense pain and he almost blacked out. When he opened them Cardoni was standing over him, tapping a tire iron against the palm of his hand.

'Hi,' the surgeon said. 'How you doing?'

Pritchard was in too much pain to answer. Cardoni added to his pain by breaking his left kneecap.

'Rule number one: Remove your opponent's legs.'

Cardoni walked around Pritchard slowly. He was sprawled on his back, gritting his teeth and fighting to stay conscious.

'A blow to the kneecap ranks as one of life's most painful experiences. It rivals a thrust to the genital area. Shall we make a comparison test?'

Cardoni's foot flashed. Boxers are used to pain, but this was pain on a new level. Pritchard made no effort to stifle his scream.

'I bet that smarts. In fact, I know it does. Doctors know every place on the human body that can cause suffering.'

Pritchard wanted to say something brave in response to Cardoni's taunts, but he was weak with fear. If Cardoni wanted to inflict more pain, he knew he would be helpless to stop him.

'Do you know where you are, little man?'

When Pritchard did not answer, Cardoni gave his right kneecap a casual tap. Pritchard arched his back as if electricity had shot through him.

'You're in the House of Pain, and I run the establishment. There's one rule in the House of Pain: Anything I say goes. Disobedience is punished swiftly. Now, here's my first question. It's an easy one. What's your name?'

'Fuck you—' Pritchard started, but the sentence was cut short by a scream when Cardoni gripped his left wrist and extended his arm out at an awkward angle, forcing Pritchard to roll onto his injured knees.

'The hand is a marvelous creation designed by God to

do the most wonderful things,' Cardoni said. 'I use my hand to wield instruments that save lives. I bet you use yours to pick your nose and beat off.'

Pritchard tried to struggle, but Cardoni brought him to heel with a small amount of pressure on his wrist. Then the surgeon gripped the man's index finger tightly. He tried to resist, but Cardoni had no trouble prying it out straight.

'There are twenty-seven bones in the hand. That gives me twenty-seven opportunities to inflict excruciating pain on you.'

Cardoni tightened his grip on Pritchard's index finger.

'The bones of the fingers and thumb are called phalanges. A single phalange is the length of bone from one knuckle to the next. There are three phalanges in your index finger.' Cardoni bent the index finger backward. 'All of them are going to be broken if you don't become more cooperative.'

Pritchard screamed.

'Now, what is your name? Even a moron like you should be able to answer that question.'

Cardoni applied pressure.

'Gene, Gene Pritchard,' he gasped.

'Good boy.'

Pritchard lunged suddenly. Cardoni backed away and jerked hard on his wrist. Pritchard's feet splayed out and he howled like a dog. Cardoni snapped Pritchard's index finger. As the bone cracked, the man sagged, almost passing out.

'The next time you decide to pick on someone, make

sure you're man enough for the job,' Cardoni said as he pried Pritchard's pinkie away from his fist.

'Now, Gene, who sent you to follow me?'

Pritchard hesitated for a second and paid for it. The last time he remembered crying was when he was eight. Tears trickled down his cheeks.

'Martin Breach,' Pritchard gasped without having to be asked again.

'That's a very good boy. And what does Martin want you to do besides tail me?'

'We're . . . supposed to . . . bring you . . . to him.'

'Dead or alive?'

'Alive, in good condition.'

'Why?'

'The money he paid for the heart. He wants it back.'

Cardoni studied Pritchard for what seemed like an eternity to the crippled enforcer. Then he released Pritchard's hand, backed into the shadows and disappeared without another word.

27

Bobby Vasquez knocked an empty bottle of whiskey into two empty beer bottles as he rolled onto his side. The three bottles crashed to the floor, and the sound of breaking glass brought Vasquez partway out of his drunken stupor. He opened his eyes and blinked. His first thought was, What time is it? Then, What day? Then he wondered why he cared. Since his suspension every day had been shit.

Vasquez struggled into a sitting position, squeezed his eyes shut against the light and waited for the throbbing to subside. After his humiliation and destruction at the motion to suppress, action had been swift. Vasquez had been placed on suspension, and Internal Affairs was conducting an investigation. Milton County would probably

181

indict him for perjury, obstruction of justice and any other crime they could stick him with. The union lawyer represented him in front of Internal Affairs, but he had to foot the bill for his criminal lawyer, and that would probably wipe out his savings. If he was convicted or thrown off the force, he could kiss his pension goodbye.

Vasquez looked for something to drink. All the bottles he could see were empty. He lurched to his feet and stumbled into the kitchen. He smelled. He had not shaved in days. He didn't care. He wasn't going to see anyone, and no one was going to see him. Yvette had called, but he had been drunk and insulted her. She did not call again. So much for true love. There had been calls from some of his cop friends, but he let the machine take them. What could he say? He had no excuses. He'd just gotten caught up in the thing. First there'd been his desire to avenge Mickey Parks. Then he'd found the heads, and he'd wanted Cardoni so badly that he had broken the law. To make matters worse, it was Breach's man who had brought him down. Now he was probably going to go to jail, and a man who had butchered nine human beings was walking free.

Vasquez went through the kitchen cabinets until he located the only liquor bottle left with something in it. He tilted it up and sucked down all of the remaining whiskey as his last thought echoed in his head. He would be in jail soon, and Cardoni would be free. His life was over, and Cardoni's would continue. The psycho fuck would kill again, and Vasquez would be responsible for each new death. Why go on? Why face disgrace and jail?

He was starting to believe that the answer to his problems was a single shot through his brain when an alternative suddenly occurred to him. The brain in question did not have to be his own. If he was really willing to end his life, he could do anything he wanted to do. It was like having a terminal disease. No one could punish you worse than you were going to be punished. There was no threat that could deter you. The rules no longer applied. If he killed himself, Cardoni would still be free to cause untold suffering. If he killed Cardoni, he would be a hero to some and his conscience would be clear.

28

Art Prochaska entered Martin Breach's office in the Jungle Club and yelled, 'Ed and Eugene are in the hospital,' so that Breach could hear him over the blaring heavy metal music to which a buxom ecdysiast named Miss Honey Bush was disrobing.

'What happened?'

'Cardoni surprised them.'

'Both of them?' Martin Breach asked in disbelief.

Prochaska nodded. 'They're in pretty bad shape.'

'Motherfucker!' Breach screamed as he leaped up from behind his desk and started pacing. When he stopped, he leaned forward on his knuckles and glared across the desk at his enforcer. Breach's fists were clamped so tightly that his knuckles were white.

'You take care of this personally. When I'm through with Cardoni he's going to beg to tell me where he's hiding my money.'

29

The phone was ringing. Amanda sat up in bed and groped for it in the dark.

'Frank, I'm in trouble.'

It was Vincent Cardoni, and he sounded desperate.

'This is Amanda Jaffe, Dr. Cardoni.'

'Put your father on.'

'He's in California taking depositions. If you give me a number where he can reach you, I'll have him call tomorrow.'

'Tomorrow will be too late. There's something that I have to show him right away.'

'The best I can do is give my father your message.'

'No, you don't understand. It's about the murders.'

'What about them?'

Amanda heard heavy breathing as Cardoni whispered into the telephone.

'I know who committed them. I'm at the cabin in Milton County. Get up here, right away.'

'The cabin? I don't—'

'You're my lawyer, goddamn it. I pay your firm to represent me, and I need you up here. This is about my case.'

Amanda hesitated. Frank would never refuse to help a client who sounded this desperate. If she didn't go, how could she explain her inaction to her father? How could she practice criminal law if she would not help a client because he frightened her? Criminal lawyers represented rapists, murderers and psychopaths every day. They were all frightening people.

'I'll leave right away.'

The line went dead, and Amanda instantly regretted telling Cardoni she would meet him. It was midnight, and it would take her a little over an hour to drive to the cabin. That meant that she would be alone with Cardoni in the middle of nowhere in the middle of the night. Her stomach churned. Amanda remembered what had happened in that cabin. She saw Mary Sandowski's face drained of all color and all hope. What if Cardoni had done those things? What if he wanted to do them to her?

Amanda went downstairs to the den. Frank liked guns, and he'd had her on a pistol range as soon as she was old enough to hold one. Amanda enjoyed target practice and knew her way around weapons. Frank kept a .38 snub-nose in the lower drawer of his desk. Amanda loaded it and slipped it in her jacket pocket. She had never shot a handgun off a range. She'd heard and read that shooting a person was totally different from shooting at a metal cutout, but she was not going to meet Vincent Cardoni in the woods after midnight without protection.

The temperature was in the thirties, so Amanda had thrown her ski jacket over jeans and a dark blue turtleneck. The rain started shortly before one and changed to snow near the pass. Amanda had a four-wheel drive, so she was not worried, but she was still relieved when the snow fell away to a light rain. She was within eyesight of the turnoff to the cabin when a car suddenly swept out of the narrow dirt road and sped past her. Amanda thought she recognized the driver in the brief moment when the two cars were side by side. Then the taillights of the other car faded in her rearview mirror.

As soon as her headlights illuminated the house Amanda was certain that something was wrong. The lights were on in the living room and the front door was wide open. The wind had picked up and was blowing sheets of rain slantwise into the house. Common sense told her that she should turn the car around and speed toward safety, but she knew her father wouldn't turn tail and run. Amanda sucked in a deep breath, took her gun out of her pocket and walked toward the cabin.

The first thing that Amanda noticed when she entered

the house was the blood that dampened the planks of the hardwood floor in the living room. The stain was not large, but it was wide enough to let her know that something bad had happened in the room.

'Dr. Cardoni,' Amanda called in a trembling voice. There was no response. She scanned the large front room cautiously and saw nothing else that was odd. The other lights on the main floor were off, but the lights were on in the stairwell that led to the bottom-floor operating room. A blood trail led toward the stairs.

Amanda eased down the stairway, the .38 leading the way. The door to the operating room was wide open. Amanda edged along the wall. She stopped opposite the entrance to the horror chamber and stood in the door frame, her heart hammering in her chest.

It took a moment for Amanda to understand what she was seeing. The operating table was covered with a fresh white sheet. Drops of blood radiated outward from one large stain that covered the middle of the sheet. In the center of the stain was a severed hand.

Amanda bolted up the stairs and through the door. She covered the space between the house and her car in a flash and dove inside. The ignition would not catch. Amanda panicked. She looked toward the house while she fumbled with the key, half expecting to see an apparition streaking toward her, blood pumping from its severed limb.

The engine started. The car burned rubber. Amanda was shaking. She was cold. Terror forced her to drive faster, never slowing even when the road curved or the car went airborne after bouncing out of a pothole. She stared in the rearview mirror and almost fainted with relief when she did not see headlights bearing down on her. She brought her eyes forward and spotted the highway. The car careened onto it, and she drove as fast as she could for five minutes before her heart rate slowed and she started to think about what she would do next.

Amanda parked in front of the cabin and waited for the sheriff's deputies to pull in before getting out of her car. Fred Scofield had ridden from Cedar City to the cabin with her. He got out of the passenger side and turned up his collar against the wind, which had turned fierce while Amanda was giving her statement at the sheriff's office. The DA gestured through the storm toward the still-open front door.

'Are you sure you want to go back in there?' Scofield asked solicitously.

'I'm fine,' Amanda answered with more confidence than she really felt.

'Let's go, then.'

Clark Mills and four deputies fought their way through the gusts of snow and entered the cabin. Amanda and Scofield followed the policemen inside. Amanda surveyed the brightly lit front room. As far as she could see, except for a dusting of snow just inside the front door, everything was as she had left it.

Scofield looked over his shoulder at the front yard. 'It's too bad that the snow waited until after that car drove off.

We might have gotten some tracks.' He looked back at Amanda. 'How certain are you that the driver was Art Prochaska?'

'My window was streaked with rain, the interior of the other car was dark and it went by very fast. All I had was a momentary impression. I don't know if I could swear that it was Prochaska in court. But I think the man I saw was bald and his head was unusually large.'

'This floor is clear,' Sheriff Mills said to Amanda and Scofield after his deputies completed a sweep. 'We're going downstairs. You can wait up here if you like, Miss Jaffe.'

'Let's go.'

Amanda hung back and let the sheriff, the DA and two armed deputies precede her down the stairs. When she reached the lower hall, she saw that the door to the operating room was still open and the lights inside were still on.

'Everyone but Clark please wait in the hall,' Scofield said before entering the room. The men who crammed the narrow hallway blocked Amanda's view. She edged along the wall behind them until she found a spot where she could see between two of the deputies.

The hand still sat in the center of the operating table. Drained of blood, it looked chalky white. Scofield and Mills approached it cautiously, as if afraid that it might spring from the table and grab them. They leaned over it and stared intently. The amputated hand was large and a man's, judging from the hair on the back. Scofield lowered his head until he could make out the letters on a ring that covered part of one finger. Vincent Cardoni had graduated from the medical school in Wisconsin whose name was engraved on the ring.

Amanda crossed the Multnomah County line a little after four in the morning and, without a second thought, headed toward Tony Fiori's house. The house was dark when she parked in Tony's driveway at four-thirty. She walked onto the porch and rang the doorbell. A light went on after the third ring, and Amanda heard faint footsteps coming down the stairs. A moment later Tony peered through the glass panel in the front door. Then he opened the door a crack.

'What are you doing here?' Tony asked uncomfortably, and she knew instantly that she'd made a big mistake. Over Tony's shoulder, Amanda saw a woman wrapped in a silk dressing gown descending the stairs. The gown parted to reveal bare legs. Amanda looked from the woman to Tony. Then she backed away from the door.

'I'm sorry . . . I – I didn't know,' Amanda stuttered, turning to go.

'Wait,' Tony said. 'What's wrong?'

But Amanda was already opening the door of her car. As she backed out she saw Tony staring at her. Then the woman was beside him in the doorway, and Amanda got a second look at her. While she was finding Vincent Cardoni's severed hand in the cabin in Milton County, Tony Fiori had been spending the night with Justine Castle.

30

Amanda spotted her father coming off the 9:35 P.M. plane from LA before he saw her in the crowd at the gate. He looked agitated, and his head swung back and forth as he searched for her. Amanda stepped forward, and Frank threw a bear hug on his daughter. Then he held her at arm's length.

'Are you okay?'

'I'm fine, Dad. I was never in any danger. How was your flight?'

'Damn the flight. You don't know how upset I've been.'

'Well, you shouldn't have been upset. I told you I was fine this morning.'

They started moving with the crowd toward the

baggage claim. Now that he saw that Amanda was in one piece, Frank's face darkened.

'What were you thinking, meeting Cardoni in that place in the middle of the night?'

'I was thinking of what you would have done. I even brought your thirty-eight with me.'

'You're not serious, are you? Did you think Cardoni would stand in front of you and let you shoot him?'

'No, Dad, I thought he was a client in trouble. Don't tell me that you would have stayed in bed with your covers over your head and told Vincent to come to your office in the morning. He sounded desperate. He said he knew who murdered the victims at the cabin. It looks like he may have been right.'

Amanda had given Frank a capsule version of her Milton County adventure early Friday morning. He had wanted to fly straight home, but Amanda convinced him to finish his deposition. As they waited for Frank's luggage Amanda told him everything that had happened at the cabin.

'Do they know yet if the hand is Cardoni's?' Frank asked as he hefted his bags and headed toward the parking garage.

Amanda nodded. 'Mr. Scofield called me at work. The prints match.'

'Jesus.' Frank sounded subdued. 'You must have been scared out of your wits.'

'If I could move as fast in the pool as I moved when I ran out of the cabin, I'd have Olympic gold on my wall.'

That got a grudging smile out of Frank.

'What about the body?' he asked.

'They're digging up the property, but they hadn't found a thing when Scofield called.'

Frank and Amanda walked for a while without talking. He loaded his bags in the trunk, and Amanda started the car. On the way back to town Frank told his daughter about the deposition and asked about the office. When they were halfway home on the freeway, he asked Amanda twice about a research project he'd given her before getting an answer.

'Is something besides what happened at the cabin bothering you?'

'What?'

'I asked if something else is worrying you besides what happened to Cardoni.'

'What makes you think that?' Amanda asked warily.

'I'm your father. I know you. Do you want to tell me what's wrong?'

'Nothing.'

'You forget who you're trying to con. Some of the best liars in the state have tried to fool me.'

Amanda sighed. 'I feel like such a fool.'

'And what's made you feel that way?'

'Not what, who. Last night the police let me go around three in the morning. I was still upset, and it was dark when I got back to Portland. I just didn't want to be alone, so I drove to Tony's house.'

Amanda colored. It was so embarrassing. Frank waited patiently while she collected herself.

'He wasn't by himself. He . . . There was a woman with him.'

Frank felt his heart tighten.

'It was Justine Castle. I . . . I ran off without talking to him. I shouldn't have. It was immature. We just went out a few times and we never . . . We weren't intimate. It's academic now, anyway. Tony was just accepted into a residency program in New York and he's not even going to be here.'

'How do you know that?'

Amanda's color deepened.

'I called him to apologize.' Amanda sighed. 'I really liked him, Dad. I guess I'm just disappointed,' she said in a way that broke Frank's heart.

'Tony might not be the best person for you to get serious with.'

Amanda turned toward Frank for a moment before bringing her eyes back to the road.

'You don't like Tony?'

'Did he tell you that he was seeing Justine Castle at the same time he was seeing you?'

'We weren't serious. He never even made a pass at me. If he was seeing Justine, that was his business. He didn't lead me on. I . . . I just got my hopes up. Anyway, like I said, it's all over. Tony is going to New York.'

31

The first thing that Bobby Vasquez noticed when Sheriff Mills ushered him into the long, narrow interrogation room was the hand. It had been printed and cleaned up, then placed in a large jar, where it floated in preservative that gave the skin a faint yellow cast. The jar was at one end of a long table in front of Fred Scofield. Scofield was in shirtsleeves, his collar undone and his tie yanked down away from his fleshy neck. It was warm in the room, but Sean McCarthy was still wearing a suit jacket and his tie was knotted. To McCarthy's right was a guy named Ron Hutchins from Internal Affairs who dressed like a mortician and sported a goatee. Sheriff Mills was in uniform.

Scofield pointed at the hand. 'What do you think, Bobby?'

'Ugly mother,' Vasquez answered. 'Whose is it?'

'Don't you know?' Scofield asked.

'What is this, Twenty Questions?'

'Sit down, Bobby,' McCarthy said in a kind, non-threatening way.

Vasquez slouched onto an unoccupied chair. The sheriff sat behind Hutchins's shoulder. They were all facing him now. The theory was that he would feel over-whelmed, but he didn't feel anything at all.

'How are you doing?' McCarthy asked with real concern.

'As well as anyone whose career has been ruined and who's facing bankruptcy and jail,' Vasquez responded with a weary smile.

The homicide detective smiled back. 'I'm glad to see you've kept your sense of humor.'

'It's the only thing I still own, *amigo*.'

'Where's your lawyer?' Scofield asked.

'He charges by the hour, and I don't need him. I know how to plead the Fifth if I have to.'

'Fair enough,' Scofield said.

'You want something to drink?' McCarthy asked. 'Coke, a cup of coffee?'

Vasquez laughed. 'Who's playing the bad cop?'

McCarthy grinned. 'There isn't any bad cop, Bobby. Besides, how are we going to con you? You already know all the tricks.'

'I'm not thirsty.' Vasquez turned his attention back to the hand. 'You still haven't told me who this belongs to.'

'This is the right hand of Dr. Vincent Cardoni,' McCarthy said, watching closely for his reaction. 'We found it in the basement of the Milton County cabin.'

'You're kidding!'

McCarthy thought that Vasquez's surprise was genuine.

'Dr. Death himself,' Scofield answered. 'The prints check out.'

'Where's the rest of him?'

'We don't know.'

'Poetic justice.'

'I call it cold-blooded murder,' Scofield responded. 'We have the rule of law here, Bobby. Guilt is decided at a trial. You remember, a jury of your peers and all that shit?'

'You think I did this?' Vasquez asked, pointing at the jar and its ghoulish resident.

'You're a suspect,' McCarthy answered.

'Mind telling me why?' Vasquez asked. He leaned back in his chair, trying to look cool, but McCarthy could read the tension in his neck and shoulders.

'You had a real hard-on for Cardoni. You screwed up your career to get him. Then Prochaska shot you down and Cardoni walked.'

'What? I'm gonna kill everyone who beats one of my cases?'

'You wanted this guy bad enough to burglarize his house and lie under oath.'

Vasquez looked down. 'I'm not sorry Cardoni is dead, and I'm not sorry he was chopped up. I hope the sick son-of-a-bitch suffered. But I wouldn't do it that way, Sean. Not torture.'

'Where were you on Thursday night and Friday morning?' Scofield asked.

'Home, by myself And no, I don't have anyone who can vouch for me. And yes, I could have driven to the cabin, killed Cardoni and returned unnoticed.'

McCarthy studied Vasquez closely. He had means, motive and opportunity, just like they say in the detective movies, but would Vasquez saw off a man's hand for revenge? There McCarthy was undecided. And if they could not decide, they were left where they started, with suspects but no grounds for an arrest. Art Prochaska denied murdering the physician and even had an alibi. Prochaska's lawyer had faxed over a list of five witnesses who would swear that they were playing poker with Prochaska from six P.M. on Thursday night until four A.M. Friday morning. The problem with the alibi was that all five witnesses worked for Martin Breach.

'What's your next question?' Vasquez asked.

'We don't have any for now,' Scofield answered.

'Then let me ask you one. Why are you so certain that Cardoni is dead?'

McCarthy cocked his head to one side, and Scofield and Mills exchanged glances.

Vasquez studied the hand. 'You've moved to reopen the motion to suppress, right, Fred?'

Scofield nodded.

'What's the chance that Judge Brody will grant the motion and reverse the decision to suppress?'

'Fifty-fifty.'

'If you win, Cardoni goes back to jail. What are your chances at trial?'

'If I get to trial with what we found in the cabin and his house in Portland, I'll send him to death row.'

Vasquez nodded. 'There's a rumor that Martin Breach has a contract out on Cardoni because he thinks Cardoni was Clifford Grant's partner and stiffed him on the deal at the airport.'

'We've heard the rumor. Where is this going?'

'Can a doctor amputate his own hand?' Vasquez asked.

'What?' Sheriff Mills exclaimed.

'You think Cardoni chopped off his own hand?' McCarthy asked simultaneously.

'He's got a contract out on him placed by the most relentless son of a bitch I've ever dealt with. If he escapes Breach's hit men, he's looking at a stay on death row. The only way the law and Martin Breach will stop looking for Cardoni is if they believe that he's dead.'

'That's ridiculous,' Mills said.

'Is it, Sheriff?' Vasquez paused and looked at the hand again. 'There are animals that will gnaw off their own limb to get out of a trap. Think about that.'

Part 2

Ghost Lake

32

At eight o'clock on a blustery Friday evening, Amanda Jaffe parked on the deserted street in front of the Multnomah County courthouse, showed her bar card to the guard and took the elevator to the third floor. Two weeks ago it had taken only one hour for the jury to find Timothy Dooling guilty of a horrible crime. The same jury had been out two and a half days deciding whether Dooling would live or die. What did that mean? She would soon find out.

In the five years she had been working in her father's firm, the county courthouse had become Amanda's second home. During the day its corridors and courtrooms hummed with drama, high and low. Every so often there was even a little comedy. At night, absent the hustle and bustle, Amanda could hear the tap of her heels on the marble floor.

As Amanda approached Judge Campbell's courtroom, she remembered the mob of reporters that had filled the Milton County courthouse during *State v. Cardoni*, her first death penalty case. The sad truth was that death penalty cases had become so common that Dooling's case merited the attention of only the *Oregonian* reporter with the courthouse beat.

This was not the first time that Amanda had thought about Vincent Cardoni during the four years that had passed since his mysterious disappearance. The case had made her wonder whether she really wanted to practice criminal law. She stayed on the fence for two months. Then her legal arguments helped win the dismissal of unwarranted rape charges against a dirt-poor honor student who now attended an excellent college on scholarship instead of rotting in a cell for a crime he did not commit. The student's case convinced Amanda that she could do a lot of good as a defense attorney. It also helped her understand that every defendant was not like the deranged surgeon, although her present client came pretty close.

Amanda paused at the courtroom door and watched Timothy Dooling through the glass. He was sitting in his chair at the counsel table, shackled and watched by two armed guards. It seemed absurd that anyone would be wary of a slip of a man barely out of his teens who tipped the scale at 140 pounds, but Amanda knew the guards had good reason to keep a careful watch on her client. The slight build, the wavy blond hair and the engaging smile did not fool her, as it had the young girl he had murdered. Even during those times when she felt relaxed in his company, the presence of the jail guards made her feel a lot more comfortable. She liked to think that Tim would never hurt her even if he had the chance, but she knew that was probably wishful thinking. The psychiatric reports and the biography Herb Cross had compiled made it very clear that Dooling was so badly broken that he could never be put together again. From the earliest age, his alcoholic mother had abused him physically. When he was barely out of diapers, one of her boyfriends had sexually assaulted him. Then he'd been abandoned and placed in one foster home after another, where he had been the victim of more sexual and physical abuse. It was not an excuse for the rape and the murder, but it explained why Tim had become a monster. No one in her right mind would argue that Dooling should ever be let out of maximum security, but Amanda had argued that he should be allowed to live. There were good arguments against her position. Mike Greene, the prosecutor, had made all of them.

Dooling turned when Amanda walked in and looked at her expectantly with big blue eyes that begged to be trusted.

'How are you feeling?' Amanda asked as she set down her attaché case and took her seat.

'I don't know. Scared, I guess.'

There were times, like now, when Amanda actually felt sorry for Dooling, and other times when she actually liked him. It was the craziest thing, something only another criminal attorney would understand. He was so dependent on her; in all likelihood she was Tim's only friend. How pathetically sad must a man's life be, Amanda thought, when his attorney was the only person in the world who cared about him?

The bailiff rapped his gavel, and the Honorable Mary Campbell entered the courtroom through a door behind her bench. She was a bright, no-nonsense brunette in her early forties with short hair and a shorter temper who ran a tight ship. With Campbell running the show, her client had received a fair trial. That was bad news if the verdict was death.

'Bring in the jury,' the judge told the bailiff.

Across the way, Mike Greene looked grim. Amanda knew that he was feeling the tension as much as she was. She found this comforting, because Greene was a seasoned prosecutor. Amanda liked Greene, who had barely heard of her father when he moved to Portland from LA two years ago. It had been hard for Frank Jaffe's daughter to establish her own identity and reputation. Mike was one of the few DAs, lawyers or judges who did not think of her initially as Frank Jaffe's little girl.

When the jurors filed in, Amanda kept her eyes forward. She had long ago quit trying to guess verdicts by studying the expressions on the faces of the jurors.

'What happens now?' Dooling asked nervously, even though Amanda had explained the process to him several times.

'The judge gave the jurors four questions to answer.

The questions are set out in the statute that governs sentencing in an aggravated murder case. The jury's answer to each question must be unanimous. If all of the jurors answer all of the questions with yes, the court has to impose a death sentence. If the answer of any juror to any of these questions is no, the judge has to give you life.'

A slender, middle-aged woman with gray hair stood up when Judge Campbell asked if the jury had a verdict. This was Vivian Tahan, a CPA with a large accounting firm. Amanda would never have let Tahan on if she'd had a choice, but she had run out of peremptory challenges by the time Tahan was called and she had discovered no reason to ask for her dismissal for prejudice. The fact that the strong-willed Tahan was the foreperson made Amanda very nervous.

Judge Campbell took the verdict forms from the bailiff and read through them. Amanda's eyes were riveted to the stack of paper.

'I'm going to read the questions posed to the jurors and their answers to each,' Judge Campbell said. 'I note for the record that each juror has signed the verdict form. On the first charge in the indictment, to the first question, "Was the conduct of the defendant, Timothy Roger Dooling, that caused the death of Mary Elizabeth Blair committed deliberately and with the reasonable expectation that death of the deceased would result?" the jurors have unanimously answered yes.'

During the guilt phase, the jury had found that Dooling acted intentionally when he strangled Mary Blair to death. There was a legal distinction between intent and deliberation, but it was the width of a hair. While the yes finding did not surprise Amanda, it still caused her heart to skip a beat.

'On the second question, "Is there a probability that the defendant, Timothy Roger Dooling, will commit criminal acts of violence that would constitute a continuing threat to society?" the jurors have unanimously answered yes.'

There were still no surprises. Timothy Dooling's first violent act occurred in third grade, when he set a dog on fire. They had never stopped, and they had gotten progressively more serious.

The third question asked whether the defendant's action in killing the deceased was an unreasonable response to the provocation, if any, of the deceased. The only time this became an issue in a case was in situations of self-defense or long-term abuse. Dooling's victim had been kidnapped, held hostage for days and systematically raped and murdered. It was no shock that the jurors had unanimously found Dooling's conduct unreasonable.

Amanda and Mike Greene leaned forward when Judge Campbell started to read the last question and the jury's answer to it. Question four was the only important one in most cases. The question, 'Should the defendant receive a death sentence?' opened the door for defense counsel to present any argument against death that could be supported by evidence. Amanda had presented witness after witness to attest to the horrors of Timothy Dooling's childhood, and she had argued that the mother who gave him life had handcrafted him from birth to be the monster he had become. If one of the twelve jurors agreed with her arguments, Tim Dooling would live.

'To question four,' Judge Campbell said, 'the jury has answered no by a vote of three to nine.'

Dooling sat stone still. Amanda did not move either. It was only when she saw the prosecutor's head bow that she knew that she had convinced three of the jurors that Dooling's life was worth saving.

'Did we win?' Tim asked her, his eyes wide with disbelief.

'We won.'

'Ain't that something.' Tim was grinning. 'That's the first time I ever won anything in my whole life.'

Amanda returned to her loft at ten-thirty, exhausted but ecstatic at having beaten back her first death verdict. The loft was twelve hundred square feet of open space in a converted red-brick warehouse in Portland's Pearl District. The floors were hardwood, the windows were tall and wide and the ceiling was high. There were two art galleries on the ground floor and good restaurants and coffee-houses nearby. She could walk to work in fifteen minutes when the weather was good.

Amanda had filled the loft with furniture and fixtures she loved. A solemn Sally Haley pear in a pewter bowl that cost a month's salary hung across from a bright and cheery abstract painted by an artist she had met in one of the street-level galleries. Amanda had discovered her oak sideboard in an antique store two blocks away, but her dining table had been crafted in a woodworker's studio on the coast. It was made of planks the artisan had salvaged from a fishing vessel that had run aground in Newport during a storm.

Amanda flipped on the lights and threw her jacket onto the couch. She was too excited to go to sleep and too distracted for TV, so she poured herself a glass of milk and put two slices of bread in the toaster before collapsing in her favorite easy chair.

Tim Dooling's case was her first capital murder as lead counsel. The pressure on her during the past nine months had been tremendous. Nothing had prepared her to handle a case where one mistake could result in the death of a client. When the verdict was read Amanda had not experienced the manic surge she'd felt when she won her first PAC-10 swimming title; she had simply felt relieved, as if someone had removed an immense burden from her shoulders.

The toaster dinged, and Amanda dragged herself to her feet. As she crossed the room she suddenly noticed how quiet it was in her loft. Amanda enjoyed her solitude, but there were times, like tonight, when it would have been nice to have someone with whom she could share her triumph. She had dated a few men since moving back to Portland. There had been a six-month affair with a stockbroker that had died a mutually agreeable death and a longer relationship with a lawyer from one of Portland's large firms who had asked her to marry him. Amanda had asked for time to consider the proposal, then realized that she wouldn't have to think at all if he was 'the one.'

Amanda wouldn't have minded having Frank to crow

to, but he was in California with Elsie Davis, a school-teacher who had been a character witness for a student Frank had defended. While interviewing her, Frank discovered that she had lost her husband to cancer and had stayed single for twelve years because she had never found anyone to take his place. Their cautious friendship had blossomed into a serious relationship, and they were on their first vacation together.

Amanda buttered her toast at the kitchen table. While she sipped her milk she took stock of her life. On the whole she was happy. Her career was going well, she had money in the bank and a place she loved to live in, but she was lonely at times. Two of her girlfriends had married during the past year, and she was beginning to feel isolated. Couples went out with couples. Soon there would be children to occupy their time. Amanda sighed. She didn't feel incomplete without a man. It was more a question of companionship. Just having someone to talk to, who would be around to share her triumphs and help her up when she fell.

33

Andrew Volkov performed his custodial duties at St. Francis Medical Center diligently. Tonight, as he cleaned the floor outside the offices of the Department of Surgery, he moved slowly and deliberately, making certain that his mop covered every inch of the corridor. Volkov was tall, but it was hard to guess his height because he slouched and shuffled as he worked. He rarely spoke and never met the eye of anyone who spoke to him. His own eyes were gray-green, his hair was close-cropped and blond, and he had the broad cheekbones, wide nose and brooding brow of a Slav. Volkov rarely showed any emotion, maintaining a stolid expression that reinforced the impression that he was as much a mule as a man. When told to do something, he obeyed immediately. His superiors had learned quickly to be precise in their instructions because Volkov demonstrated little imagination and followed orders literally.

The offices of the Department of Surgery were quiet and deserted at two A.M. Volkov pushed his cart against the wall and straightened slowly. He rested his mop against the wall, checked the corridor and shuffled toward the door to the next office. He opened it and turned on the light. The office was narrow and not very deep, a windowless cubicle, really, hardly wider than a closet. A gunmetal gray desk took up most of the floor. It was covered with medical journals, textbooks, mail and miscellany. Volkov was under strict instructions never to touch anything on a doctor's desk, but he was supposed to empty the wastebasket under the desk.

Volkov took a duster from his cart and ran it over the shelves of a bookcase that stood against one wall. When he was through dusting, he looked down at the patch of floor that was not covered by the desk, the bookshelves and the two visitor chairs. It was an area so small that it was hardly worth dealing with, but Volkov's boss had instructed him to clean any surface that could be cleaned, so Volkov shuffled outside, emptied the wastebasket, then took his vacuum cleaner off the cart. He plugged it in and ran it back and forth across the floor. When he was satisfied that he had done all he could do, Volkov placed the vacuum cleaner back on the cart.

Volkov reentered the office one last time. He closed and locked the door and drew a pair of latex gloves out of one pocket and a Ziploc bag out of the other. Then he stepped behind the desk and opened the bottom drawer. The coffee mug was right where he had seen it on other nights. Volkov placed the mug in the Ziploc bag, left the office and relocked the door. He placed the bag under a pile of towels along with the gloves. Then he grabbed his mop and began pushing it slowly and deliberately toward the next office.

34

On this moonless Sunday night, even with his high beams on, all Multnomah County sheriff's deputy Oren Bradbury could see through his rain-streaked windshield was the yellow line that divided the two-lane country road and an occasional glimpse of farmland.

'You know this is a bullshit call, don't you?' his partner, Brady Paggett, griped. 'The place has been deserted since . . . Hell, I can't remember when.'

'It could be kids.'

'On a night like this?'

Bradbury shrugged. 'We weren't doing anything anyway.'

They rode in silence until Paggett pointed toward a

rusted mailbox whose post leaned precariously toward the tall grass on the side of the road.

'There it is.'

A dilapidated wooden fence bordered the road. Its slats were unpainted. Several had broken loose on one end and dangled from the few nails that were still in place. Bradbury spotted the break in the fence and turned through it. The patrol car bounced along a rutted dirt track. There were tall trees on either side. After a quarter mile the headlights picked up a farmhouse with peeling brown paint and a front yard overgrown with weeds. When they drew closer, the deputies could make out a dim glow through a front window.

'Maybe this isn't a bullshit call,' Paggett said.

'What exactly did dispatch say again?' Bradbury asked.

'Someone phoned in to report screams.'

'Who?'

'Dispatch couldn't get a name.'

'The caller had to be right here. The next neighbor is half a mile down the road. There's no way you'd hear anything if you were driving by, and no one's gonna be walking along the road tonight.'

As the patrol car swung into the front yard, its light swept across a dark blue Volvo that was parked at the side of the house.

'Someone's here,' Bradbury said just as a person in a hooded jacket and jeans burst through the front door and streaked for the Volvo. Bradbury hit the brakes, and Paggett jumped out of the car with his gun drawn.

'Stop, police!'

The runner skidded to a halt and froze in the police car's headlights.

'Hands in the air,' Paggett commanded.

Bradbury drew his weapon and got out, keeping the car between him and the hooded apparition. Paggett squinted to keep the rain out of his eyes.

'Step over to our car, put your hands on the roof and spread your legs.'

As soon as the person was in position, Paggett reached out and pulled back the hood. A cascade of honey brown hair fell across a woman's shoulders. The deputy kept his gun on her as he patted her down. He noticed that her chest was heaving, as if she had run a distance.

'Is anyone else inside?' Paggett asked.

The woman nodded vigorously.

'I . . . I think he's dead,' she managed. The words came out in gasps.

'Who's dead?' Paggett demanded.

'I don't know. He's in the basement.'

'And who are you?' Paggett asked.

'Dr. Justine Castle. I'm a surgeon at St. Francis.'

'All right, Dr. Castle, you can put your hands down.' Paggett opened the back door of the police car. 'Why don't you get in out of the rain and try to calm down.'

Justine sat down in the backseat. Bradbury walked around the car and joined Paggett at the rear passenger door.

'What are you doing here, Dr. Castle?' Paggett asked.

Justine's saturated hair hung along her damp face. Her breathing was still not under control.

'There was a call. He said that he was from St. Francis, that it was about Al Rossiter.'

'Who is Rossiter?' Bradbury asked.

'One of the surgeons.'

'And who was the caller?'

'I'm not sure. I think he said that his name was Delaney or Delay. I really don't remember. It wasn't someone I knew.'

'Okay, go ahead.'

'The man said Dr. Rossiter was working on someone who was badly injured and needed my help. He said that it was urgent. He told me to come here and he gave me directions.'

'Do you usually drive to the scene of an injury?'

'No, it's definitely not routine. I asked why they didn't send for an ambulance. I said I would meet them at the hospital. That's where all our equipment and staff are. This Delaney or Delay said that he couldn't explain over the phone but that it was a matter of life and death and I would understand when I got here. He said that the man's condition was desperate. Then he hung up.'

'Where's everyone else? Where's Dr. Rossiter?' Paggett asked.

Justine shook her head. She looked upset and confused.

'I don't know.'

Justine squeezed her eyes shut and took a deep, shuddering breath.

'Are you okay, Dr. Castle?' Paggett asked.

Justine nodded slowly, but she did not look okay.

'Is anyone besides the dead man inside?' Bradbury asked.

'I . . . I don't know. I didn't see anyone. When I saw him . . .' Justine swallowed hard. 'I panicked. I ran.'

'You stay with Dr. Castle,' Bradbury said. He walked toward the farmhouse, his gun at the ready.

Paggett closed the rear door of the patrol car. There were no handles on the inside. Justine was effectively a prisoner, but she made no protest and seemed content to sit with her eyes closed and her head against the back of the seat.

The drops were pounding harder. Paggett put on his hat to keep the rain off. He checked his watch and wondered what was keeping Bradbury. When Oren came out, he looked glassy-eyed and pale.

'You got to see this, Brady. It's horrible.'

Paggett and his partner had seen car wreck victims, abused children and other mangled and degraded human beings. It would take a lot to put Oren in this state. He headed for the farmhouse with Bradbury close behind. The first thing that struck him as odd was the cleanliness. Weeds ruled the front yard and the exterior walls were in disrepair, but every inch of the entryway and the front room appeared to have been vacuumed clean. There was no furniture in the entryway and only a cheap coffee table and a straight-back chair in the living room.

'The stairs to the basement are in the kitchen,' Bradbury said. 'The kitchen lights were on when I came in the house.'

'Those must have been the lights we saw when we drove up.'

The kitchen was as clean as the other rooms. There was a card table and two straight-back chairs standing on the yellow linoleum floor. Paggett opened one of the cupboards and saw a few plastic plates and cups. A half-filled coffeepot and a coffee mug were on a drain board next to the sink. When Paggett drew closer, he saw that there was still some coffee in the mug.

'The body is down there,' Bradbury said, pointing through the open basement door. His voice was shaky.

'What's it look like?'

'Bad, Brady. You'll see.'

As Paggett walked down the wooden steps that led to the basement, he noticed the suffocating odor that permeates the air when death has been a visitor. A bare 40-watt bulb threw dim shadows over the unpainted concrete floor and walls. Paggett could see a mattress next to the furnace. Lying on the mattress was a figure. The light was too dim to make out details, but there was enough light to see that the body was naked and cuffed at the wrists and ankles by manacles that were attached to the wall by lengths of thick chain.

Paggett walked slowly toward the corpse. When he was a few feet away he saw the body clearly for the first time and almost lost it. The deputy blinked, not quite trusting his eyes. The mattress was saturated with blood; so much of the body was covered with dried blood that it was very difficult to tell its race. An ear and several digits were missing. Paggett's stomach heaved. He turned away, squeezed his eyes shut and took deep breaths. The smell almost overpowered him, but he struggled to keep his food down.

'Are you okay?' Bradbury asked anxiously.

'Yeah, yeah.' Paggett was bent over with his hands on his knees. 'Give me a second.'

When he was ready, Paggett straightened up and took a closer look at the corpse.

'Holy Jesus,' he whispered reverently. Paggett had seen a lot of bad shit in his day, but nothing like this.

The deputy turned away from the body, relieved to have it out of his sight, and surveyed the rest of the basement. At first the dimensions of the room confused him. The basement seemed smaller than he expected. Then Paggett realized that a gray concrete wall with a narrow doorway divided the basement in half. He walked through the doorway. Inside a second room was an operating table. A tray of surgical equipment stood next to the table. Among the tools was a scalpel encrusted with blood. Paggett turned and headed back up the stairs.

'I'm gonna check out the rest of this place. You call it in. We need homicide and forensics.'

'What about the woman?'

'After what we saw, I'm not letting her out until we know for sure that she didn't do this guy.'

Paggett shook his head again, as if to clear it of the image of what he had just seen. Bradbury left the house. Paggett took a deep breath and started to explore the main floor. After taking a second look at the kitchen and living room, Paggett walked toward the rear of the house and found two empty rooms with closed doors. They had been vacuumed clean.

As he started to climb the stairs to the second floor, something occurred to Paggett. He turned around and went through the main floor again. He was right. There weren't any telephones in the house. The deputy wondered if he would find a phone on the second floor.

He didn't, but the second floor did yield a discovery. In one of the rooms were a bookcase, an armchair and a single bed with a mattress and a pillow. A lamp stood between the bed and the armchair. There was no sheet on the bed and no pillowcase on the pillow. Paggett guessed that the killer had used the bed but had taken the sheet and pillowcase because they might contain trace evidence like hair or semen stains.

Paggett read some of the titles in the bookcase. He found *The Torturer's Handbook*, *Cleansing the Fatherland: Nazi Medicine and Racial Hygiene*, and *Sweet Surrender: A Sadist's Bible* mixed in with medical texts and other books on torture.

Also in the bookcase was a black three-ring binder. Paggett used his handkerchief to take it out of the bookcase and open it. A computer had generated the pages.

Tuesday: Watched from dark as subject revived. 8:17 p.m.: Subject disoriented. Realizes that she is naked and manacled to wall. Struggles for less than minute before commencing to sob. Screams for help commence at 8:20, end 8:25. Watched subject until 9:00. Went upstairs to eat. When kitchen door opened and closed, subject commenced begging. Listened from kitchen while I ate. No fighting spirit, pathetic, subject may provide little new data.

Wednesday: Approached subject for first time. Begging, pleading, questions: 'Who are you?' 'Why are you doing this?' etc. Subject is extremely docile, drew into fetal position at touch. Moved head slightly, but accepted training hood with little struggle. When released from manacles obeyed commands immediately. No challenge.

Saturday: After two days without food and with sensory deprivation, subject is weak and lethargic. I am disappointed at lack of resistance. Have decided to commence pain tolerance experiments immediately.

8:25: Remove manacles and lead subject to operating table. No resistance, subject obeys command to mount table and submits to restraints. 8:30: hood removed, subject's head secured to table. Begging, pleading. Subject sobs quietly. I have decided to start with the soles of the feet.

Paggett felt light-headed. He could read no further. Let the DA and the homicide detectives find out what happened to . . . It hit him suddenly. The journal referred to the subject as 'she.' The corpse in the basement was a male. Paggett flipped through the journal. There were more entries.

35

It took three rings to drag Amanda out of a deep sleep. The phone rang again, and Amanda groped for the receiver in the dark while reading the bright red 2:13 on her digital clock.

'Miss Jaffe?'

'Yes?' Amanda answered groggily.

'This is Adele at the answering service. I'm sorry to disturb you.'

'That's okay.'

Amanda swung her legs over the side of the bed and sat up.

'I have a woman on the line. She's calling from the police station. She asked for your father.'

'Mr. Jaffe is out of town.'

'I know. I told her that you were taking his calls. She said that was okay.'

'Did she say what this is about?'

'No. Just that she had to talk to you.'

Amanda sighed. The last thing in the world she wanted to do was talk to a drunk driver at two o'clock on Monday morning, but middle-of-the-night calls came with the territory when you practiced criminal law.

'Put her through, Adele.'

Adele's voice was replaced by Tony Bennett singing 'I Left My Heart in San Francisco.' Amanda closed her eyes and rubbed her lids.

'Is this Amanda Jaffe?'

Amanda's eyes opened. She knew that voice.

'This is Justine Castle. We met several years ago.'

Amanda felt a chill pass through her.

'You're Vincent Cardoni's wife.'

Amanda suddenly flashed on a vision of the doctor descending Tony Fiori's staircase on the evening she had discovered Cardoni's hand. Her hand tightened on the receiver.

'Why are you calling my father at this hour?'

'Something terrible has happened.'

Amanda detected a tremor when the doctor spoke.

'I . . . I've been arrested.'

This time the tremor was more pronounced, as if Justine was barely holding herself together.

'Where are you calling from?'

'The Justice Center.'

'Is anyone with you?'

'Detective DeVore and a deputy district attorney named Mike Greene.'

Justine had her attention now. DeVore was homicide, and Mike rarely handled anything but capital cases.

'Are DeVore and Greene listening to this call?' Amanda asked.

'They're in the room.'

'Answer my questions yes or no and do not say anything else unless I say it's okay. Do you understand?'

'Yes.'

'Have you been arrested for a serious crime?'

'Yes.'

'Some type of homicide?'

'Yes.'

'I'm coming down. From this point on you are not to speak with anyone but me. Is that clear?'

'Yes, but – '

'Dr. Castle, Alex DeVore and Mike Greene are very nice men, but they are also specialists in sending people to death row. One way they do that is by befriending confused and frightened people who are under tremendous stress. These people trust them because they're so nice. They say things to Mike and Alex that they do not realize are going to be used to crucify them in court.

'Now, I am going to repeat my instructions. Do not – I repeat – do not talk to anyone about this matter except me unless I say it's okay. Do you understand my instructions?'

'Yes.'

'Good. Please give Mr. Greene the phone.'

'Hi, Amanda,' Mike Greene said a moment later.

Amanda was in no mood for small talk.

'Dr. Castle says you've arrested her. Mind telling me what for?'

'Not at all. Two sheriff's deputies caught her fleeing the scene of a homicide.'

'Did she confess?'

'Claims she didn't do it.'

'But you arrested her anyway?'

'Of course. We always arrest people when we can prove they're guilty.'

36

Prior to 1983 the Multnomah County jail was an anti-quated, fortresslike edifice constructed of huge granite blocks that was located several miles from the Multnomah County courthouse at Rocky Butte. When the Rocky Butte jail was torn down to make way for the I-205 free-way, the detention center was moved to the fourth through tenth floors of the Justice Center, a sixteen-story, state-of-the-art facility one block from the courthouse in the heart of downtown Portland. In addition to the jail the Justice Center also housed the Portland police central precinct, a branch of the Multnomah County district attorney's office, state parole and probation, the Portland police administrative offices, the state crime laboratory, two circuit courts and two district courts.

Before Amanda could visit Justine Castle she had to check in with a guard on the second floor of the Justice Center and go through the metal detector. The guard led Amanda to the jail elevator and keyed her up to the floor where Justine Castle was being held. When the elevator stopped, Amanda found herself in a narrow, brightly lit hallway. At one end a telephone without a dial was attached to the wall next to a massive steel door. Above the door was a surveillance camera. Amanda used the telephone to summon a guard. A few minutes later a corrections officer opened the door and let Amanda into another narrow corridor. On one side of this hall were three visiting rooms. Amanda could see into each room through a plate of thick glass. The guard opened the heavy metal door of the room nearest the elevators. On the other side of the room was another steel door that opened onto a hall that led to the cells. A black button stuck out from the bottom of an intercom that was recessed into the yellow concrete wall. The guard pointed to it.

'Press that if you need assistance,' he said as he closed the door behind him.

Amanda sat on an orange molded plastic chair. She took a legal pad and a pen out of her attaché case and placed them in front of her on a small, round table that was secured to the floor by iron bolts. From experience Amanda knew that it would take a while for the guard to bring Justine to her. While she waited Amanda thought about the last time she'd seen Justine Castle.

Four years ago, finding Justine with Tony Fiori had

been a shock, but the incident was ancient history. There hadn't been anything between her and Tony, anyway. She was honest enough to admit that she wished that there had been but realistic enough to know that they had just been friends.

The locks snapped, and a uniformed jail matron led Dr. Castle into the visiting room. Amanda studied her for the changes that time might have wrought. Justine was exhausted, and no one looks chic in an orange jailhouse jumpsuit at three in the morning. Justine's hair, ruined by the rain, was unkempt, but Justine was still beautiful, even under these trying circumstances, and the strength was there, even if it was being sorely tested.

'Thank you for coming,' Justine said.

'Dr. Castle—'

'Justine, please.'

'My father's in California. He won't be back for a week. If you want another lawyer to represent you, I can give you a list of several excellent attorneys.'

'But you're a criminal lawyer, too, aren't you?' Amanda sensed a hint of desperation in the question. 'The district attorney told me that you just beat him in a murder case. He thinks you're very good.'

'Mr. Greene was being kind. I didn't win the case. My client was found guilty. I just convinced the jury to give him a life sentence instead of a death sentence.'

'I read about what your client did to that girl. It can't be easy to convince a jury to save the life of someone like that.'

'No, it's not.'

'So Mr. Greene wasn't being charitable when he said you were good.'

Amanda shrugged, uneasy with the compliment. 'I work very hard for my clients.'

'Then you're the lawyer I want. And I want you to get me out of here as soon as possible.'

'That might not be easy.'

'You don't understand. I can't be charged with murder. My reputation will be ruined, my career would be . . .'

Justine stopped. Amanda could see that she hated to sound needy and desperate.

'This has nothing to do with my ability as a lawyer. It has to do with the way that the law is written. In Oregon every crime except murder has automatic bail. Remember your husband's case? My father had to ask for a bail hearing when the DA objected to release. We'll have to hold a similar hearing for you unless the DA agrees to release you.'

'Then get him to agree.'

'I'll try. We're meeting as soon as I finish talking to you. But I can't guarantee anything.'

Justine leaned forward and focused all of her energy on Amanda. It made Amanda feel uncomfortable, but Justine's stare was so intense that she could not look away.

'Let me make two things clear to you. First, I did not kill anyone. Second, I have been set up.'

'By whom?'

'I don't know,' Justine answered with obvious frustration, 'but I do know that I was lured to that farm, and the police turning up when they did was no coincidence.'

Justine told Amanda about the phone call that convinced her to rush to the farmhouse and what happened after she arrived.

'Do you know the victim?'

'I don't think so, but I can't say for sure. I only had a brief look, and his face was so disfigured.'

Amanda noticed that Justine's hands were folded in front of her on the table and she was clasping them so tightly that the knuckles were white. If the mental image of the dead man could freak out a surgeon, Amanda was not looking forward to viewing the autopsy pictures and crime scene photos.

'Besides finding you at the scene, can you think of anything that would make the police believe that you killed the man in the basement?'

'No.'

'Did you say anything that could be interpreted as a confession?'

Justine looked annoyed. 'I told you I didn't kill anyone. The man was dead when I got there.'

'Were you arrested at the crime scene?'

'No. The two officers who found me were very polite. Everyone was, Mr. Greene and the detective, too, after I arrived at the Justice Center. They brought me coffee, got me a sandwich. They were very sympathetic. Then they got a call from the crime lab and everything changed. DeVore and the DA went into the hall and talked. When they came back DeVore read me my rights.'

'Did they say what had happened?'

'They said that they knew I'd killed that man. They insisted I was lying when I denied it. That's when I called you.'

Amanda made a few notes.

'When did you get the call about Dr. Rossiter?'

'Around nine on Sunday night.'

'Where were you?'

'At my house.'

'Were you alone?'

'Yes.'

'Were you with anyone earlier in the day? Someone who can give you an alibi?'

'No. I was away for the weekend. I have a cabin on the coast. It's been hectic at the hospital, and I drove out Friday evening to get away from everyone and watch the storm. I got home shortly before the call.'

'You said that was about nine.'

Justine nodded.

'Where is the farmhouse located?'

'Out in the country on a two-lane road in the middle of nowhere. I got really concerned when I drove into the front yard. The place looked like it hadn't been lived in for years.'

Justine looked unsettled again.

'Go on,' Amanda urged.

'You were involved in Vincent's defense, weren't you?'

'I assisted my father.'

'And you've been to that cabin in Milton County? You're the one who found Vincent's hand?'

'Yes,' Amanda answered softly.

235

Justine took a deep breath and closed her eyes for a moment.

'It wasn't seeing the body that made me run.'

Justine exhaled slowly and gathered herself while Amanda waited patiently.

'The farmhouse basement is divided in two by a cement wall. There is a room on the other side of the wall. When I walked into the room I saw the table.'

'What table?' Amanda asked as a sick feeling formed in her stomach.

'An operating table.'

Amanda's mouth gaped open. 'This sounds like . . .'

Justine nodded. 'It was the first thing I thought of. That's why I ran, and that's why I called your father.'

Amanda stood up.

'I've got to talk to Mike Greene. He was a DA in Los Angeles when Cardoni was arrested. He wouldn't know about the case.'

'Wouldn't DeVore have heard?'

'It wasn't his case, and most of the action was in Milton County.'

Amanda rang for the guard, then turned to Justine.

'The worst part of being in jail isn't what they show you on TV,' she said. 'It's the boredom. Sitting around all day with nothing to do. I'm going to give you a job that will keep you occupied and help your defense. I want you to write an autobiography for me.'

The request seemed to take Justine by surprise.

'Why do you need that?'

'I'm going to be blunt with you. I hope I win this case

236

and you go free, but a good lawyer always prepares for the worst. If you're convicted of aggravated murder, there will be a second phase to your trial: the penalty phase. That's when the jury decides your sentence, and one of the sentences that can be imposed is death. In order to convince a jury to spare you I'll need to get them to see you as a human being, and I do that by telling them the story of your life.'

Justine looked uncomfortable.

'If you don't use the biographical information unless I'm convicted, why don't I wait to write it?'

'Justine, I hope I never have to use any of the material you give me, but I know from experience that I can't wait until the last moment to prepare for the penalty phase. The judge usually gives you only a few days between the trial and the penalty phase. There won't be enough time to do a thorough job unless we start now.'

'How far back do you want me to go?'

'Start when you were born,' Amanda answered with a smile.

The locks snapped, and the door started to open.

'I'll come back this afternoon for the arraignment. While you're waiting, write the bio. You'll thank me for giving you something to take your mind off your troubles.'

37

Mike Greene dealt with rapists, killers and criminal defense attorneys all day but always seemed to be in a good mood. He had curly black hair, pale blue eyes and a shaggy mustache. His head was large but did not seem out of proportion because he was six-five with the kind of massive body that compelled males to ask if he had played basketball or football. He had not; he didn't even watch sports on TV. He did play chess and was a rated expert during his days on the chess team at the University of Southern California. Greene's other passion was tenor sax, which he played proficiently enough to be asked to sit in on occasion with a jazz quartet that entertained at local clubs.

Alex DeVore was a dapper little man who always

dressed well and looked fresh and alert even at three-thirty in the morning. He had been the lead detective in two cases Amanda had cocounseled with Frank. She remembered him as being low-key and businesslike.

The deputy DA and the detective were sipping coffee from foam cups at DeVore's desk in the homicide bureau when Amanda walked in. A Dunkin' Donuts box with its lid folded back sat in front of them.

'I saved a jelly doughnut and a maple bar for you, just to show that there are no hard feelings over Dooling,' Greene told her.

Amanda was hungry and exhausted. 'Can I get some coffee?' she asked as she grabbed the maple bar.

'We'll even give you powdered creamer if you'll plead out your client.'

'No deal. I don't cop my clients for anything less than a grande caramel latte.'

'Damn,' Greene answered with a snap of his fingers. 'All we've got is industrial-strength caffeinated.'

'Then it looks like we'll have to go to the mat.'

Greene filled a cup with a sludgy black liquid. Amanda took a sip and grimaced.

'What is this stuff? If I ever find out that you gave it to one of my clients, I'll sue you.'

DeVore smiled, and Greene let out a belly laugh.

'We brew this specially for defense attorneys.'

Amanda took a big bite out of her maple bar to cut the taste of the coffee.

'What do you say to some form of release for Dr. Castle?'

Greene shook his head. 'Can't do it.'

'C'mon, Mike. She's a doctor. She has patients to tend to.'

'That's regrettable, but you have no idea what's going on here.'

'Tell me.'

Greene looked at DeVore. The detective nodded. Greene leaned back in his chair.

'Your client's been using the farmhouse as a torture chamber.'

Greene waited for Amanda to react. When she didn't, he continued.

'We found a man in the basement.' Greene shook his head and the pleasant smile disappeared. 'Count yourself lucky that you'll only have to look at the photos. What makes it even more evil is the journal.'

'What journal?'

'Your client has kidnapped other victims. The journal is an account of her torture sessions with each of them. She kept them in pain for days. It takes a lot to get to me, but I could not read the journal straight through.'

'Is the journal in Dr. Castle's handwriting?'

Greene shook his head. 'No, the pages were generated by a computer. Her name's not in it, either. It would have made our job easier if Dr. Castle had signed it, but she didn't.'

'So how can you be sure she wrote it?'

'We found a section of the journal in Castle's house when we executed a search warrant, earlier this evening. It contains a graphic description of what she did to the poor bastard we found in the basement. A copy will be included in your discovery. I'd wait a few hours after you eat to read it.

'By the way, the medical examiner's preliminary finding is that our John Doe committed suicide by chewing through the veins in his wrist. When you read the journal entry you'll see why he killed himself. Can you imagine how desperate and how terrified a person has to be to kill themselves like that?'

The blood drained from Amanda's face.

'Did anything else at the crime scene connect Dr. Castle to the murder?' she asked quietly.

'You'll get our reports when they're ready.'

'Dr. Castle believes that she's been set up.'

'Does she have a suspect in mind?' Greene asked skeptically.

'Actually, we both do. You told Justine that the cops came to the farmhouse in response to an anonymous nine-one-one call. The farmhouse is a quarter mile from the road, isn't it? How did this anonymous caller get close enough to hear screams?'

'Good question. I'm sure you'll ask the jury to consider it.'

'Come on, Mike. Doesn't this sound like a setup to you? The police just happen to get a call that sends them to a murder scene at the precise moment that the killer rushes out.'

'You can argue that, too.'

Amanda hesitated before plunging in.

'You've found more victims at the farm, haven't you?'

DeVore had been half listening, but the question got his attention. Mike's eyebrows went up.

'Did you get that from your client?'

'So I'm right.'

'How did you know?'

'I'll tell you that if you'll tell me whether you arrested Justine Castle because you found items with her finger-prints in the house.'

The detective and the DA exchanged looks again.

'Yes,' Greene answered.

'What items?'

'A scalpel with the victim's blood and a mug half filled with coffee.'

Amanda controlled her excitement. 'Was the mug found in the kitchen?'

'How did you know that?' DeVore asked.

She ignored the question. 'Was there anything else with trace evidence on it?'

'We found a surgical gown, cap and booties in a closet in the bedroom. They're at the lab and the technicians are going over them for hair and fibers. Now it's your turn to answer a few questions. How did you know about the other bodies and where we found the mug?'

Amanda took a sip of her coffee while she thought about the best way to answer Greene's question.

'Do you know anything about the Cardoni case?'

Mike Greene looked blank.

'The guy in Milton County with the hand,' DeVore said.

Amanda nodded. 'This was about four and a half years

ago, Mike, before you moved up here. Dr. Vincent Cardoni was a surgeon at St. Francis, and he was married to Justine Castle.'

'That's right!' DeVore exclaimed.

'A Portland vice cop named Bobby Vasquez got an anonymous tip that Cardoni was storing cocaine in a home in the mountains in Milton County. He couldn't corroborate the tip, so he broke into the house. Guess what he found?'

DeVore was sitting up, and Amanda could see that he was remembering more and more about the Cardoni case.

'What are you getting at?' the homicide detective asked.

'There was a graveyard in the woods near the house with nine victims. Most of them had been tortured. There was an operating room in the basement and a bloody scalpel with Cardoni's prints on it. Cardoni's prints were also found in the kitchen on a coffee mug. A video-tape that showed one of the victims being tortured was found in Cardoni's house. Is this starting to sound famil-iar?'

'Are you suggesting that Cardoni killed the people at the farmhouse?' Greene asked.

Before she could answer, DeVore said, 'He couldn't. Cardoni is dead.'

'We don't know that,' Amanda said to the detective before turning back to Greene. 'Not for sure.'

'You guys are going too fast for me,' Greene said.

'My father represented Dr. Cardoni. There was a

motion to suppress. Vasquez lied under oath to cover up his illegal entry, and Dad proved that he perjured himself. The state lost all its evidence, and Cardoni was released from jail. A week or so later Cardoni called me at home, at night, and said that he had to meet me at the house in Milton County.'

'I remember now,' DeVore said. 'You found it!'

'Found what?' Greene asked.

'Cardoni's right hand. It was on the operating table. Someone cut it off.'

'Who?' Greene asked.

'No one knows.'

'So it's an unsolved murder?'

'Maybe, maybe not,' Amanda said. 'Cardoni's body was never found. If he cut off his own hand, it wouldn't be a murder, would it?'

38

By the time Amanda staggered home to her loft it was almost five in the morning. Her eyes were bloodshot, and her head felt as though it were stuffed with cotton. Amanda would have given anything to dive under the covers, but there was too much to do, so she tried to fool her body into believing that she had slept by following her morning routine. She doubted that she would have been able to sleep, anyway. Her head was spinning with ideas for Justine's defense, and the possibility that Vincent Cardoni was back made her skin crawl.

After twenty minutes of calisthenics and an ice-cold shower, Amanda donned one of her dark blue court suits and walked two blocks to a hole-in-the-wall café that had been in the neighborhood since the fifties. It was still pitch black outside, and the raw, biting wind helped her stay awake. So did the flapjack breakfast she ate hunkered down in one of the café's red vinyl booths. As a swimmer, Amanda always stoked up on carbohydrates the night before a big race. Swimming distance and trying cases were a lot alike. You stored up as much energy as you could, then you dove in and kept driving.

During breakfast, Amanda could not stop thinking about Cardoni. What if he was alive? What if he was lurking in the dark, killing again? The idea terrified her, but it also thrilled her. If Cardoni was back from the dead – if Justine was an innocent woman, falsely accused – this case would make her reputation and bring her out of her father's shadow.

The moment that thought intruded Amanda felt guilty. She focused on the torment Cardoni's victims had to have experienced and forced herself to remember what she'd seen on the Mary Sandowski tape, but she could not suppress the excitement she felt when a secret part of her whispered about a future in which she would be as acclaimed and sought after as Frank Jaffe.

Amanda fought down these thoughts. She told herself that she was ambitious but that she also cared more for her clients than she did for success. Saving Justine Castle was her first, and only, priority. Fame might follow, but she knew that it was wrong to take a case for the notoriety it would bring. Still, the idea of her name in headlines was tough to ignore.

Then a disturbing thought occurred to her. Her father would be back from his vacation in a week. What would she do if he tried to grab her case? Could she stop Frank from moving her aside? She was only an associate at Jaffe, Katz, Lehane and Brindisi. Frank was a senior partner. If Frank wanted the Castle case, Amanda could not stop him from taking over. Maybe Justine would insist on Frank's being lead counsel. When Justine phoned from the Justice Center she had asked for Frank Jaffe, not his daughter.

Amanda chastised herself for thinking this way. She was putting her needs ahead of her client's. If Justine wanted her father to represent her, she would step aside. Right now she shouldn't even be thinking about anything but getting Justine out of jail.

By six-forty-five Amanda was in the basement of the Stockman Building looking through the firm's storage area. The files in *State v. Cardoni* filled three dusty, cobweb-covered cartons. There would have been many more boxes if the case had gone to trial. Loading the boxes on a dolly while keeping her suit clean was not easy, but Amanda managed. As soon as she rolled the boxes into her office she stripped off her suit jacket and started piling their contents on her desk.

Frank's case files were always well organized. One three-ring binder was for memos discussing legal issues that might be raised in the case. After each memo there were photocopies of the cases and statutes that supported each argument. Another binder contained police reports arranged chronologically. A third binder held reports generated by the defense investigation. A fourth binder was set up alphabetically for potential witnesses and contained copies of every report generated by either side that made any reference to the witness. A typed sheet with potential direct or cross-examination questions and areas of investigation that needed to be pursued preceded the reports. A final binder contained press clippings about the case.

Amanda opened the binder that had been compiled for the motion to suppress. It contained an inventory of the items found at the Milton County house. There was also an envelope with photographs of the crime scene. Amanda spread the photos across her desk and referred to the report. It took her only a moment to find the coffee mug and scalpel in the inventory and the photographs that showed where each item had been found in the house. Mike Greene had promised to give Amanda a set of crime scene photographs this afternoon at Justine's arraignment. She was willing to bet that those photographs would be similar to the photos spread across her desk.

At eight o'clock Amanda sent her secretary to the district attorney's office to get the keys to Justine Castle's house so that she could select clothes for Justine's court appearance. At eleven-thirty she wolfed down a sandwich and drank more coffee at her desk. By the time Amanda headed to the Justice Center at one o'clock for Justine's arraignment, she was exhausted but up to speed on Vincent Cardoni's case.

Amanda made it through the glass-vaulted lobby of the Justice Center and up the curving marble stairs to the third floor before someone from KGW-TV called her by name; instantly she became the focus of a mob of shouting reporters. An attractive brunette from KPDX asked Amanda if she was a stand-in for her famous father, and a short, disheveled reporter from the *Oregonian* wanted to know if there was a connection between the murders at the farmhouse and the infamous Cardoni case. Amanda ducked to avoid the mikes and the glare of the TV lights while repeating 'No comment' to each question. When the doors of the arraignment court closed behind her, sealing her off from the press, she sighed with relief.

The courtroom was packed. Attorneys sat with their clients. Anxious wives bounced children on their knee, trying desperately to keep them quiet so the guard would not expel them before their husbands were brought out of the holding area. Mothers and fathers held hands, watching nervously for a child who had gone wrong. Girlfriends and gang members shifted in their seats while they enjoyed the excitement of seeing someone they knew in court, just like on TV.

A row of chairs inside the bar of the court was reserved for lawyers from the public defender's office, private attorneys who were waiting for court appointments and retained counsel. Amanda took a seat in this section and waited for Justine's case to be called. Arraignment, a defendant's first court appearance, was the time when the judge informed the accused about the nature of the charges filed against him and his right to counsel. If the defendant was indigent, counsel was appointed at the arraignment. Release decisions were sometimes made.

Amanda had been to arraignments many times, and they were all the same. She paid attention to the first few cases because it gave her something to do, but she soon lost interest and glanced back at the spectator section out of boredom.

Amanda was about to return her attention to the front of the room when she sensed someone watching her. She scanned the crowd and was ready to chalk up the incident to her imagination when she noticed a large, muscular man with close-cropped blond hair. The man sat with hunched shoulders and his hands folded tightly in his lap, giving the impression that he was uncomfortable being in court. He wore a flannel shirt buttoned to the neck, khakis and a stained trench coat. Something about him was vaguely familiar, but Amanda had no idea where, or if, she had seen him before.

The door to the hall opened, and Mike Greene fought his way past the reporters. Once inside, he used his height to scan the room and spotted Amanda. Greene was still dressed in the brown tweed sports coat, rumpled white shirt and gray slacks that he had been wearing at three in the morning.

'I see you went home,' Mike said when he was seated beside Amanda.

'I've got on new duds, but I never got to sleep.'

'That makes two of us. The sleep part, that is.'

Mike handed Amanda a thick manila envelope.

'The complaint, some of the police reports and a set of the crime scene photographs. Don't say I never gave you anything.'

'Thanks for not being a hard-ass.'

Mike smiled. 'It's the least I can do after making you drink that foul sludge the homicide dicks call coffee.'

'Have you given any more thought to release?'

'Can't do it. Too many bodies, too much evidence.'

'*State v. Justine Elizabeth Castle*,' the bailiff called out.

Mike Greene walked to a long table at which another assistant district attorney sat. Its top was almost obscured by three gray metal tubs filled with case files. While Greene took out Justine's file, Amanda went to the other side of the room. A guard led Justine out of the holding area. Her client had on no makeup, but she looked good in her dark suit and silk shirt.

The arraignment moved swiftly. Amanda entered her name as attorney of record and waived a reading of the complaint. While the judge conferred with his clerk about a date for a bail hearing, Amanda explained what was going on. Justine listened carefully and nodded in the appropriate places, but Amanda had the impression that her client was barely holding herself together.

'Are you okay?' Amanda asked.

'No, but I won't break. You do your best to get me out as fast as you can.'

The judge ended Justine's arraignment, and the guard started to lead her away.

'I'm working on your case full time,' Amanda told her client. 'I won't see you again today, but I'll be by tomorrow. Don't lose faith.'

Justine held her head high as she walked through the door that led to the elevator that would transport her back to jail. Amanda wondered if she'd be able to carry herself with that much dignity if she was in Dr. Castle's shoes.

The reporters swarmed around Amanda in the corridor outside the courtroom. She refused to comment and fought through the crowd to the street. The rain had stopped but it was still cold and blustery. Amanda hunched her shoulders and crossed the street to Lownsdale Park, hurrying past the war memorial and the empty benches. While she waited for the light at Fourth and Salmon to change she cast a glance behind her and thought she saw movement near the small red-brick rest room on the edge of the park. The light changed and Amanda crossed the street, heading down Fourth toward her office. She had the sense that someone was behind her. Could one of the reporters be following her? Amanda stopped and turned around. A man in a trench coat ducked into the entrance of the office building across the way. Amanda stared at the entrance. She even walked back up the block a few steps for a better view. Two women walked out of the building. Amanda stared at the door they exited, but no one else came out. Suddenly a wave of fatigue hit her, and she leaned against a parking meter. She closed her eyes for a moment and still felt a little dizzy when she opened them. She chalked up her feeling of being followed to exhaustion, took a deep breath to clear her head and walked down Fourth to the Stockman Building.

39

Mike Greene grew up in Los Angeles, married his high school sweetheart and graduated from the law school at UCLA. Everything was going wonderfully, his life was perfectly on course. Then one day in his fourth year as a prosecutor for the Los Angeles district attorney's office Mike ate a bad burrito for lunch. When court resumed he was too sick to go on, so the judge recessed for the day. Mike thought about calling his wife, Debbie, but he didn't want to worry her, so he rested for an hour and drove home.

Mike walked through the door of his split-level three hours earlier than usual and found Debbie astride his next-door neighbor. He stood in the bedroom door-way, too stunned to speak. While the guilty couple scrambled for their clothes, he turned without a word and left.

Greene moved in with a fellow DA until he found a gloomy furnished apartment. He'd loved his wife so much that he blamed himself for her betrayal. The divorce was over in a flash. Debbie got the house, most of their savings and everything else she wanted because Mike would not fight. After the divorce, Mike tried to concentrate on his job, but he was so depressed that his work suffered. His supervisor recommended a leave of absence. Mike had never been out of California except for his honeymoon in Hawaii and a vacation or two in Mexico. He sold his car and bought a ticket to London.

Six months in Europe, which included a brief fling with a lovely Israeli tourist, gave Mike some perspective. He decided that Debbie's extracurricular sexcapades were not his fault and that it was time to get on with his life. A friend in the Multnomah County district attorney's office set up a job interview. Now Mike lived in a condo near the Broadway Bridge, across the Willamette River from the Rose Garden, where the Trailblazers played.

As Greene walked from the Justice Center to the Multnomah County courthouse after Justine Castle's arraignment, he fantasized about showering, eating a light meal and going to sleep on the flannel sheets of his king-size bed. That dream went up in smoke when he found Sean McCarthy waiting for him in the reception area of the district attorney's office, his nose buried in a book.

'A cop who reads Steinbeck,' Greene said. 'Can't that get you fired?'

McCarthy looked up, amused. He was just as gaunt as he had been four years before, but his red hair was thinner.

'How you doing, Mike?'

'Dreadful. If I don't get some sleep soon, you're going to be investigating my demise.'

McCarthy marked his place in *The Grapes of Wrath* and followed Greene through a waist-high gate and down a narrow hall to Mike's small office. A poster advertising last year's Mount Hood Jazz Festival adorned one wall. It showed a tenor sax superimposed on the snow-covered mountain. Mike had sat in for a set with a local trio during the festival. A chess set decorated a credenza that ran under Greene's window. The deputy district attorney was studying a variation of the king's Indian defense in his spare time, and the position reached by white after thirteen moves was displayed on the board.

Sean McCarthy took a chair opposite Mike's desk. Greene closed the door to his office and slumped in his chair.

'About four years ago a doctor named Vincent Cardoni was accused of torturing several victims in a house in Milton County. That was your case, right?'

'It was a Milton County case, but I assisted,' McCarthy answered.

'Frank Jaffe represented Cardoni. His daughter, Amanda, is representing Justine Castle, Cardoni's ex-wife, in a case with several similarities to the old case. Amanda thinks her client has been set up by Cardoni.'

'Cardoni is dead.'

'That's what Alex DeVore said, but Amanda says that no body was ever found.'

'That's true.'

'So . . . ?'

McCarthy was quiet for a moment. 'How similar are the crime scenes?'

'Amanda says they're almost identical.'

'Really. Identical how?'

Greene found the crime scene photographs and handed them to McCarthy. The detective shuffled through them slowly. He kept one picture and set the stack down on Greene's desk.

'What do you think?' the deputy DA asked.

McCarthy turned over the picture he was holding. It showed the half-filled coffee mug that had been found on the drain board in the farmhouse kitchen.

'Did the lab find Justine Castle's fingerprints on this mug?' McCarthy asked.

Greene nodded. 'They were on a scalpel with the blood of one of the victims on it, too.'

'That really bothers me.'

'Why?'

'We found more or less the same thing in the house in Milton County four years ago. The press knew about the scalpel, but we never told them about the coffee mug.'

'What about the motion to suppress?'

'A list of the items seized was submitted, but there was no mention that prints were found on any of them.'

'So you think that someone who knew about the mug set up Justine Castle?'

256

'Or she poured herself some coffee while she was working. A year or so after Cardoni disappeared I had a drink with Frank Jaffe. At one point the conversation turned to the Cardoni case. Frank told me that Justine Castle had given the coffee mug to Cardoni as a present and Cardoni claimed the mug had been stolen from his office at St. Francis. Cardoni thought that Justine Castle had used the mug and the scalpel to set him up.'

40

The weather front that had bedeviled Oregon for the past week was attacking again. Sheet after sheet of heavy rain bombarded Amanda's car. Even with the wipers on full, the visibility was so poor that Amanda counted herself lucky when she spotted the gap in the fence that bordered the farm. As soon as she turned onto the driveway the car started hitting puddles and potholes. Rain pounded the roof. Amanda's high beams raked the darkness, illuminating trees and shrubs before spotlighting the yellow crime scene tape that stretched across the door to the farmhouse.

Amanda shut off the engine and sat listening to the rain. She had convinced herself that she would know if Cardoni had created both chambers of horror simply by walking through the farmhouse. Now that she was here, the idea sounded ridiculous. Amanda turned on the interior light and took another look at the pictures that Mike Greene had given her. One showed the graveyard surrounded by trees and far from the boundaries of the property: a place that would be hard to find accidentally. She flipped to the next shot. Three bodies, all showing marks of torture, lay stretched out on a ground sheet. A tarp had been erected over them to keep the corpses as dry as possible. A close-up of a female victim showed the abuse the frail body had taken in the days before she died.

Another set of photographs showed the interior of the farmhouse. Amanda shuffled quickly past the close-ups of the body in the basement. One long look when she first saw the photos had been enough. She reviewed the other pictures before realizing that she was stalling. Amanda grabbed a flashlight and ran through the rain until she reached the overhang that covered the front door. She ripped away the bright yellow tape and walked inside.

Amanda played the beam of her flashlight over the entryway and the living room. They were as bare and sparsely furnished as the house in Milton County had been. Amanda found the bedroom. The police had left the furniture after dusting it for prints and scouring it for trace evidence, but they had taken the books and the journal from the bookcase. Amanda tried to imagine the killer sitting in the armchair and thumbing through the manuals in preparation for the next torture session. What type of monster could coldly plan the ritual degradation of another human being?

Amanda walked back through the living room to the kitchen. Outside, the wind gusted, rattling the shutters and skittering across the roof. Amanda felt a flutter in her stomach when she turned the knob of the basement door and looked into the dark space below. She flicked a light switch, and a bare bulb lit the lower part of the basement stairs. An oil-burning furnace stood in one corner. In another corner a rectangular patch of floor, cleaner than the area surrounding it, told her where the mattress had lain before forensics had removed it. She saw holes in the wall where the manacles had been secured; these too had been moved to the crime lab. Then she noticed the crudely mortared concrete wall that divided the basement in half.

The wall looked as if it had been constructed by a do-it-yourselfer from a how-to book. Amanda descended the stairs and peered through an opening that led into a dark space where the light from the 40-watt bulb barely reached. Amanda turned on her flashlight and shone it through the doorway. The operating table was there. Above it was another bulb. Amanda pulled the string attached to it, and the light illuminated a space bare except for the operating table. Everything else from the room had gone to the crime lab. Suddenly she flashed on an image of Mary Sandowski's tearstained face, and a wave of nausea surged through her. She shut her eyes for a moment and breathed deeply. There was no way that she could prove it, but there was absolutely no doubt. The person who had turned the mountain cabin into a place of horror had been at work here.

Amanda circled the table. Fingerprint powder darkened the steel legs. She knelt down and saw a dark brown fleck. Was that blood? She stared at it for a moment, then stood up.

A man was standing in the doorway.

41

The man stepped out of the shadows, blocking the only way out. He was wearing a rain-drenched trench coat. Amanda raised the flashlight and retreated.

'I'm not here to hurt you,' the man said, raising an empty hand, palm outstretched. 'I'm Bobby Vasquez.'

It took a moment, then Amanda recognized the intruder. Vasquez's face was fleshy. Rain dripped from his long, unkempt black hair; a bushy mustache covered his upper lip. Under the open raincoat Amanda could see faded jeans, a flannel shirt and a threadbare sports jacket.

'I didn't mean to scare you,' Vasquez told her. 'I tried to talk to you at the Justice Center, but I couldn't get close with all the reporters.'

Vasquez paused. He saw that Amanda was frightened and wary.

'Do you remember me?' he asked.

'The motion to suppress.'

'Not exactly my shining hour,' Vasquez said grimly. 'But I was right about Cardoni. He killed those people in Milton County and he killed these people, too. You know it, don't you? That's why you're here.'

Amanda forgot her fear. 'What makes you think he's alive?'

'Look at this place. When I read about the graveyard and the operating room, I knew.'

'What about the hand? Cardoni was a surgeon. He wouldn't cut off his hand.'

'Cardoni counted on everyone buying into that notion, that a surgeon would never amputate his own hand. But most surgeons aren't being hunted by a maniac like Martin Breach.'

'Or facing a death sentence.'

'That too. Plus, this guy is flat-out insane.'

Amanda shook her head. 'I want to believe Cardoni did this. The crime scenes are so alike. But I always come back to the hand. How could he do it? How could he cut off his own hand?'

'It's not as difficult as you might think. Not for a doctor, anyway. I asked around. All Cardoni had to do was tie a tourniquet around his biceps and run an IV filled with anesthetic into his forearm. That would put his arm to sleep. He could amputate the hand without feeling a thing. After the hand was off he would have covered the stump with a sterile cloth until the bleeding stopped, then bandaged it and used more anesthetic to block the pain.'

Amanda digested what Vasquez had said, then made a decision.

'Okay, Mr. Vasquez, I'll level with you. I am here because of Cardoni.'

'I knew it! So tell me, what else was in the police reports? You're not just here on a hunch.'

Amanda hesitated.

'Look, Miss Jaffe, I can help you. Who knows more about Cardoni than I do? I never believed that he was dead. I still have my file on him. I know Cardoni's life story; I can tell you what the police knew four years ago. You'll need an investigator.'

'Our firm has an investigator.'

'This will just be another case for him. It's my chance at redemption. Cardoni ruined my life.'

'You ruined your own life,' Amanda answered curtly.

Vasquez looked down. 'You're right. I have to take the blame for what I did. It took me a while to figure that out.' Vasquez swung his arm across the operating room. 'I take the blame for this, too. If I hadn't screwed up, Cardoni would be in prison and these people would be alive. I've got to make this right.' He paused. 'Besides, if we prove that Cardoni killed these people, your client goes free.'

Vasquez sounded desperate and sincere. Amanda took a final look around the operating room.

'Let's get out of here,' she said. 'We'll talk upstairs.'

Amanda pulled the cord attached to the lightbulb and plunged the makeshift operating room into darkness.

'What can you tell me?' Vasquez asked as they climbed the stairs. 'Are there other similarities between the crime scenes?'

'I don't think I should get into that.'

'You're right. Sorry. I'm just anxious. You have no idea how I felt when I saw Dr. Castle's name in the paper this morning and read about the operating room. All of a sudden there was hope that this nightmare might finally end.'

Amanda turned off the basement light and shut the door behind her.

'Look, Mr. Vasquez, let's be straight here, okay? I heard rumors about you after you were fired. My father heard them, too. If I ask my father to let you work with us on this case, he's going to want to know if you're reliable.'

Vasquez looked as though he had been down this road before.

'What do you want to know?' He sighed.

'What did you do after you were kicked off the force?'

'I drank. That's what you're after, right? Being a cop was my whole life. One moment I was and the next I wasn't. I couldn't cope. There's a year and a half in there that's still very blurry. But I came out of it and I stopped drinking on my own. I don't drink anymore, not even a beer. Tell your father that I'm a licensed investigator. It's how I've been earning my living. I'm good at it, and believe it or not, there are still some people on the job who'll talk to me.'

'We'll have to see.'

'When you're thinking about hiring me, think about this. I've already got a jump on the cops.'

'What do you mean?'

'Four years ago I figured I'd nail Cardoni by tying him to the Milton County house. You know, get the deed, show he owned it. Only I couldn't. He was very clever. The property was owned by a corporation, and the corporation was set up by a shady attorney named Walter Stoops, who was hired by someone he never met and paid in cashier's checks. The whole thing turned out to be a dead end, because we couldn't identify the person who purchased the cashier's checks. But it did establish an MO.

'This morning, as soon as I read about the farmhouse, I went through the records for this property. Guess what I found?'

'The land is owned by a corporation and was purchased by a lawyer.'

'Bingo. The sale went through two years ago, which would give Cardoni enough time to set up a new identity and prepare for his return to Portland.'

'Is the purchaser the same corporation that bought the land in Milton County?'

'No. And the lawyer's different. But the MO's the same.'

'What makes you think you'll be able to prove who purchased the property this time?'

'I don't know that I can, but Cardoni screwed up four years ago and we almost got him. I'm hoping he'll screw up again.'

42

That night Amanda slept like the dead and through her alarm. It was too late for her morning calisthenics or breakfast, so she took a fast shower and picked up a latte and a piece of coffee cake to go. When she walked into her office at eight-thirty her father was sitting behind her desk reading through the file on Justine Castle. He looked up and smiled. Amanda froze in the doorway.

'Good morning, Amanda.'

'You're supposed to be on vacation. What are you doing here?' she asked, fighting to keep the disappointment out of her voice.

'Didn't you think I'd be interested in your latest case?'

'I was sure you would be. That's why I left strict

instructions that no one was to tell you about it if you called in.'

'No one did.'

'Then how did you find out?'

'It's in the California papers. Somebody figured out the connection to the Cardoni case and, presto, we've got another sensation on our hands. Did you check your phone messages?'

'Not yet.'

'I glanced through them. If you want to be a media celebrity, *20/20*, *60 Minutes*, Larry King and Geraldo are all standing by.'

'You're kidding.'

Amanda set her attaché case, the latte and the bag with the coffee cake on the edge of her desk and sat in one of her client chairs.

'Isn't Elsie pissed that you've ruined her vacation?'

'Elsie is a wonderful woman. She ordered me to come back and help you.'

'Thanks for the vote of confidence,' Amanda answered sarcastically. 'I was perfectly able to save Dooling's ass all by myself. What makes you think I'm not competent to represent Justine Castle?'

'Hold on,' Frank said, raising a hand defensively. 'No one's saying you're incompetent, and don't get huffy on me. You know damn well that it takes two lawyers to handle something this complex.'

'Are you going to be lead counsel?' Amanda asked, bracing for the worst.

'I wouldn't think of it.'

Amanda tried to hide her surprise, but she must have failed, because Frank's lips twitched as if he was suppressing a grin.

'Justine might want you to be,' Amanda said warily. 'She asked for you when she was arrested.'

'Is she satisfied with you calling the shots?'

'I think so.'

'Then let's see how things go. Right now it's your case. Why don't you bring me up to speed?'

Between sips of her latte and bites of her coffee cake, Amanda laid out the details, starting with Justine's late-night phone call. When she told Frank about her visit to the farmhouse she didn't mention her encounter with Vasquez.

'I wish you hadn't gone inside, Amanda,' Frank said when she was finished. 'It was a sealed crime scene.'

'I know, but the forensic experts had gone through it already, and I had to see the place before it changed too much.'

Frank leaned back. 'What was your impression?'

'It's either the same killer or someone who knows an awful lot about the Cardoni case. I'm sure of it.'

Amanda paused a moment to think of how to broach the subject of Vasquez. She decided to plunge in.

'When I was looking over the basement at the farmhouse, Bobby Vasquez showed up.'

'The cop who lied at Cardoni's motion?'

Amanda nodded. 'He wants to work with us on the case. He's convinced that Cardoni faked his death four years ago and is responsible for the new murders.'

'Did you know that Vasquez was one of the leading suspects in Cardoni's disappearance? He was obsessed with Cardoni. The theory is that he went vigilante when the court set him free.'

Amanda tried to picture Vasquez as Cardoni's killer.

'It makes no sense for Vasquez to tell me that Cardoni killed the people at the farm if he knows that Cardoni is dead. Why would he follow me to the farmhouse? Why would he offer to work on the case?'

'I don't know and I don't care,' Frank snapped.

'You have every right to be angry about what Vasquez did in Cardoni's case. But you shouldn't let that stop you from thinking about what he can do in this one.'

'He's dishonest, Amanda. He's a drunk.'

'He says that he's not drinking anymore, and he looked sober. I think you should remember why Vasquez lied under oath. He did it because he thought it was the only way to put a very bad person in prison.'

'That doesn't excuse what he did.'

'I'm not saying it does. I just think you should look at this with an open mind. Vasquez knows everything the police knew about Cardoni, and he's already uncovered some useful information.'

'Such as?'

Amanda told Frank about Vasquez's investigation into the ownership of the farm.

'That's nothing Herb or the cops wouldn't have discovered,' Frank said dismissively. 'I don't know why Vasquez wants to work this case, but I'm not going to associate with a perjurer and a drunk.'

Amanda gathered herself. Then she looked directly at her father.

'Either I'm lead counsel or I'm not. If I am, then I choose my team.'

Frank wasn't used to being told what to do, and Amanda could see that he didn't like it.

'I'm not sure about Vasquez myself,' Amanda added quickly while she had the edge, 'but I want the right to decide if he's in or out.'

Frank let out the breath he'd been holding.

'Let's talk about this later.'

'I want it decided now. Do you think I'm competent to run this defense?'

Frank hesitated.

'Do you, Dad? We've worked together for five years. You've had a lifetime to evaluate my abilities. If you don't think I can hack it, I'll resign from the firm today.'

Frank put his head back and roared with laughter.

'You make me long for the good old days when little girls were courteous to their fathers and studied home economics.'

'Screw you,' Amanda said, fighting hard but failing to suppress a triumphant grin.

'Where did you learn such language?'

'From you, you old bastard. Now let's get back to Justine's case.'

'I'd better before you try to get a raise, too.'

Amanda lifted an eyebrow. 'Not a bad idea.'

'Quit while you're ahead, you ingrate.'

Amanda laughed. Then she grew serious. 'Were there

other suspects in Cardoni's disappearance?'

Frank nodded. 'Martin Breach's enforcer, Art Prochaska, the guy you thought you saw driving away from the cabin.'

'Of course.'

'Breach had a reputation for dismembering people he didn't like, and he had a contract out on Cardoni because he thought Vincent had double-crossed him in a deal involving the blackmarket sale of organs. The rest of Cardoni may have been in the trunk of Prochaska's car when he passed you.'

'That's a pleasant thought.'

'You asked.'

'Do you know Prochaska well enough so he would talk to you?'

'Why?'

'I'd like to know what he was doing at the cabin on the night I found the hand. If he didn't kill Cardoni, he might tell us.'

'Prochaska claimed that he wasn't at the cabin. He had an alibi.'

'He's lying, Dad. I couldn't swear in court that it was Prochaska I saw, but he was in that car.'

Frank thought for a moment. 'Martin always trusted me. I'm certain he told Art to be a witness for Cardoni. Let me see what I can do. I'll let you know what Martin says as soon as I talk to him.'

Frank left to work his way through the mail that had piled up while he was away. Amanda wandered out to the front desk, picked up a thick stack of phone mes-

sages and returned to her office. Frank hadn't lied about
the calls from Geraldo and company, but the message
that made her pause wasn't from New York or LA.
Amanda tapped the slip against her palm, uncertain
whether to call the number or not. She swiveled her
chair and stared out the window. The name on the slip
aroused mixed emotions. Suddenly Amanda said, 'Why
not?' and dialed St. Francis Medical Center. She told
the operator her caller's name and was put on hold.
After a moment the voice of Tony Fiori came on the
line.

'Amanda?' he asked hesitantly.

'Long time, Tony,' Amanda said evenly. 'I didn't know
you were in town.'

'Yeah. I'm back at St. Francis.'

'How was New York?'

'Good. Actually, I was so busy most of the time that I
didn't take as much advantage of being there as I should
have.'

'So, what's up?' Amanda asked, dying to know why he
had called but unwilling to ask.

'I was in New Orleans since last Friday and didn't see
a paper until this morning. I read about Justine being
charged with those killings.'

Amanda flashed on a vision of Justine and Tony standing side by side in Fiori's doorway four years ago.

'So that's why you called, because of Justine?' she
asked, fighting to mask her disappointment.

'Your name was in the paper, too, Amanda.' He
paused. 'Look, I've got to be in surgery in three minutes,

so I don't have much time. I'd like to see you. Could we have dinner?'

Amanda's pulse gave an unexpected flutter.

'I don't know.'

'If you don't want to, I'll understand.'

'No, it's not that.' She did want to see Tony. 'I'll be up to my neck in Justine's case for the next few days.'

'How about this weekend?'

'Okay.'

'I'll make a dinner reservation at the Fish Hatchery for Friday night. Is that okay?'

'Sure.'

'See you then.'

Amanda hung up the phone. Tony Fiori. Wow! Now here was a blast from the past. Amanda laughed. She'd really acted like a schoolgirl when she found out he'd been sleeping with Justine, but that was years ago and she was a lot tougher now. And she had enjoyed the time they'd spent together. Amanda stared out the window for a moment. Then she smiled. It would be interesting to see how well Tony had aged in four years.

43

The view from Carleton Swindell's office had not changed, but Dr. Swindell's blond hair was thinning, and Sean McCarthy suspected that a facelift had been performed on the hospital administrator of St. Francis Medical Center during the past four years.

'Detective,' Swindell said as he rose from behind his desk to extend a hand. The administrator's grip was still strong, and the detective noticed several new rowing plaques and medals had been added to the trophies that graced Swindell's credenza. 'I assume you're here about Justine Castle.'

McCarthy nodded as he handed Swindell a subpoena for the doctor's records. Swindell examined it briefly. He looked as though he hadn't been sleeping well.

'After that business with Vincent Cardoni I thought I'd seen everything. But this . . .' He shook his head in dismay. 'Frankly, Detective, I find it hard to believe that Justine could do the things I read about in the paper.'

'She was arrested at the scene of the murders, and we have other evidence connecting her to them.'

'Even so.' Swindell hesitated. Then he leaned forward. 'I followed Cardoni's case. Of course, I only had access to the media accounts, but these new murders, aren't they similar to the murders Cardoni was supposed to have committed? The newspaper even commented on it.'

'I'm afraid I can't discuss the evidence.'

'Oh, of course. I didn't mean to pry. It's just that, well, when Cardoni was arrested, no one was shocked. But Justine . . . We've never had any reason to suspect that she would be capable of anything like this. Her record is spotless.'

Swindell shifted uncomfortably. 'I know this isn't my area of expertise, but with such bizarre circumstances, wouldn't you suspect that the person who committed one set of murders also committed the others?'

'That's a possibility that we're investigating, along with several others.'

The administrator flushed. 'Yes, I should have guessed that.'

'Dr. Swindell, the last time we spoke, you mentioned a connection between Dr. Castle and Clifford Grant.'

'He was her attending, her supervisor during her residency.'

'So they would have been close?'

'Professionally, yes.'

'Four years ago, would Dr. Castle have had the skills to harvest a human heart for use in a heart transplant? If you know.'

'I trained as a surgeon before I decided to become a hospital administrator, so I'm well aware of the technique,' Swindell said with some pride. 'Justine is a highly skilled surgeon. I believe she would have been able to perform the operation.'

McCarthy considered Swindell's answer for a moment. Then he stood. 'Thank you, Doctor.'

'Feel free to call on me for help anytime.'

'We appreciated the way you sped things along the last time I asked for your help. If you could do the same with this subpoena . . .'

Swindell held up his hand. 'Say no more. I'll get on it immediately.'

44

The reservation at the Fish Hatchery was for eight, but Amanda was intentionally late. When she spotted Tony in the upscale crowd in the lounge at eight-twenty she was pleased to see him casting anxious glances toward the door. He was wearing a dark sports jacket without a tie, a white shirt and gray slacks, and he was every bit as handsome as she remembered. Amanda worked her way through the crush at the bar. Tony saw her and flashed a wide smile. Amanda extended her hand but Tony ignored it, pulling her into a quick bear hug.

'You look great,' Tony said enthusiastically. He pushed her back. 'God, look at you.'

Amanda felt herself flush.

'Our table won't be ready for a few minutes. Do you want a drink?'

'Sure.'

Amanda ordered a margarita. The bar was packed, and she and Tony were pushed hip to hip. The contact felt good.

'When did you get back to Portland?' she asked while they waited for the drinks.

'I've been at St. Francis for almost a year.'

'Oh,' Amanda answered coldly, stung by the fact that he'd taken so long to call her. 'I guess you've been busy.'

'You've got every right to be mad. It's just that . . . Well, I guess I was embarrassed because of what happened the night you showed up at my house. I didn't know if you'd want to hear from me.'

'You have nothing to be embarrassed about,' Amanda said, keeping her tone neutral. 'I certainly had no right to assume that you would be alone.'

'You needed someone to comfort you, and you came to me. When I found out what you'd gone through in the mountains I felt like a complete shit.'

'There wasn't any reason for you to feel that way,' Amanda said, answering more sharply than she had intended.

Tony looked upset. He took a deep breath.

'We were friends, Amanda. You don't have to sleep with someone to care for them.'

The hostess chose that moment to tell them that their table was ready. Amanda was grateful for the interruption and followed her in embarrassed silence. The hostess gave them menus and a wine list. As soon as she left, Tony put down his menu.

'Let me clear the air, okay? Otherwise we're both going to be blushing and mumbling all evening. I'm going to start with Justine. I'd seen her around the hospital, but I never spent much time with her until Cardoni attacked Mary Sandowski. I happened to be passing by when Justine confronted him. I was afraid that he might hit her, so I asked if there was a problem, just to let Cardoni know that Justine wasn't alone. After we calmed down Mary, Justine and I talked. One thing led to another. When I ran into you at the Y, we were already sleeping together.'

Tony paused and looked down at the table.

'I don't want you to take this the wrong way. I'm not someone who flits from woman to woman. But Justine and I . . . Well, I don't know any other way to put this. Our sex was recreational. She was going through a hard time, and I was a distraction. I liked her and I think she liked me, but it didn't mean anything.'

'Tony . . .'

'Let me finish. You did mean something to me. I've always liked you, even when we were kids. But it was more like a big-brother-little-sister thing then. When I saw you at the Y it was confusing. You weren't a kid any-more. You were a woman. I didn't know how to treat you. After we spent those two evenings together I could-n't stop thinking about you, and I wanted to see you again.'

'So what stopped you?'

'I was accepted into one of the best residency programs in the country, and it was in New York. A long-distance romance didn't make any sense. And I had no idea how you felt about me. We'd only dated a few times. You were starting a career.' Tony shrugged. 'Then you saw me with Justine. The only thing I want to know is how badly I hurt you, because I always hoped that you didn't care enough for me for my leaving to matter.'

A welter of emotions confused Amanda. She was thrilled that Tony felt strongly enough about her to bare his soul, but his frontal assault was coming so fast that it didn't give her time to think.

'I don't know how I felt when you left, Tony. It's been years, and a lot has happened in between.'

'Maybe that's best,' he said. 'Maybe we should just start over and see what happens. Would that be okay? Could you do that?'

Amanda smiled. 'I'm here, aren't I?'

'I guess that's right. You didn't shoot me down.'

'And I didn't shoot you, either.' She smiled. 'Not yet, anyway.'

The waiter arrived, and Tony seemed grateful for the interruption. Amanda opted for a safe topic of conversation as soon as the waiter left with their orders.

'What are you doing at St. Francis?'

'I've finished my residency and I'm an attending plastic surgeon. I just gave a paper in New Orleans, last Friday, at the annual meeting of the American Society of Plastic and Reconstructive Surgeons,' Tony said proudly.

'What was it about?'

'The long-term aesthetic effects of immediate versus delayed breast reconstruction using the pedicled TRAM flap.'

'In English, please, for the scientifically impaired.'

Tony laughed. 'Sorry. It's not that complicated, really. You can do breast reconstruction after a mastectomy in a number of ways. The pedicled TRAM flap involves taking abdominal tissue to use in the reconstruction. You don't have to do the reconstruction at the same time as the mastectomy. You could do it a year later, if you wanted to. But I've concluded that immediate reconstruction looks better, and I talked about the basis for my conclusion. Impressed?' Tony asked, sipping his margarita.

'Not bad for a college dropout,' Amanda answered with a smile.

'Now that you know all about pedicled TRAM flaps, fill me in on what you've been up to. It said in the paper that you just won a death penalty case. Are you specializing in criminal law like your father?'

'Yup. I think I'm genetically programmed for it.'

'Do you like representing criminals?'

'I don't know if *like* is the right word. Criminal law is exciting, and I think the work is important. With a case like Justine's I feel I can do some real good.'

'How is she holding up?'

'She's a strong woman. But no one really does that well under these circumstances. She's worried about her career and her future. Jail is a lousy place to be even if you're guilty. It's hell if you're innocent.'

'So you don't think she's guilty?'

'No, I don't.'

'Why?'

Amanda was not certain how much she should reveal about the case to someone who was not involved in Justine's representation. But Tony was very bright, and it would be interesting to see how a nonlawyer saw the case after hearing the facts.

'You have to promise to keep what I tell you to yourself.'

'Of course. Doctors have confidentiality restrictions, too.'

Amanda laid out what she knew. Tony tensed when she described the similarities between the Milton County and Multnomah County crime scenes, and his brow furrowed when she explained that an anonymous caller had summoned the police to the farmhouse.

'It looks like a setup,' Tony concluded when Amanda was done. 'I can't believe that the cops don't see it.'

'A setup doesn't fit into their scenario. It complicates matters, and the cops like their cases to have simple solutions.'

'What about the anonymous call that sent the cops to the farmhouse? How do they explain that?'

'The DA says he doesn't have to explain it, that it's my job to construct a defense for Justine.'

'That's bullshit. It's obviously a frame. And you know what I think? It's got to be someone with access to the hospital. Think about it. The scrubs, the cap, the scalpel – all that stuff came from St. Francis, and they aren't something a casual visitor could pick up. You'd have to know when Justine was going to be in surgery, you'd have to have access to the room where Justine discarded her cap and scrubs.'

'That means Justine has an enemy at St. Francis,' Amanda said. 'Do you know anyone who hates her so much he would do something like this?'

Tony thought for a moment, then shook his head.

'The only person I can think of . . . No, it's not possible.'

'You're thinking about Vincent Cardoni.'

'Yeah, but he's dead.'

'We don't know that for sure,' Amanda said. 'His body was never recovered.'

'You think Cardoni is working at St. Francis?'

'I think it's possible. He'd have to have had plastic surgery and he couldn't be working as a doctor. He doesn't have a hand.'

'Actually . . .' Tony started, then stopped, lost in thought.

'What?'

Tony looked up. He leaned toward Amanda.

'A hand transplant,' he said excitedly. 'It's possible to transplant a hand. They tried it for the first time in Ecuador in 1964. The operation failed because the tissue was rejected, but there are new antirejection drugs and advanced surgical techniques that have resulted in several successful hand transplants.'

'Of course,' Amanda answered, echoing Tony's excitement. 'I remember reading about them.' She sobered suddenly. 'A transplant would be so spectacular that everyone would know about it. The one I remember was front-page news. If Cardoni had a hand transplant in the past four years, we'd have heard.'

'Not if it was done clandestinely. Didn't Justine believe that Cardoni had money stashed away in offshore accounts?'

'Yes.'

'With enough money, Cardoni could find a doctor who would change his appearance and try a hand transplant. And he doesn't have to be working as a doctor. Maybe he has a prosthesis and is working at some other job.'

Tony thought for a moment. 'Do you know when the farmhouse was purchased?'

'About two years ago, I think.'

Tony leaned forward. He looked intense.

'That's it, then. I'll get someone in personnel at St. Francis to give me a printout of every male employee who was hired in the past two years. Cardoni could change his appearance and his weight. He could also change his height, but I'm betting he didn't. I'll look for white men about six-two who are roughly Cardoni's age.'

Tony reached across the table and covered Amanda's hand with his.

'If Cardoni is at St. Francis, I'll track him down. We'll catch him, Amanda.'

The waiter arrived with their wine and the first course, and Amanda had a chance to calm down. She ate her salad in silence while she thought about getting Tony involved in Justine's case.

'Maybe I should have our investigator get the personnel records.'

'Why?'

'If Cardoni is our killer, you'd be putting yourself in danger by looking for him.'

'Your investigator wouldn't have the expertise to spot a really good facial reconstruction. I'd recognize one in an instant. And believe me, I'm not going to take any chances. If I find Cardoni, we'll go straight to the police.'

Amanda hesitated.

'Amanda, I like Justine. I don't want to see an innocent person suffer. But I like me, too, and I'm too young to die. I appreciate how dangerous this can be. I'm not going to put myself at risk.'

'Promise?'

'Promise.'

'You know what?' Tony asked.

'What?'

'I think we should stop talking shop for the rest of our meal.'

Amanda smiled. 'I agree. What shall we talk about?'

'I just had an idea. Have you seen the new Jackie Chan flick?'

'I haven't seen a movie in ages.'

'It's showing at the Broadway Metroplex at ten-thirty. Are you in the mood for some mindless violence?'

'You bet.'

Tony smiled. 'You're a girl after my own heart.'

45

When Bobby Vasquez had called earlier for an appointment, Mary Ann Jager had answered her own phone. Now he knew why: The lawyer's tiny waiting room reeked of failure. There was no receptionist, and the top of the receptionist's desk was bare and covered with a light layer of dust. Vasquez knocked on the doorjamb of an open doorway. A slender woman with short brown hair looked up, startled, from the fashion magazine she was reading.

Vasquez had learned a lot about Jager from the Martindale-Hubbell Law Directory listing of attorneys' résumés and the file of complaints against Jager that he had obtained through the Oregon state bar. She had gone to work for a midsized firm for a decent salary

Phillip Margolin

after graduating high in her law school class. There were no problems until shortly before her divorce, when a client complained about irregularities in her trust account and rumors of substance abuse began to circulate. Jager was suspended from the practice of law for a year and fired from her firm. When she could practice again, she opened her own office. Jager's history was very similar to that of Walter Stoops, and Vasquez wondered if Cardoni found his lawyers by studying complaints filed against members of the bar.

'Ms. Jager? I'm Bobby Vasquez. I called earlier.'

The lawyer stood up quickly, walked around her desk and extended a damp hand. Vasquez noticed a slight tremor.

'I hope you weren't waiting outside long,' Jager said nervously. 'My receptionist is out with that flu that's going around.'

Bobby smiled sympathetically, though he was certain that there was no receptionist – and very little business, to judge from the empty state of Jager's in-box and her bare desktop.

'I'm interested in contacting the owner of some land you purchased approximately two years ago for Intercontinental Properties, a corporation you formed,' Vasquez said when they were seated.

Jager frowned. 'That was a farm, right?'

Vasquez nodded, breathing a silent prayer of thanks that he had beaten the police to Jager and that she did not know that the land she had purchased had been turned into a slaughterhouse.

'I'd like to help you, but I have no idea who owns the

288

property. The owner contacted me by mail. I was paid to form Intercontinental Properties for the sole purpose of buying the land. My retainer and the money for the property were paid in cashier's checks. I forwarded the title to a post office box in California.'

'If you could give me the owner's name, I can try to trace him.'

'I don't have a name. There was no signature on my instructions.'

'This all sounds very mysterious.'

'It is, but it's completely legal.'

'Of course.'

Vasquez paused, then acted like a man who has just gotten an idea.

'Could I see your file? Maybe there's a clue to the owner's identity in it.'

'I don't know if I can do that. The information in the file is privileged.'

Vasquez leaned forward and lowered his voice, even though he and the lawyer were alone.

'Ms. Jager, my client is very intent on negotiating for this property. He has authorized me to compensate you for your time and for reasonable copying costs. I don't see where a problem would arise. Most of the information is public record anyway.'

The mention of money got Jager's attention.

'I charge one hundred and fifty dollars an hour.'

'That sounds reasonable.'

Jager hesitated, and Vasquez knew that she was desperate for more money. He hoped that she didn't go crazy on him. Until the Jaffes hired him, he was fronting his expenses.

'My copying costs are rather high. I would need another fifty dollars to cover them.'

'That's fine.'

Vasquez slid two hundred dollars across the desk.

'May I see the file?'

Jager rotated her chair and retrieved a manila folder from a cabinet behind her desk. Inside, Vasquez found copies of documents he'd seen in the Multnomah County file. He only asked for copies of the checks. Jager was gone for a few minutes. When she returned, she handed a stack of photocopies to Vasquez.

'What's so important about this farm?' Jager asked. 'You're the second person who's been interested in it. Is someone going to build a subdivision?'

'Someone else asked about this property?'

'Yeah, about a week ago.'

Vasquez put the photocopies away and dug a photograph of Cardoni out of his attaché case.

'Was this the man?'

Jager studied the photograph for a moment. Then she shook her head.

'The man who came in was blond and looked different. More like a Russian.'

'How tall was he?'

'Over six feet.'

'Did he say why he wanted to buy the property?'

'No. He was more interested in how it was purchased.'

'Can you tell me any more about him?'

'No. He just showed up and asked about the farm.'

'Did you show him the file?'

'Yes.'

Vasquez was stumped. Who else would be interested in the farm?

'If this guy shows up again, try to get some more information about him.'

'How will I let you know?'

Vasquez gave Jager his business card and another fifty.

Ten minutes later Vasquez was on the phone with Amanda Jaffe.

'Have you had a chance to talk to your father about me?' Vasquez asked anxiously.

'I'm lead counsel on Dr. Castle's case, so it's my decision.'

'Look, I know you're worried, but I'm good and I've already got a jump on the cops.'

Vasquez eagerly related what he had learned during his meeting with Mary Ann Jager. Amanda only half listened until Vasquez told her that someone else had been asking about the property.

'Do you think he was just interested in buying the farm?' Amanda asked.

'I don't know. I showed Jager a photograph of Cardoni. The person who came to the office was his height, but Jager said that he looked different.'

'If he's alive, Cardoni may have had plastic surgery.'

'If he's alive, I'll find him. It doesn't matter what he looks like.'

Vasquez's determination pushed Amanda toward a decision. Frank might not trust Vasquez, but she did. He had a burning desire to get Vincent Cardoni, and you could not buy that kind of drive.

'Mr. Vasquez, I think you can help Dr. Castle. I want you to work for me.'

'You won't regret this. What do you want me to do?'

'Serial killers refine their techniques. Our murderer has used a unique MO twice. I want you to see if he's used it before. Start searching for unsolved murders involving mass graves. Maybe you'll find another property purchased in a similar way. Maybe we'll get lucky and Cardoni has made a mistake that will let us nail him.'

46

Mike Greene had asked Fred Scofield to send him a copy of the Milton County file in the Cardoni prosecution shortly after Justine Castle's arrest. It arrived on Monday afternoon. Greene was reading the file when Sean McCarthy walked into his office a little after five. The homicide detective looked depressed. He dropped a sheaf of police reports on Greene's desk and lowered himself into a chair.

'Jesus, you look terrible,' Greene said. 'You want some coffee?'

McCarthy dismissed the offer with a despondent wave.

'We have a real problem, Mike. Everything we've got so far makes me believe that the person who committed the murders in Milton County also committed

the murders at the farm. Both properties were purchased at the behest of an anonymous buyer through
dummy corporations set up by a lawyer who's been in
deep trouble with the bar. The crime scenes are so similar that it can't be a coincidence.'

Greene looked confused. 'Why is that a problem?'

'If Dr. Castle murdered the victims at the farm, we
screwed everything up four years ago.'

'Then we'll make everything right.'

'That might not be so easy. If we can't prove Cardoni's
dead, the Jaffes will argue that he's returned to frame
Castle. They can call Fred Scofield and Sheriff Mills as
witnesses to testify that they were convinced that Cardoni
murdered the victims in Milton County. Hell, Mike, they
can call me and I'd have to swear that I was certain that
Cardoni did it.'

Greene thought about that. He pointed at the papers
that were strewn across his desk.

'The evidence against Cardoni was pretty convincing.'

'And there was none implicating Dr. Castle.'

Greene was lost in thought for a moment. When he
turned his attention back to McCarthy he looked concerned.

'Have you been able to identify the victims at the
farm? Are any of them connected to Castle?'

'The poor bastard who died in the basement was a
male prostitute named Zach Petrie. He showed up at the
emergency room at St. Francis a week before he died, but
there's no record of Castle being involved with the case.'

'What about the others?'

'Diane Vickers was a prostitute who was treated for a sexually transmitted disease at St. Francis, but as far as we can tell, Castle didn't treat her. David Capp was a run-away, and we can't find any link between him and St. Francis or Justine Castle.

'Now, no one reported Petrie, Vickers or Capp missing, but we'd been treating the disappearance of Kimberly Lyons, the other female victim, as a possible homicide since she went missing a few months ago. Lyons was a student at Portland State. From what we can tell, she was abducted at the Lloyd Center mall. Her car was found there, and she told her friends that she was going to shop for a birthday present for her boyfriend.'

'Do you think the others were also random kidnappings?'

McCarthy shrugged.

'How about taking a new look at the old victims to see if we can link them to Castle?'

'I'm already doing that.'

Greene smiled. 'Sorry, I should have assumed you would be. Anything else new?'

'The DNA test identified the hair in the surgical cap as Castle's. I also talked to the lawyer who was representing Cardoni in his divorce. Castle went through with the divorce after Cardoni disappeared and made out like a bandit.'

'How well?'

'She cleared around two million dollars.'

Greene whistled. 'Two million dollars is a good motive for murdering Cardoni.'

'The lawyer also told me Castle was certain that Cardoni had set up secret bank accounts in Switzerland and the Cayman Islands, but she never found them. When I asked when she started looking for them, he said it was well before she filed.'

'Why is that important?'

'Four years ago Castle testified at her husband's bail hearing. She said she left him when he raped her, but it looks like she may have been checking into his finances way before that.'

'So what do we have, a black widow?'

'It's beginning to look that way, Mike. If she killed Cardoni, it won't be the first time she's offed a husband.'

'Oh?'

'It might not even be the second time.'

47

The matron closed the door to the visiting room behind Justine Castle, and Amanda motioned to the chair across from her. Justine had lost weight, and there were dark circles under her eyes.

'We've got a problem, Justine,' Amanda said.

Justine watched Amanda warily.

'The DNA tests of the hair found in the surgical cap came back positive for you.'

Justine seemed to relax a bit, as if she'd expected Amanda to say something else.

'I assumed it would,' Justine told Amanda. 'Whoever planted the coffee mug and the scalpel obviously took a cap I used during surgery.'

'There's more. Mike Greene's developing a theory that

you married Vincent Cardoni for his money and killed him to get it.'

Justine smiled wearily. 'That's utterly ridiculous.'

'Greene thinks he can prove it, and he's not simply going to describe you to the jury as a gold digger. He's going to characterize you as one of the most depraved serial killers in history.'

Justine leaned back in her chair. Her smile widened.

'Isn't that what they said about Vincent? Aren't they going to have a hard time explaining how I murdered the victims in Milton County when all of the evidence points to him?'

Amanda was surprised that her news had not upset Justine more. She studied her client for a moment. Justine did not blink under the scrutiny.

'You've been thinking about this, haven't you?'

'Why does that surprise you, Amanda? My life is at stake, and I have nothing but time on my hands.'

'Well, you're right. The Milton County case hurts Mike, but he can overcome it if he has evidence that you've killed before for money.'

Justine's smile faded. 'What are you talking about?'

'I reread the autobiography you wrote for me. You left out some things. Like the fact that you shot your first husband to death.'

Amanda watched the color drain from Justine's face.

'And I didn't see anything in your bio about the one hundred thousand you cleared on his insurance or the several hundred thousand dollars you inherited when your second husband died a violent death within a year of marrying you. Didn't you think I would be interested in these little tidbits?'

'I shot Gil in self-defense,' Justine said, her voice barely above a whisper, 'and David's death was an accident. They have nothing to do with this.'

'That isn't what Mike Greene thinks. Damn it, Justine, you can't hide something like this. I've got to be prepared. This isn't a shoplifting case. If we make one mistake, the State is going to kill you. And you can be damn sure that the DA will find out every little secret you decide to keep from me.'

'I'm sorry.'

'Sorry doesn't cut it. Anything you tell me is confidential. Remember me saying that? I don't care how bad it is, you tell me. No one else gets to know, but I've got to know if I'm going to save your life. Okay?'

Justine didn't answer. She just stared past Amanda, who let her collect herself.

'How did they find out?' Justine finally asked.

'The same way Herb Cross did when my father was representing Vincent.'

Justine's head snapped up. 'Your father had me investigated?'

'Dr. Cardoni told my father that you killed the victims in Milton County. We followed up on the accusation.'

'How can you represent me if you think I framed Vincent?' Justine asked angrily.

'I don't think that, and neither does my father. He never believed Cardoni. He was just doing his job.'

'Can the DA bring up Gil's and David's deaths?'

'He'll sure as hell try.'

'Will it be in the papers?'

'Of course. Even if we keep the evidence from the jury, the legal arguments will be in open court.'

Justine squirmed in her chair and her shoulders hunched.

'This is no good,' she said, more to herself than Amanda. Then she looked across at her attorney. 'You can't let them do this,' she pleaded. 'No one knows about my past here.'

'The DA does. He knows that you insured Gil Manning for a hundred thousand dollars less than a year before you shot him.'

'That was for the baby,' Justine said desperately. 'When we got married, Gil was working construction. He wasn't making enough for us to have our own place. I had to think about how I'd take care of our baby if something happened to him.'

'You didn't cancel the policy after your miscarriage,' Amanda said softly.

Justine looked stunned.

'After my baby . . . After he . . . I . . . I wasn't thinking very clearly for some time after that happened.'

'Alex DeVore interviewed Gil's parents. They believe you murdered Gil.'

Anger restored color to Justine's cheeks. She glared at Amanda.

'Do you know why Gil thought it was okay to use me as his private punching bag? He watched his father use his mother that way. Living in that house was like living in hell. Gil and his father were both abusive drunks, and the drinking got worse when high school ended. All of a sudden Gil wasn't a god, and neither one of them could take that. Then I lost my figure when I got pregnant, and Gil wasn't married to the most desirable girl in Carrington anymore. I became an inconvenience, except when Gil needed someone to blame for his problems.'

'Why didn't you leave when he started to beat you?'

'Where could I go? My parents wouldn't look at me after Gil knocked me up. I had no money.'

'Gil's parents say you drove him to drink and tormented him until he lost his self-control.'

'Of course they say that.'

'There's an interview with David Barkley's parents in which they accuse you of setting him up.'

'That's not true. I loved David.'

'They say they warned David that you were after his money. They also say that David didn't drink.'

'His parents didn't know the first thing about him. The autopsy showed that David's blood alcohol was point-two-oh. He hated them, and he drank because of the pressure they put on him. I loved David, but he was an alcoholic. I thought I could change him, but I couldn't and he died.'

'The neighbors say you and David quarreled the night he died.'

Justine looked down at the tabletop.

'He was drinking too much,' she said softly. 'We had words, and he stormed out and drove away. I couldn't stop him.'

'You inherited David's trust fund and the proceeds of another life insurance policy when he was killed.'

Justine looked directly into Amanda's eyes when she said, 'Yes, I did.'

'And there was another policy on Dr. Cardoni.'

'Which the insurance company refuses to pay.'

'Nevertheless, you see how this looks.'

'No, Amanda, I see how the district attorney wants to make it look. I'm counting on you to make a jury see the way it really is.'

48

Amanda broke into a smile when the receptionist announced that a Dr. Fiori was calling on line two.

'Hi,' Tony said. 'I had a great time Friday.'

'That makes two of us.'

'I got home late from the hospital. That's why I didn't return your message sooner. I was afraid I'd wake you.'

'Actually, I was probably up. I've been working on Justine's case into the wee hours. Any luck at the hospital?'

'Hey, I'm a regular Dick Tracy. Not only did I come up with a list, but I've already eliminated a few suspects.'

'How?'

'I followed them.'

'Don't do that!'

'I thought I'd save you some trouble.' Tony sounded hurt.

'I'm serious,' Amanda insisted. 'It's dangerous. Fax me the list and let my investigator do the rest.'

'Don't panic. I'm being very careful.'

'Damn it, Tony. Promise me you'll stop.'

'Okay, okay, I promise.' Tony paused. 'Seeing as you're pissed, is this a bad time to ask you out for this Saturday?'

Amanda laughed in spite of herself.

'You're on,' she said, 'but only if you behave yourself.'

'Listen, I've got to run. Think of something nice for Saturday and get back to me.'

'Hey, brother, you get back to me.'

'Anyone as aggressive as you are can take care of dinner reservations. That'll teach you to bust my balls. And it better be a nice place.'

'What ever happened to take-charge guys?'

They both laughed and said goodbye. Amanda was still beaming when Frank rapped on her doorjamb.

'There's a Cheshire cat grin,' he said. 'Good news, I take it?'

Amanda blushed. 'It could be worse.'

'Well, I've got good news of my own. Art Prochaska is willing to meet with us.'

'When?'

'Now. Grab your coat.'

The night that Berkeley won the PAC-10 swimming championships Amanda went carousing with her teammates. One of the bars they hit was a male strip joint. Amanda had cheered and hooted with her friends, but secretly she'd been embarrassed. She felt even more uncomfortable when she entered the Jungle Club with Frank. Onstage, a woman with unnaturally large breasts danced unenthusiastically to a blaring ZZ Top tune. Amanda averted her eyes and followed Frank past the bar to a short hall at the end of which was an office. A man with a bull neck and massive shoulders stood outside the door.

'We're here to see Mr. Prochaska,' Frank told him.

'He s expecting you.'

Art Prochaska was squeezed behind a desk at one end of the narrow room. He had put on weight since the motion to suppress, but he was no less intimidating. Prochaska's tailored suit gave him an air of quasi-respectability. He and Frank shook hands across the desk.

'It's been a while, Art.'

'A coupla years.'

'This is my daughter, Amanda.' Amanda's hand disappeared in the gangster's massive paw. 'You may remember her. She assisted me during the motion in Cedar City.'

'Nice to meetcha,' Prochaska said. Then he returned his attention to Frank. 'Martin said you wanted to talk.'

'And I appreciate the quick response.'

'I ain't sure I can help, but I'll try. What can I do for you?'

'I'd like to know what happened at the cabin in Milton County four years ago,' Amanda said.

Prochaska looked surprised that Amanda had asked a

question. When he answered, he turned away from her and spoke to Frank.

'I was never there. I was playing cards that night. I had five witnesses.'

Amanda wanted to disabuse Prochaska quickly of the idea that she was Frank's secretary.

'I'm sure they were wonderful witnesses, Mr. Prochaska,' she said firmly, 'but I was at the cabin, too, and I saw you drive away just as I arrived.'

Prochaska turned his attention back to Amanda. She met his stare and held it.

'You're mistaken.'

'Probably, if you have five witnesses,' Amanda answered with a smile that said that she wasn't buying his bullshit. 'But let's say, for the sake of argument, that I wasn't. Why would you have been at the cabin at that time of night?'

'What would it matter?'

'I'm representing Vincent Cardoni's ex-wife, Justine Castle. She's been charged with committing several murders at a farmhouse in Multnomah County. There's a makeshift operating room in the basement of the farmhouse. Other victims were found buried in a graveyard on the farm.'

'So?'

'The murder scene is almost identical to the scene of the crime in Milton County.'

'Why should I care?'

'It's possible that Vincent Cardoni cut off his own hand four years ago to make everyone think he'd been murdered. If Cardoni was trying to convince everyone that he was dead, it would be convenient for me to see you leaving the cabin just before I discovered his hand.'

Prochaska stared at them like a gangster Buddha.

'I'm not interested in getting you in trouble, Mr. Prochaska. In fact, it's my understanding that Martin Breach would be very interested if Cardoni is alive. You should be too if Cardoni tried to set you up.'

Prochaska mulled over Amanda's information.

'Anything you tell us will go no further, Art,' Frank assured him.

When Prochaska spoke, he directed his remarks at Amanda.

'I was never at that cabin, understand?'

Amanda nodded.

Prochaska leaned forward and spoke so softly that it was almost impossible to hear him over the club's loud music.

'Martin did some business with a doctor at St. Francis. This doctor stiffed Martin for a lot of money, and he wanted it back. Then the doctor turned up as one of the corpses the cops found at that cabin, but the money didn't show up. Martin thought Cardoni had it.'

Prochaska waited to see if Amanda was following him. When Amanda nodded, he continued.

'The night you found that hand, outa the blue Cardoni calls and says he wants a truce. He's got the dough at the cabin. Martin should send someone up. Martin sent me. As soon as I saw the hand I knew it was a setup. I got in the car and left. That's all there is to it.'

'You didn't find the money?' Amanda asked.

'If Cardoni set me up, there wouldn't be no money, would there?'

Prochaska was on the phone as soon as his visitors closed the door behind them.

'Guess what, Martin? Vincent Cardoni might not be dead.'

'That's why Jaffe wanted to see you?'

'He's representing Cardoni's ex-wife.' He told Breach about the meeting with the Jaffes.

'Son of a bitch,' Breach said when Prochaska was through. 'If Cardoni's back in Portland, I want him found before the cops get him.'

49

Andrew Volkov moved his cleaning cart against the wall to make way for two internists. They were deep in conversation and didn't even glance at the invisible man in the gray custodian's uniform. When they passed, Volkov moved his cart forward. As he did so, he noticed another doctor watching him from the end of the hall. He ducked his head and the doctor averted his eyes, but it was obvious that Volkov had been the object of his attention.

The physician walked toward Volkov, who turned his cart and pushed it in the opposite direction. A hall led off to the right and he entered it. Halfway down the corridor was the entrance to a stairwell that led to the basement. He left his cart next to it, waited several beats before opening the door, then pushed it wide so that it would take time to close. If the doctor was following him, the door would bait him. If he missed it swinging shut the cart would provide a clue to where he'd gone that only an idiot would miss.

Volkov moved down the stairs slowly, pausing at each landing until he heard the hall door open. He had been right. He was being followed. He waited a moment, then continued to descend the stairs, making certain to step heavily enough so that his footsteps created echoes in the stairwell. When he reached the basement, Volkov opened the door and let it slam shut. In front of him was a narrow hallway made narrower by the exposed steam pipes that were attached to the walls. Low-wattage bulbs, spaced far apart, kept most of the corridor in shadow. The air was damp and cool. Volkov moved down the corridor at a steady pace until he was almost at a side hall that led to the boiler room. He paused until he heard the basement door open before turning into the side passage and pressing against the wall. Volkov heard footsteps drawing closer. They stopped at the entrance to the hallway. Then the doctor stepped around the corner.

'Why are you following me?' Volkov asked.

The doctor's eyes widened with fright. He pulled a scalpel out of his pocket and lunged. Volkov blocked the thrust and lashed out with a front kick. The doctor leaped back, and the janitor's toe only grazed him. Volkov's body flowed forward behind the kick. His fist caught the doctor's shoulder, slamming him against the concrete wall on the other side of the hallway. Volkov's next kick should have shattered his foe's kneecap, but he was surprised when his attacker moved into him, nullifying its power.

Volkov felt a sharp pain in his side and realized that he'd been stabbed. The doctor lashed out again, and the scalpel ripped through Volkov's shirt, slicing through skin. Volkov grunted, slashed upward with an elbow and saw blood gush from a broken nose. The doctor struck out blindly and stabbed Volkov in the cheek. The janitor unleashed a kick that connected solidly, driving the doctor backward until he lost his balance and fell to the floor.

'Andy?'

Arthur West, another janitor, was standing at the far end of the corridor.

'What's going on?' West shouted.

The doctor still held the scalpel and was struggling to his feet. Volkov hesitated. West started walking toward him. Volkov kicked the doctor again and ran toward the exit door at the end of the hallway. He tore it open and fled across the street to the employee parking lot.

50

Amanda walked from the Stockman Building toward the river for several blocks and found Vasquez waiting for her in a booth at the back of O'Brien's Clam Bar.

'What's up?' Vasquez asked.

Amanda handed him the list of employees that Tony had faxed to her.

'A friend of mine is a doctor at St. Francis. I told him a little about our case. He thinks that there's a good possibility that the person who planted the scalpel, clothing and coffee mug at the farmhouse works at St. Francis, since all of the evidence came from the hospital. This is a list of men who have been hired at St. Francis during the past two years. I want you to check them out.'

'I'll get right on it.'

'Great.'

A waitress arrived, and Amanda ordered fried clams and an iced tea. Bobby asked for a BLT and coffee.

'Now I have something for you,' he said as soon as the waitress left. 'I've been trying to find similar killing grounds in the United States and abroad. I went on the Web initially and found newspaper and periodical stories about serial murders that were like our cases. The reporters who wrote the stories gave me more information about each case and the names of the detectives who worked them. Most of the cops talked to me. They'd sent their case information to the FBI's National Center for the Analysis of Violent Crimes for investigation by the Investigative Support Unit and VICAP, the Violent Criminal Apprehension Program.'

The waitress brought their drinks and Bobby continued.

'I know a former FBI agent who owes me a favor. He talked to some friends at the Bureau and got me more details on the domestic cases. With the international cases it was harder, but I know someone at the Interpol office in Salem. She was able to get me information on the foreign cases.'

Vasquez handed Amanda a multipage document. 'This is my preliminary list. I've found murders that are similar to ours in Washington, Colorado, Florida, New Jersey, Canada, Belgium, Japan, Peru, and Mexico. And it turns out that there was another case right here in Oregon,' he concluded, pointing to the synopsis, which explained that fourteen years ago two young women had been found buried in the forest near Ghost Lake, a ski resort in the Cascades.

Something about the entry bothered Amanda, but her cell phone rang before she could figure out what it was. She took the phone out of her purse and answered it.

'Is something wrong?' Vasquez asked when she hung up.

'My friend at St. Francis, the one who got me the list, has been attacked. I have to go to the hospital.'

Amanda rushed through Emergency until she found Tony slouched in a chair in an examining room. He had black-and-purple bruises under both eyes and a bandaged nose. There was dried blood on his shirt, which was open, revealing ribs wrapped with tape. Amanda stopped in the doorway, shocked by his appearance. Tony stood up when he saw her. The effort made him grimace. Amanda's eyes widened with concern.

'How badly are you hurt?'

'Don't worry. Nothing's broken that can't be fixed.'

'What happened?'

'I was on my way to see a patient when I noticed a janitor named Andrew Volkov standing next to a cleaning cart. He's one of the employees on my list. Volkov saw me watching him and got flustered. I followed him into the basement, which was pretty stupid. If I had any brains, I would have realized that he was luring me downstairs. He jumped me and was beating the crap out of me when another janitor came along and scared him off.'

'Is Volkov Cardoni?'

'I couldn't honestly say. The body type is right, but I was too busy defending myself to get a good look at him.'

Amanda thought for a moment. Then she took out her cell phone.

'I'm going to call Sean McCarthy. He can arrest Volkov for assault and take his prints. We'll know pretty soon if he's Cardoni.'

51

It had been three days since the crime lab had matched the prints on Andrew Volkov's custodian's cart to the prints taken four years before from Vincent Cardoni's left hand. Prints found in Volkov's apartment also matched the doctor's. A thorough search of Volkov's locker at the hospital and his apartment provided no clue to Cardoni's whereabouts.

Mike Greene was trying to distract himself while he waited for an update on the case by analyzing a chess game played between Judit Polgar and Viswanathan Anand in a recent tournament in Madrid. He was studying the pivotal position in the game when the phone rang. Greene swiveled his chair and picked up the receiver.

'This is Mike Greene.'

'Hi, Mike. This is Roy Bishop.'

Bishop was an overbearing criminal defense attorney who was strongly suspected of being a little too friendly with some of the people he represented.

'What's up, Roy?'

'I'm calling on behalf of a client, someone I know you want to talk to. He wants to meet with you.'

'Who are we talking about?'

'Vincent Cardoni.'

Greene sat up straight.

'If you know where Cardoni is, you better tell me. Harboring a fugitive will get your ticket yanked.'

'Ease up, Mike. I've only talked to Cardoni on the phone. I have no idea where he is.'

'Does he want to turn himself in?'

'Absolutely not. He made it very clear that he won't meet with you unless he gets a guarantee in writing that he will not be arrested if he shows up and that nothing he says will be used against him.'

'That's impossible. The man is a mass murderer.'

'He says that he's not. But even if he is, from what he tells me, you don't have grounds to hold him.'

Mike Greene looked pale and drawn when Alex DeVore and Sean McCarthy entered his office at ten the next morning.

'Vincent Cardoni will be here in half an hour,' Greene announced. He sounded exhausted.

DeVore looked stunned. McCarthy said, 'He's turning himself in?'

Greene shook his head. 'He's coming here to talk. I had to guarantee that we would not take him into custody.'

'Are you nuts?' DeVore exclaimed.

'You're joking!' McCarthy said simultaneously.

'I was here until ten last night and I was back here at seven this morning hashing this out with Jack, Henry Buchanan and Lillian Po,' Greene answered, naming the district attorney for Multnomah County, his chief criminal deputy, and the head of the appellate section. 'There's no way we can hold him.'

'He killed four people at the farmhouse,' McCarthy said.

'He changed his features and lied to get a job at St. Francis so he could steal the coffee mug, the scalpel and the clothes,' DeVore argued. 'He killed all those people in Milton County.'

'It won't wash. Cardoni had access to the items we found at the farmhouse, but there is no way we can prove that he stole them and planted them there. There isn't a single piece of evidence connecting Cardoni to the farmhouse or any of the victims. Believe me, guys, we went round and round on this. I'm as frustrated as you are.'

'What about Milton County? He's still under indictment there,' McCarthy said.

Mike looked grim.

'There was a massive screwup in the Milton County case, an unbelievable screwup. The judge signed an order granting Cardoni's motion to suppress, which he filed in the clerk's office. Fred Scofield had thirty days to appeal the order if he didn't want it to become final. During the thirty days, Cardoni disappeared and his hand was found in the cabin. Everyone thought that he was dead, and Scofield forgot to file the appeal. That means that Judge Brody's order is final and no evidence seized from the cabin or Cardoni's home in Portland can be used at a trial. Without that evidence, there is no Milton County case.'

'I don't believe this,' McCarthy said. 'You're telling me there's no way to put Cardoni in jail? He's killed at least a dozen people.'

'Unless you've got proof that's admissible in court, that's just speculation. I can't arrest a man on a hunch.'

'Damn it, there's got to be a way,' McCarthy muttered to himself. Suddenly he brightened. 'Fiori! Cardoni attacked Dr. Fiori. We can hold him for assault.'

'I'm afraid not. Cardoni says Fiori was stalking him. Fiori admits he followed Cardoni into the basement with a scalpel and made the first aggressive move. Cardoni's claiming self-defense.

'Look, guys, we went through these arguments a million times. It always comes out the same way. There isn't a person in this office who doesn't believe that Vincent Cardoni is a homicidal monster, but the sad truth is that there isn't enough evidence to hold him. We've already faxed Bishop our written assurance that we won't arrest Cardoni within twenty-four hours of this meeting.'

'If he knows you don't have the evidence to arrest him, why does Cardoni want to meet with you?' DeVore asked.

Before he could answer, the intercom buzzed and the receptionist announced that Dr. Cardoni and Roy Bishop were in the waiting area. Greene told her to show them to the conference room. Then he turned to DeVore.

'You can ask him yourself.'

Vincent Cardoni took a seat opposite Mike Greene at the long table in the conference room. A row of stitches crossed Cardoni's cheek. Roy Bishop, a large man with styled brown hair, sat next to his client. Sean McCarthy studied the surgeon carefully. It was hard to believe that this was the man he had arrested four years before.

'Good morning, Dr. Cardoni,' McCarthy said.

'I see you're still as polite as you were when you arrested me.'

'Except for growing a little grayer, I haven't changed. But you certainly have.'

Cardoni smiled.

'Why don't we get down to business, Roy?' Greene said. 'I'm dying to know why your client wants to talk to me.'

'It's a mystery to me, too, Mike. Dr. Cardoni has not confided his reasons to me.'

'I hope you're planning to confess, Doctor,' Greene said. 'It'll save us a lot of trouble.'

'There isn't a thing for me to confess. Contrary to what you believe, I never murdered anyone. Justine killed the people at the farmhouse, and she's responsible for the victims in Milton County.'

'Who's responsible for cutting off your hand?' McCarthy asked.

Cardoni held up his right hand and slid down his cuff. Everyone in the room stared at the jagged scar encircling his wrist.

'I did this,' Cardoni told McCarthy.

'Plastic surgery, a false identity and self-mutilation? That's pretty extreme behavior for an innocent man.'

'I was desperate. I couldn't see any other way to stay alive.'

'Want to explain that to us?' Greene prompted. Cardoni looked at the DA and the two detectives.

'I can tell that you don't believe me, but I swear I'm telling the truth. Justine was Clifford Grant's partner in a black-market organ scheme. She killed him, then set me up so that Martin Breach would think I was the one who ripped him off.'

Cardoni took a deep breath. He looked down at the conference table when he spoke.

'You've seen Justine. She's beautiful and brilliant, and she was always two steps ahead of me. Justine knew every one of my weaknesses.

'Look, I know I'm no saint. The pressure in medical school was too intense for me. I used all sorts of pharmaceuticals to cope with it, and they almost destroyed me. Fighting my addiction was exhausting, and it was easy to give in when Justine brought me cocaine. I didn't even realize that she was trying to break me down until it was too late.

'I also didn't know why she saw so much of Clifford Grant until Frank Jaffe told me that Grant was harvesting organs for Martin Breach. He told me about the raid at the airfield. Justine was Grant's silent partner. She framed me to make Breach think I was. Shortly after Frank got me out of jail two of Breach's men attacked me. I was able to get the better of them, and I made one of them tell me why I was attacked. This was the same day I learned that the Milton County DA was trying to reopen the motion to suppress and that there was a good chance I would have to go back to jail. I was strung out on coke, and I figured I was either going to be tortured to death by Martin Breach or end up on death row. My only way out was to convince everyone that I was dead.'

'So you chopped off your hand,' McCarthy said.

Cardoni fixed on McCarthy. He seemed exasperated.

'Imagine you're accused of a crime you didn't commit. The state of Oregon wants to give you a lethal injection, and a vicious criminal doesn't think that would be a violent enough death. Don't you think you might take desperate measures to save your life?'

'I've got too many real-life problems on my plate to worry about hypothetical ones, Doctor. Maybe you can give me the answer to one of them. Did you steal a coffee mug and a scalpel with Dr. Castle's fingerprints on them and plant them at the farmhouse to implicate her?'

'Haven't you been listening to what I said? She's insane. She's a mass murderer. You've got her now. I'm begging you, don't let her get away with this.'

'Dr. Cardoni,' Greene said, 'I agreed to this meeting in the hopes that you would surrender yourself or at least admit your guilt. Instead you've told us a story that you can't support with one shred of evidence.'

Cardoni's head dropped into his hands. Greene continued.

'I'll be frank with you. I don't believe a word you've said. I think you framed Dr. Castle for your own bizarre reasons and set up this meeting in the hopes that you could manipulate me into furthering your plan to send an innocent woman to death row. It's not going to work.'

'If you let Justine out, she'll kill again. She is the most dangerous murderer you've ever dealt with. You've got to believe me.'

'Well, I don't. Unless you want to surrender or confess, this meeting is over.'

52

The guard let Justine Castle into the interview room at the jail. She looked at Amanda expectantly. Amanda waited a beat, then smiled.

'I've got great news. We're holding another release hearing this afternoon. The DA's recommending your release.'

'I'll get out of here?' Justine said in disbelief.

'By tonight.'

Justine sat down heavily. After a moment she reached across the small table and gripped one of Amanda's hands.

'Thank you, thank you. You have no idea what it's meant to have you as my attorney. I don't think I could have made it through this ordeal without you.'

The warmth and intensity of Justine's response caught

Amanda by surprise and made her heart swell with pride. She covered Justine's hands and squeezed them.

'You've been incredibly brave, Justine. I think we've turned the corner on this case. With luck, it will be behind you very soon.'

Justine was about to say something else when her features changed from relief and happiness to concern. She released Amanda's hands.

'Why are they letting me go?' Justine asked abruptly. 'Have they arrested Vincent?'

Amanda stopped smiling. 'No, but they've spoken to him.' She related what Mike Greene had told her earlier in the day.

'They just let him walk away?' Justine asked incredulously.

'They can't prosecute him, Justine. They don't have any evidence connecting him to the murders at the farmhouse.'

'What about the murders in Milton County?'

'All of the evidence from that case was suppressed.'

'This is bad,' Justine muttered to herself. 'This is very bad.'

'You'll be okay, Justine.'

Justine fixed Amanda with her eyes. A pulse was throbbing in Justine's temple, and her skin was so tight from tension that Amanda could imagine it ripping.

'You don't understand the way Vincent's mind works. He's insane, he's relentless and he believes that he is infallible. No matter what the odds are against him, he'll come after me.'

'He won't try anything with everyone watching.'

'That's the worst part, Amanda. Vincent will bide his time before making his move. He waited four years to frame me. Now he'll disappear and wait until everyone has forgotten about him. I'll never be able to sleep, I'll never be able to lead a normal life.'

Amanda wanted to comfort her client, but she knew that Justine was right. Cardoni was insane and he was patient, and that was a deadly combination.

'I have an idea,' Amanda said. 'Do you remember Robert Vasquez, the detective who searched the cabin in Milton County? He's a private detective now. He's been doing some work on this case for me. You might consider hiring him as a bodyguard. I could have him drive you home from the jail.'

'He's responsible for Vincent being free, and you want me to hire him?'

'Justine, Bobby Vasquez has been living with his guilt for four years. He's dedicated himself to getting Vincent. This wouldn't just be a job for him. You won't be able to find anyone who would be more committed to protecting you.'

Amanda was getting ready to go to the courthouse for the hearing when Vasquez returned her call. Amanda told him about Cardoni. He sounded devastated.

'Cardoni won't be able to control his impulse to kill. There'll be new victims if we don't do something.'

'Look, Bobby, I hired you to help on Justine's case. Our job was to clear her, and that's been accomplished.'

'Your job was to clear Justine. Mine is to get that motherfucker.'

'Don't even think like that. The last time you took the law into your own hands, you blew the State's case out of the water.'

Amanda paused to let what she'd said sink in.

'Bobby?'

'Yes?'

'Promise me you won't go after Cardoni on your own.'

'Don't worry,' Vasquez said a little too quickly. Amanda was not reassured.

'I had another reason for calling you. Justine is going to be released from jail this afternoon. She's worried that Cardoni will come after her. I think she's smart to worry, and I suggested that she hire you for protection.'

'As a bodyguard?'

'Right. Will you do it? It'll keep you in the case, and she's really scared.'

'With Cardoni out there, she's got a good reason to be.'

53

In order to develop expertise, the judges in Multnomah County were assigned to rotations where they heard particular types of cases for set periods of time. There were three judges who handled only homicide cases for one or two years, depending on the judge's preference. Justine Castle's case had been assigned to Mary Campbell, the judge who tried the Dooling case.

At four o'clock the parties met in Judge Campbell's chambers so Mike Greene could explain why the State was willing to release Justine Castle on her own recognizance, even though she was charged with four counts of aggravated murder. Justine, Amanda and Frank were present for the defense. The Multnomah County district attorney accompanied Mike Greene.

'The grand jury had enough evidence to indict Dr. Castle,' Judge Campbell said when Greene was through. 'That means that you were able to establish probable cause.'

'Yes, Your Honor. Our problem is that there is a very real possibility that Dr. Castle was set up by her ex-husband.'

'And there was no way to hold him?'

'No, Your Honor. Not at the present time.'

'This is very troubling. The idea of releasing the perpetrator of these crimes is repulsive to me, but it is equally repulsive to keep an innocent woman locked in jail.' The judge stood up. 'Let's go into court and put this on the record. I'm going to grant release on Dr. Castle's recognizance. Keep your statement tight, Mr. Greene, but make certain that the press understands the basis for this motion. Ms. Jaffe, you may speak if you feel the need, but I'll ask you not to use my courtroom as a pulpit. You've already won.'

'Don't worry, Your Honor. I don't plan on making any statement in court.'

'Very well.'

Amanda preceded Justine and her father into the courtroom. Someone had leaked news of the hearing, and every seat was taken. Amanda scanned the faces and saw several that were familiar. Vasquez had found a seat near the front. Amanda nodded to him moments before spotting Art Prochaska in the last row. Seated two rows in front of him was Dr. Carleton Swindell, the hospital administrator, whom Amanda had interviewed as a possible character witness. But the person who captured and held her attention was sitting beside his attorney in the front row, directly behind the defense table. When their eyes met, Vincent Cardoni smiled coldly. Amanda stopped short.

Cardoni shifted his attention to Justine. Amanda had described Cardoni's new look to her client, but Amanda could tell that seeing it in person was a shock. She started to comfort Justine but stopped when she saw that would not be necessary. Justine returned Cardoni's stare with a look of intense hatred. Frank saw what was happening and walked between Justine and Cardoni.

'Good afternoon, Vincent,' Frank said in a calm and measured tone.

'I see you're representing a less desirable class of client these days,' Cardoni responded.

'I'm going to ask you to act like a gentleman. We're in a court of law, not a barroom.'

'Chivalry is usually reserved for the protection of ladies.' Frank's features darkened. 'But I'll behave myself, out of respect for our friendship.'

'Thank you.'

Frank took the seat beside Amanda, directly in front of Cardoni. This put Justine as far from her ex-husband as possible. Judge Campbell entered the courtroom. As soon as the judge was seated, Mike Greene moved to have Justine's release conditions changed. He gave the judge a severely abridged version of the reasons he had outlined in chambers for the reversal of the State's position on bail. Amanda found it hard to concentrate on what Mike was saying with Cardoni so close.

Judge Campbell made her ruling swiftly and left the bench. As soon as the judge was gone Justine turned slowly and walked to the rail, her face inches from Cardoni's. Amanda had never seen a face so white with anger. When Justine spoke, her voice was barely audible, but Amanda thought she heard Justine say, 'This isn't over, Vincent.'

54

Reporters swarmed around Vincent Cardoni as soon as he left the courtroom. Roy Bishop cleared a path, chanting, 'No comment.' The reporters kept shouting questions as Cardoni descended the marble stairs to the ground-floor lobby. A Town Car was waiting in front of the courthouse. Cardoni and his lawyer ducked inside and the driver took them to the Warwick, a small luxury hotel a few blocks from the Willamette River, where Cardoni had booked a suite. He had no plans to return to the cramped basement apartment he had lived in as Andrew Volkov now that his identity had been discovered.

A mobile van from one of the TV stations followed the Town Car, but the driver phoned ahead and hotel security blocked the reporters from entering the lobby. After a brief consultation, Bishop drove off in the Town Car, and Cardoni took the elevator to his rooms. As soon as he locked the door, he stripped off his clothes and showered under steaming hot water. After the shower, he put on a terry cloth robe and ordered room service. The restaurant at the Warwick was one of Portland's best. The meal was exquisite and the wine superb, but the food and drink could not dull the rage Cardoni felt. Justine would soon be back in his old house, luxuriating in the bath the way she had when they were married. She would be washing away the smell of jail and gloating because she was free and his plan had been thwarted.

By the time room service brought him a bottle of twelve-year-old single-malt scotch and cleared his trays, the sun had fallen below the horizon. Cardoni stood at the window, watching the lights of the city glitter and gleam. The sight soothed him and helped him to put his feelings of failure behind him. Negative thoughts had to be banished. Positive thinking was required if he was going to avenge the loss of his hand and his profession, and his years in exile.

55

Bobby Vasquez was waiting when Justine Castle came out of the jail elevator. He was wearing a sports jacket, a clean blue Oxford shirt and pressed khakis. He had even shaved to make a good impression. Justine paused to study the private detective. He shifted nervously. Justine held out her hand.

'You must be Mr. Vasquez.' Her grip was firm, and her hand was cool to the touch.

'Yes, ma'am,' Vasquez answered, thinking that she was remarkably composed for someone who had spent several weeks in jail.

'Is your car outside?'

Vasquez nodded.

'Then get me away from here. We can talk while you drive.'

Vasquez owned a ten-year-old Ford. It usually looked like a garbage dump, but he had gotten rid of the empty chip bags, old socks and other refuse before driving to the jail. Justine Castle was classier than his usual clientele. She also made him a little nervous. He had seen her confrontation with Cardoni earlier in the day.

'Do you know where I live?' Justine asked when Vasquez drove away from the jail.

'Yes, ma'am. I was at your place when we arrested Dr. Cardoni.'

They rode in silence for a while. Vasquez glanced at Justine. She had closed her eyes and was savoring her first moments of freedom.

'So, Mr. Vasquez,' she said after a few moments of silence, 'tell me what you think of my ex-husband.'

'Didn't Miss Jaffe tell you?'

'I want to hear it from you,' Justine said, turning so she could observe Vasquez when he answered.

'I don't think he's human. I think he's some kind of mutant, a monster.'

'I see we share the same view of Vincent.'

'I can't think of many people who wouldn't think that way.'

'Will he try to kill me, Mr. Vasquez?'

'I think he has to kill, and he won't stop with you,' Bobby answered without hesitation.

'Will the police be able to stop him?'

'Honestly, no. He's going to disappear. Then he's going

to surface someplace else. Sooner or later he'll buy another property and start his experiments again. I don't think he can stop himself. I don't think he wants to stop.'

'Then what can be done to stop him?' Justine asked. There was a determined set to her jaw.

'What do you mean?' he asked, even though he was certain he knew.

'We both hate Vincent, Mr. Vasquez, and neither one of us thinks the police are capable of dealing with him. I'm certain that he'll try to kill me. If not today or tomorrow, then someday when I least expect it.'

Vasquez could feel Justine's eyes boring into him.

'I do not want to live in fear.'

'What are you suggesting?'

'How badly do you want to stop Vincent, Mr. Vasquez? How far would you be willing to go?'

56

Vincent Cardoni slept through the night and awoke at nine. He wanted to take a run, but he didn't want to deal with the reporters who were certain to be lurking about, so he moved some furniture and worked up a sweat with calisthenics. After his workout, Cardoni showered, then ordered a light breakfast from room service. He tried reading the newspaper but found that he couldn't concentrate. Cardoni walked to the window. A tanker was passing under the Hawthorne Bridge on the way to Swan Island against the magnificent backdrop of Mt. Hood's snowy slopes. The scene should have brought him peace, but thoughts of Justine kept intruding.

The day passed slowly. By late afternoon Cardoni was thoroughly bored and still had no plan for dealing with his ex-wife. It was soon after the room service waiter cleared his dinner that he spotted the cheap white envelope someone had slipped under his door. The envelope bore no return address. His name was typed on the front. He sat on the sofa in the sitting room and opened it. Inside were two pieces of paper. The first was a map of I–5. A rest area several miles south of Portland was circled. '11:00 P.M.' was typed on the map.

The second sheet was a photocopy of a journal entry.

Thursday: Subject is still combative after four days of applied pain, sleep deprivation and minimal food. 8:10: Subject bound and gagged and placed in upstairs closet at end of hall. Turned out lights in house, drove off, then parked and doubled back. Watched from woods. 8:55: Subject exits house, naked and barefoot, armed with kitchen knife. Remarkable strength of character. Breaking her will be a challenge. 9:00: Subject stunned by my sudden appearance, attacks with knife but Taser stops her. Subject in shock when told that bonds had been intentionally loosened to permit escape as test to see how fast she would get out compared to other subjects. Subject sobs as I put on the training hood and handcuffs. Will begin pain resistance experiments immediately to test whether crushing subject's expectation of escape has lowered her resistance.

Cardoni checked his watch. It was eight-forty-five. He read the journal entry one more time before going into his bedroom. DAs and cops said that Roy Bishop was a criminal lawyer in the truest sense of the phrase. One

advantage of retaining Bishop was the attorney's willing-
ness to render services that other, less pricey lawyers were
unwilling to provide. Cardoni opened a small valise that
Bishop had left for him and took out a handgun and a
hunting knife.

Mike Greene answered his phone after the second ring.
'Hey, Sean. I hope this is good news.'

'Would you consider it good news if I could prove
that Vincent Cardoni phoned in the nine-one-one on the
evening of Justine Castle's arrest and made the call that
lured her to the farm? I was rereading the report of the
first officer on the scene. There were no phones in the
farmhouse, so I asked myself how Cardoni called Dr.
Castle and phoned in the nine-one-one. Volkov owned a
cell phone. His records show he placed calls to the emergency operator and Dr. Castle's apartment on the evening
of Dr. Castle's arrest.'

'Great work, Sean!'

'Do we have enough for a warrant for Cardoni's
arrest?'

'Meet me at Judge Campbell's house. Let's see what she
thinks.'

Vasquez knew a maid who worked at the Warwick. Her
boyfriend delivered room service. For fifty bucks they
were willing to call Vasquez on his cell phone when the
doctor left his room. For fifty bucks more one of the
garage attendants at the hotel let Vasquez park in a space
a few slots down from Cardoni's car. At 9:10 the maid

told him that Cardoni was on the move. Vasquez ducked down in his seat and waited. Moments later the surgeon emerged from the elevator and got into his car. He was dressed in jeans, a black turtleneck and a dark windbreaker.

Vasquez had no trouble following Cardoni onto I-5 south. There wasn't much traffic, so he kept a car or two between him and his quarry. When Cardoni turned off at a rest area Vasquez followed him. Cardoni parked near the concrete rest room. The only other vehicle in the rest area was a semi hauling a load of produce. It was parked near the rest room. As he passed by, Vasquez saw that the cab of the truck was empty.

Vasquez parked at the far end of the lot and turned off his engine. Moments later the trucker walked out of the men's room and drove off. Cardoni left his car and entered the rest room. Fifteen minutes later he had not reappeared.

Vasquez got out of his car and moved through the picnic area toward the rest room, using the trees as cover. He circled behind the concrete building and paused to listen. He was about to move again when he heard the sound of someone struggling. Vasquez edged along the side of the building and chanced a quick look around the corner. Something was huddled in the shadows under a bench. It looked like a body. Vasquez was certain that it had not been there when he drove into the lot. He was debating whether to check out the body or wait in the shadows when he heard a noise behind him.

57

Amanda was working on a discovery motion when the intercom buzzed.

'Mary Ann Jager is on line one,' the receptionist said.

Amanda recognized the name of the attorney who had purchased the farm.

'This is Amanda Jaffe. How can I help you?'

'I, uh, I'm not sure if I'm calling the right person.' Jager sounded nervous. 'You represent Justine Castle, right?'

'Yes.'

'Is Robert Vasquez working for you?'

'Yes.'

'He, uh, he visited my office recently and wanted to know about some property. It's the place where all those

people were murdered. I read that Castle was charged
with the murders and that you're her lawyer. I can't get in
touch with him, so I decided to call you.'

'About what?'

'There was someone else who came around asking
about the property. Mr. Vasquez showed me a picture
but it wasn't him. He, uh, he said there was some money
in it if I could tell him who it was. Are you still interested?'

'Yes.'

'I never told anyone but Mr. Vasquez about this man,
not even the cops, so you'll be the only one who knows.'

'Who was it?'

'Vasquez said that he would pay me for that information.'

'How much did he say he'd give you?'

'Why don't you come to my office with three hundred
dollars? I'm just a few blocks away.'

Amanda knocked on Frank's doorjamb.

'Got a second?' she asked when Frank looked up from
his work.

'Sure. What's up?'

'I just visited Mary Ann Jager, the attorney who
bought the farm where the bodies in the Castle case were
found. When Bobby Vasquez interviewed her, she told
him that someone else had asked about the property
shortly before he did. Bobby showed her an old picture of
Cardoni, but she couldn't identify him. Last night she
saw the man on the evening news in a story about

Justine's case. When she couldn't get in touch with Vasquez, she called me.'

'So who is it?'

'Cardoni.'

'I thought you said—'

'The picture Vasquez showed her was taken before he had plastic surgery.'

Frank's brow furrowed. 'That makes no sense. Why would Cardoni expose himself to Jager if he already owned the farm?'

'He wouldn't.'

'You're saying . . . ?'

'There are some loose ends in Cardoni's case that always bothered me. For instance, who made the first anonymous call to Vasquez?'

'Martin Breach. Justine.' Frank shrugged. 'It could have been anyone Cardoni pissed off.'

'It couldn't have been Breach,' Amanda said. 'Why would he want Cardoni in police custody, where he could cut a deal to testify against him? Breach would be more likely to put out a contract on him.'

'You're probably right,' Frank answered thoughtfully. 'And the caller couldn't have been Justine.'

'Why?'

'She didn't know about the mountain cabin. Cardoni bought that in secret.'

'The police were never able to prove that Cardoni owned the cabin. What if he didn't? What if Justine did?'

'You think Justine is responsible for the murders in Milton County?'

'That's what Cardoni always claimed.'

Frank drew into himself for a moment. Then he shook his head.

'It doesn't work. Even if Justine knew about the cabin, how did she know about Martin Breach? The caller said that Cardoni bought his cocaine from Breach.

'In any event, you shouldn't be trying to prove Justine Castle is a murderer. First off, that's a job for the police. Then there's the little fact that Dr. Castle is our client. Even if you had the proof you needed, most of it, like the information you just learned from Jager, is privileged either as an attorney–client confidence or work product. Besides, you're sniffing up a false trail. I don't have any doubts that Cardoni is guilty.'

'How can you be so certain?'

'You remember the coffee mug with Cardoni's prints that the police found in the cabin in Milton County?'

Amanda nodded.

'The fact that Cardoni's fingerprints were found on the mug was never made public.'

'It wasn't?'

'No. The police always hold something back to weed out false confessions. I became suspicious when a coffee mug was found at the farmhouse with Justine's prints on it. The public didn't know about the coffee mug, but Cardoni did.'

'How do you know?'

'I told him his prints had been found on the mug when I was representing him. Only someone who knew about the coffee mug from the Milton County case would go to the trouble of stealing Justine's mug from the hospital and planting it at the farmhouse.'

'If it was planted. What if Justine brought the mug with her and drank coffee while she worked?'

Frank's smug look disappeared. 'That's a chilling thought.'

It dawned on Amanda that another of Frank's conclusions could be wrong as well. He had said that Justine could not have made the anonymous call to Vasquez, because the caller knew about Martin Breach and Justine did not. But Justine would know a great deal about Breach if she was Clifford Grant's partner in the black market organ scheme.

Amanda was about to explain this to her father when the intercom buzzed and the receptionist announced that Sean McCarthy was in the waiting room and needed to talk to Amanda. Frank told her to show McCarthy to his office. The detective looked paler than usual and he moved slowly.

'Good afternoon, Frank, Miss Jaffe,' the detective said.

'Good afternoon, Sean,' Frank answered. 'You look like you can use some coffee. Can I get you some?'

'I'd appreciate it. I haven't been to bed and I'm running on fumes.'

Frank buzzed his secretary and asked her to bring a cup of coffee for McCarthy while the detective settled into a chair.

'So, what brings you here?' Frank asked.

'Bobby Vasquez.' McCarthy looked at Amanda. 'A

trucker found him in a rest area on the interstate. He's at
the county hospital.'

Amanda paled.

'What happened?' Frank asked.

'He was knocked unconscious. The blow to the head
was pretty severe. His condition is serious.'

Amanda felt dead inside. 'Did Cardoni . . . Was he the
one who . . . ?'

'We think so,' McCarthy answered. 'We went to his
hotel room to talk to him. He wasn't there, but we
found a map in his trash with the rest area circled and a
journal excerpt that's similar to the accounts in the
journal we found at the farmhouse. We also found your
business card in Vasquez's wallet. I thought you might
be able to tell me what Bobby was doing in the rest
area.'

Amanda was about to tell McCarthy that Vasquez was
working as Justine's bodyguard, but she stopped herself.
Why was Vasquez in the rest area when he was supposed
to be guarding Justine? Had Justine sent Vasquez to kill
Cardoni? Amanda had no proof that Justine had done
anything wrong, and she remembered what Frank had
said about her duty to her client.

'Mr. Vasquez was working with me on Dr. Castle's
case, but I don't know why he was at the rest area,'
Amanda told the detective. 'Will Bobby be okay?'

'When I left the hospital, the doctors didn't know.'

Amanda felt terrible.

'Are you going to arrest Cardoni?' Frank asked.

'We're looking for him. Until we find him, you two

should keep your eyes open. We have no reason to believe that Cardoni will go after you, but we're concerned for the safety of anyone connected to him.'

Amanda normally dealt with stress by exercising, but she did not have the energy for a workout. Going home was out of the question, because she could not handle being alone. She hesitated a moment, then picked up the phone and called Tony Fiori at the hospital.

'How are you feeling?' she asked.

'Like Sly Stallone at the end of *Rocky*.'

'Should you be working?'

'Hey, if Sly could go fifteen rounds with the champ and not quit, I can't let a couple of cracked ribs stop me. What's up?'

'Bobby Vasquez was working with me on the case. Now he's in the hospital. The police think that Cardoni did it.'

'Oh, shit. How bad is he?'

'I don't know, but I feel awful.'

'Do you need someone to talk to?'

'Yeah, Tony, I do.'

'I get off in an hour. Why don't you drive to my place? I'll meet you there.'

'That would be great.'

'See you in a few hours.'

Tony gave Amanda directions to the house he'd purchased when he moved back to Portland. It was in the country, south of the city, several miles east of the interstate on two acres of secluded woodland. Amanda found the curving country lane that led to it. As soon as she got out of her car Tony put his arms around her. They held each other for a moment, then Tony pulled back so he could see Amanda's face.

'You okay?' he asked.

Amanda nodded somberly. 'Better now. Thanks.'

Rain started to fall, and they hurried inside a modern log cabin with a huge stone fireplace and a high, peaked roof crossed by massive raw beams. No walls separated a large living room from a modern kitchen. On either side of a short hall were an office, a bathroom and the stairs to the basement. A wide stairway led to a sleeping loft that overlooked the first floor.

Logs were stacked in the fireplace, and there was a pile of old newspaper in a wicker basket next to the hearth. Tony used the paper to start a blaze. Amanda listened to the patter of the rain on the roof and the crackle of the flames. The heat from the fire soon took the chill from the room.

'Can I fix you a drink?' he asked when the fire was going. 'You look like it might help.'

'I don't want a drink.' She sounded dragged out.

'Tell me what happened.'

'Bobby Vasquez asked me if he could work on Justine's case. My father didn't trust him, but I did, so I argued with Dad until he gave in and let me hire Bobby.' Amanda sounded like she had the weight of the world on her shoulders. 'When Justine was released from jail I got Vasquez a job as her bodyguard. Now he's badly hurt and I . . . I don't know, it feels like my fault somehow.'

Tony sat beside Amanda and took her in his arms.

'It's not, you know. Vasquez is an adult. You just told me that he wanted to work on the case.'

Amanda pressed against him, feeling safe and comforted.

'I know you're right. It just doesn't make me feel any better. What if he dies?'

Tony stroked Amanda's hair and kissed her forehead. It was the right thing to do. Amanda wanted to forget Cardoni, Justine Castle and the terrible thing that had happened to Bobby Vasquez. She tilted her face up and their lips met.

'Whatever happens to him, it won't be your fault,' he whispered.

That was the right thing to say. Amanda grabbed Tony and kissed him hard. He kissed back just as passionately as they sank onto the white shag rug in front of the fireplace. Tony winced. Amanda drew back, alarmed. She had forgotten Tony's injuries.

'Did I hurt you?'

'A little,' he answered with a laugh. 'Can you do this gently?'

Amanda placed a hand on Tony's chest. 'Lie back.'

Tony lowered himself onto the rug as Amanda stripped off her clothes. Tony reached out and played with her nipples while she tried to undo the buttons on his shirt. The touch of his fingers made it hard to concentrate, and she fumbled a few times. Then she gave up altogether.

Tony pulled her to his side. He stroked her thigh with a feathery touch, working his way upward until he slipped his fingers inside her. Amanda closed her eyes and lost herself in Tony's touch. His hands seemed to be everywhere at once, and each stroke made her quiver or flex. Amanda's senses were soon jumbled. Her breath came in gasps, and her body moved involuntarily. When she came the first time she squeezed Tony's fingers tight to keep them in her, straining for more. After a while her legs relaxed and Tony slipped his hand out. She opened her eyes. It took a few seconds to focus. He was watching her, still fully clothed. Her breathing was ragged. Tony smiled.

'You've got strong legs.' He shook his fingers slowly. 'These might be broken. I'm not sure I can finish unbuttoning my shirt.'

Amanda flushed.

'Think maybe you can do the job this time?' he asked.

Amanda nodded, still too wasted to speak. Tony lay down beside her and she started undressing him. As she worked he played with her body. By the time they were both naked, she had no idea where she was.

Amanda lay in Tony's arms. She could feel the heat from the fire on her back. The rain beat a tattoo on the roof.

'Maybe it would be a good idea if you stayed here for a while,' Tony said. 'I don't like the idea of you being alone with Cardoni on the loose.'

'I don't think he'll go after me. Why would he?'

'Why did he go after any of the people he killed? Cardoni doesn't think logically.'

Amanda remembered the way Cardoni had stared at her at the release hearing. She also remembered McCarthy's warning.

'Hey, it's not like going to prison,' Tony said. 'I make much better meals than they serve in the joint.'

Amanda smiled. 'Okay, I'm sold.'

'Speaking of food, I'm starving. There's a shower upstairs and a warm-up suit in the closet that you can slip on. While you're showering I'll whip up some dinner.'

It occurred to Amanda that she had not eaten for hours. Tony grabbed his jeans and shirt and limped toward the downstairs bathroom to wash up. Amanda picked up her crumpled clothes from the floor and climbed the stairs to the loft. A king-size bed sat beneath high windows. Amanda straightened her clothes as best she could and folded them over a chair. A blue warm-up suit was hanging in Tony's closet.

Amanda turned on the light in the bathroom. Tony had a large shower stall with multiple shower heads, and a Jacuzzi. Amanda set down the suit on the tiled counter next to the sink and turned on the shower. She watched the rain spatter on the skylight for a moment before stepping into the shower stall. It was chilly in the bathroom, and the cascade of hot water felt wonderful. Amanda closed her eyes, tilted her head back and let it run over her, trying to lose herself in the pulsating spray. But she couldn't. The Castle case kept intruding on her thoughts.

For all intents and purposes, her involvement in Justine's case was over. Justine was out of jail and the charges against her would soon be dismissed. She should feel triumphant, but she didn't. And the case wasn't really over. Cardoni was somewhere in the night, and Bobby Vasquez, his latest victim, was suffering in a hospital while Justine Castle lived in fear. The ending was unsatisfactory, not at all like a work of fiction where all the loose ends were tied up with a well-constructed knot.

58

In the morning Tony left for St. Francis and Amanda returned to her apartment to dress for work and pack some clothes to take to Tony's at the end of the day. Amanda called the county hospital, only to find that the doctors weren't letting Vasquez have visitors. Then she tried Justine to find out why Vasquez was following Cardoni instead of guarding her. She got the machine and left a message asking Justine to call.

Tony phoned Amanda shortly before noon and told her to come by at nine. By the time she pulled into Tony's driveway, she was ravenous. The aroma of simmering tomatoes, herbs and spices assaulted Amanda as soon as she walked through the front door. Tony was dressed in jeans and a T-shirt spotted with tomato sauce.

'Let me at the food, I'm starving,' Amanda said, slipping an arm around his waist.

'You're going to have to show maturity and self-control. I just beat you home.'

'Do you have any tree bark I can chew on?'

'No,' Tony replied with a laugh, 'but there's a loaf of olive bread sitting on the counter next to a great bottle of Chianti. If you want white, there's a bottle of Orvieto chilling in the fridge. Now, give me your bag.'

Tony took Amanda's valise from her and carried it up to the loft. Amanda shucked her coat and wandered across the living room to the kitchen. A cast-iron pot filled with tomato sauce was bubbling on the stove next to a larger pot of boiling water. A fire crackled in the hearth. Amanda poured a glass of Chianti, cut a slice of bread and wandered over to the couch. She remembered curling up with Tony after dinner on their first date, four years ago. That had been a great evening, an evening she had replayed in her mind many times.

'What are you daydreaming about?' Tony asked as he came down the stairs from the loft.

'How nice it is to be with you.'

Tony smiled warmly. 'Me too.'

A timer bell went off in the kitchen. He groaned. 'Duty calls.'

Ten minutes later the pasta was ready. When they were through with dinner, Amanda carried the dishes into the kitchen. Then they settled down in front of the fire.

'Tell me about Justine Castle,' Amanda asked abruptly.

Tony looked surprised. 'What do you want to know?'

'What's she like?'

'I don't know, really. I see her at the hospital, but we aren't intimate anymore, if that's what you're worried about.'

'I'm not jealous. I just want to get a handle on her.'

'And you haven't while you've been representing her?'

'She's very controlled most of the time. And she lies, or at least she withholds information. What was she like when you were close to her?'

'You want to know what she was like when we were lovers?' Tony sounded uncomfortable. Amanda nodded, flushing slightly because she was embarrassed to pry and worried that Tony would think that she was jealous.

'I was only with Justine a few times. The sex was okay, but sometimes I wasn't sure if she knew I was there. And she was tough to talk to if we weren't talking shop. She's a brilliant surgeon, but she didn't seem to have any interests outside medicine. I don't know what else to say.'

'Do you think that Justine is capable of murder?'

Tony paused and gave the question some thought.

'I guess anyone is under the right circumstances,' he answered finally.

'I'm talking about something else. I'm talking about . . . Cardoni always claimed that Justine was framing him, that she killed the people at the cabin.'

Tony shook his head. 'I just can't see her as a serial killer.'

Amanda wanted to tell Tony about the way Justine's

first two husbands had died, but her duty to her client sealed her lips.

'What makes you think that Cardoni isn't responsible for the killings?' Tony asked.

'I can't tell you very much. A lot of what I know is confidential.'

'Have you thought of a way to prove your suspicions?'

'Vasquez compiled a list of other serial murders with possible similar MOs. I can see if Justine lived in any of these places when the murders were committed.'

'I'm not a lawyer, but don't you have a duty to Justine? She's your client. Should you be investigating her?'

'No, I shouldn't.' Amanda sighed. 'It's just that I feel responsible for what happened to Vasquez and that I should do something.'

Tony yawned. 'Well, I know what to do,' he said. 'We should get to bed. I'm beat and I've got to get up at the crack of dawn.'

'Let me help you clean up.'

'Not necessary. Why don't you use the bathroom while I load the dishwasher? It'll only take me a minute.'

Amanda walked over to Tony. He took her in his arms, and she leaned her head against his shoulder.

'It's nice being here.'

He kissed her forehead. 'It's nice having you.'

Tony patted her on the butt. 'Now let me clean up before I fall asleep.'

Amanda gave him a quick kiss and went upstairs to the loft. She heard the disposal run as she started to enter the bathroom. It stopped. She opened her valise and took out her makeup case. She was headed for the bathroom when her cell phone rang. It was in her purse, and it took a moment to find it.

'Hello?'

'Amanda?'

'Justine?'

Amanda heard heavy breathing on the other end.

'You have to come to my house, now. We have to talk. It's about Vincent. It's . . . it's urgent.'

Justine was speaking in gasps. She sounded very upset.

'What do you—'

'Please come right away.'

'Justine, I can't—'

The phone went dead. Downstairs the dishwasher started. Amanda leaned over the loft wall and yelled down to Tony.

'What is it?'

'Justine just called me on my cell phone.'

Tony walked to the bottom of the stairs, a damp dishrag dangling from his hand. Amanda repeated the phone call as she descended.

'Should we call the police?' she asked when she reached the bottom.

'What would you tell them? Wouldn't she have called the cops if she was in danger?'

'She sounded so upset.'

Tony thought for a moment. 'Let's drive over.'

He walked to a drawer in the kitchen and took out a pistol. Amanda's eyes widened.

'Do you know how to use that?'

'Oh, yeah,' Tony said. 'The care and use of handguns is one of the things my father taught me. He was a gun nut. I never liked shooting, but now I'm glad I know how.'

Justine s Dutch Colonial looked eerie and deserted. The limbs of the barren shade trees swayed in the chill night air like skeletal hands. There were no lights on in the downstairs rooms, but two of the upstairs dormer windows glowed pale yellow like cat's eyes.

'Justine should be expecting us. Why is it dark downstairs?'

'I don't like this,' Tony said as they climbed out of the car.

He rang the doorbell as Amanda glanced nervously over her shoulder and to either side. When Justine did not answer after the second ring, Tony tried the door.

'It's locked.'

The curtains on the front windows were drawn, but Amanda pointed out a small gap between the sill and the bottom of the curtain. Tony slipped through a row of boxwood hedges and squatted so that he could see into the front room. Amanda started to say something, but Tony put his finger to his lips and hurried back to her.

'Go to the car and lock yourself in,' he whispered urgently 'Call nine-one-one. Justine is in there. She's tied to a chair.'

'Is she—'

'Go now,' he said, pushing her away from him. 'Ask for an ambulance. Go!'

Tony disappeared around the side of the house.

Amanda ducked behind the car and called 911 on her cell phone. The dispatcher took the information and told her that help was on the way. As soon as she hung up Amanda reached for the door handle, but she stopped when she realized that Tony had the ignition key. If she locked herself in, she would be trapped with no way to escape if Cardoni came for her.

Amanda hesitated for a moment, then followed the path that Tony had taken to the rear of Justine's house, crouching low and listening for any sound. Just as she reached the backyard Amanda heard a shot. She froze, terrified. A second, louder shot followed. Amanda edged along the side of the house until she was able to see through the windowpanes into a large, modern kitchen. Vincent Cardoni was sprawled against the wall next to the refrigerator. Tony stood over him, gun in hand. Amanda opened the door. There was a smell of gunpowder in the air. Tony swung the gun toward her, his eyes wide with panic.

'It's me,' Amanda yelled, thrusting her arms toward him, hands out.

'Jesus!' Tony lowered the gun. 'I told you to stay in the car.'

'I called nine-one-one, but I didn't want to stay alone.'

'I could have shot you.'

Amanda remembered the first shot. 'Are you okay?'

Tony nodded.

'What happened?'

'He tried to kill me,' Tony said, pointing to a head-high hole in the wall next to the back door. 'He was in

359

the kitchen. He fired when I stepped through the door.' Tony shook his head. He looked dazed. 'I shot him.'

Amanda flipped on the kitchen light and knelt beside Cardoni. There was a gun lying near his hand, and blood was spreading across his shirt. Cardoni's eyes were closed, and his head lolled to one side. He was alive, but just barely. Tony took a handkerchief out of his pocket and picked up the gun. Amanda looked at him quizzically.

'Cardoni's prints will be on the gun. I don't want the police thinking that I shot him in cold blood.'

Amanda suddenly remembered the reason they'd driven to the house in the middle of the night. She took Tony's hand.

'It's okay. It was self-defense. Now we've got to check on Justine.'

Amanda pushed through the door that led to the living room. As she groped for a light switch she could see a figure silhouetted against the shaded window, and she could smell the rustlike scent of blood.

Amanda stopped searching for the light and crossed the room. When she drew closer, she saw that Justine's arms and legs were secured to a straight-back chair with thick strips of masking tape in a way that made the front of her naked body vulnerable to assault.

'Justine,' Amanda whispered in a trembling voice.

Justine's head was down and her chin rested on her chest. A lamp sat on an end table near the chair. As Amanda switched it on she noticed a blood-smeared hunting knife resting next to the base.

Weak yellow light illuminated the room. Amanda's

back was to Justine, and it took all her courage to turn around. A sob caught in Amanda's throat, and her stomach clenched. She wanted to turn away, but she'd lost control of her body and could only stare with horror at what had once been a beautiful woman.

Tony knelt beside Justine and checked for a pulse. Then he turned to Amanda with sad eyes and shook his head.

59

They waited in the kitchen for the ambulance and the patrol cars that were coming in response to Amanda's 911 call. While Tony watched Cardoni, Amanda phoned homicide. Sean McCarthy arrived soon after the ambulance and the first patrol car. While the medics were loading Cardoni onto a stretcher, McCarthy took the couple into the den where Amanda had watched the videotape of Mary Sandowski's torture four years before. The TV and VCR were still there. Amanda could not bring herself to look at them.

McCarthy could see that Amanda and Tony were emotionally drained and made arrangements to talk to them at the Justice Center. Amanda's father arrived soon after the police. Frank insisted that Amanda spend the night in her old room. He also offered to put up Tony for the night.

Amanda was in bed by three. For the first time since she was a little girl, she kept a light on. The horror of what she had seen and her guilt at suspecting Justine tormented her every time she shut her eyes. When she did drift into sleep she found herself in a pitch-black room. She tried to sit up, but her body was secured by leather restraints. As she struggled to get loose a door opened, admitting a bright, blinding light. When her eyes adjusted, Amanda saw that she was strapped to an operating table.

'Who's there?' she called, her heart beating faster.

A bare lightbulb dangled from the ceiling over Amanda's head. A face covered by a surgical mask suddenly moved between Amanda and the light. A cap covered the doctor's head. In one of his hands was a shiny scalpel, in the other a coffee mug.

'I see our patient is awake,' the surgeon said. Then the mug slipped from the doctor's fingers and fell in slow motion, spilling its contents. Blood, not coffee, flew through space. The mug smashed against the concrete floor and exploded into ceramic shards. Amanda lurched up in bed, her heart pounding. It took her half an hour to fall asleep again.

Amanda was up by seven-thirty, feeling ragged and bleary-eyed but unable to get back to sleep. Through the front windows she saw a crowd of reporters massing near the curb. Frank had taken the phone off the hook and asked McCarthy to send an officer to keep the mob off his lawn.

Tony was very subdued when he came downstairs. No one had much of an appetite. Frank had put up a pot of coffee, and the couple carried their mugs onto the back porch where the reporters could not see them. The shade trees in the backyard were denuded of leaves, and the gray weather had bleached the color out of the grass and hedges. It was cold and blustery, but it was not raining.

'Couldn't sleep?' Tony asked. Amanda shook her head. 'Me either.'

They were quiet for a moment.

'Whenever I closed my eyes I saw myself shooting Cardoni.' Tony shook his head as if to clear it of the image. 'I don't know why I feel bad. I mean, the guy was a monster and I stopped him. I should feel great, but I don't.'

Amanda laid a hand on his arm.

'That's only natural, Tony. Cops who shoot criminals in the line of duty feel guilty even when they know they've done the right thing.'

Tony stared straight ahead, nodding bravely.

'He would have killed again.' Amanda put her hand over his. 'Think of the lives you've saved.'

Tony looked away.

Amanda grabbed him by the chin and forced him to look at her.

'You're a hero, do you know that? Not everyone would have gone into Justine's house knowing that Cardoni might be inside.'

'Amanda, I—'

Amanda put her finger on his lips. She kissed him, then laid her head on Tony's chest.

'Amanda, you don't still think that Justine killed all those people, do you?'

'No. I feel terrible for suspecting her.'

Amanda remembered what Cardoni had done to Justine. She fought back tears. After a moment, she took a deep breath and pulled away from Tony.

'We should get ready,' she said, wiping her eyes. 'We have to go downtown and talk to Sean McCarthy.'

McCarthy had instructed Frank to park under the Justice Center in the police garage so they could avoid the media. As soon as they arrived at the homicide bureau, Alex DeVore escorted Tony into one interrogation room and McCarthy escorted Amanda into another. McCarthy was kind and his questions were gentle. Three-quarters of an hour after he started, the detective told Amanda that he was done. As he opened the door for her, Mike Greene stepped into the room.

'Can we have a minute?' Greene asked.

'Sure, I'm done. Thanks, Amanda,' he said closing the door behind him.

'Am I going to need an attorney?' Amanda asked with a weary smile.

'Yeah, I'd get the Dream Team on this, right away.' He smiled. 'How you doin'?'

'I'm okay.'

'You have no idea how horrible I felt when Sean told me what Cardoni did to Justine Castle.'

'Why should you feel responsible?'

'I'm the one who decided that we didn't have enough evidence to hold that lunatic.'

Amanda's weary eyes softened. 'You didn't have a choice. You'd have been breaking the law if you'd done anything different.'

'The worst part is that we had enough evidence to arrest Cardoni. We just couldn't find the son of a bitch.'

Mike told her about the cell phone bill that proved that Cardoni had phoned in the 911 and called Justine's house on the evening of Justine's arrest.

'We were also following up on an idea Sean had four years ago but stopped pursuing after Cardoni disappeared. You know that Cardoni practiced at a hospital in Denver before he came to Portland?'

Amanda nodded.

'I just heard from the Colorado state police this morning. Two years ago they uncovered a killing ground similar to ours in a rural area about an hour outside of Denver. The bodies had been buried for some time. A Colorado lawyer, who has since been disbarred, purchased the property where the graves were found. He was contacted by an anonymous buyer through the mail and paid in cashier's checks.'

'Cardoni's MO.'

Mike nodded.

'I might have some extra ammo to use against Cardoni,' Amanda said. 'You know that Bobby Vasquez is working for me, right?'

'Sean mentioned it.'

'He gave me a preliminary list of serial murders that might have the same MO as Cardoni's killings. I'll get it to you in case he found something that your investigators missed.'

'Great,' he answered distractedly. 'Listen, about Bobby . . .'

'Have you gotten an update on his condition?'

'It's not good. The doctors don't know if he's going to make it.'

Amanda's shoulders slumped. 'What about Cardoni?'

Mike looked grim. 'The bastard's doing fine. That's the bad news. The good news is that he'll be fit for trial soon, so I'll be able to send him to death row. I trust you won't be representing him this time.'

Amanda forced a smile and shook her head.

'Am I done here? I'd love to get home and take a long, hot bath.'

'You're done,' Mike said, holding her chair for her as she stood. Then he took her hand and gave it an affectionate squeeze.

'If there's anything I can do, let me know,' Greene said quietly with a warmth that surprised her. She looked at the DA quizzically, and he blushed.

'I enjoy butting heads with you,' he said, 'so take care of yourself.'

60

Even with Cardoni locked in the secure wing at St. Francis, Amanda was afraid to stay by herself. But she turned Tony down when he invited her to stay at his house. Amanda never ran from something that scared her, and she wasn't going to start now.

That night, alone in her apartment, Amanda watched an old movie until her eyes grew heavy, then went to bed around one. She dreamed again about the operating room, the masked surgeon and the coffee mug filled with blood. When the mug slipped from the surgeon's fingers, a wave of blood arced through the air. Amanda jerked up in bed when the mug shattered. It was the second time she'd had that dream, and both times she had woken feeling at loose ends.

No reporters were lurking outside the offices of Jaffe, Katz, Lehane and Brindisi when Amanda arrived at eight the next morning. She had been putting off work on her other cases while she concentrated on Justine Castle. Before she could get to them she had to put Justine's files in order. It was while she was performing this chore that Amanda spotted Bobby Vasquez's list of possible killing grounds. She remembered her promise to send it to Mike Greene. As she scanned the list her eye lit on the Ghost Lake, Oregon, entry. Something about Ghost Lake tickled her memory again, but she was interrupted before she could give it much thought.

'There's a call for you on line three,' the receptionist told her.

'Who is it?'

'He says he's Vincent Cardoni,' the receptionist answered nervously. 'He asked for Mr. Jaffe. When I told him he was out of town, he insisted on speaking to you.'

Amanda hesitated. It would be easy to have the receptionist tell Cardoni that she would not take the call, but her curiosity got the better of her.

'Why are you calling this firm, Dr. Cardoni?' Amanda demanded as soon as she picked up the receiver. 'Roy Bishop is your attorney.'

'Bishop has no credibility with the district attorney or the police.'

'That may be, but we are no longer your lawyers.'

'I paid your father a lot of money to represent me. He's still under retainer.'

'You can discuss that with him when he comes back to

Portland at the end of the week. As far as I'm concerned, our professional relationship ended when you murdered my client.'

'But I didn't. Please come to St. Francis. I have to talk to you.'

'You must be insane to think that I would come anywhere near you after what you did to Justine.'

'You have to come.' Cardoni's voice was raw and needy.

'The last time I agreed to meet with you, it didn't turn out so well. I think I'll pass.'

'This is more important than you know,' Cardoni pleaded. 'You're in danger, and you're the only person who knows enough to understand.'

Amanda hesitated. She had no interest in meeting Cardoni. The idea of being in the same room with him scared the hell out of her. But he sounded so disturbed and unsure of himself.

'Listen carefully, Dr. Cardoni. You think we still have an attorney–client relationship, but we don't. If you say anything incriminating, I'll walk straight from your hospital room to police headquarters and tell them every word you told me.'

'I'll take that chance.'

Amanda was surprised by the response. 'Let me make myself clear, Doctor. I would like nothing better than to be the one who gives you your lethal injection.'

'I said I'll take that chance.'

Amanda thought for a moment. She could hear Cardoni's ragged breathing on the other end of the line.

'I will talk to you on one condition. I am going to bring a release with me. Once you sign it, the attorney-client privilege will no longer apply and I'll be free to tell the police anything you tell me. I'll also be free to testify against you in court. Will you sign the release?'

'Yes, I will.'

A massive steel door separated the secured ward at St. Francis from a small entry area opposite the elevator. An orderly manned a desk in front of the door. He inspected Amanda's ID and briefcase, then pressed a button. Another orderly studied Amanda through a window made of bulletproof glass that was centered in the top half of the door. When he was satisfied, he let Amanda into the ward, relocked the door and escorted her to Cardoni's room. A policeman was sitting outside. He stood up when he heard footsteps tapping down the narrow hallway. Amanda handed her bar card and driver's license to the policeman.

'I'm Dr. Cardoni's attorney.'

'Can you please open your briefcase?'

Amanda complied, and he thumbed through her paperwork and inspected all of the compartments.

'You'll have to leave the briefcase out here. You can bring in your papers and a pen, but don't give the pen to Dr. Cardoni.'

'I have a paper he has to sign.'

'Okay. I'll come in with you. He can sign in my presence.'

Cardoni was dressed in a hospital gown and propped

up on a hospital bed with his head slightly elevated. His arms were lying on top of his blanket, and Amanda saw the jagged scar that circled the surgeon's arm just above his right wrist. Cardoni's eyes followed Amanda as she crossed the room. She moved a chair near the bed but was careful to stay far enough away so he could not reach her. The policeman positioned himself at the end of the bed. Cardoni glanced at him.

'You don't need a bodyguard,' he said quietly. 'I'm not going to hurt you.'

Cardoni looked tired and subdued. The bravado she had so often noticed was not present.

'The policeman will leave as soon as you sign the release.'

Cardoni held out his hand, and Amanda gave him the document and a pen. He read it quickly, signed and returned the pen.

'I'll be watching through the window,' the officer assured Amanda before leaving the room. Amanda sat stiffly, feeling very uncomfortable in the doctor's presence.

'Thank you for coming,' Cardoni said as soon as the lock clicked into place.

'What did you want to tell me?'

Cardoni closed his eyes and rested for a moment. He seemed weak and exhausted. 'I was wrong about Justine.'

'Clever move, Doctor. Who are you going to blame for your crimes now?'

'I know I'm fighting an uphill battle trying to convince you that I'm innocent, but please hear me out. Four years ago, after Justine buried me at my bail hearing, I was certain that she had framed me. And after I did this,' Cardoni said, pointing at his scarred wrist, 'all I could think about was revenge for my hand, the time I'd spent in jail and the destruction of the life I'd built. I wanted her to suffer the way I was suffering.'

Cardoni held his wrist out. 'Do you have any idea what it's like to saw off your own hand, to lose a part of yourself? Can you imagine what it would be like for a surgeon whose life is his hands? And the new hand.' Cardoni laughed bitterly. 'Picking up a glass was like climbing Everest. Holding a pen, writing; my God, the hours I spent trying to master that simple task.'

He paused and rubbed his eyes. 'And, of course, there were the victims. I believed that Justine would continue to kill and that no one would try to stop her because everyone thought that I was guilty.

'I returned to Portland and took a job at St. Francis so I could keep an eye on Justine. I was certain that she had a new killing ground. It took me almost a year to find it. I spent hours looking at records, visiting properties that fit the profile, talking to attorneys until I discovered Mary Ann Jager on the Thursday before Justine was arrested. That night I went to the farm and found that poor bastard in the basement. He was already dead.'

Cardoni closed his eyes again and took a deep, rasping breath before continuing. He looked as though he were trying to banish a bad dream.

'I went back to the hospital and took the coffee mug.

I already had a surgical cap with some of Justine's hair and a scalpel with her prints. I'd been saving them.

'After planting everything at the farmhouse, I parked down the street from Justine's house and phoned her from my cell phone. She left and I followed. When I saw her make the turn from the highway onto the road that led to the farm, I called in the nine-one-one. I hoped that the police would find her at the farm. If she got away before they arrived, her prints would be on the items I left and everything she touched when she was there. An anonymous tip would lead the police to her.'

Cardoni paused again. He looked depressed.

'When I found the victim in the basement, I studied him so I could write a journal entry detailing what I was certain she had done to him. I learned the writing style when I read the journal in the farmhouse bedroom. As soon as I was sure that Justine was going to the farm, I wrote the journal entry on the computer in her house and left a copy.'

Cardoni rubbed his eyes and sighed.

'I was so certain that I was doing the right thing. I was so certain that Justine had framed me and killed all of those people. Seeing that man in the basement . . . I was so certain . . .'

Cardoni's voice trailed off.

'Everything was going exactly the way I planned it until Tony Fiori blew my cover. I knew the police would release Justine as soon as they realized that I was alive. I was desperate, so I had Roy Bishop set up that meeting with Mike Greene to try to convince him that Justine was guilty.'

'It didn't work.'

'No, it didn't, but something did happen. I received instructions to come to a rest area off the interstate. A diary excerpt was enclosed. It was an account of the torture of one of the victims. Only the killer would have that journal. So I went to the rest area early to lay a trap, but I outsmarted myself. The killer was there ahead of me, and I was hit with a tranquilizer dart.'

Amanda held up her hand as though she were stopping traffic.

'Please. If you're going to tell me that Bobby Vasquez is the killer, I'll walk out right now.'

'No, no. I didn't even know that he had followed me to the rest area until McCarthy questioned me after Justine's murder.'

'So who is it now? The butler?'

Cardoni answered her sarcasm with a murderous glare. Then his anger faded and he looked defeated. Amanda folded her arms across her chest but stayed seated.

'The first time I woke up after being tranquilized I was in total darkness and disoriented. I'm not even certain that this really happened. I thought I saw light and I think that someone gave me a shot, then I was out again.

'The next time I came to I was in Justine's kitchen. I remember Fiori shooting me. The next thing I remember, I was in the hospital.'

Amanda stood up. 'This has been a very interesting story, Dr. Cardoni. I suggest you try selling it to

Hollywood. Perhaps you can start a writing career while you're on death row.'

'I have proof. Have them test my blood. The hospital draws blood before an operation. Have the hospital run a screen for tranquilizers. I was still heavily sedated when Fiori shot me.'

'You can have your attorney do that. My firm doesn't represent you anymore.'

Amanda pressed a button next to the door.

'I know who killed Justine,' Cardoni shouted at her. 'It's your boyfriend, Tony Fiori.'

Amanda burst out laughing. 'If I were you, I'd go with the butler. It's a hell of a lot more believable.'

'He tried to kill me at the hospital,' Cardoni cried out desperately. 'Then he shot me at Justine's house. I was on the floor when he came through the door. I was barely conscious. Why would he shoot someone who was no threat to him? I think he needed me dead to stop the investigation. I think he was afraid that the police would figure out that I'm innocent if they kept looking into these murders.'

Amanda turned to face Cardoni. The fear she'd felt was long gone, replaced by a cold hatred.

'He shot you because you tried to kill him, Dr. Cardoni. I saw your gun.'

'I never fired a shot. I swear.'

Amanda banged on the door and the guard opened it immediately. She turned back to face Cardoni.

'I was with Tony when Justine called from her house and asked me to come over. She was alive then, but she was dead when Tony and I arrived. You were the only other person at the house. You tried to kill Tony and you murdered Justine.'

'Miss Jaffe, please,' Cardoni pleaded. But Amanda was already out the door.

61

Amanda was furious with herself for visiting Cardoni and furious with the surgeon for thinking so little of her that he would try to fool her with his ridiculous story. During the return trip to the Stockman Building, she thought about things Cardoni had said that would help nail him. He'd confessed to planting the mug, scalpel and surgical cap at the farmhouse. This tied him to the scene of four murders, but it didn't prove that he'd killed anybody. Amanda wanted something more. Justine's death demanded it.

It was while she was parking that Amanda remembered the Ghost Lake murders that Bobby Vasquez had included on his list. Back at her desk, she ran an Internet search. She found several stories about Betty Francis, a senior at Sunset High School, who had disappeared seventeen years before during a winter break ski trip, and Nancy Hamada, a sophomore at Oregon State, who had disappeared the next year, also while skiing at the Ghost Lake resort during winter break. Their bodies had been discovered fourteen years ago when a cross-country skier stumbled across them.

Amanda phoned the sheriff's department in Ghost Lake. No one in the department had been with the sheriff's office fourteen years earlier, but the secretary, who had grown up in Ghost Lake, remembered that Sally and Tom Findlay's boy, Jeff, had been a deputy when the bodies were discovered. Amanda called the Findlays and learned that their son was working in Portland.

Zimmer Scrap and Iron was an ugly stretch of chain-link fence, piles of twisted and rusting chunks of iron and herds of monster cranes that spread along the shores of the Willamette River. Just after four-thirty Amanda parked her car in front of the corporate headquarters, a three-story brick building surrounded by chaos and ruin. Amanda asked the receptionist if Jeff Findlay was in. Moments later a tall, square-jawed man with sandy hair walked into the waiting area. His pale blue eyes fixed on Amanda, and he flashed her a confused smile.

'What did you want to see me about, Miss Jaffe?'

'Two murders you helped investigate at Ghost Lake fourteen years ago. You were a deputy with the county sheriff's office at the time.'

Findlay stopped smiling. 'What's your interest in those cases?'

'They may be connected to a larger series of murders that were committed over the past four years.'

'Let's go inside.'

Amanda followed Findlay to a small, unoccupied office.

'I can see you remember the case.' Amanda said.

'That was the worst thing I've ever seen. Two months after the girls were dug up I quit law enforcement for good. I enrolled in an accounting program at a community college, then finished up at Portland State. I think I was trying to find a profession that would keep me as far away from dead bodies as I could get.'

'If Betty Francis and Nancy Hamada looked anything like the victims I've seen, I don't blame you.'

Amanda told Findlay about the Cardoni and Castle cases.

'We've always thought that the killings in Milton and Multnomah Counties weren't Cardoni's first,' Amanda concluded. 'We were hoping to find an earlier murder that we could connect to him.'

'And you think this is it?'

'It might be.'

'Cardoni's name never came up in our investigation,' Findlay said.

'Where were the bodies found?' Amanda asked.

'In separate graves in the forest that borders the ski resort.'

'Who owned that land?'

'Ghost Lake Resort.'

'Cardoni's practice has been to buy property in a remote area and bury the bodies near the house where he tortures his victims. Was there private property near the burial site?'

Findlay shook his head. 'No, there . . . Oh, wait. There was a cabin a couple of miles away. Funny thing is, there was a double murder at the cabin a year before we found the bodies. We looked hard for a connection, but the only one we could find was that all four murders were during winter break.'

'Did the double murder at the cabin involve torture?'

'Not that we could tell. The cabin was torched and the bodies were badly burned. If I remember, the medical examiner concluded that the man had been bludgeoned.'

Amanda frowned. There was something very familiar about this case.

'Who were the victims?' she asked.

'One was a young woman. She'd gone up to the ski resort with her boyfriend and disappeared. Or at least that's what the boyfriend said. They were having problems. We interviewed several witnesses who heard loud arguments on the evening the woman disappeared.

'The popular theory was that she'd been upset with her boyfriend, met the guy who owned the cabin and gone off with him. The boyfriend finds out, goes to the cabin, kills them and burns the place down. Trouble was, we never had any evidence to support the theory, so no one was ever arrested.'

A thought flickered through Amanda's mind, but she could not hold on to it.

'Do you remember the names of the victims?'

'No, but I seem to remember that the man was a lot older than the woman. I think he was an attorney with a Portland firm.'

The blood drained from Amanda's face.

'Are you okay?' Findlay asked, concerned by Amanda's ash gray coloring.

Amanda did not answer. It dawned on her suddenly that she knew the name of the attorney who died at Ghost Lake, and, just as quickly, she understood the significance of her dream about the blood-filled coffee mug.

The meeting with Jeff Findlay had taken half an hour, and it took another hour before Amanda was sufficiently composed to return to the office. Frank was still working at six o'clock when she knocked on his doorjamb.

'Hey, princess.'

'What're you working on?' Amanda asked, to see if she was in control of her voice.

Frank leaned back and folded his hands across his stomach.

'You know that drug bust in Union County?'

Amanda nodded.

'We've picked up one of the defendants.'

Amanda forced a smile and sat down across from her father. Outside, the lights of downtown Portland shone bright, but storm clouds covered the moon.

'Thank God for the rising crime rate, huh?'

'It does help pay the rent,' Frank said. 'How come you're here after quitting time?'

'I wanted to ask you something.'

'Shoot.'

'Remember the night I picked you up at the airport? The day after I found Cardoni's hand?'

Frank laughed. 'How could I forget? It's not every day a father gets a call from his daughter informing him that she's discovered the amputated limb of a psychopath.'

'I guess it was a memorable occasion. Anyway, on the ride back I told you about finding Tony with Justine Castle and you said that Tony might not be the best person to get serious with. What made you say that?'

'Why do you want to know?'

'Tony and I, we've gotten pretty close since he returned from New York.'

Frank's eyebrows went up.

'When you said that about Tony, four years ago, he was leaving Oregon and I didn't see any reason to press you. But now . . . I mean, is there some reason you don't like him?'

'No, I guess I just didn't like him hurting my little girl.' Frank smiled ruefully. 'You know, it doesn't matter whether that little girl is five or twenty-five when you're her father.' Frank paused. 'So, how serious is this?'

Amanda forced a smile and shrugged. 'I don't know, Dad. But there was nothing specific, right?'

Frank hesitated. Then he sat up straight.

'You know that Dominic, Tony's father, was one of my original law partners?'

Amanda nodded.

'Dom was in my study group in law school. So was Ernie Katz. We called ourselves the Three Musketeers because we were all young guys with families who were working our way through night school.

'Dom was the life of the party, the hardest drinker, the one who always wanted to go for a beer. I never understood how he could always be on the go without collapsing, but you do that sort of thing when you're young and never think about it. Nowadays they have names for Dom's problem: bipolar disorder, manic-depression. We just thought of Dom as an iron man, and we rarely saw him when he was down.

'Once we formed our partnership it became obvious that Dom had problems. His wife left him and Tony when Tony was in high school. There were rumors that he was abusive to both of them. Tony was pretty wild by then. I helped him out of two scrapes in high school, and I was able to keep his record clean. When he went to Colgate I hoped that being away from Dom would help him get his life together.

'Dom was very smart and he was a good lawyer when his motor was going, but he was arrogant and lazy. He was also a heavy drinker and a womanizer. He cost us two good secretaries before we caught on. You were a sophomore in high school when Ernie and I asked Dom to leave the firm. It was a bad scene.

'Two days later a detective came to the office. It was winter break and we were supposed to go skiing, but I had to call off the trip, remember?'

Amanda nodded.

'Dom had a cabin in the mountains—'

'Near Ghost Lake, wasn't it?'

Frank nodded, and Amanda felt sick.

'The detective told us that it had burned to the ground. Dom and a young woman were inside when the fire started. The police determined that it was arson.'

'Where was Tony?' Amanda asked, using every ounce of will to keep her tone casual.

'He was in Mexico for winter break. I'm the one who had to phone him and tell him that his father was dead.' Frank shook his head sadly as he remembered the call.

'So you talked to him, you spoke to him?'

'Not right away. If I remember, I left a message at his hotel asking him to call. I think he got in touch a day or so later. Then he flew home.'

'What does his father's murder or his problems have to do with you not liking Tony? You can't blame him for his father's sins.'

Frank thought for a moment before replying.

'What Tony's done, becoming a doctor, is admirable, but growing up the way he did can affect a young man; it leaves scars. Sometimes they're permanent and they prevent a man from ever figuring out how to relate to a woman. Tony's father was a drunk and a womanizer, and he was physically abusive. That's the lesson he taught Tony. When you told me he was dating you and seeing another woman at the same time, it made me think of the way Dom treated women.'

Amanda stood up. It was all she could do to keep her legs from shaking.

'Thanks, Dad. I've got to go now.'

'Sure. I hope I didn't upset you.'

'No, I'm fine.'

Amanda flashed a smile and hoped it masked her fear. Then she turned and left the office, fighting hard to keep from running.

62

The orderly on duty outside the secured ward looked up when two men wearing white coats over casual clothes got out of the elevator. Dimitri Novikov and Igor Timoshenko were arguing about this year's prospects for the Seattle Mariners. They both carried cups of coffee. Timoshenko had a stethoscope around his neck. The guard relaxed. That's when Novikov pressed his silenced pistol against the guard's temple.

'Please ring for your friend who is inside,' Dimitri asked politely in barely accented English. 'I will be lowering my pistol as soon as you do, but my companion is also armed and he will kill you if there is any trouble.'

As soon as the guard pressed the button, the weapon

disappeared. A moment later a face pressed against the bulletproof glass in the door to the ward.

'We're here to examine Dr. Cardoni,' Novikov said into the intercom next to the door. Then he turned to Timoshenko and continued to press his position that the Mariners had no chance of winning their division.

'Their relievers are pathetic,' he said emphatically.

He was midway through listing the earned-run averages of the team's relief pitchers when the door opened. He stopped arguing long enough to press his gun against the orderly's stomach.

'One word and I will kill you. Lead us to Dr. Cardoni's room.'

The orderly's eyes widened. He turned without speaking and started down the corridor. He was so frightened that the *pfft* made by Timoshenko's silenced pistol did not register. Timoshenko closed the door to the ward, locked it and followed Novikov and the orderly. On the other side of the door, blood from a fatal head wound spread over the surface of the guard's desk.

Timoshenko and Novikov were Russians who lived in Seattle. Martin Breach had used their talents before for special jobs. The previous evening they had met Art Prochaska in a video arcade in Vancouver, Washington. Prochaska had paid them $25,000 and promised another $25,000 if they delivered Vincent Cardoni to Breach alive and relatively unharmed. He had given the Russians a floor plan of the hospital and a detailed diagram of the secured ward. An elevator inside the ward was used to move prisoners. An ambulance driven by another Russian was parked outside a ground-floor door of the hospital. All Novikov and Timoshenko had to do was gain access to Cardoni's room, sedate him and take him down the elevator. Breach did not care how they accomplished their task as long as they delivered their package.

The policeman who was sitting outside Cardoni's room was surprised to see two doctors following the orderly down the corridor. He knew the schedule by heart, and no one was supposed to be examining the prisoner at two o'clock in the morning. The officer stood and took one step forward before Timoshenko shot him in the forehead. Blood from the exit wound splattered across the window in the door to Cardoni's room. The orderly made a half turn, but he was dead before he could complete it. It was always best to leave no witnesses.

Novikov took the orderly's keys and opened the door. He put his pistol in the pocket of his white coat and withdrew a syringe. The room was dark, but Novikov could make out a large shape under a blanket and sheet. He moved quietly, not wanting to wake Cardoni. Prochaska had made it clear that there would be no more money if Cardoni was killed or badly injured, and Novikov did not want to have to explain failure to Martin Breach.

Cardoni's blanket covered him from head to toe. Novikov was standing over the bed before he could make out the top of the surgeon's head in the darkened room. The Russian pulled the covers back slowly. He was leaning down to inject Cardoni when the surgeon plunged a bedspring through Novikov's ear and into his brain. It was the same bedspring he had broken off from the underside of his bed and spent hours straightening and sharpening in the dark while planning his escape. The hypodermic fell to the floor and shattered. Cardoni propped up the Russian, who twitched for a moment before becoming limp.

Timoshenko glanced down the hall, then looked through the window to see how his partner was doing. Novikov's body was bent forward, shielding Cardoni from Timoshenko, whose view was partially obscured by the blood that had spattered across the window in the steel door. Cardoni slid out from under his attacker and lowered Novikov's body onto the bed. He found the Russian's weapon while Timoshenko was figuring out that something unplanned had occurred in the darkened room. Cardoni shot the Russian while he was charging through the door.

When Cardoni was certain that his assailants were dead, the surgeon stripped Novikov, who was closest to his size and whose clothes were unstained by blood. In a few minutes Cardoni was dressed in street clothes covered by a doctor's white coat. A stethoscope was draped around his neck. He took the elevator to the ground floor and walked out of St. Francis Medical Center.

Sean McCarthy's call awakened Mike Greene from a deep sleep at five-thirty. He had been bleary-eyed when he picked up the receiver, but the news of Cardoni's escape acted like a double shot of espresso. Greene was so distracted that he recalled little of the drive through the darkened streets of Portland. The first thing that did make an impression was the large bloodstain that covered the desk outside the secured ward. He shivered involuntarily as he walked through the law enforcement personnel who jammed the corridor outside Cardoni's room.

Sean McCarthy was talking to a fingerprint expert. A policeman and a man in an orderly's clothes lay on the green linoleum floor in pools of blood a few feet from the detective. Greene smelled the dead men before he saw them. He looked up so that the bodies were only in his peripheral vision.

As soon as he spotted the deputy district attorney, McCarthy walked to meet him.

'Let's get out of here,' McCarthy said. 'I need some coffee.'

'How did he get away?' Greene asked as soon as they were in the elevator.

'We're not sure yet. We found five bodies. We've identified three of them: the orderly who mans the desk in front of the elevator and the policeman and orderly who were found outside Cardoni's room. Here's where it gets weird. There are two dead men in Cardoni's room. One man was shot as he came through the door. He was dressed like a doctor, but he was holding a pistol with a silencer. The techs think it's the weapon that was used to kill the cop and the two orderlies.

'The second man was killed with a sharpened bedspring. Cardoni worked it off the bottom of his bed. The second man is only wearing underwear, and we found Cardoni's hospital gown on the floor. We assume Cardoni's wearing the dead man's clothing.'

'Was the guy a doctor?'

'We don't know, but no doctors were scheduled to visit Cardoni and no one from St. Francis has been able to identify either man.'

The elevator doors opened. McCarthy bought two coffees from a vending machine while Greene took a table in the deserted cafeteria.

'One interesting thing,' McCarthy told the DA after taking a sip from his cup. 'Cardoni had a visitor yesterday afternoon, Amanda Jaffe.'

'What was she doing with Cardoni?'

'Her firm represented him when he was charged in Milton County. Maybe he wants her to continue the representation.'

'There's no way the Jaffes could do that,' Mike said. 'She's a witness, and he murdered one of the firm's clients. There's a clear conflict. Have you talked to her?'

'I phoned her apartment, but her answering machine was on.'

'Have someone go there. It's a long shot, but Cardoni may have said something to Amanda that will give us a clue to where he's gone.'

Before McCarthy could answer, McCarthy's partner, Alex DeVore, walked into the cafeteria.

'We've got an ID on the two men in Cardoni's room,' he said. 'Dimitri Novikov and Igor Timoshenko, Russian Mafia from Seattle.'

'What were they doing down here?' McCarthy asked.

'Remember the Colombians who tried to move in on Martin Breach two years ago?'

'I still have trouble eating when I think about the crime scene,' Greene answered.

'The word is that Novikov was in on that.'

'So you think Breach brought in out-of-town talent to do Cardoni?'

'Breach never forgives and he never forgets,' McCarthy answered.

Mike Greene's pager started to beep. He took a look at the number on the screen, then pulled out a cell phone and dialed immediately.

'Amanda? It's Mike.'

'We've got to talk.'

She sounded upset, almost near tears.

'I can't right now. I'm at St. Francis. Cardoni's escaped.'

'What! How?'

'We're not really certain.'

'We still have to talk. Please. What I have to say may be more important than the escape.'

'I find that hard to believe.'

'There's a possibility that Vincent Cardoni is innocent.'

'Come on, Amanda. Cardoni murdered Justine Castle almost under your nose. We've got five dead men here. The man is a homicidal maniac.'

'Listen to me closely, Mike. Before a patient has surgery the hospital draws a blood sample. You have to find out if there was any trace of sedatives, anesthetic or tranquilizers in Cardoni's sample. If his blood wasn't tested for those substances, I want you to run one and tell me the results. If the test results are what I think they'll be, you'll change your opinion.'

63

Sean McCarthy and Alex DeVore followed Mike Greene into the conference room at the district attorney's office. Greene stared at Amanda Jaffe. Her shoulders slumped and her complexion was ashen.

'What the hell happened to you?' Greene asked as he took a seat next to her. When Amanda answered, he had to strain to hear her.

'We've all been fools.' Her voice caught, and she paused to collect herself. Mike thought that she might begin to cry. 'Cardoni is innocent. So was Justine.'

'It's going to take a lot to convince me of that.'

Amanda took a deep breath, as if the mere act of speaking had wasted her. She sipped from a glass of water.

'Fifteen years ago a member of my father's law firm

drove to a cabin he owned near the Ghost Lake ski resort. A few days later my father learned that he had died in an arson fire. The body of a young woman was also found in the cabin.'

'What does this have to do with Cardoni?'

'Nothing. The lawyer's name was Dominic Fiori. He was Tony's father. The following year, the bodies of two young women were found in shallow graves a mile or so from the Fiori cabin. One had been reported missing the year before the arson during winter break. The other was reported missing two years before, also during winter break.'

Amanda paused. She ran her hand hard back and forth across her forehead and fought to regain control of her emotions.

'Are you okay?' Mike asked, concerned by Amanda's obvious distress.

'No, Mike. I feel sick. I can't . . .'

Greene cast a quick glance at McCarthy, who looked equally concerned.

Amanda gathered herself. When she spoke, Greene was certain he'd misunderstood her.

'What did you say?'

'I said the women at Ghost Lake were Tony Fiori's first victims.' Amanda's voice broke as tears flooded her eyes. 'He killed them, Mike. He killed them all.'

'How is that possible, Amanda? Tony was with you when Justine called you for help. The medical examiner said that Justine died within an hour of your arrival at her house. You told Sean that you were with Fiori for two hours before Justine called.'

Amanda wiped her eyes. When she spoke, her voice was devoid of emotion.

'When I visited him at the hospital, Cardoni told me that he was knocked out with a tranquilizer dart at the rest area. I think Tony kept him a prisoner somewhere, then brought Cardoni to Justine's house before I came over to Tony's house on the night Justine died.'

'But what about the phone call?' Mike asked. 'How could Tony kill Justine? He was never out of your sight.'

'That's not true. I didn't see Tony while I was making the nine-one-one call at Justine's house. I've given this a lot of thought. What if Tony tortured Justine earlier in the afternoon and forced her to make a tape? He could have left Cardoni sedated in Justine's kitchen and Justine sedated and tied to the chair in the living room. I took Justine's call in the loft on my cell phone. Tony could have played the tape over his phone in his kitchen. I couldn't see Tony when I spoke to Justine. None of her statements was responsive to anything I said. The call was short. She said my name, then she told me to come over and she hung up.'

'I don't know,' Greene said. 'That's quite a stretch.'

Amanda sat up straight in her chair and her features hardened.

'Cardoni had traces of heavy-duty tranquilizers in his blood. That's what you told me. Why would he tranquilize himself?'

Greene didn't answer.

'After Tony told me that Justine was tied up in the living room, he told me to stay in the car and lock myself in when I called 911. He was counting on my following his orders. I think he ran into the house and cut Justine's throat. He'd calculated when the anesthetic he'd given Cardoni would wear off. Maybe he even gave Cardoni something to bring him around. After that, all he had to do was place the second gun in Cardoni's hand while Cardoni was still groggy and fire the first shot. Then he shot Cardoni with his own gun. I'm betting that Tony would have finished him off if I'd stayed in the car. Tony needed Cardoni dead so you'd stop investigating his crimes. He was afraid you'd stumble onto something that would prove he was the killer.'

'This sounds crazy, Amanda,' Greene said.

'Tony Fiori has been killing since he was a junior in high school and no one has ever suspected him. He was supposed to be in Mexico during winter break when his father died, but that was his alibi. I think his father walked in on him while he was working on his third victim and Tony killed him. My father is the one who called Mexico to tell Tony that Dominic was dead. I asked him about that last night. He said it took the people at his hotel a day to find him.'

'You have to do better than this.'

Amanda reminded Mike Greene of the killing ground in Colorado and told him about the killing ground in Peru. She also told him her dream about the blood-filled coffee cup and what it meant.

'It's possible,' McCarthy said when she was through, 'but there's nowhere near enough for an indictment.'

'There's no concrete evidence at all,' Mike added.

'I know,' Amanda answered, her voice unsteady but filled with determination. 'That's why you have to let me get you your evidence.'

64

'God, it's good to see you, Tony,' Amanda said, reaching up to give him a hug. 'Thanks for letting me stay here.'

In a van parked on a side road a short distance from Tony's house, Alex DeVore, Sean McCarthy and Mike Greene heard every word broadcast through the listening devices that had been planted while Fiori was at the hospital.

'To tell the truth, I haven't felt like staying alone, either, since I heard Cardoni escaped.'

'We probably don't have anything to worry about. Sean McCarthy's convinced that Cardoni is long gone.'

'You wouldn't be staying here if you believed that.'

Amanda smiled coyly. 'I might have ulterior motives.'

'You are such a slut.'

Tony put his hands around Amanda's waist, pulled her close and kissed her. She pulled back slightly, and he looked confused.

'Everything all right?'

'Sure,' she said, fighting to keep from sounding nervous. 'Cardoni's escape just has me rattled. Say, I'm starving. What's for dinner?'

'Veal piccata, but I just got home fifteen minutes ago, so I don't have dinner up yet.'

'Busy day at the hospital?' Amanda asked, to keep Tony talking.

'It was a madhouse. All anyone was talking about was Cardoni's killing spree. Then we had a five-car pileup on the interstate.'

Amanda followed Tony into the kitchen. He filled a pot of water, then took two strips of veal scaloppini out of a shopping bag and laid them between sheets of wax paper.

'I may have proof of Cardoni's guilt soon,' Amanda said as Tony pounded the veal lightly to flatten it.

'Oh?'

'Bobby Vasquez discovered two murders that occurred in Oregon that are very similar to the killings in Milton County and the murders at the farm.'

'No kidding. When was this?'

'One woman was killed seventeen years ago and the other sixteen years ago.'

'Where were the murders?'

'The Ghost Lake ski resort. The women were found in

the forest, half a mile from one of the runs. This could have been Cardoni's first killing ground, so he may not have been as careful as he is now.'

Tony blended flour with salt and pepper, then dipped the meat in the mixture until there was a light coating of flour on the veal.

'Did you tell McCarthy that Cardoni accused me?' he asked casually.

'No. Why should I waste his time with that ridiculous story? Cardoni was just desperate. He even claimed that he was drugged when he was at Justine's house. He wanted me to have the blood that was drawn prior to his operation screened for tranquilizers.'

'Who was supposed to have drugged him? Me?' Tony asked as he put olive oil and butter in a skillet, placed the skillet on a burner on the stove and turned on the heat under the pot of water.

'Yeah,' Amanda answered, shaking her head in disbelief. 'He said that he was coming to when you shot him.'

'Coming at me is more like it. What did McCarthy think about that little gem?'

'I didn't mention it to him. Like I said, why waste his time with Cardoni's crap?' Amanda shook her head. 'I do have to give Cardoni credit, though. He had me going for a minute.'

'You've got to be kidding.'

'He's a skilled liar, Tony. You have no idea how convincing he can be.'

Tony looked alarmed. 'You actually thought I . . . that I could do that?'

401

'No, but he made a pretty good case against you.'

'How, if I didn't do it?'

'Whether you did it or not is irrelevant. Lawyers convince juries all the time that things that didn't happen are true.' Amanda smiled. 'I bet I could convince you that you're guilty, using my exceptional forensic skills.'

'Bullshit.'

'That's not a challenge, is it?'

'Loser does the dishes.'

'You're on.'

'Okay, Ally McJaffe. Prove I did it.'

'Let's see.' Amanda stroked her chin dramatically. 'First, there's the killing ground in Colorado.'

'What killing ground?'

'It was on the list that Bobby Vasquez compiled for me of murder cases with MOs similar to the Oregon cases. The bodies of several torture victims were found on farmland near Boulder. The farm was purchased using the MO used to purchase the farmhouse in Multnomah County and the home in Milton County.'

'How does that prove I'm a killer?' Tony asked with a skeptical smile.

'You were a ski instructor in Colorado, and you went to school at the University of Colorado at Boulder.'

'That's true, but Cardoni worked in Denver. And, come to think of it, so did Justine. You won't get much mileage out of that point. Next?'

The water started to boil. Tony turned the heat up under the skillet.

'There's the coffee mug.'

Tony looked puzzled. 'What coffee mug?'

'The one the police found at the cabin in Milton County.'

'What about it?'

'The police never told the press or the public that Cardoni's prints were on it.'

'So?'

'You knew.'

'I did?'

'Four years ago, at your house, we were talking about Cardoni's case after dinner. I told you about serial killer profiles, and I mentioned that organized nonsocials have active fantasy lives that enable them to visualize their crimes in advance. I said that this trait helped them anticipate errors that could lead to their capture. You commented that Cardoni did not anticipate the errors that led to his capture. You said that it was really dumb to leave a scalpel and a coffee mug with his fingerprints at the scene of the crime.'

'I don't remember saying that.'

'Well, you did.'

'Come on.' Tony laughed. 'How can you possibly remember what we talked about four years ago?'

Amanda stopped smiling. 'It was our first date, Tony. I remember everything about it. I was really taken with you and replayed the evening in my head a lot of times. It meant something to me.'

'Well, you got the conversation wrong. I never mentioned anything about a coffee mug. I don't think I even knew the cops found a mug at the cabin, unless you told me about it. That might be where I heard about it, if I did. You said yourself that we talked about the case.'

The butter and olive oil were heating up, and Tony put the veal in the sizzling pan.

'There was another killing ground in Peru.'

Tony froze.

'Cardoni was living in the States when the victims disappeared and Justine was never in Peru, but you were in medical school in Lima then.'

'There were similar murders when I was studying in Peru?'

Amanda nodded.

'Wow. That's amazing.' Tony shrugged and smiled. 'Well, I didn't do it. Besides, you're forgetting that Cardoni admitted framing Justine by planting evidence at the farmhouse. That proves he was at the scene of the crime.'

'Ah, but it doesn't prove he committed the crime. Cardoni claimed that he framed Justine because he believed that she framed him four years ago.'

'Why would Justine do that?'

'Clifford Grant made a deal with Martin Breach to deliver a heart that was supposed to be transplanted into a wealthy Canadian. The police raided the airport when Grant arrived with it, but Grant escaped with the money and the organ. Grant had a partner. Breach didn't know the partner's name. The partner killed Grant to keep him from talking and buried him at the cabin. Cardoni's story is that the partner created a fall guy to throw Breach off the scent. With his addiction to cocaine and erratic behavior, Cardoni was the perfect patsy. Cardoni thought Justine was Grant's partner, so he framed her to get even. Now he claims that you were Grant's partner.'

'Of course he does. With Justine dead, he couldn't very well carry on with his ridiculous story that she framed him.'

'Oh, it's pretty clear that Cardoni was framed.'

'Yeah?' Tony said as he dropped several handfuls of pasta into the boiling water.

'Cardoni didn't know about the farm until shortly before he framed Justine. I talked to Mary Ann Jager, the lawyer who bought the property. She said that Cardoni showed up at her office a few days before Justine was arrested and tried to find out who owned it and how it had been purchased. Why would he do that if he already owned it?'

Tony clapped his hands and laughed. 'Very impressive, Amanda. You're a terrific lawyer. You almost have me convinced that I killed everyone.'

'That's why I get paid the big bucks,' Amanda said, making a small bow.

'Still, when you add everything up, your case against me is purely circumstantial and pretty skinny.'

'I've won with less,' she answered with a confident smile.

Tony sighed. 'Are you taking me in before dinner or do I get a last meal?'

Amanda pointed to the skillet. 'That smells too good to waste. I think I'll wait until after we eat to bring you in.'

'Here's a reward for your kindness.'

Tony secured a slender piece of veal on the tines of a fork and held it just out of reach of Amanda's lips.

'Take a taste,' he said, feeding the slice to Amanda. As soon as it was in her mouth, Tony swung his fist as hard as he could and caught Amanda flush on the jaw. She staggered. Tony pulled her to the ground and applied a choke hold. Amanda was unconscious in moments.

'How about opening the wine?' Tony said as he pressed tape over Amanda's mouth. He kept up a dialogue about his day at work, interspersed with cooking instructions, while he searched Amanda for a wire. If she was here on her own, he had no problems. If she was wired or the police had gotten into the house and planted listening devices, he would have to disappear. He didn't think the police were watching him on a concealed camera because they would have moved as soon as he hit Amanda.

Amanda began to stir. Tony rolled her over and secured her hands behind her back with a set of plastic restraints. He hastily scribbled a short note and took a sharp knife out of a drawer while regaling Amanda with a funny story about a screwup by a new intern. As soon as Amanda's eyes opened Tony pressed the knife to her throat and held up a note: ONE SOUND AND I WILL BLIND YOU.

Amanda's eyes showed her fear, but she did not make a sound. Tony motioned her to her feet. Amanda scrambled up and stood unsteadily, still groggy from being rendered unconscious. Tony had removed all of her clothes during the search, but she was too terrified to be embarrassed.

He pointed toward the basement door with his knife. Amanda hesitated, and he stabbed her in the arm. Amanda gasped. Tony put the knife to her eye and she stumbled down the hall.

'Is that a great Chianti or what?' Tony asked cheerfully.

65

'Something's wrong,' Mike Greene said. He, Alex DeVore, Sean McCarthy and a technician were squeezed in the back of a van jammed with electronic equipment.

'They're talking,' Alex DeVore said.

'No, *he's* talking. She hasn't spoken in more than five minutes. I put a watch on them. She's got to be nervous. Hell, she's got to be terrified. Someone in that state should be talking a blue streak. It's her only contact with us.'

'Mike might be right,' McCarthy said.

'If we send the men in now, we blow it,' DeVore cautioned.

'If we don't and something happens to Amanda, I—'

'Hold it,' the tech interrupted. 'They're in the basement. I can hear them going down the stairs.'

'Send the men in, now,' McCarthy yelled, ripping off his headset.

DeVore yanked the mike from the tech's hand.

'Go, go, go,' he yelled. 'They're in the basement.'

SWAT team members rose from their positions in the woods surrounding Tony's house and moved in. The first group went in the back door and the second through the front. When they experienced no resistance, the first group opened the cellar door. It was pitch black. The first man through the door crouched low and scanned the basement with night vision goggles. He edged down the stairs, weapon at the ready. Two other SWAT team members followed. They fanned out when they were in the basement. There was little to see: a floor-to-ceiling wine rack, the furnace, a water heater, a racing bike.

'Lights,' the team leader ordered. The men removed their goggles and the man at the top of the stairs flipped the switch.

'Where are they?' one of the men asked.

'There has to be another way out,' the team leader said. 'Find it.'

'Over here,' one of the men yelled. He was kneeling next to a trap door that was flush with the floor. It had been covered with a rug. Three of the men surrounded the door and aimed their assault rifles at it. The fourth man opened the door in one smooth movement while the team leader looked on. There was a narrow depression in the earth no wider or deeper than a coffin. There were blood spots on the dirt. A rank smell issued forth.

'The basement is deserted,' the team leader reported to the men in the van.

'So is the rest of the house,' the tech in the van answered. The second team had already briefed him.

'We found a hidden trap door covering a coffin-size hole with what appears to be dried blood and excrement in it. He may have been holding people down there.'

'Keep looking for another way out,' McCarthy said. 'If there's one hidden door, there might be another.'

Tony Fiori had met his first victim on the slopes of the Ghost Lake resort. He had taken her to the family cabin, tortured her to death and buried her in the woods. Everything went so smoothly that Tony gave no thought to being caught. Teenagers don't do much planning, anyway. Tony's luck held with his second victim. Then Dominic Fiori walked in on his son in the act of torturing victim number three, and it suddenly occurred to Tony that it would be wise to take precautions.

Tony had enough money from his father's estate and life insurance to secure a private place to conduct his experiments in pain, and he soon developed a foolproof technique for purchasing his 'research facilities.' Then he studied forensic techniques to avoid detection by police specialists. Finally he created an escape plan if the worst-case scenario occurred.

As soon as they were in the basement, Tony placed a hood over Amanda's head, slid the moveable wine rack aside and pushed her into the escape tunnel. A flashlight hung on a hook just inside the door. Beneath it was a backpack with a pistol, cash, a change of clothing, materials for a disguise, a fake passport and other false identification.

Tony barred the entrance to the tunnel from the inside, grabbed the flashlight and located the backpack. The tunnel extended a quarter of a mile under the woods behind his house. Amanda ran stooped over because of the low ceiling. Stones and roots cut her bare feet; her buttocks and the backs of her thighs bled from gashes made by Tony's knife as he jabbed her when she slowed. A half mile from the tunnel exit a car purchased with false ID was waiting. Several hundred miles away in a small Montana town was his new laboratory. Amanda Jaffe would be its inaugural subject. It was stocked with enough food to last several months. When the search for him and Amanda died down, he would leave the country and plan his future. Amanda, or what was left of her, would stay behind in Montana.

Tony felt energized by the chase. He'd heard the back door crash open seconds before he closed and bolted the door to the tunnel, and it gave him a sense of satisfaction to know that he had outwitted the police.

As they hustled along, Tony admired the way Amanda's buttocks moved ahead of him. They were lithe and well muscled, like her legs. Tony thought about the time he would spend with Amanda. Tony liked best those first lovely moments when his subjects fully appreciated the horror of their situation. He watched with night vision goggles as they awoke in the dark, confused, frightened and unaware that they were under observation. There was always a widening of the eyes, a racing of the pulse, the mad attempt to break free from their bonds. He would lose this moment with Amanda. In her case, though, there would be other compensations.

'You present me with a rare opportunity,' Tony told Amanda as he prodded her forward. 'Most of my subjects have been runaways, addicts or prostitutes. They haven't been in the best of physical condition, and I've often wondered what effect that had on their ability to tolerate pain. I'm interested to see how much pain a well-conditioned athlete can endure. We'll both learn a lot about pain in the weeks to come.'

Tony suddenly grabbed Amanda's arm and yanked her to an abrupt stop while he listened for movement in the tunnel. When he was certain they were not being followed, he slapped her with the blade of his knife. She lurched forward and collided with the tunnel wall before Tony set her straight.

'You were so easy to fool,' Tony taunted, breathing easily as they ran. 'I dated you to milk you for information, just as I used Justine to find out what I needed to know to frame Vincent. Did you think our reunion at St. Francis was a coincidence? Justine told me about the interview.'

Tony chuckled. 'You weren't much of a challenge,

though I must say that your reactions to sexual stimulus were often interesting. I may see if I can bring you to climax while you're in pain. I've tried it before on male and female subjects with interesting results.'

Amanda was becoming exhausted and disoriented. It was hard to breathe in the hood with the tape across her mouth, and her fear was quickly sapping her strength.

'You can take some comfort in the fact that you're aiding science. You know, it was my father who inspired my interest in pain, but he wasn't very scientific or imaginative. Belts and fists were the limits of his creativity. I've far surpassed him, as you'll soon learn.

'I would have loved using Vincent as a subject, but I couldn't because the medical examiner would have seen the marks. If you hadn't stopped me from killing Cardoni, the investigation would have ended and I wouldn't have had to worry about someone like you discovering my work in Peru and Ghost Lake. I bet you wish you'd stayed in the car.'

They were almost at the end of the tunnel when they heard the explosion.

'Looks like the police have found my escape hatch. But don't get your hopes up. They're a quarter mile behind.'

Tony shoved open a trap door concealed under a layer of earth. He pushed Amanda up a short ladder, closed the door and rolled a boulder over it. Then he urged Amanda through the woods. There was no trail, but Tony knew every inch of the route to the car by heart. He did practice runs each month.

Amanda gasped for air as she stumbled forward over

the stones that cut her feet. Only fear of what Tony would do if she slowed down kept her moving. Her legs trembled and she stayed upright by sheer force of will. Finally, just when she was certain that she could not go another step, she ran into the side of a car.

'Stop,' Tony ordered.

Amanda doubled over. Her lungs heaved. She heard the trunk pop open. Once she was in the trunk, it would be all over. Tony would drive away and her fate would be sealed.

Amanda broke away from the car and was in the woods before Tony could react. She hit a tree with her shoulder, spun and drove forward blindly. She expected to feel Tony's grip any moment, but she was still running free when a log sent her sprawling. Pain shot through her shins as she flew through space. Her head cracked against a tree trunk. She lay on the ground, stunned, yet somehow gathered herself, rolled to her side and regained her feet. A car motor started. She heard tires spinning and distant shouts. Amanda raced toward the voices, stumbled and fell to her knees.

'She's over here,' someone shouted.

'It's okay,' someone else said.

Amanda collapsed as kind hands took hold of her. Someone cut through the plastic restraints that bound her hands behind her, and someone else draped a coat over her shoulders. Another person removed the hood and the tape that sealed her mouth. With eyes blurred by tears and exhaustion, Amanda saw the SWAT team members who were scouring the woods.

'Do you have him?' someone shouted.

'He's gone. He's disappeared,' someone else answered.

'Amanda, it's me.'

Amanda opened her eyes and saw Mike Greene leaning over her in the back of the ambulance.

'Is she okay?' Greene asked the medic.

'She'll be fine,' he answered. 'She's disoriented and frightened, but her cuts are all superficial.'

'Did they get him?' Amanda asked.

Greene shook his head.

'But don't worry. He won't get far,' Mike said bravely, though without conviction. He sat next to Amanda, trying to think of something else to say. The medic gave Amanda a cup of steaming tea. She thanked him automatically and took a sip while her eyes stared ahead vacantly. Finally, at a loss for words, Mike Greene laid a reassuring hand on her shoulder and gave it a squeeze.

66

Tony Fiori came to slowly. His vision was blurred, his cheek pressed against cold, damp concrete. Fiori's hands were bound tightly behind his back. Tape covered his mouth; he tried to stand, but his ankles were also bound.

'Good, you're awake.'

Fiori recognized the voice. He rolled over and saw Vincent Cardoni watching him.

'We're in a warehouse in Portland, if you're interested,' Cardoni said as he reached down to check the ankle and wrist restraints. Fiori tried to wrench away from him, but it was useless.

'I'd conserve your strength if I were you. You're going to need it.'

Cardoni saw fear in Fiori's eyes and smiled. 'Oh, no, you don't have to worry about me. But you do need to be afraid.'

Cardoni took out his cell phone.

'I followed Amanda Jaffe to your house and spotted the SWAT team, so I stayed in the woods to see what would happen.'

Cardoni listened to someone on the other end of the phone. 'Mr. Breach, please.'

'It was luck that I saw you emerge from your tunnel,' he continued as he waited for Breach to take his call. 'Bad luck for you.' Cardoni smiled. 'You've made my life hell since the day you framed me. But you're going to put things right. You're going to square me with Martin Breach.'

Cardoni's attention returned to the phone. 'Mr. Breach,' he said, 'have you checked with your police friends?' Cardoni paused. 'Good. Then you know that Tony Fiori was Dr. Grant's partner and that I had nothing to do with the heart?'

Cardoni paused again and nodded at something Breach said. When he spoke, he looked at Fiori so that he could enjoy his reaction.

'No, no, Mr. Breach, I don't want any money. Dr. Fiori cost me my hand and my career, and he made me live underground like an animal for four years. What we both want, I believe, is revenge: something more fitting than a quick and painless death by lethal injection.'

Cardoni watched with great satisfaction as understanding, then terror, registered in Fiori's eyes. He tried to speak, but the tape muffled his words. As he thrashed on the ground Cardoni gave Breach the address of the warehouse, then disconnected.

'They'll be here soon, so I have to leave,' Cardoni said. 'Mr. Breach did want me to tell you something, though. It seems that a contact in the police department gave him a copy of your pain journals. He says he found them quite interesting and is looking forward to trying the techniques you found most effective.'

Fiori's eyes stretched open as far as possible. He strained uselessly against his bonds. Cardoni watched him for a moment more, then threw his head back and began to laugh. His laughter continued to echo in the cold, hollow space as he disappeared into the night.

67

Two weeks after her escape, Amanda was reviewing case notes in the corridor outside a courtroom when she looked up to find Mike Greene smiling down at her.

'Mr. Greene, are you spying on me?' she asked, matching his smile with one of her own.

Mike sat beside her on the bench. 'Nope, I'm just checking to see if you're okay.'

'Thanks, Mike, I'm fine.'

'This must be really hard for you. You were very close to Fiori, weren't you?'

Amanda smiled sadly. 'He used me to find out about the investigation, Mike. I never meant anything to him, and he doesn't mean a thing to me now. I'll tell you one thing, though – I'm through dating serial killers.'

419

Mike barked out a laugh. Then he sobered and looked at Amanda uneasily. She sensed that he wanted to say something, but Greene looked uncharacteristically nervous.

'Have you heard anything more about Bobby Vasquez?' Amanda asked when the silence went on too long.

'He'll be out of the hospital by next week,' Greene said. He seemed grateful for the easy question. 'He's made a great recovery.'

'Thank God for that.' She paused. 'Have you . . . ?'

Mike shook his head. 'There's nothing new on Fiori. He's dropped off the face of the earth.'

Amanda sighed. She nodded toward the police officer sitting a few benches away.

'It sure would be nice to know that I didn't need protection anymore.'

'Well, you're going to get it until we know you're safe. I don't want anything happening to you – at least outside court.'

Amanda smiled. 'I think I can take pretty good care of myself there.'

'That you can,' Mike agreed. Then he hesitated. 'You know, I could take over as your bodyguard this Saturday if you're interested.'

Amanda looked confused. Mike smiled nervously.

'Do you like jazz?'

'What?'

'There's a really good trio playing at a club in Old Town next week.'

Amanda couldn't hide her surprise.

'Are you asking me out, like on a date?'

'I've wanted to ask you out for a long time.' Mike blushed. 'No guts. But I figured if you could be brave enough to go up against Fiori, I could muster the courage to ask you out.'

'I love jazz.'

Mike's face lit up. 'Okay.'

'Give me a call and let me know when we're going.'

'I will. This is great.'

Amanda laughed. 'Does this mean you'll go easier on me the next time we have a case together?'

'Not a chance,' Mike answered, grinning unabashedly. 'Not a chance.'

Epilogue

The three men who were playing cards looked up when Martin Breach walked through the door to the warehouse.

'Hey, Marty,' Art Prochaska said.

Breach waved, then glanced down at the man who lay on the bloodstained mattress. It was almost impossible to tell that he was human. After a moment Fiori looked up listlessly with his one good eye. Breach lost interest and walked to the card players.

'You think we got everything out of him?' Breach asked Prochaska.

'Our guy in the islands cleaned out the account. I don't think he's got another one. If he ain't talked by now, nothing else we do is gonna make him. It's been a month.'

Breach nodded. 'Get rid of him,' he told Prochaska.

Prochaska breathed a sigh of relief. His enjoyment in torturing Fiori had waned considerably after the first few days, although Marty's enthusiasm had lasted much, much longer.

'Oh, and Arty,' Breach said, pulling a can of beer from a cooler, 'let's leave a little something so the cops know he's dead. I don't want them to keep wasting their time on a big manhunt. Those are my tax dollars they're spending.'

'How about we send them a hand?' Prochaska asked with a smile. Breach considered the suggestion for a moment, then shook his head.

'That would be poetic, but I want the cops to know he's really dead. And Frank's daughter, I want her to know, too. She's a good kid, and Frank's always done right by me. I don't want them worrying.'

Breach popped the tab on his beer and took a long, satisfying drink.

'So what's it gonna be, Marty?'

Breach thought for a moment. Then he looked down at Fiori and smiled.

'The head, Arty. Send them the head.'